Got It Bad

By Christi Barth

For my husband, who may *have secretly pined for months just like Kellan before finally asking me out…*

Acknowledgments

THANK YOU *so much* to all the readers who have embraced this series. My bad boys were a bit of a new direction, and I'm beyond grateful to everyone who took the leap with me.

Thanks to Jessica Alvarez for not only finding the right publisher for the series, but also being a stalwart rock of wisdom and calm throughout its creation. Thanks to Nicole Fischer for having the vision to point out the myriad ways I could make it better. And big hugs to all my friends who supported me during the late nights and head-banging moments I wrestled with these bad boys!

Prologue

Northwestern University Law School, Chicago
November 1, 2:30 p.m.

KIERAN MULLANEY PUSHED through the double glass doors of the Northwestern University Law School and sucked in a deep breath. Other people might think he was nuts, what with the exhaust fumes, pollution, general downtown stink of Chicago in the air. But Kieran only smelled *freedom*.

No more notes on his iPad. No more trying to hide his side-eye when that douche canoe Pietro cut off every woman in the class when they tried to answer.

Law school didn't suck. It was sometimes interesting. It just wasn't fun. Or rewarding. Or, you know, not even his *choice*. Not that he'd get pissy about that now. Nope, Kieran planned to celebrate his freedom, for the next few hours at least, by finding someone sexy and sassy and talking her into a drink. No talk about tort law. No case law. No law, period.

Flirting. That's what was on the docket. Kieran didn't need his four years of undergrad or three years of law school when it came to his mastery of romancing the fairer sex. He'd been charming women out of their tops, bottoms, and everything underneath since . . . well, since long before his brothers actually *thought* he'd lost his virginity.

He looked down Superior Street for a hot prospect. Pretty much any woman that he didn't recognize from law school would do. Kieran almost jolted when his gaze connected with two blue eyes staring right at him. Very blue, long-lashed, and with a single, *I'm interested* raised eyebrow.

"Oh, hey there," the woman said and then she added an upward, flirty-as-hell tilt to her mouth that sealed the deal. She had *noticed* him.

This was a million times better than trying to stay awake in Criminal Procedures class. Plus, she was unexpected. Kieran fucking *loved* surprises.

"Hi yourself, beautiful. Are you hanging around the law school because you need a lawyer? Or because smart men with enormous earning potential turn you on? Either way, I'm your man."

Her smile flipped downward into a disapproving smirk. "Wow. Has that line ever worked? I mean, *ever*? There's four huge problems with the four sentences you just smarmed at me."

Kieran was equal parts pissed that she'd called him out on his lazy come-on . . . and intrigued that she'd called him out on his lazy come-on. "*Smarmed* isn't a word."

"Didn't you hear? You can make anything a verb these days. The grammar police officially gave up when *squeed* got added to the OED."

Surprise Girl was definitely around his age. Definitely his type, what with the sass and the smarts.

Definitely hot, with those wide, pink-glossed lips that begged to be kissed and thick blond hair that fell just below her shoulders. Kieran really wanted to slide his fingers through it, tug just hard enough so that her head tilted back and he could skim his lips along her throat. And he'd glimpsed one hell of a body wrapped up in a cream sweater and jeans before locking his eyes respectfully above her chin. Oh, and those knee-high brown leather boots that were the best god-damned thing about autumn in the Midwest.

He crossed his arms over his chest. "So what are your official complaints with what I said?"

A super slo-mo blink indicated that she'd expected an apology, and been surprised by his challenge. Then she shoved up the sleeves of her sweater with a determined squint. Game on.

"You can't assume I'm 'hanging around' the law school. I just saw you come out the door, which means you have zero knowledge of where I'm coming from or going. And I just came from a walk on the lakeside trail, so in fact, you're wrong."

Feisty was more fun than overtly flirty in Kieran's book. He shrugged, just to egg her on. "Okay, that's one."

She tossed her head. The motion sent her hair rippling in the late-afternoon sunlight. Exactly the way it'd ripple if Kieran flipped her on top of him in a bed. It was also the classic hair toss he'd seen a thousand times from women trying to get his attention. "If I did need a lawyer, I'd go find an actual lawyer. Not some student who may or may not pass the bar exam on the fifth try."

He held up two fingers, spread in a wide V. "Two." Kieran barely bit back a snort. No way would he be one of those idiots who didn't prep enough to pass on the first try.

"As for that presumed earning potential?" She patted the bulge of her fat, pumpkin-colored purse. Geez, that thing was big enough to hold a gun. Most women he knew stuck a credit card in their iPhone case and called it a day. What could she be lugging around in there?

Kieran widened his stance and tucked his thumbs into the front pockets of his jeans. Arguing with the pretty stranger was a hell of a lot more fun than arguing in mock trials. "It's a well-known fact that even the dumbest lawyer can pull in the big bucks. Why do you think so many people suffer through three years of law school hell?"

A smile slipped past her guard faster than a meteor streaking across the sky. Surprise Girl was enjoying this argument as much as he was. Looking up at him from beneath half-lidded eyes—another top-level flirt move—she asked, "What if you become a public defender?"

"If I planned to be poor and principled, I'd be a teacher already."

A motorcycle missing its muffler roared by, and the sharp blast it made whipped her head around as fast as if she'd thought it was a sniper. Guess in today's world you couldn't be too careful. Just as fast, she zipped her attention back to Kieran. "Or you took out loans for all seven years of college and won't actually turn a profit on your super fun eighty-hour work weeks until you're pushing forty?"

"Three." He conceded her point with a nod. And wiped a hand across his mouth to hide his grin.

Finally, the woman crossed her arms just beneath her breasts, lifting them to his attention. Not like he needed the help, but Kieran appreciated all her subtle physical indications of attraction while she tried to win the argument. "Either way, why assume that *you're* the man who can meet my needs? You don't know anything about me."

"Four." Kieran moved closer. So close that he smelled her perfume. Something fresh, like rain in a forest. Close enough that, yeah, he could see straight down the V of her cleavage to a *thank you, God* amount of creamy skin surging against the lace edge of her bra. "And now I've got an answer for you."

She tilted her head up, her chin jutted forward in an ongoing challenge. Which, yeah, exposed even more cleavage. And that couldn't be an accident. Especially not when she practically purred her next words. "Go on."

"Yes, apparently all of that does work—because you're still standing here arguing with me." Kieran let his arms swing forward just enough so the backs of his hands brushed the backs of hers. A jolt—tiny, but visibly noticeable—ran through both of them at the touch. So he did it again. "Arguing invariably leads to kissing."

Those pretty pink lips parted. Then they closed again, and she licked them. God, the woman was *killing* him with this non-flirting flirting. "Is that so?" It came out all husky, the way he imagined her voice sounded at midnight. In the dark. In bed.

Kieran spread his fingers to interlace, backward, with hers. Just the tips. Just to tease both of them a little. "Well, you have two choices. We could skip right to the kissing. Or we could go for a drink first. Do something old-school like—and I'm just spitballing here—learn each other's names."

"I'm intrigued." Another toss of her thick blond hair. "Looks like I've found an actual gentleman."

Not like he'd had a choice. "Believe me when I say I've had chivalry literally beaten into me."

Her mouth formed a silent O of shock. Then her hands flipped over to lace even tighter, and she squeezed. "Your mom hit you?"

"Never. Not once," Kieran said emphatically. "But

after she died, my big brothers raised me. At that point, we'd been wrestling and beating each other up for years. It was better to get an atomic wedgie as a reminder to hold the door open for a girl than because Ryan and Frank thought I looked weird at them when passing the ketchup."

Her whole face softened. Thick, dark brown lashes batted in double time over those wide blue eyes. "I'm sorry to hear she died."

Crap.

Usually Kieran remembered to keep the whole *dead parents* thing under wraps. Women tended to focus on it. To abandon all other topics and be the comforter, the soother. Soothing wasn't sexy, though. If he wanted to share memories, he'd turn to Ryan and Frank. Because those memories weren't something he casually discussed. Ever.

"It was a long time ago." He'd learned to use the technique of deflection on this topic long before officially learning its usefulness in law school. "And wedgies aside, I couldn't ask for better brothers. They both work like dogs so that I can go to law school and just study, instead of splitting focus with a job or worrying about loans."

Something in her eyes flickered. "They sound great." Another flicker. Like thoughts were racing fast behind them. Kieran didn't know what that was about. Did mystery woman have brothers? That she missed? Maybe off in the armed forces?

All he knew was that he wanted to find out.

"Ryan and Frank are the best guys in the world. I'd lay down my life for them, but they'd move heaven and earth to beat me to it."

Flicker number three. "I'm impressed."

Uh-oh. Kieran lifted a hand to brush away a stray leaf the November wind had just blown into her hair. "Before I ruin my chances and send you running into my not-nearly-as-hot-as-me brothers' arms, how about that drink?"

"You stayed both polite and charming while you stood up to me. That's a fine line most men can't balance on." She stroked a single finger slowly down his sternum. "I think I'd really enjoy going out with you."

It was the middle of the afternoon. Luckily, they were in Chicago, so finding an open bar day or night wasn't exactly a problem. "Let's walk to Navy Pier. Hit the Tiny Tavern, soak up the view of the lake and the city?" Because Kieran absolutely wanted to keep talking to this fun, feisty woman.

"How about we drive?" She pointed to a huge black SUV half a block down. The oversized, darkened-window kind that usually alerted you to the presence of movie stars. "I rolled my ankle skidding on some leaves at the entrance to the tunnel under Lakeshore Drive."

"Then you shouldn't be standing on it." Kieran lifted her into his arms with a fast but smooth swoop. It did not at all suck to have his forearm squeezed between her calf and thigh. And he wouldn't begin to let himself notice the softness of her breast pressed to his chest.

Okay, he'd *notice*, because he wasn't fucking dead. And this woman snuggled tight against him was the best thing he'd held in a very long time.

Her arms lifted to wrap around his neck. "Before we go any further, I have to say that meeting you was an unexpected pleasure. Truly, the best part of my day."

"Same here."

A megawatt smile lit up her face. "I'm Delaney Evans."

"Kieran Mullaney."

"I guess that makes this an official date. Now that we know each other's names."

"Nope. Not official yet." Kieran tilted his head to just barely brush her lips with his as he walked. At least, that's what he'd intended. But she tasted like coconuts and freedom. Kieran slid his tongue along the crease of her lips, and hell if they didn't part right away. His grip tightened on her, hand splaying wide across her taut stomach.

"You hang on to me while I get the door open."

But then the big door opened to his left. Kieran twisted at the noise, instinctively tucking Delaney a little bit behind him. Then he gaped when he saw his *brothers* inside.

"Get in, K.," Ryan ordered.

There was someone in the driver's seat. Delaney slid out of his arms, stepped around him—without any limp—and climbed in to sit next to Frank. Confused as all hell, Kieran followed her, dropping his backpack on the floor. She closed the door. The car merged into traffic, moved down the block, and was on Lakeshore Drive before Kieran could do more than squint in confusion at his brothers as he buckled up.

"What the hell is this? Where are we going?" Then he twisted around to look, *really* look at Delaney. The residual softness in her expression from their kiss was gone. She'd added a brown blazer before fastening her seat belt. And now? She'd just pulled a gun out of the side pocket to her seat and tucked it into the back of her pants.

A *gun*? A freaking gun? He'd hit on a woman who carried a gun? Yeah, that struck Kieran a little harder than wondering how she knew his brothers. Or why anybody needed a gun in the middle of the afternoon. Which, as a soon-to-be lawyer, was probably a dumb thought. Criminals didn't punch a time clock. Was she a criminal?

"Who are you—really?" he demanded.

"Delaney Evans. U.S. Marshal."

No shit? Marshals were way hotter than he'd ever imagined. Kieran was also pretty fucking off-balance if that was his first response to whatever the hell was going on right now.

"I'm sorry, Kieran." Ryan shook his head and let his hands dangle off his knees. His oldest brother hadn't looked that sad and serious since . . . hell, probably since their dad died. "It's a shitty way to do this, but I can't think of a good way."

"To do what?" Because Kieran was fucking *worried* at this point.

"To tell you that we're in the Chicago mob. Both of us." Frank pointed back and forth between himself and Ryan. "Or we were, until this morning."

No. No fucking way. Kieran shook his head, trying to shake Frank's words back out of his ears. "That's one hell of a sick joke."

"Notice how we're not laughing."

Yeah, he'd noticed alright. The pair of them matched head to toe. Kieran catalogued the oddness of all of it. Their mussed dark hair—and they both liked to hog the mirror *a lot* to be ready for any hot women that might cross their paths on a given day. Black jeans and tees, on a weekday when they should at least be sporting ties. Most of all, the hangdog downward tilt to their whole faces. This . . . whatever *this* was, it was deadly serious.

He tried to lunge sideways to get to Delaney, but the damned seat belt snapped him back in place. Kieran white-knuckled the armrest as he torqued his body around. "Holy shit, did you arrest my brothers?"

"No."

"Then why—oh." His brain finally revved past the shock. If what Ryan and Frank alleged was true, there was only one reason there'd be a U.S. Marshal in the car with them. "You fuckers are going into Witness Protection, aren't you?"

"Yeah. I'm so, so sorry, K."

"Cut the apology crap." He didn't have time for it. Because Kieran had the feeling he was already on borrowed time. That any second *Marshal* Evans would kick him out of the car and he'd never seen his brothers again. "You're leaving me? This is you two saying goodbye? Forever?"

Damned if there wasn't a lump in his throat. This couldn't be happening. The Mullaney brothers were tight. Tight in a way that only happened when you lost both your parents before you could shave. He'd never even thought about what life would be like without them.

"No." Ryan fought briefly with his seat belt before just reaching over and gripping Kieran's upper arm. Squeezing it like a python. "We stay together. Always. Keeping the three of us together is the only thing that matters. It's the reason we're joining WITSEC."

"I don't understand. You're ratting on the mob . . . for us?"

"The head of the mob, Danny McGinty—"

Delaney cut him off with a buzzer-like noise. "Hey. Remember the ground rules. Kieran doesn't need details. The less he knows, the better."

Ryan's eyes burned with blue fire he aimed back at the marshal. "He needs to know the name of the man who fucked us over. The man who was behind the death of our parents."

Kieran's suddenly upside-down world did another one-eighty. Nobody had ever said their parents were *murdered*. What else about the life he thought he knew was a total lie?

The woman he still—unfuckingbelievable—wanted to kiss gave a sharp nod. "Fair enough. But watch yourself."

"McGinty had some deals fall apart. He needed someone to take the rap, do time in prison. He picked Frank to be the fall guy. When he oh-so-generously gave me the heads-up, I decided to take action. No brother of mine would rot behind bars for something he didn't do."

The repeated honk of the taxi in the lane next to them bought Kieran time to figure out how to ask the obvious question. "You're a mobster—but you *didn't* commit a crime?"

"Pretty much no. I really do—" Frank grimaced "—*did* run the construction company you know about. Kept my nose clean. It was the front for the mob, but legit. I sure as hell didn't do what McGinty wants me to cop to."

Ryan held up two fingers. "No prison. And we stay together. Those were my terms when I went to WITSEC and asked for protection. They gave their word. It's all going down today. The raid on McGinty's crew. And the three of us disappearing forever."

Forever? Talk about dramatic overkill. Ryan always did like to tell stories. Kieran looked out at the enormous, overwhelming blue of Lake Michigan. The lake that had anchored his whole life. They weren't leaving Chicago. No way.

He pushed off Ryan's hand. "Wait a minute. You mean we'll be holed up in some boring safehouse in the suburbs for a few weeks while you get questioned."

"No." And Delaney actually looked at him with pity—fucking *pity*!—as she continued. "That's only step one. The Irish Mob is bigger than McGinty, bigger than Chicago."

Frank glanced out the window, then deliberately turned his back on the view. "It won't ever be safe for us to come back here. Or ever be Mullaneys again. But that's just a fucking name, right? We'll be together, wherever we end up. *Whoever* we end up."

He was right. Nothing else mattered but sticking with his brothers. The rest was just details. Really fucking weird and impossible details, but still. Practically immaterial compared to the Mullaneys being side by side.

Kieran couldn't process any of this. Like . . . how big of criminals *were* his brothers?

What did they do?

What would they do now?

Even with traffic at a crawl, he knew they were too far down Lakeshore Drive to see Northwestern anymore. Still, Kieran craned his neck out the back window, trying to get one more peek of the law school. Because it was all he knew. All he'd planned and worked toward for years.

Stretching out her arm, Delaney said, "Hand over your wallet."

When a woman with a gun down her pants issued a command, Kieran obeyed. He gave it to her, but kept his hand on top, so his fingers brushed the inside of her wrist. That electric charge of awareness tingled in him again. Then she pulled out everything but the cash and gave it back, tucking his ID and credit cards into her bag.

"Right now is the moment your life as Kieran Mullaney ends. Officially."

Well, *shit*.

Chapter One

Maguire House, Bandon, OR
June 10

KELLAN MAGUIRE KNEW better than to ask a favor of his brothers without offering something in return. Oh, no doubt that Rafe and Flynn would go to hell and back for him—that'd been proven over their last seven months spent crisscrossing the country.

They'd get planted in a town, be given new identities and jobs and a home (all on the government dime), and they'd . . . stick it out until they invariably fucked up. Stir and repeat.

Bandon, they'd been warned, was their last chance. Make it work here or they were out of WITSEC. On their own . . . with what was left of the Chicago Mob eager to find them.

So, yeah, they were on their best behavior here in this tiny spot between ocean, sand, and forest. Kellan's concerted effort at being good was at cooking. Because, eventually, his mad kitchen skills would impress the pants—and panties—right off some hot chick. For now, it'd hopefully get the perma-frown off Flynn's grumpy face.

He slid a steaming plate of eggs and toast in front of Rafe, then added the oversized mug of coffee with a sprig of cranberries painted on it. They hadn't gotten to pick out anything in this house the government dumped them in and it was all cutesy, with carved wooden plaques on the walls and placemats shaped like pine trees.

But hey, it was better than a jail cell or a pine box six feet under, which apparently were their only other alternatives. Or so Rafe and Flynn claimed.

Kellan didn't buy it. But then, how could he buy a story spun by the two people he trusted most in the world who'd *evidently* spent half their lives lying to him?

"What's this? It's not Saturday." Rafe tilted his head sideways, instantly suspicious.

Or maybe that was just Kellan's knee-jerk reflex to the man he'd learned had been the number two guy in the mob. The "fixer." Whatever that meant. Kellan hadn't asked much, because he still, after seven long months of turning it around in his head, wasn't entirely sure he wanted to know the scope of the crimes his brothers had committed.

He turned a plate upside down over the rest of the eggs and sat down, straddling the ladderback chair across from Rafe. "True that. Impressive calendar-reading skills, bro. Or is it that if it's Thursday, it must be a *make out with Mollie* night?"

"Don't be a douche about my girl." He scraped butter across the toast. "And don't begrudge me hot sex just because the only action you see is in the shower with your own hand."

"You know I'm jealous as hell. Doc Mollie's too good for you." Kellan was thrilled the pretty hometown doctor had fallen for his older brother. He really just begrudged the missed opportunity for a metric shit-ton of jokes about a doctor and lawyer hooking up.

Wrong.

Almost lawyer. That was still hard for Kellan to swallow. That he'd spent all the time, slaved for all those years, to never do anything with that knowledge.

He shook it off. Which is what he always did because his brothers were all he had left. It wasn't like he could bitch and rant to them about, well, *them* and their nefarious pasts. Kellan lifted his own mug in a toast. "Plus, everyone knows *I'm* the handsome brother."

Rafe snorted. "Funny stuff. Especially this early in the morning. *Everyone* knows that I got the looks, Flynn got the charm, and you got the brains."

"I'll take two out of three, now that Flynn and his charm have permanently parted ways. He's had a cactus up his ass for months."

With a long sigh, Rafe said, "It's too damn early

to talk about Flynn's moodiness. Try me again in, oh, twenty years from never on that one." He dug into his eggs. "Why'd you make me breakfast?"

The Maguires didn't play games with each other. Or so he'd always thought. Kellan launched right into it. "I want to borrow your car this afternoon."

"Why?"

He was tempted to channel his twelve-year-old self and say *why not?* But law school had taught him the finer points of logical argument over plain old stubborn pissyness. Especially when the whole truth was that he wanted to ask their WITSEC handler for a gun.

Which needed to stay a secret from his overprotective oldest brother.

"Why does it matter? When we agreed to share one car between the three of us, we agreed we'd each get equal time. Frankly, you've been hogging it."

Rafe stabbed the air with his fork. "Don't start with me. We live in a town the size of a burp. We barely drive as it is. If you haven't been taking your third of the time in it, that's not on me."

Riiiight. They both knew damn well that Rafe had gone from zero to defensive in the blink of an eye because he mostly used the car as a makeout spot with his girlfriend, Mollie.

She lived with her grandmother and teenaged nephew. Rafe shared this house with Kellan and Flynn, so privacy for the couple was damn hard to come by.

Kellan took pity on them once a week and hung out with Flynn while he bartended at the Gorse. Still, who wanted to wait a whole week to have sex?

Gritting his teeth, Kellan forced a smile. "Well, I'm asking for it today."

"Don't you have to work?"

Work. That was a laugh. Total drudgery was more like it. No, total brain death. "There's a health inspection at the cranberry plant, so most of us were given the afternoon off."

"Where are you going?"

Clearly he hadn't put enough cheese in the eggs to distract Rafe from giving him the third fucking degree. Kellan smiled again. Sipped at his kick-ass coffee. And lied through his teeth. Since apparently lying was how this family rolled.

"I just need some time with the wind in my face. You've got the beautiful doc as an outlet. Let me drive up the coast for a few hours. I'll bring it back washed and detailed." Their shared car happened to be Rafe's dream car—a 1970 Camaro with T-Tops. Kellan knew that giving it some TLC would guarantee Rafe's assent.

"Fine. But if you're going to take it, stay gone past dinner."

"You're going to cook for Mollie?"

"I'll heat things up. Just not in the kitchen." And then Rafe flashed a wolfish, smug smile.

Lucky bastard.

Kellan would give, well, a lot to be heating up the

sheets, but he only wanted the one woman he couldn't have. The woman he'd kissed once on a sun-dappled November day.

The woman he'd get to see this afternoon.

DELANEY WAS ALWAYS happy to meet with her protectees. Her job wasn't simply to keep them safe. It was also making sure that they were settled and content. That often entailed many sessions of listening, helping them to come to terms with accepting their new lives. She enjoyed being their sounding board. Giving people a safe space to rant could make all the difference.

Today's visit with Kellan Maguire, however, promised to be equal parts enjoyable and horrible. That was true of any and every interaction with him, let alone a meeting without the buffer of his brothers. Because she'd gone and committed the worst mistake possible for a marshal.

She'd fallen for her protectee.

Oh, not in a *let's run away together* idiotic way. No man was worth giving up her career. Delaney had made that vow to herself by the ripe old age of ten. Watching her mother demean herself, lose jobs and self-respect and ultimately, her life, all to keep the love of a man? That had been one heck of a deeply ingrained lesson.

This thing with Kellan was more of a nagging awareness. Like when you felt a pimple coming up, beneath the skin. One you couldn't see, couldn't do anything about, but was all hot and inflamed to the touch.

So she sat in the car after parking for another minute, steeling herself against his charm. Delaney stared at the pink walls and bright blue awning of the walk-up coffee shop and bit back a grimace. It looked more like a cotton candy kiosk at a Six Flags park. Undoubtedly Kellan, with his typical Maguire overdeveloped masculinity, would assume Delaney was punishing him with this cutesy, girly location for their meet.

Which made no sense, since he was the sole non-criminal Maguire brother. The one who hadn't gotten them kicked out of any towns.

On the other hand, he did flirt with her harder than a soldier just back from a six-month deployment. Which forced Delaney to work very hard to make it appear that his flirting annoyed her.

Which invariably just made him do it more.

Even though, every time, she was *actually* annoyed at her inner reaction to his flirting. As well as not being able to give in and enjoy it.

It made Delaney remember those two minutes of perfect kissing they'd shared. Maybe it was the shock of how right he'd felt when they met. Maybe it was all tied up with how those had been the last moments of his life as Kieran Mullaney, and she'd been breaking every rule to engage with him like that. But she couldn't stop thinking about kissing Kellan.

Kissing him *again*.

Not like that would ever happen.

She tightened her ponytail and swung out of the car.

Then she tugged up the scoop neck of her yellow sundress. Because she could literally feel his gaze burning into her breasts from across the parking lot.

Even that imagined heat seared straight through to her core.

Damn it. Talking to Kellan, staying ahead of him by at least two steps, required all of her focus. Delaney dragged her gaze off his muscled legs dusted with dark hair, past the biceps straining against the sleeves of his tee, and back to the pink walls of the coffeeshop. Mission accomplished. Nothing sexy about a building that looked like Oompa Loompas might charge out of it, waving donuts.

She waved at him, a wide smile breaking across her face. Time to play the part. The chance that anyone had followed her from the U.S. Marshals Field Office in Eugene to the long-term hotel where she'd changed, *and* would recognize Kellan, and *then* would rat out his location to the Chicago mob? Infinitesimal.

But she didn't take chances, no matter how small, with the lives of her protectees. So Delaney would play the part of his girlfriend. It was why she'd worn such a short, flirty dress. All part of her undercover look.

Nothing to do with wanting to see Kellan's ice-blue eyes smolder as they raked up the length of her bare legs.

Nope.

Delaney locked her mental chastity belt. Almost heard the snick as the walls around her heart locked into place. Then she rushed across the last twenty feet separating them to throw her arms around him in a tight hug.

The man was a flirting machine. He was no dummy when it came to taking advantage of a moment. Kellan cinched his arms around her waist, lifted her, and twirled to make her hang on even tighter. He even used the opportunity to sniff at her hair. Right under her ear lobe, which chased chills across her neck.

"Hello, Sunshine."

Delaney tilted her head back to look at him adoringly. She licked lips slick with an orange gloss. "I'm undercover, Kellan. Don't be an idiot, and don't you dare cop a feel."

The only way to resist him was to go over-the-top in the opposite direction. Every time he extended the most miniscule olive branch, she brought a wood chipper to the table.

Kellan seized the advantage. Widened the spread of his fingers to sit just below the curve of her breast. Then he put his mouth right at her ear and breathed warm air over it until she shivered. "I'm not fully versed in Oregon dating rituals. But where I come from? Most coffee dates—"

"You know full well this is only supposed to *look* like a date," she said, cutting him off. "You asked to meet me privately. To discuss something mysteriously official." Wondering what that might be had kept her mind spinning through the possibilities all night.

With perhaps a two-minute break to spin through

the possibilities of what it'd be like to have him in bed next to her.

"Non-official marshal business coffee dates," he continued, "aren't full contact. Gotta ask if you're using this whole undercover thing as an excuse to grope me." Kellan moved to breathe on her neck, and goose bumps popped up immediately. "Not that I object to being used as a sex object. I just want to know the parameters." Then he put her down right away. Probably because they'd danced this dance enough for him to realize she was one more comment away from connecting her knee to someplace painful.

A woman had to keep up appearances, after all.

Delaney *wanted* to linger on the suggestion of using his toned and tanned body as a sex object. That want, that temptation, pushed her to respond in a clipped, cold tone. Because pushing him away was her emotional Kevlar. The only protection she had from his charm. His sexy-as-sin smarts.

"You want parameters?" she snapped. "Coffee. Walk and talk. That's it."

"I know you take your coffee with one sugar and an obscene amount of milk. But since you're undercover and all, I'm going to get you a girly, sugary Frappuccino drink that matches that sweet concoction of a dress."

So he *had* noticed the dress. Delaney's feminine wiles did a fist pump.

It took no time to get their strawberry-swirled fraps. Kellan deliberately put the plastic cup in her left hand, then interlaced his fingers with her right hand. "This is a fun change from meeting in the sheriff's office."

"Fun is relative. Do you have any idea how much a thigh holster chafes under this dress?"

"I don't, actually." Flashing a quick wink, he added, "But I will volunteer to kiss it and make it better."

"Kellan. Seriously." Delaney tugged her hand free and flashed him the absolute opposite of a wink—a side-eye so sharp it had corners. "When will you stop flirting with me as if you actually have a shot?"

"We had a shot. It went well. I'm just lobbying for round two."

The almost-lawyer nailed all the facts. Which made it such a shame that she had to push back with the cold, hard truth. The facts that she used as a shield.

Despite said facts doing nothing to snuff out the connection that had sparked between them that autumn day.

"For the hundredth time, even if I wanted to date you, which I do *not*, marshals are not allowed to have relationships with their protectees. I'd lose my job. You and your brothers would be kicked out of the WITSEC program. Can you really stand there and say that sleeping with you would be worth losing my job?"

"Yes." He raised his drink to cut off her protest. "I've never once backed down from a challenge, Marshal. Four-point-oh average through high school, college, and law school. When I put my mind to something, I excel at it. So, yeah, it isn't hubris to say that it'd be well worth your while to at least give me a shot."

"That's never going to happen. What I would like to happen is to stop having you eye-fuck me every time we're in the same room."

"Stop looking so eye-fuckable and I will."

Biting back a grin, Delaney led him to the edge of the busy road. The constant roar of cars guaranteed that nobody who pulled in for a midafternoon hit of java would overhear their conversation. "Tell me why I had to drive an hour from Eugene to meet you."

"As I said on the phone, I'd like to ask you for a favor."

"As a representative of the U.S. Government, I already pay your rent, your cost of living, and a not shabby monthly stipend. What more could you possibly want from me?" This time she was the one who whipped up a hand to stop him from talking. "And keep it clean."

Kellan turned to face her, so she could see the sudden solemnness in his eyes, the humorless set of his mouth. "I'd like you to help me obtain a gun. Then I'd like you to work with me at a gun range until I'm skilled enough to hit anything."

That came out of left field. "Why do you want a gun?"

"What do you think I want it for—to hold up convenience stores?" After a short, savage pull at his drink, he snapped, "For protection."

"That's my job," Delaney whipped back. Kellan had crossed a line. He'd tiptoed up to it dozens of times with his sexual innuendo. But he'd finally leapt across it by insulting her competency. His apparent lack of faith in her after all these months *stung*.

Kellan led them toward the pond. "Look, there are mobsters who want my brothers' heads on a plate. They could be looking for us. It was only a month ago that FBI agent tried to blackmail us. As dirty as he was? It wouldn't have been hard to go a step further and sell out our location to McGinty's crew."

"He didn't know who you were. He only knew that you were a witness, and assumed that you'd be sitting on hidden money to pay him off."

He gave her a *look* out of the corner of his eye. "Don't try to out-logic an almost-lawyer. Technically, we're on the run. In hiding. Which means there is a chance someone nefarious could find us. If that happens, I want to be prepared. I want to be able to protect not just myself, but my brothers."

"Your brothers are ex-mobsters. Flynn's such an expert at MMA he could probably kill someone by flexing his big toe. They can take care of themselves."

"Maybe. But we can't be too careful."

Delaney stopped as soon as their feet hit the gravel on the other side of the road. She planted herself, legs spread wide and her free hand fisted at her side. Slowly and emphatically she said, "I repeat, *I'm* in charge of protecting you."

"In theory, sure. But I doubt that if the mob comes for us, they'll keep it to normal business hours with a four-hour forecast arrival window like the fucking cable company."

Despite her anger, and her hurt, Delaney couldn't help but snicker. Because Kellan had a gift for diffusing tension. Perhaps it came from being the youngest of three hotheaded brothers. "That'd make my job a lot easier."

"Look, it's a simple matter of math. Miles and minutes. Most of the time you're in Eugene, a three-hour drive away. And I like to be self-sufficient."

Still pissed at the implication that she wasn't *enough*, Delaney lashed out. "Is that so?"

He'd started walking to the edge of the green scum-covered pond, but Kellan cranked his head around at the disbelief in her voice. "What's that supposed to mean?"

"Your brothers treat you like a spoiled prince. I'd be shocked if you were self-sufficient enough to change a toilet paper roll."

"Over or under?"

Delaney huffed out a breath that fanned her bangs off her forehead. Suddenly tired of sparring, she said, "Just don't, Kellan. A gun is no joke."

"Neither is my desire to stay alive."

"Are you sure it isn't just a desire to keep up with your badass brothers?"

"This is war. This is survival." He speared his fingers through his black hair. "Rafe and Flynn may have put me in this situation, without my knowledge or consent. But now that I *am* in it? I intend to fully participate.

I made friends at the cranberry plant. I'm a model-fucking-citizen of Bandon. That's not enough, though. I need to prepare for the worst. I need to learn how to use a gun."

She slurped down almost half of her drink while looking out across the still water. The tactic he'd chosen had been perfect. Talking about saving not just himself, but his brothers. Stamping the whole situation with the mob as a war. Because it was. And because he'd unwittingly painted a picture, a nightmare vision, of the Maguires being pinned down in Bandon while she slept, unaware, up in Eugene.

That vision already tormented her at least once a week. Kellan's request was unorthodox. It was also utterly logical. "Fine."

"Really?"

"Yes." Delaney put her cup on the ground and crossed her arms. "You're smart enough to get one under the table without my help. I don't want you going down that road. I also don't take gun ownership lightly. If you're going to have one, I want you fully trained and able to hit a body mass on a dime. Because if you half-ass this and end up shooting Rafe in the leg on the way to the bathroom one night, it'll mean a hellish amount of paperwork for me."

Kellan let out the breath she hadn't realized he'd been holding. "Thank you. Sincerely."

Her lips pursed again. His sincerity had a way of slipping in past her defenses. "Don't make me regret it."

"Protection only. You have my word."

"Great. The word of an *almost*-lawyer," Delaney said mockingly. "That and twelve dollars will buy me a martini."

Then she instantly regretted pushing his buttons. It was habit. It was fun.

It was *dangerous*.

One thick dark eyebrow winged up, like an arched frame around his stunning ice-blue eye. "First you call me spoiled, and now you're insulting my near lawyerness? If I didn't know better, I'd say the lady doth protest too much."

"The lady has her hands full dealing with your troublesome brothers. She doesn't like to waste her energy constantly fending you off, too."

"I think you do." Kellan set his cup down.

Delaney gaped at him. Because she'd been oh-so-careful never to give away with so much as a flicker the fact the she was still interested. How could he tell something that Delaney barely admitted to herself? "You think I *want* to keep fending you off?"

"Yes." Kellan stepped closer. In fact, he moved in way past what would be polite. Invaded her personal space just as much as he'd been invading her mind. "You like fighting with me. You could ignore my compliments, my flirty remarks. You don't. You rise to the bait every time. I think you're every bit as frustrated as I am."

"You don't know anything about my life outside the time I spend working on your case." Heat flashed across her cheeks and chest. And she stepped in, too. To where the tips of her breasts brushed his chest, and her feet bumped against his. "Don't begin to think you know me."

"I don't *think*. I *know*. I know that you may have been on dates since you met me. But none of them distracted you from whatever's simmering between us. You want to turn back the clock to the day I asked you out and follow through on it."

"I don't." Her words were the verbal equivalent of a foot stamp. Then, softer, as if she didn't mean to speak it out loud at all, Delaney said, "We can't."

In response, Kellan framed her face with his hands, tilted her head back more, and kissed her.

Not the light, polite, introduction kiss they'd shared the first time. Delaney had obviously pushed him past that step. Kellan kissed as if he needed her to *know* just how badly he wanted her. His lips worked across her mouth, moving and kneading. Kellan nipped at her wide bottom lip. It felt like punishment for her making him wait so long.

It also felt like a reward, so she rewarded *him* with a tiny moan.

Delaney's hands fisted in his thick hair, pulling and tugging. It undoubtedly showed him the insta-heat burning her up inside as much as the way her leg wrapped around his calf.

She wanted more.

His tongue teased at the seam of her lips, and Delaney opened for him like they'd already done this dance a hundred times. She tasted the sweetness lingering from his drink. Desire rocketed through her, turning her nerves to lava. From the way his penis had hardened to pure steel against her belly, Kellan felt the same.

He streaked the backs of his knuckles down the undersides of her raised arms. Kept going to just lightly brush them along the sides of her breasts, her ribs, the flare of her hips to finally land on the curve of her ass.

Kellan dug his fingers in and lifted. Just high enough to press her center against his penis. Instantly, she got on board with the position, rocking against him even as her tongue twined and teased.

It was impossible to stop the little breathy moans that kept escaping from her. It was impossible not to undulate against his rock-hard abs and dig her fingers into the sculpted muscles of his back. Kissing Kellan wasn't foreplay. It was a sex act all by itself. Utterly satisfying even as it drove her hunger up immeasurably.

And while Delaney would've sworn it was impossible, he was a million times better in reality than all the ways she'd fantasized being with him over the past months. Kellan ripped his mouth away to burn a trail of kisses down the side of her neck.

A semi rolled by, and the driver honked for a long time. It had been easy to ignore the white noise of the cars passing, but the horn broke through to Delaney. It reminded her they were on the edge of a green-scummed pond, across from a strip mall. The world could see them making out. And they'd already shot way past a reasonable stopping point.

So she unwound her leg and put her foot back down on the ground. Kellan seemed to get the signal. He dialed back the intensity on his kisses and rained them up the side of her face, down her nose, to end with a light peck on her mouth before easing back. Then he moved his hands to her shoulders.

It took a moment for her eyes to reopen. When they did, it took another moment before Delaney fully focused on him.

"Not only *can* we kiss," Kellan said with enough authority to make her realize he wouldn't allow her to pretend this hadn't happened. To pretend that she hadn't just climbed him like a tree and responded with a fervor that matched his own. "We're *absolutely* doing it again."

Chapter Two

THE U.S. COURTHOUSE in Eugene was pretty new, as federal buildings went. Snazzy glass outside, good lighting, excellent air-conditioning that kept you cool without requiring a parka in June.

So why was Delaney burning up? Hot flashes weren't an obvious explanation at twenty-eight years. But she couldn't stop fanning herself with the ubiquitous bail bondsman notepad.

Hot. So hot. And the more she stabbed at the keys of her laptop, inputting all of Kellan Maguire's vital information, the more heat prickled beneath her skin.

Age: 25
Height: 6'1"
Eye color: the blue of a blue jay's wing, with lighter

flecks that glinted in the blue of the Pacific on a
sunny day . . .

Her screen beeped. Repeatedly. Apparently, the box
for eye color didn't allow for the ramblings of a kiss-
drunk woman.

And how embarrassing was it that she was still
googly-eyed over a kiss that had happened twenty-four
hours ago?

"That's annoying," her partner-for-now said calmly.
Everything Kono Cheeska said came out calmly. Delaney enjoyed that about him. It was especially fun to
watch that calmness beat down a suspect.

Delaney furiously tapped the delete button to clear
the box. "Sorry." She deliberately circled the cursor,
then plopped it back in place.

Eye color: *blue.*
Sex: *yes, please.*

Delaney let out a groan.

Kono pushed his waist-length black hair over his
shoulder. "What's blowing up your screen?"

"I'm getting one of my protectees a gun. Obviously
I want to circumvent the background check, as well as
the wait period, so I'm doing all the paperwork myself."

One eyebrow lifted on his placid face, which was the
equivalent of anyone else shrieking and running in a
circle. "That's a new one."

No kidding. There weren't any actual rules against it because no marshal with a lick of common sense would provide a former criminal with a firearm. Delaney didn't want Kono to think she'd lost her mind. Especially since he was more than just her partner here in Eugene.

Rafe and Flynn were poised to take down one of the largest, once-thriving crime syndicates in the country. If she got the Maguires safely—aka *alive*—to Chicago to testify against Danny McGinty, there'd be a promotion. She'd figured out fast that Kono was officially keeping an eye on her for *someone*. Making sure she truly deserved the promotion, even if he didn't know the specifics of why or what.

So it seemed prudent to make her case for this decision. Delaney stacked her hands on top of each other on the desk. "He's not a criminal. Kellan's the good Maguire. The one who got dragged along with his brothers."

Kono, like everyone else in the Eugene field office, didn't know the actual details of the *Mullaney* brothers and their connection to the Chicago mob. Not to mention the multiple different identities they'd worked through before landing in Bandon. All he knew was that she was in charge of the *Maguire* brothers, two of which were actual witnesses with a somewhat shady past that needed to testify in a few months.

That's how it worked in the Marshals Service. The fewer people who knew the real story lessened the risk to their new lives exponentially.

"Hmm. Was this your idea?"

She understood why he asked. While she was assigned to the Eugene office, they were partners. Kono needed to be able to trust her judgment.

"No. Definitely not. Their covers are rock-solid. There's been no hint that anyone connected to their case is looking for them. The Maguires are in no danger."

"Why'd you agree to it?"

Kono was asking all the right questions. The same ones that ran through her head the moment Kellan brought it up. There wasn't a single reason in the extensive rulebook for a protectee to be armed, but there were innumerable reasons why they *shouldn't* be armed.

Except that Kellan was different. He was whip smart and honest and loyal and all the man wanted to do was pull his weight in protecting the family. Okay, so there was probably some pride in the mix that was bruised from his brothers keeping such huge secrets from him. That he hadn't been allowed to be part of the decision-making process that enrolled them in the program. The process that ripped away any possibility of the law degree he'd worked so hard and come so close to getting.

Mostly, though? She knew it wasn't at all about keeping himself alive. It was about not being a liability to Rafe and Flynn if there was a fight. The one thing that was indisputable about the Maguire brothers was their obvious love and loyalty to each other. Kellan's loyalty, despite everything his brothers had done? It was one of the qualities she most admired in him.

Delaney pushed out of her chair, suddenly too antsy to stay seated. The bare-bones office they shared had a Keurig right around the corner. She nipped into the hallway, popped in a pod, and shoved a mug underneath the spigot, buying enough time to figure out how to express her unshakeable belief that Kellan wouldn't cause trouble in a way that Kono would understand.

"Here's the thing." She paced back in to his desk in the sensible heels that matched her sensible navy suit. Over three steps to straighten her chair, then back to look at that nonjudgmental face the color of wet sand. "I'm considering it as a placebo. You and I?" Delaney waved a hand back and forth between them. "We both know he's never going to need this gun, let alone use it. But it'll give Kellan strength. Confidence."

"That's pretty touchy-feely. Since when do you care about a protectee's inner strength?"

Damn it. Another three steps back to perch on the edge of her chair. She drummed her fingers on the black padded arm. "Not . . . usually."

"You're affected by them. Not just the one who wants the gun. All of these brothers."

A jolt ran through her and Delaney sagged against the back of the chair. It squeaked and rolled off the edge of the plastic mat underneath the wheels. Kono's oh-so-casual assessment hit her as hard as the shoulder to the diaphragm he'd given her in their hand-to-hand practice that morning.

"I should only care about the job, not the people,"

she murmured. "That's one of the most basic rules." One she'd oddly had trouble following for the last year.

Protectees lives were messy and leaving them didn't automatically remove the messy feelings. There were department shrinks to talk them through their problems, officially. Her job was to give them unbreakable covers, decent-enough jobs, and make sure they rode the straight and narrow.

But she'd had trouble recently, drawing the line. She *liked* listening to them. Delaney had discovered that helping gave her as much satisfaction as protecting.

Too bad that wasn't in her job description.

The Keurig beeped. Kono retrieved her mug and set it on her desk. Then he laid a heavy hand on her shoulder and squeezed, once. "Caring's not a bad thing, Evans. Getting attached *is*."

"I know." She'd already stuck her neck out for the Maguires a few times. They had a way of finding trouble— although Rafe claimed trouble found them more easily than flies to a shit pile. They'd grown on her. Their dogged loyalty and love for each other was irresistible. So, yeah, they'd carved a soft spot onto her heart.

One that Kellan had sealed with a kiss.

"Is this going to be a problem?" Kono asked as he sat back down. She didn't think he'd complain about her to the district supervisor. Not yet, anyway. He was probably filing away everything for the final report he'd submit on her to someone in HR. On the other hand, she'd known him for only a little over a month.

Either way, Delaney did *not* intend to let this ridiculous soft spot endanger her career.

Because her career was all she had.

This favor for Kellan was for his peace of mind. Period. Gun ownership wasn't too difficult to obtain in Oregon. She wasn't bending the rules.

Technically, anyway.

So she'd finish the paperwork because she'd given Kellan her word. And then she wouldn't communicate with *any* of the Maguires again until their next scheduled check-in. Aside from the training she'd agreed to give Kellan.

Crap.

More to the point, Delaney wouldn't *think* about any of the Maguires, aside from the coordination with her team in Chicago as they put the pieces in place for their return to testify.

That kiss with Kellan was an aberration. A mistake. Yes, something that had been coming down the pike, if she hadn't stubbornly had blinders on to it, for a good long while. But it was over. Done with.

Kellan was out of her system.

No matter how many of his traits she admired, no matter how many muscles she ogled. He was her job, and nothing more.

Delaney shook her head so hard that her ponytail whipped her cheek. "Plumbers don't get sappy about the toilets they snake. It's simply a responsibility to check off the list. Which is how I need to compartmentalize again. I'm just tired. This has been a long haul with the Maguires—longer than my other assignments. Exhaustion probably blurred my lines a bit."

"You said the trial should start early October? Only a few more months. Then you'll get a whole new protectee to keep in line."

"Yes. A fresh challenge. That's what makes this job so great. There isn't usually the chance to get bored, get in a rut." Or to connect to anyone. Which was also starting to bug her, truth be told.

Kono slapped his hands together, like he was clapping erasers to get rid of detritus. "A new assignment will solve that. No doubt it'll be somewhere far away."

"Yes. And maybe I'll put in for a week of vacation first, to recharge." Delaney spun her chair back around, infused with fresh resolve. The job mattered. Protecting her charges, protecting the public. It was the least she could do to balance the scales. To make up for all the heinous crimes her father had committed that had earned him a life sentence.

It was clear-cut. She'd decided a long time ago to devote herself to her career above all else. Because her mother had taught her that love—lust—whichever it was, didn't keep a roof over your head or food in the fridge. It didn't guarantee safety.

A job did that.

She'd get the Maguires to the trial. She'd do it so well that, if not a full promotion, she'd at least earn a commendation for her file. That lasted. That mattered. A few stolen kisses did *not*.

Her phone vibrated, skittering across the desk. Delaney flipped it over and swiped it open. A text from Kellan filled the screen.

K: Yesterday? I just planned to ask you for a favor. Nothing more. Didn't want you to think I made you fight traffic for more than an hour so I could steal a kiss.

Oh. That hadn't even crossed her mind.

Kellan was spontaneous and flirty and lighthearted, but he wasn't frivolous or self-centered. He wouldn't have done such a thing. But it *was* nice of him to go to the effort of making sure she knew that.

D: Okay.

K: I'm sorry if you're stirred up right now about it. Sitting at your desk, wondering if we did the wrong thing. I'm sorry if you're second-guessing something that felt so right.

Geez, had he implanted a microcamera during that kiss? How did he know? How did he know what she was feeling when she hadn't been able to identify it for a full day?

Was it possible that all those months of sniping and fighting and herding him and his brothers across the country had brought them closer?

Was it possible that Kellan was right about her *liking* the fighting? About rising to the bait every time because she did, indeed, want to go on that date he'd offered on a cool November afternoon? When—if truth be told—she'd let her guard down and just interacted with him as herself.

Not as a marshal, undercover and working to get him inside a stranger's car so he wouldn't make a scene.

But as a woman. As one who'd connected with him and enjoyed it.

Before Delaney could figure out an appropriate non-response response, the phone buzzed in her hand again.

K: I'm not sorry that we kissed.

In addition to the nearly uncountable rules she followed as a federal employee, as a marshal, as a law enforcement official, Delaney had one hard-and-fast personal rule that she stuck to with all her protectees.

She never, *ever* lied to them. Since they were literally trusting her with their lives, it was incumbent upon her to make sure that trust was deserved. She was up front and honest, no matter what.

Usually, the *no matter what* revolved around upsetting the protectee's peace of mind.

This time, the whole truth and nothing but the truth

was more about Delaney's whirling thoughts. After only a small hesitation, she bit her lip and raced her thumbs across the screen.

D: I'm not sorry, either.

His answer came before she could drag in her next shaky breath.

K: I won't be sorry the next time, either.

PASQUALE ELBOWED KELLAN in the ribs. "Man, your brothers are the best things to happen to this town in a long time."

It was end of shift at the cranberry-processing plant, and they were changing out of their coveralls. All he'd heard, all day, was the telling and retelling of the way Flynn had bounced a drunk out of the Gorse last night.

Yeah, he'd been there. He'd seen the whole damn thing. Helped with the broken wrist that lowlife had given his date until the ambulance arrived, too. But nobody mentioned *that* part. All they could talk about was Flynn the hero. Keeping their town safe from the transient scum of the earth.

And when they got tired of talking up Flynn? It invariably circled back around to revisit the way Rafe and Flynn had caught a pair of burglars last month.

Oh, Kellan had been there for that one, too. On the sidelines. Watching as his badass brothers stopped the creeps who'd stolen a bunch of jars of weed from the coffeeshop and pot dispensary Mollie's grandmother ran.

Nobody told stories about the guy who called 911. Even though that was the responsible choice. The law-abiding response to wrongdoers. The heroically smart response to mayhem and danger.

A part of him itched to blurt it all out. That the so-called town heroes were, essentially, thugs and criminals in their own right.

It kept him up more nights than not. Kellan was torn in two. He loved his brothers, would until his dying day. But he'd spent his whole life thinking they were great men, the heroes all of the guys here at the plant thought them to be.

It turned out they were flawed, regular men. Men whose actions he'd judge severely in anyone else and Kellan didn't know what to do with that feeling. Didn't know how to move past it.

He sure as hell didn't need to hear the entire plant label them damn heroes.

Back in the day, Kellan had dreamed about delivering closing statements at trials. Ones so powerful that the people in the jury would well up, just a little. And then they'd let his victimized and almost impossible-to-prove-innocent client off the hook in record time. *He'd* be the one to save the day.

Yeah. Kellan stomped around the lockers to the

doorway to toss his coveralls in the giant hamper. He was pissed.

To be fair, a good portion of it was how much he hated his job. As Delaney had said—*repeatedly*—the government provided them with stable jobs. Not fantastic ones. When your entire background was made up and you were cut off from using any of the life skills you'd acquired, the choices were . . . not great.

He wasn't allowed to take the bar out here in Oregon. Hell, he wasn't even allowed to be a paralegal. So what did the government decide he was best suited for, most capable of doing without any training or experience?

Boxing up cranberries. By the bajillion.

It was monotonous, repetitive, soul-sucking work that bored him to death. It wasn't even physically taxing. Just fucking boring.

There was almost nothing Kellan loathed more than being bored. Which equated to him being pissy for pretty much eight straight hours, five days a week since they'd moved to Bandon six weeks ago.

Maybe some of his crappy attitude was from wanting to see Delaney again and not being able to come up with an excuse. Her job had brought them together, but it was also the ultimate cock block.

No, it wasn't all his blue balls. He was pissy about the nonstop praise being heaped on his brothers. His ex-*criminal* brothers. Because he'd spent so long planning to champion victims and prosecute wrongdoers. All the praise they received made a mockery of everything he believed in, had planned to spend an entire lifetime fighting for.

When the fuck would *he* get the chance to be a hero? Sure, becoming a lawyer hadn't been his choice. But once decided, he'd put his heart and soul into it. He wanted to stand up for a victim, make a difference, take down wrongdoers, big and small.

Kellan leaned his forehead against the bank of lockers. He kind of wanted to bang it against the metal. Guess he'd have to settle for this moment of peace while everyone else gathered their shit on the other side.

Keys jingled. A deep voice said, "Mike, do you want a ride to the resort tonight?"

"Nah. I'm going to skip it. I can't afford to be cleaned out again."

Huh? Kellan straightened, wondering why his fellow plant workers would go to one of the priciest resorts on the West Coast. It seemed like while half the town worked here, the other half worked at the world-famous golf resort. It was not a place where anyone raking in an hourly wage could afford to so much as order a beer.

Aside from the beautiful marshal, nothing had given his brain a reason to flicker in months.

"You have to. It's the only way to stop him. We'll all be there. We'll pay attention, and not let him win at all. Or catch him cheating red-handed."

"Yeah? And then what? It isn't like we can take a freaking member out by the dumpsters and give him a beating."

This was interesting. Kellan craved *interesting* the way a drug addict craved their next hit. He shoved his hands in the pockets of his loose work pants and ambled, all casual-like, around the corner.

"What are you guys talking about?"

"None of your business, College Boy" Pasquale said it with a sneer in his voice, like accusing Kellan of having a college degree was an insult. Pasquale was a first-class asshole. Kellan got along fine with almost everyone. But Pasquale had sneered the first week when Kellan used the word *bloviate*. Ever since then, he'd been up his ass. Clearly it was a case of jealousy.

Or it could be that the man had a micro-penis. That had been Mollie's giggling guess when Kellan complained about him at dinner one night. Yeah, he adored her in a big-sister way. Hopefully Rafe wouldn't fuck it up.

Mike shook his head. "Maybe he could help. Kellan's smart. We all know it."

He put on the smile he used to win the regional debate championship. The one he'd used to seal the deal when he convinced Melissa Watkins to go all the way in her parents' pool house after junior prom. The one he'd used in his final interview before making law review. "I'm happy to help. What's the situation?"

Pasquale scowled. But Mike barreled ahead. "We're in a poker game with some of the guys at the club. Gardeners, waiters—and some of the guests."

The guests fell into two camps. Oregonians with

more money than God who came out every weekend. And people from around the world who'd appear either for a weekend or to settle in at an over-the-top "cabin" for weeks at a time. Either way, he'd heard the buy-in to the club was a cool million, along with annual dues, and required restaurant minimums. The money it took to be a member/guest was no joke.

Kellan leaned against the locker, ankles crossed. "How can you afford to be in a game with high rollers?"

"They play our stakes, nothing higher."

"Why would they bother?" Slumming it with the help was a long-established, albeit crappy, tradition in clubs. But wasn't that about sex, not card games? It didn't add up.

"They claim the club members play pansy-ass poker. Games with all wild cards that get crazier and crazier. We play hard-core poker. Nothing wild. Nothing stupid. We just like to play a good game."

Begrudgingly—because he hated to be left out of anything, Pasquale chimed in. "It's been going on for years. A semisecret game that anyone can buy into if they want some honest, no-frills action."

Interesting, indeed. Not to mention right up Kellan's alley. "Can I play?"

"You don't want to, College Boy." Pasquale hocked up a loogie and spat in . . . well, the general direction of the sink. "We've got a cheat. Three weeks in a row now. We're sure it's a club member. We just can't prove it."

Mike shrugged, hunched forward and lowered his

voice as if worried a wealthy member might actually appear in their locker room out of the blue. "We can't accuse him unless we figure out how he does it. We can't even tell him not to come back." Eyes downcast, mouth downturned, the guy looked beaten down.

Even Pasquale must've noticed, because his cocky demeanor faded away. He looked back and forth between Kellan and Mike. Finally, he jerked one shoulder forward. "You really think that if we bring Kellan in, he can help us figure it out?"

This sounded like *fun*. Not just fun. It was his chance to be a hero. To be freaking Robin Hood. To take from the rich and give back to the poor they'd fleeced.

To stand up for a victim and take down a wrongdoer.

"I can take him down. Teach him a lesson."

"Big talk, College Boy. How?"

"I can count cards."

Mike didn't look like he got the significance of Kellan's statement. Pasquale, on the other hand, laughed and offered up a high five. "No shit? You've done it before?"

"Oh, yeah. Even at casinos. And we got away with it." His brothers didn't know. But some of his friends had gone to MIT. There, they'd heard the legend of the MIT students who outsmarted casinos up and down the strip. They'd studied and practiced and figured out how to do the impossible—beat the house.

Which only brought out Kellan's competitive side. No way were MIT math nerds going to one-up the best and brightest of Northwestern's pre-law class. So they worked it out, practiced at games in frat houses all across Chicagoland, and even took it to some casinos in Minnesota and Wisconsin one epic spring break.

Kellan was the best of the bunch. Not only could he count cards, but he could damn well spot anyone else doing it. They all stopped after the casino trips because nobody wanted to cheat their way through life. They'd just wanted to prove their smarts. Prove that they *were* the smartest.

And now he could do it pejoratively. In this case? Pasquale and Mike were right. They couldn't force this entitled asshole to give back the money, or even apologize.

But Kellan could catch him in a trap of his own making. He could punish him appropriately by taking all the cheater's money.

He could make a difference.

And that's when the thunderbolt of an idea hit him. What if he could make a difference every single day?

Mike bounced a little on the balls of his feet. "Dude, you would do that for us?"

"Absolutely."

"It sounds risky." Typical Pasquale. The man was all talk. No bite to back up his bark. But, to be fair, it sounded like they'd all been cleaned out. Kellan got a government stipend to augment his plant paycheck until after the trial. These guys didn't have that kind of help. They couldn't chance losing any more wages.

Good thing Kellan was dead certain he could do it.

"It sounds fun." But to reassure them, Kellan kept going. "I'll drive the bidding up, bleed him dry, and split the money with all of you. That asswipe won't know what hit him."

As they straddled the wooden bench in the middle of the locker room and talked over the details, Kellan's attention was divided. Half of his brain was caught up in the idea that had blindsided him with the force of a sucker punch.

There was a job opening in town that *did* appeal to him. One that enforced the law he'd studied and believed in wholeheartedly. One that he could qualify for now, even with his made-up background.

He could make a difference right here in Bandon.

He could become a deputy. The town sheriff was severely shorthanded, a little something Kellan knew from when Delaney used her cover as the sheriff's girlfriend to meet with them here in town.

When he got up every morning, it would matter. And that was something that had been lacking in his life.

The best part of this shiny new idea? It'd mean asking the beautiful marshal for another favor . . .

Chapter Three

DELANEY STARED AT the front door to the Bandon Sheriff's Department. Then she bent and slowly banged her head against the steering wheel of her Jeep.

Only three days had passed since her vow to keep contact with the Maguires to a minimum. Three days since she'd admitted to Kellan that she didn't *regret* their kiss.

Three days since she *hadn't* admitted that there was no chance of it happening again. Because that would only lead to an argument. Kellan would've been an excellent lawyer, if his top-notch arguing skills were anything to go by.

Delaney couldn't risk giving him the slightest chance to change her mind. To convince her to forget about rules and her own personal code of conduct—far stricter than that of the U.S. Marshals—that said a relationship, an involvement, would only weaken her and thus was to be avoided.

But here she was at the jail. The spot where, in every town, she brought the Maguires to yell at them for getting into trouble. Or announced they were pulling up stakes and being herded to a new location.

Funny how jails made her think of Kellan now. Of all the extra glances she'd snuck at him, or the jokes she'd bitten her cheek not to laugh at. Delaney had been certain that was sufficient resistance to his charm. Enough so that she could relax and enjoy reliving those moments at night. In bed. Alone.

She'd been so very wrong.

She'd been too lenient with herself. The result was giving in to a kiss so spectacular that it made her efforts at resistance *much* more difficult. More complicated. It made Delaney furious with her own weakness.

And clearly, she'd been far too lenient with her protectees, since apparently they'd gotten involved in a bar brawl. Not that any of the three of them had bothered to contact her with a heads-up.

The rules were actually pretty simple to staying in WITSEC. 1) Don't have any contact with your old life. 2) Stay out of trouble. Stay on the right side of the law.

So why, exactly, did Flynn and Kellan end up on a police incident report? Especially without feeling the need to immediately contact her with a concise explanation of said incident?

Frustration pounded in her head, but hitting the

steering wheel didn't decrease it. Nor did staying in a car that practically steamed because the air-conditioning had been on the fritz for the entire drive. So Delaney got out of the car with a downward tug at the short hem of her clingy black dress.

Whenever she came to Bandon to check on the Maguires, she used the cover of pretending to date Mateo, the sheriff. He was more than willing to assist the Marshals Service. Luckily, they enjoyed talking shop together.

Unluckily, it meant parading in front of Kellan dressed like she was trying to flirt her way into bed.

Delaney headed straight back to the multipurpose conference/interrogation/lunch room. She paused outside the open door to remind herself that Kellan was off-limits. Not tempting. Besides, she wasn't here to see him. She was here to read his brothers the riot act for risking their safety and continued participation in the program.

Again.

"Can we get back to my question?" Kellan elbowed Flynn as he sat down next to him. Throwing an elbow popped his biceps out from the edge of his burgundy Bandon Cranberry Cooperative tee. The man even looked hot in a factory uniform. How was she supposed to resist all that muscled goodness? "About sex?"

Delaney entered with a scathing frown. Going on the attack, sniping at him like she always did, seemed the best plan. It'd annoy him, keep his brothers from guessing about *the kiss that rocked her world*, and keep her on edge enough to distract from Kellan's charm.

She'd just need to amp it up about two hundred percent.

Snidely, she asked, "Don't you ever think of anything else, Mr. Maguire?"

Automatically, he stood. The man had impeccable, chivalrous manners. Which didn't count as Delaney noticing him. It was simply a fact. "I think about you all the time, Marshal. But that's all wrapped up in thoughts of sex, so I guess the answer is *no*."

She banged the door closed behind her. The gust of air blew the front strands of hair into her face. Delaney was well aware that if she tried, she couldn't have given herself more of a tousled, even *sexier* look.

What she wouldn't give to have a giant inflamed pimple growing on her chin right now.

Lacking that, Delaney narrowed her eyes dangerously. "Maybe if you stimulated that big brain of yours, instead of just what's in your pants, you'd find a job that suits you better than the cranberry plant."

Kellan froze, halfway between standing and sitting. Clearly he'd been caught off guard by her crossing the line from their usual flirtatious bickering.

Considering what had gone down between them last week, *i.e., the epic kiss that could not, would not be ignored*, Kellan probably didn't understand her reaction at all. They'd more than come to a truce. Things had changed between them.

And then she'd remembered the potential danger to that change. The way her feelings for a single man could derail everything. Watching the surprise flicker across his handsome face, Delaney didn't feel satisfaction at pushing him away.

No, she felt confusion.

This smart, nice man had done nothing but compliment her and appreciate her. For his attention, she was slapping him back with a verbal two-by-four. Why did her sound plan suddenly feel so wrong?

Slowly, Kellan shifted into the hard wooden chair. "They say the brain is the biggest sexual organ. Thanks for noticing that mine is . . . oversized."

She curled her toes in her pointy stilettos to keep from smiling. Kellan didn't back down. Ever. Delaney liked that about him. A lot. Not to mention that even when she worked her hardest at not responding, the man could put a smile in her heart.

Irresistible.

Flynn entered the fray, his voice a little too loud with a purposeful shift. "Marshal Evans. It's always a rip-roaring good time hanging with you. But if we keep being seen coming into the police station, it'll be suspicious. People will start to talk."

"Then make friends with the sheriff," she snarled. Then Delaney sagged, leaning her butt against the door and pressing her palms to it while sucking in a long breath. Because this was nuts.

Turning into a raging bitch wouldn't solve anything.

Her protectees didn't deserve that attitude. If they complained about her, that would derail her career even more than her NSFW fantasies about Kellan.

So Delaney pasted on a smile. Regrouped. "Apparently, Mateo paddle surfs. Wouldn't that be fun?"

Flynn rolled his eyes. "I literally have no fucking idea."

"Fine, then." She threw up her hands. Because the man had a point. They needed a cover as strong as her pretend dates. "Golf. Didn't I see in your files that you and Rafe golf?"

"We all do." Flynn waved a hand in a circle to include his brothers. "We also like deep dish pizza, the playoffs of any and every sport, and hate nineties grunge music. Why do our files have random information that belongs on a dating profile?"

Delaney was glad he'd asked. It steered the conversation back around to what brought them all together in this room. The Chicago mob. The case multiple agencies had worked together to build against its leader for years. The case on the brink of bringing McGinty to justice, thanks to the Maguire brothers.

The case that had changed their lives irrevocably. The one that could do the same to hers. Because it would either go well and earn her a promotion. Or end in, well, probably a shoot-out, with her protectees dead and her career tanked.

Everything was riding on them staying alive and giving testimony. Everything in their lives and in her own.

"Because your ex-boss, Danny McGinty—and many

of his high-level crew—participated in that charity golf tournament last summer."

Rafe made a two-handed snap/fist thump combo. "Whistling Straits Pro-Am. Can't believe we had to drag our asses past all those cows to Sheboygan for it. How'd that get on your radar?"

She sat down, across the table from them. "It's in Wisconsin. Someplace that McGinty did not control. Which meant we were able to bug the clubhouse and the golf carts."

Kellan's head snapped up. "That's underhanded. Strategic. Impressive."

"Thank you, Counselor." The compliment warmed Delaney's heart, since that particular plan had been her idea. But she couldn't show any signs of softening. Flynn and Rafe would be suspicious. "So glad you approve of an investigation that took us five years, seven different agencies, and which cost three undercover agents their lives."

"It was a compliment, Marshal. And an olive branch. The rules of polite society require that you accept it as both."

Was she overdoing her attempt at their standard level of bickering? Delaney lifted her hair off the back of her neck. Then she shook her head side to side. "I'm sorry. I'm in a bad mood. Traffic down here from the Eugene field office was hideous. My air-conditioning's on the fritz. And this dress means I have to wear a thigh holster, which just isn't comfortable."

She watched Kellan while she continued to chat with his brothers. Watched him watching her. And hoped he knew that their *kiss* wasn't the cause of her behavior.

Then grumpy, ever-sullen Flynn cracked a joke. He'd adjusted the least to any version of their new lives. Delaney wasn't a psychiatrist, but she guessed he carried about three hundred and sixty pounds of guilt for being the reason his brothers had gotten their lives ripped away. It was a complete change of pace to see him smiling and teasing.

She knew how much it would mean to Kellan to have their old dynamic restored. He idolized his brothers. Sure, they'd tarnished a bit in his eyes after the reveal that they were criminals. It didn't appear to change his love for them at all, though. She snuck a glance to, yes, see him smiling at Flynn proudly, like the guy had finished a marathon instead of merely cracking wise.

Delaney shifted in her seat to face Rafe. "What's up with your brother? He's not being a stick-in-the-mud. He's downright . . . friendly. Has he been sampling the medicinal wares at that coffee and marijuana shop? I warned you guys to steer clear of it."

Rafe held up his hands. "We only go for the coffee. Norah's given me her word that she won't ever 'spice up'—her language, not mine—anything the Maguires order. We're clean, Marshal."

"Flynn's high on life." Kellan made a heart with his hands and held it up to one eye to look at Delaney through. Which was adorable. Not that she noticed.

Again, simply a fact that deserved to be catalogued by a trained observer. "Or love, to be more specific. He's got a girl."

Both of her eyebrows shot upward. Delaney couldn't resist teasing Flynn a bit. Maybe her comments would end up teasing another easy grin out of Kellan, too. "Is she aware of this development? And willing? You know, there are rules in this state about locking women in the basement."

"Very funny," Flynn ground out between clenched teeth.

Delaney propped her elbows on the table and cradled her chin in her hands. "Ooh, I'm intrigued. Tell me all about her."

"Her name's Sierra. She's pretty great. And that's all you get."

Her arms fell to the scarred wood. Why did everything have to be so complicated with the Maguires? "Sierra Williams?"

"Yeah." Kellan drilled her with a suspicious stare. "How'd you know that?"

"Because she's in the police report as a witness to the event that brings me down here tonight."

His already-light eyes iced over. Glacially so. "You came to talk to us about what happened at the Gorse on Saturday."

"No. Not 'what happened.'" Delaney made air quotes with her fingers. Because Flynn had apparently used his MMA skills on a drunk who'd attacked his own girlfriend in the Gorse, where Flynn tended bar. He might as well have brought a semiautomatic to a rock/paper/scissors game. "More 'what you did.' A hailstorm *happens* to you. When you repeatedly punch and then kick a man out a door, that's a conscious choice."

Kellan stood and lifted one upraised finger to hammer home his point. "Rosalie O'Hearn is the one who made a choice. She *chose* to put her faith in the wrong man. Flynn didn't have a choice to make. He had a *responsibility*—as a man, as a concerned citizen, and as the bar's official bouncer—to help her out of a tight spot. To prevent her from getting a worse injury than just her broken arm."

Oh.

Oh, *my*.

Oh, he was *good*. Was there anything sexier than standing up for what he believed? And for defending his brother, on top of it? If she'd been standing, Delaney's panties might very well have just dropped to the floor from the power of that speech.

Delaney allowed herself to give Kellan a brief nod. But then she was right back into it. Because she had a job to do. Rafe and Flynn had a history of fighting in their previous towns. Not to mention Flynn's very long string—undefeated—of underground fights in Chicago. She had to do her due diligence and be sure this wasn't the first sign they might need to be relocated.

For the sixth time.

"While I appreciate your vociferous defense of your

brother, I need to hear from Flynn himself." Palms up, she placed one hand on top of the other and laid an icy cool stare straight across the table. "What was your intent that night? Did you have any prior interactions with Mr. Neal before bloodying his face?"

While Flynn said all the right things about helping a defenseless woman, about not wanting to fight but needing to stop her attacker, Delaney watched Kellan some more. Just out of the corner of her eye, because she still had to carry through with yelling at Flynn for fighting. But the side-eye glimpse was enough to catch Kellan staring at her face. Drinking her in. With a few very complimentary dips downward to her cleavage.

It felt so good to be looked at like that. Like he was appreciating everything about her.

It felt . . . decadent.

Delaney didn't want it to stop. Didn't want him to stop.

What on *earth* was she supposed to do about that?

It threw her off track, off the foundation of pushing away most chances at relationships. She'd back-burnered her love life since college. Dating other marshals was out of the question. And Delaney didn't want to date civilians and have to withhold so much of her secretive job from them.

But mostly? She was terrified of the right man weakening her. Of *love* weakening her, like it had her mother.

How could she now be tempted by what scared her

the most? Even worse, by the one man that she absolutely could not have without giving up everything else?

Utterly uncomfortable, she pushed up from the table. Delaney needed to get out of there. To get away from the velvety lure of Kellan's gaze. It was time to take off the gloves and deliver the hard-assed message she'd driven down here to make sure they received.

"If McGinty goes free? He'll rebuild in a matter of months. And if we don't get a conviction on any of the charges? It'll be almost impossible to justify keeping your whole family in the program."

That should scare them into behaving. For at least, oh, a week.

In a low growl, Flynn asked, "Is that a threat or a promise?"

"It's motivation. You've had a break, boys. Gotten comfortable. Seen how good life *can* be here. Now you've got to do the work to earn this new life." Delaney walked out without another word.

DELANEY'S THUMBS RACED across her phone screen as she rounded the corner.

I just made a total fool of myself, Em.

The best thing about her college roommate's job as social media manager for a huge soda company? She was always on her phone, and always responded at a moment's notice.

> D, what's wrong? Did you drop your gun down the toilet?

Her heels tapped loudly against the concrete floor, heading for anywhere with privacy. Another corner took her to the hall that led to the three empty cells. Perfect. Why is that your first question every single time? No. And there will never be a scenario where my gun goes in the toilet, FYI.

> Then what?

I yelled at . . . a guy I protect. The worst thing about her job as a marshal? Having to completely censor conversations with Emily from pretty much everything work related.

> Did he scratch your car? Use full-fat milk in your latte?

Delaney leaned her forehead against the cool steel of the bars. He kissed me. Really, really well. But he's off-limits, Em. So I yelled at him.

> That's dumb. Everyone know that kisses you shouldn't have are the hottest ones. So stop yelling and use your tongue for something else.

It's against all the rules.

Will it hurt anyone? If not—break 'em. Oh wait—
you already did. ROFLMAO

Kellan's voice echoed a little as it traveled down the
hallway. "What the hell was that?"

Delaney could've played it coy. Pretended not to
know what he meant. But that wasn't her style. She was
a straight shooter—both in handguns and life. Not that
you could tell that from the ridiculous way she'd be-
haved the last fifteen minutes. "I believe the technical,
psychological term is 'overcompensating.'"

Kellan stalked closer, work boots slamming loudly
with every step, barreling ahead as if he hadn't heard
her, his voice quieter but more cold and focused. "You
bit my head off multiple times for no reason whatsoever.
If nothing else, I deserve more basic respect than that."

"You're right. I owe you an apology." Reluctantly,
she flipped around to lean back against the cell door. "I
didn't want your brothers to figure out that we kissed.
So I made sure that we squabbled, like usual. I just, ah,
kicked it up a few dozen notches. To not leave anything
to chance."

Her stilettos added a good four inches to her 5'7"
frame. Yet Kellan was still able to glower down at her
as he stopped, eye to eye, toe-to-toe. "Did you think
I'd stick my tongue down your throat in front of them?
That I wouldn't be able to control myself?"

"No. Not exactly. I mean, you are an outrageous flirt, so . . . maybe?" When his glacially blue eyes narrowed to slits, she rushed out the rest of the truth. God, this was humiliating. "It was *me*, okay? I was worried about acting different. About . . . indicating, somehow, that I like you."

"Well, I happen to be a likeable guy. Charming. Easygoing. I don't think anyone would be shocked at that revelation."

He was baiting her. It was laughably obvious. Trying to get her to admit things that Delaney hadn't been brave enough to fully admit to herself yet.

It worked.

"If you must know, I wanted to call you. Multiple times since Thursday. It's been difficult to resist the urge."

"Is that so?" He eased back to lean against the opposite wall. Legs crossed at the ankle, jeans hugging his muscular thighs, Kellan looked like a worker ready to kick back and have a beer. Good thing she was all too aware—and on guard against—that whip-smart, enormous brain of his. The one that intrigued her so darned much. "Well, it just so happens that I was about to call you when you summoned us in here."

"Why?" He'd only texted that one time. A phone call . . . that was more *serious*. It had to be about more than their kiss. Didn't it?

"Remember that cheap shot you took about me finding a better job than the plant? I did. Find one that I want. But I'll need your help to get it."

The call wouldn't have been about their kiss . . . or whether or not there'd be a next kiss? So she'd been twisting herself up in knots about what may or may not be evolving between them, and Kellan just wanted a favor?

Oh, that wasn't humiliating at *all*. Even with all her years of training, she'd read him completely wrong?

Delaney lashed out, all wounded pride under a sharp veneer of by-the-book government official. "First a gun, and now a job. Is there anything else you need me to hand you on a silver platter, Mr. Maguire?"

Delaney regretted the super-snarky words the minute she said them. Feeling rejected wasn't a reason to be rude. She regretted them even more when Kellan didn't snap back. No, he just stood there, one dark eyebrow arched, waiting.

Waiting for her to stop being a bitch.

"God, I'm sorry."

"We need to compartmentalize this conversation, before I piss you off for the wrong reasons again. Set aside everything personal. This is a legitimate favor, protectee to government handler, that I'm requesting. One well within the scope of the rule book."

The *wrong* reason? So maybe she had read Kellan right. Maybe there was no rejection. Maybe he did still want her, want to have things progress between them. He'd just changed gears away from the personal into an official capacity, and she hadn't kept up. Delaney wiped her hands down her thighs. "I won't even fall back this time and say it's habit. It's because I'm nervous. You make me nervous."

"You're the one with the gun strapped to your thigh, Marshal. How could I make you nervous?"

Swallowing hard, she forced the honesty from deep in her heart. "Because you make me want to break all the rules." The U.S. Marshals Service rules. And her own.

"You mean the one you already did—the *first* time we kissed?"

"Yes."

His mouth opened, as if to either rebut or kiss her again. And then, with a twitch of his lips that looked a lot like a wince, he said, "There's an opening for a deputy here in the Bandon sheriff's department."

Yes. Compartmentalize. Get the official stuff out of the way. Then his words sank in, and Delaney's eyes popped wide. "You want to be a deputy?"

"Yes." Kellan held up long, strong fingers to tick off points. Fingers that she could still feel a sensory echo of along her ribs from their embrace . . . "I'll get to enforce the law, be on the side of might and right, help people, and make a difference."

"That's one heck of a mission statement."

"It's one heck of a job. I meet the basic qualifications, and then some. The sheriff knows we're in WITSEC, but he'll probably want some guarantee on your part that I'm *not* a criminal in hiding before he'll even let me interview."

"I'll do it."

"Just like that? I had a whole statement prepared."

This was the kind of emotional win that a marshal had maybe once a year, at best. A protectee not just going along with the new life he'd been handed. Not just accepting. But striving for *more*. Working toward a better new life. Delaney was proud of him. No coercion necessary. It'd be a natural fit.

"I think it's a great idea. You clearly have a proclivity toward justice, you're smart, strong, good with people." The list wasn't just why he'd make a good deputy. It also happened to be a list of all the reasons why she wanted Kellan so darned much. "I'll talk to Mateo and give you a recommendation. This is the kind of thinking we encourage all our protectees to do when it comes to starting a new career. Well done."

And, God help her, it couldn't be overlooked how smoking hot Kellan Maguire would be in a uniform . . .

"Thank you."

Kellan stepped forward, trapping her against the bars. He grabbed her hands, pulled them overhead, behind the bars, and interlaced their fingers to hold her there. "Now stop being a marshal. Slam the door on that compartment and say why you wanted to call me."

"I . . . I don't know." Because Delaney didn't have it figured out at all. How they could be together. Where they'd even *meet*. How she'd flip-flopped so many times, refusing to admit the desire that had been there from day one. Or feeling it but ignoring it. Heck, she had whiplash just from how her thoughts had snapped back and forth since arriving at the jail.

"I'm damn sure that you do." His lips were right there, taunting here, a breath away and yet not coming any closer.

"Because our kiss wasn't enough," Delaney blurted out.

"Agreed. We need to do something about that." Then he kissed her. Kellan's hips ground against hers. His muscled thighs pressed tight against the outsides of hers. And his magical, sensual, *talented* lips ravaged her mouth.

Kellan took nips along the very edge. Swiped his tongue along the inner edge of her lower lip as though he were licking cream off her. He thrust and swirled and danced his tongue around hers, along her cheeks, in a constant, driving motion that suddenly matched the thrust of his hips. Heat bloomed in every cell of her body.

"Come on a date with me," he whispered into her ear. The hot breath chased tingles down her neck, straight into her nipples. When he bit the rim of her lobe, those tingles went even lower. "A real date. We'll talk, we'll have dinner, we'll try like crazy to keep our hands off each other."

It sounded intriguing. It sounded inevitable. All of Kellan's nonstop flirting, all of Delaney's secret fantasies, all their fighting that barely balanced on the microthin line between frustration and passion—all these months *had* to have been leading up to this. It had been sheer lunacy to try and fight it for so long.

"It'd have to be a secret," Delaney cautioned. "Because of the whole completely-against-the-rules thing."

"Of course." Kellan's easy acceptance pushed her resolve over the edge. He hadn't offered a quickie behind the station. He wanted to *talk* to her.

Wasn't that just the hottest thing ever?

So she'd go. Have fun. Nobody would ever need to know. They'd work it out of their systems with some casual sex, nobody would be the wiser about the utter disregard for regulations, and nobody would get hurt.

In fact, they'd probably clear the air of all this tension that had been building between them since last November. Then taking the Maguire brothers back to Chicago would go much more smoothly.

Put that way, going on a date with Kellan was the smartest move she could make.

"Okay."

Chapter Four

―――――――――――――――――――――――

Two NIGHTS LATER, Kellan was grateful as hell for the distraction of the big poker game. It gave him something to do instead of counting the hours until his date with Delaney tomorrow. Action helped. So rather than kicking back counting his winnings, he was helping to clean up.

Kellan looked under the counter for a trash bag. And then under the cash register shelf. And in the row of low cabinets that held nothing but boxes of golf balls and tees. Granted, it was the clubhouse of Sunset Shoals Golf Resort, but even the über-wealthy had to throw things out, right?

"Here." Mike pulled a bag out of his backpack. "We're like the national parks. We bring in what we need, and don't leave anything behind. That's how we've kept this poker game off management's radar for so many years."

Pasquale grabbed it before Kellan could. "No trash

duty for this guy. Not tonight. Not after winning the way he did."

"I made you a promise. The only way to stop a cheater is to make sure he doesn't win." The modesty wasn't false. It hadn't even taken that many hands before Kellan had turned the tables on the guy who'd been fleecing his friends.

One man—early thirties, athletic, and with a fucking attitude that said he'd gotten his way from the day he slid out of the womb—got noticeably ticked off as hands kept falling to Kellan. Then super quiet, while he tried to figure out what the hell was going on. Then, belligerent. Especially when he got up to get more pretzels, go the bathroom—obvious ploys to sneak a good card into his hand—and he *still* didn't win.

Not just a cheat. A *bad* one. Kellan smirked, thinking of how Delaney would be tempted to arrest the guy for pure stupidity. If she played poker. With her sharp mind, he'd love to see her in a game. Or go up against her one-on-one. Chess, maybe.

Strip chess.

Yeah, probably not the best idea for their first date. Save that for date three. Because they'd get there, he'd make sure of it. Getting Delaney to agree to a date at all was the big hurdle. Everything else would be easy after that.

Hopefully.

"Dude. Did you see his face when Mr. Yamada told him it was time to leave?" Mike laughed and slapped his thigh.

Kellan almost rolled his eyes. Everyone's money was the same color green at this game, but the plant workers and resort employees called the club members by their last names. Like their shit didn't stink just because their homes had heated toilet seats. He'd said hell, no, to that tradition. Pointedly asked for first names until they were given, and kept using them. Cheating wasn't the only bad habit he intended to fix at this game.

"Hey." A group of three guys across the room lifted the collapsed table, turning it sideways and heading for the door. "We're taking off. See you next week."

"Hang on." Kellan jogged across the wide tan carpet with the club's logo of a sunburst dipping into the ocean. He didn't need or deserve the money. He had his victory. And not the victory of winning two-thirds of the hands. No, Kellan's victory was in setting the score straight. Defending the wronged. It might not technically be *heroic*, but it felt damn good to make a difference. He fished out the handfuls of cash he'd stuffed into his cargo shorts. "Here."

"What are you doing?"

"I came here to stop a cheater. Means I didn't exactly play on the up-and-up. This money's not mine to keep. You guys split it between all the regulars."

Shockingly, Pasquale stepped in front of everyone else and shook his head. "We can't do that. You did us a favor. Mr. Jackson got the message, loud and clear. He won't mess with us again. You deserve to keep the money."

Wow. An asshole he might be, but an *honorable* one. Which made him okay in Kellan's book. "Nah. It was too much fun. And this'll go a little ways to replacing all the money he took from you over the last few weeks."

Pasquale took the money out of one of Kellan's hands, but pushed the other back toward him. "We'll split it. You keep half. Keep our secret, too."

"Scout's honor."

Predictably, Pasquale's lip rolled down into a sneer. "Boy Scout? With the sissy rolled up handkerchief around your neck and merit badges for washing your hands after you pee?"

Kellan stuffed his money back into his pocket. Wished—for a split second—that he *was* in the mob like his brothers and could just pop the guy in the nose for being a jerk. He should've known Pasquale's honorable streak wouldn't supersede his already well-established douchebaggery.

"Yeah. I was a Boy Scout." It was cool to be able to share one fact—however small—about his *first* life, back in Chicago. "But my first aid badge means I can save your life if you lose a finger at the plant. The emergency preparedness badge means I can save your life in a zombie attack. I'd say that's worth having to wear a stupid uniform."

The table-bearing crew clapped him on the back and murmured thanks as Kellan left the room. If he stayed he'd just go another round with Pasquale, and that would flatten the high of his victory.

Kellan didn't want to fight with the guy, but he didn't want to put up with his small-minded insults, either.

He'd bitched the least about settling into small-town life. But it took some getting used to. Living in a city the size of Chicago intrinsically gave people broader perspectives, a bigger worldview. Some of the men he worked with at the plant were third generation employees and hadn't gone any farther than Portland their entire lives. They were loyal, hardworking, good guys.

But guys who thought a neckerchief was "sissy."

Kellan trailed his fingers against the grass cloth wallpaper lining the hallway to the back offices and parking lot. Aw, who was he kidding? The very word *neckerchief* was ridiculous. He should've just laughed it off. Let Pasquale's dig roll off him like fog rolling off the ocean right outside the clubhouse.

Delaney would poke at him for rising to the bait. Then he'd poke back. Then she'd get that spark in her eyes that always kindled when they sniped at each other. That same spark that he now knew came to life when he kissed her . . .

Blue boat shoes came into his line of vision, and Kellan jolted into the wall to avoid walking into a man rounding the corner.

Not just any man. Lucien Dumont, the heir apparent to the Sunset Shoals Golf Resort empire. Best friend to Mollie. Which probably explained why he'd given Rafe an arctically cold shoulder from day one. Guess being a girl's best friend pulled out a protective streak almost as strong as being her father or brother—neither of which the Doc had, so Lucien took his duty to look out for her *seriously*.

Since Kellan wasn't in Mollie's pants, however, Lucien had always been decent to him. He was a funny guy who didn't walk around with a silver spoon up his ass even though he could buy and sell half the town.

But someone who would—rightly so—want to know why Kellan was wandering around his clubhouse late on a Wednesday night. Sure enough, one of those surfer-blond eyebrows shot up to his hairline. "Maguire. Surprised to see you here."

"Not as surprised as I am to see you," Kellan muttered.

Shit. He wasn't a member. And given that Lucien *knew* he worked at the cranberry plant, "interested prospective member" didn't fly as an excuse for his presence here, either. There was no amount of fast-talking that would explain it away without getting his friends in trouble.

Or without getting him charged with trespassing. Which was *almost* tempting, if it meant a late night visit from Delaney . . . Not that even his well-developed charm could get her in a kissing mood after a two-hour drive down from Eugene at 10:00 p.m. to keep her protectee out of jail. Balancing on this tightrope between being her responsibility and trying to also be her man was already harder than he'd anticipated.

Lucien cocked his head. Then he took a couple of steps back and opened the door behind him. "Come into my office."

Great. A private smackdown.

Lucien shut the door as Kellan sat on a couch the color of the Chicago River when it swelled after a rainfall. The couch was the only comfortable touch in what was clearly a working office. Not as big as Kellan would've expected for the owner's son. Three file cabinets crowded one wall. The opposite one was a row of long cardboard boxes full of golf clubs. Drivers, from the drawings on the sides. Double monitors dominated the desk, along with an iPad, Mac, and a walkie-talkie.

From the bottom drawer of the file cabinet, Lucien retrieved a bottle of Four Roses Bourbon—*nice!*—and two rocks glasses. "Join me in a drink?"

"Sure." The bourbon probably indicated Lucien wouldn't call the cops on him. And if Kellan had to sit through a lecture, it'd go a hell of a lot better under the filter of good booze.

"Sorry there's no ice. But I can't let anyone know I've got my own nineteenth hole bar beneath the members' files."

This was . . . odd. Lucien didn't seem pissed about Kellan trespassing in his über-pricey clubhouse. He did, however, seem relaxed and happy to have somebody to knock back a drink with at the end of the day. "I'll rough it."

They clinked glasses. Took a swallow. Lucien sat on the edge of his desk, feet crossed at the ankles. "Did you by any chance just beat the pants off Ron Jackson in the secret poker game?"

Thanks to months of practice in mock trials, Kellan kept his face deadpan and responded swiftly with "What secret poker game?"

"Let me rephrase." He cocked his head again, clearly taking measure of Kellan's relaxed pose, one ankle crossed over his knee. "You know, Maguire, it'd be a huge favor to me if *somebody* stopped Ron Jackson from cheating my hardworking employees and their friends out of their money."

"Is that so?"

"Yeah. I'd be grateful as fuck if someone took care of that *unofficially*. So that I didn't have to step in and do something *officially*. Since an official step on my part would require yanking his membership—thus losing my family his considerable monthly restaurant fees. Providing a reason for canceling that cheating cock-sucker's membership would also mean acknowledging the existence of a secret poker game. That game would have to be shut down as a result."

"That'd be a shame." Kellan took another slow sip. Tried to decide exactly how much to let slip to a man who was definitely more savvy than his laid-back attitude indicated.

"Agreed. The game's a harmless way to let off steam. Why let one person ruin everyone's fun?"

So Lucien knew everything. Kind of a relief that somebody who was almost running the place had his finger on the pulse enough to see between the cracks. "Any chance that game's why you're hanging around so late? Keeping an eye out to be sure assholes like Jackson don't get angry and trash the place?"

"Wednesdays are a good night to catch up on paperwork. Tonight had the added bonus of a show when Todd Yamada pretty much kicked his sorry ass all the way out." And a very satisfied smile broke across Lucien's cheeks.

Kellan decided to trust him. Hell, he was Mollie's best friend. That meant there must be more to Lucien than the just the glad-handing, smooth-talking walking billboard for the club. "The game's fine. Jackson was the only problem. But he won't be after tonight. I took care of him."

"Thank you. Sincerely."

"It was my pleasure. Sincerely. Winning's fun. Turning the tables on a fucking cheat's even more fun."

Lucien threw back his head and laughed. Hard. A big rolling belly laugh that doubled him over for almost a minute. "Nice to hear somebody have the balls to not put all our members up on a pedestal."

"I call 'em like I see 'em." Kellan had always believed that being truthful was one hundred and ten percent the smartest choice.

Until he was forced to lie every god-damned day about who he was . . .

"That's a nice change of pace." Lucien pushed off the desk to straddle a chair. "Still, I owe you. Jackson would've been a complicated bitch of a problem to solve officially. Mollie mentioned that you golf. How about we hit the links together?"

"I don't have clubs. Anymore." The thought of some

low-level FBI schmuck using his sweet set of Calloway clubs pissed Kellan off. Officially, they'd been seized by the government. Put in a storage locker containing all belongings that wouldn't give away their real identities. But Delaney had unofficially warned them that the agents with the crap duty of boxing it all up might've cherry-picked a few good items. "They, ah, got lost when we moved out here."

Laughing again, Lucien gestured to the row of boxes along the wall. "We're a golf resort. One thing we've got in spades is clubs. I'll hook you up with a loaner pair from the pro shop."

It was tempting and not just for the golf. His friends from the plant were more of acquaintances, friendly with him only due to forced proximity. Kellan had found a way to fit in, because he genuinely liked people and took them at face value. But he still missed all his friends from Chicago, people who shared his interests and worldviews and even different cultural references.

He was lonely, damn it. Rafe had made friends with Mick, a retired Marine Corps colonel. Plus, he had Mollie. Flynn had Sierra and the guy who ran the Gorse. Kellan had . . . well, he had this inability to think about any woman besides Delaney. That was pretty much it.

Swirling the cubes in his glass, Lucien said, "I want to partner with someone I don't have to be on my best behavior with. To not be the owner's son, shaking hands and smiling and letting the rest of my foursome win a very calculated eleven holes, no matter what."

"Jesus, eleven?" How did you walk out on the course knowing you'd be *required* to not do your best? Kellan was too Type A to be able to deal with even the idea.

Delaney's head would probably implode. She took following the rules so seriously. And the rules of sport were that you played to win. Kellan couldn't wait to see her horrified reaction to this story.

He couldn't wait to see her again, *period*. On Thursday, since it couldn't look like he was actually dating anyone, or his brothers would get all up in his business and demand to know who, and this whole secrecy thing would be shot to hell.

Shrugging, Lucien said, "I win enough holes to look like I know what I'm doing, but lose enough to leave them feeling great about the round and their sky-high annual membership fee."

"If you 'let' me win a single hole, I'll kick your ass."

Lucien sighed, raised his glass in a toast. "That sounds great. Speaking of great, I saw your website overhaul for the Cranberry Festival."

Kellan barely stopped himself from rolling his eyes. He guessed that Rafe had come up with the idea of drafting Kellan at the last planning meeting for two reasons. 1) To distract the annoying festival organizer from asking *Rafe* to do more, and 2) as a lame effort to give Kellan something interesting to chew on. But he'd managed to spruce the site up with half his brain shut down. Hell, he'd made PowerPoints in high school that were more elaborate than the old site.

"How'd you see that?"

"Mollie's nephew, Jesse, helped his girlfriend with the actual blood and guts work with the website coding. He had it up when I was at her house the other night."

"My brothers roped me into helping. When in Bandon, you gotta live and die with the Festival, right?"

One dark blond eyebrow arched sky-high. "Ah, it should be 'that's right, *your majesty*.' I was King of the Cranberry Festival back in the day."

"I thought there was only a queen?"

"*Now* there's only a queen. Had to make the change when nobody was good enough to follow in my footsteps."

Kellan grinned. "Bullshit." But whatever the real story, he sure liked Lucien's style.

"Your bullshit-meter is well tuned. There was a thing a few years back where the king and queen made out. A lot. To the point where they made a baby. The town felt indirectly responsible."

"That wouldn't hold up in a court of law." The words slipped out before Kellan could stop them.

Shit.

But then he remembered that it was just a turn of phrase. Lucien had no way of knowing that Kellan could literally cite the case law backing up his assertion.

"The fear was that somebody might *try* and sue. An expansive battle to fight, even if they won. So the council decided it'd be best for the town—and the town's coffers—to not hand deliver temptation on a silver platter. Now there's just a queen."

"The Legend of King Lucien Dumont's a better story."

Leaning in, Lucien lowered his voice. "Don't *even* ask what Queen Annie Keller and I got up to underneath the bleachers at Bandon High. Talk about legendary . . ."

"At my high school we went *behind* the bleachers. In the gym. Must be a regional thing."

"Where are you from? I don't think Mollie ever mentioned it."

Such a casual question. Kellan just hated to answer with a lie. The bourbon was smooth, the couch was comfortable after standing for his entire shift at the plant, and he was relaxing, shooting the shit with someone who might turn out to be a real friend.

It brought home that on top of being sexy as shit and smart as fuck, Delaney was the only person besides his brothers that Kellan could be completely open with. His true self. Unguarded. It kicked the comfort level of everything with her up a notch. Like going from shag rug to thick pile. 7–Eleven cardboard crust slice of pizza out of the warmer to a Gino's East inch-thick deep dish.

Shit. He'd better come up with a comparison a damn sight better before he tried out that analogy on Delaney.

"Uh, we moved around a fair bit. Our dad was a long haul trucker, so when he got itchy feet, he'd uproot us and start his rig from a new spot on the map." Delaney had been particularly pleased when she'd come up with this cover story. It explained away any difference in regional accents and turns of phrase, like the infamous pop versus soda debate that raged across the country.

"I liked getting the hell out for college." Lucien waved his arm at the window and the coastline just beyond. "But I knew I'd come back, too. There's something special about Bandon."

"Aside from the deference everyone pays you as former King of the Festival?"

"Nah, that's pretty much it."

Kellan decided to jump on the opportunity presented by hanging out with a guy who knew Bandon backward and forward. "Since you're local, can you help me with something? Where would I go when I'm ready to buy a bike?"

"Ten speed or hog?"

"Motorcycle," Kellan clarified, laughing.

Lucien squinted at him in appraisal. "First one?"

"I rode a lot with my buddies. I know the ropes. But this'll be my first to own. As soon as I've saved enough to swing it."

"Take mine." He opened the top desk drawer, fished out a key, and tossed it over to Kellan.

"*You* have a motorcycle?" It didn't seem to fit the resort-heir persona. But he sure as hell wouldn't look a gift horse in the mouth.

"Yeah. I loved riding it up and down the coast. But it's been garaged since Mollie came back to town. When your best friend's a doctor and lectures you every day for a week about donorcycles and ending up a brain-dead vegetable—let's just say I lost the urge."

"To ride?" Kellan smirked, stretching his legs out

and crossing them at the ankles. "Or to listen to her nagging?"

"Very funny. It's a Harley. Great condition. It'd do it good to be used."

"That's a generous offer."

Lucien shrugged. "I've got enough toys to play with. It's good to share the wealth. Or we can barter. How about you come back once a month and check on the poker game? Make sure everyone's on the up and up?"

"Deal."

"Did you get sick of sharing the car with your brothers? Or do you have a girl you want to impress?"

More like the woman he wanted to impress lived over two hours away. No four-hour, round trip commute tacked onto a three-hour date could go unnoticed when sharing a car. "I can't tell if it'll impress her. But I need to pull out all the stops and try."

Lucien froze, halfway through refilling his glass, and shot him a knife-sharp look. "She's special, huh?"

"That's an understatement."

"Well, I haven't met a woman—besides my hard-headed Mollie—who doesn't get turned on by a giant engine rumbling between her legs. I'll get it tuned up and cleaned, and I'll leave you two helmets so you can take her for a ride."

Taking Delaney for a ride was exactly what Kellan had in mind. And he didn't mean on a bike . . .

Chapter Five

IT WAS MINUTE one of their date.

It was already fantastic.

Delaney's mouth dried out as her jaw dropped. Kellan looked just like the faceless man in the fantasies she mentally flipped through alone in hotel rooms. His dark hair was mussed from removing his helmet. But it was a good mussed. Like she'd raked her fingers through it during sex. The muscles in his thighs contracted as he swung off the bike.

Her thumbs raced across her phone's screen. Em, is there anything hotter than a man on a motorcycle?

E: Duh. Of course not. Remember, we rated ultimate hotness factors years ago. At the top were men on motorcycles, followed by men in uniform, and then men on horseback. Amended,

once you joined the Marshals Service, to stipulate
that men in uniform only covered firefighters and
the military.

True. Delaney dealt with too many police officers in
her day-to-day work. She'd had to strike that visual fantasy from her mind completely. Well, my date just pulled
into the parking lot on a big old Harley. Be very, very
jealous.

E: Think he'll give you a ride on it?

God, she hoped so. That'd be one thing to check off
her bucket list. If I'm very, very good.

E: I'll bet he'll do it for sure if you're at least a little
bit bad.

Delaney bit back a giggle as she slid her phone into
her purse. Her bulky purse, complete with service
weapon—not a cute little clutch appropriate for a first
date. Some things had to be sacrificed as a marshal. Yes,
she was off duty, but she was with her protectee—even
if *very* unofficially. Being armed on a date was a first for
her, something not exactly in the rule book.

Kellan tempted her to want to throw away the rule
book completely.

"Hi." His eyes raked down the low-cut V neck of her
white top. The top that stopped several inches short of

meeting the wide bow on her long seersucker skirt. Delaney had a killer midriff, thanks to all her training. It was fun to show it off every once in a while. Especially to a man as appreciative as Kellan. "You look gorgeous."

"Thanks. You don't look half bad yourself, getting off that bike."

"Like that, do you?"

"Mmm-hmm." Because it was too hard to form actual words to describe how *much* she liked seeing Kellan as a biker.

"A friend loaned it to me. To tide me over until I can buy one of my own."

"You're waiting until after the trial for that?" Rafe and Flynn had made it clear that fully adopting a new life was on hold until after the trial.

In case they didn't survive it.

Delaney *hated* that they lived with that in the back of their minds. It was her job to keep them alive. To protect them at all cost leading up to and during their testimony against the Chicago mob. Their actions over the past few months had proven that they had faith in her ability, that they trusted her dedication and training.

But they also trusted that Danny McGinty's need for vengeance could be greater.

Kellan's right hand clenched into a fist. "No. Hell, no. I'm not letting that fucking mobster have sway over one more piece of my life."

She loved his vehemence. Loved that all the trouble his brothers had inflicted on him since deciding to yank him out of Chicago hadn't beaten him down too far. "Good for you."

"I need to find the right bike. Take my time." Kellan pulled her snug against him with a strong hand at the small of her back. "Find one that fits between my legs just right."

Delaney licked her lips, looking up at the twinkle in his pale blue eyes. And then, she gave in to a very naughty impulse and rocked her hips back and forth against him. Because she knew he wasn't just talking about a motorcycle. "Proper fit is very important," she said solemnly.

His other hand immediately grabbed hold to still her movement. "Holy Christ, Delaney. You can't tease me like that. Not in a parking lot. Not unless you want me to throw you on that saddle, lift your skirt, and take you right here."

"I like everything about that threat except for the 'right here' part. In case that knowledge is of interest to you."

"It definitely is." After a light brush of his lips against hers that set every minuscule hair follicle on her body to tingling, Kellan pulled away. "I brought you something."

"Guess we're on the same wavelength. I brought you something, too."

Kellan lifted the back seat up and pulled a travel mug—covered with Bandon's ubiquitous cranberries— out of the compartment. "I got this from Coffee & 3 Leaves."

"You brought me coffee? Aren't we having dinner?"

"Dinner's in a bit. I thought we'd stroll through Old Town Florence first. Talk. And I brought you some stress-relieving tea. A special blend of herbs and roots that Norah swears by."

She sniffed it. But then asked in a tone dripping with suspicion, "Will I still pass a drug test if I drink this?"

"Yes. Norah promised that her special ingredient isn't in there. It's St. John's wort, chamomile, rose hips, and lemon balm."

"Do I look that stressed?" Clearly the new under-eye serum with carrot extract Emily sent from Hong Kong wasn't doing the trick. Self-conscious, Delaney dabbed at what *might* be dark circles under her eyes.

"Oh—ha, no. You look like a million dollars. You look completely edible. It's supposed to be a joke. Because being around me always jacks up your stress levels."

"That's both adorable and sweet. Thank you. But . . . I thought we had a plan? To stop the bickering and do lots of kissing instead?" Kissing was integral to lead into the next step of *casual sex to get him out of her system*. Have sex so satisfying that she wouldn't need any more for at least a year. Or at least until after the trial was over and she'd moved on to a new case, far away from Kellan and his temptation.

"Indeed. It's a solid plan. But you and I don't like to leave anything to chance. We'll call the tea a backup."

After a sip of the still-warm tea, Delaney smiled. "A tasty one. Please tell Norah that it's delicious." She set it on the roof of her car while she unzipped her big purse. "Here's your present."

"Where?"

Delaney pointed at the shiny .22 caliber gun nestled right next to her 9mm service weapon. "Right here."

"Fast work, Marshal. I'm impressed."

He should be. But Delaney didn't want to dump on him just how much paperwork and tap dancing and promising of favors she'd had to do to orchestrate this. Kellan might read too much into it.

"Well, you made a strong case for how important it was to you. You're in a situation entirely out of your control." Delaney zipped her purse and put a hand on his forearm. Tried—and failed—to resist tracing the thick ridge of vein snaking beneath her fingertips. "Whatever I can do to make you feel safe, I have to do. It's that simple."

Kellan lifted her hand to his lips and planted a soft, warm kiss just below her knuckles. "Thank you."

"Don't thank me yet. There's quite a bit of homework before you do anything with this present. Gun ownership isn't like buying a new pillow to toss on the sofa. Learn how to clean it, dismantle it, exactly what sort of damage the bullets do, shooting distance, the whole shebang. Only after that will we go to a range and put your hands on the trigger."

"Whatever you say, Marshal."

How did her title sound both sexy and teasing when it came out of his mouth? Would he say it like that when they were in bed together?

Delaney retrieved her tea so they could start walking.

It was a picture-perfect June night on the Oregon Coast. And the town they were in was a postcard itself. To the right was the wide blueish gray expanse of the Siuslaw River, spanned by the tall bridge of the Oregon Coast Highway. Ahead was a cluster of shops and restaurants that couldn't be cuter. Every one sported low, overflowing flower boxes that popped summer's bright colors against the white-shingled buildings.

"Learning to shoot now will give me a leg up on my training to be a deputy."

"Uh, the job's not yours yet, last I heard. Didn't I get your interview scheduled for next week with Mateo?"

Kellan waved off her comment with his hand before interlacing his fingers with hers. "That's a formality."

With the ease of a bad habit, the pilot light on Delaney's temper lit at his words. "Actually, it's not. I put myself on the line vouching for you with the sheriff. This job isn't a slam dunk. You have to impress him, Kellan. You have to take this seriously."

He stopped, abruptly, beneath the brown-and-tan-striped awning of the Siuslaw River Coffee Roasters. A deep growl furred over his words. "This is my entire future we're talking about. You'd better believe I'm taking it seriously. I'm as serious as a heart attack."

"Okay. Sorry. I promise that'll be the last knee-jerk snap-back of the whole night." They still needed a *little* more practice at talking like people on a date. It was all new and different and put Delaney off-balance. Maybe it was because she was jonesing for a kiss. That would smooth things right out.

Except Kellan still had the furrowed brow and intense stare of someone making a point. And in all her experiences with him, she'd seen him drop the charm and go full tilt serious probably only once before.

This was major.

"I'm *going* to be a deputy. Because when I put my mind to something, I make it happen. Nothing stops me."

Delaney licked her lips again. How could her mouth be so dry and yet her panties be so wet from the resolve and strength in every hard edge of his face? "I'll remember that."

"Good."

"I'm not trying to throw wood on a fire, I promise," she said cautiously. "But are you ready for your interview? Or do you maybe want to talk through anything with me?"

Kellan swung their hands a little between them as they resumed walking. And like a flip had switched, the intensity vanished. "I'd like that. I, uh, didn't want to ask for any more help from you. Only what was absolutely necessary. But you've got an inside perspective that would be invaluable."

Okay. This was normal. A man and a woman, just having a back and forth. "What do you want to know?"

"I don't know how to tell the sheriff the whole of why I want the job, without explaining the piece where I want my law training to not go to waste."

Delaney thought back to her interview for the Marshals Service. They'd asked her why she wanted to put her life on the line to defend witnesses who could be criminals. Like Kellan, she'd struggled to find the answer in her prep session with Em since the first answer that sprang to mind was that she had no family to speak of, so better her than someone else.

Em had refilled her wineglass, and told her to dig deeper. Which is when Delaney remembered how it felt, as a child, to be in the back of a police car with her mother after one of her dad's violent rages, and finally feel *safe*. How that had been the greatest gift she'd ever received.

When she'd told the panel of interviewers that she wanted to give everyone that same sense of safety, she'd gotten unanimous nods of approval.

"Well, that *is* only one piece of it. But let's backtrack and dig deeper. Why did you want to become a lawyer?"

"I didn't."

How could that be true? Shocked laughter skittered out of her. "Law school isn't something you fall into accidentally like slipping in the shower."

Kellan bumped their joined hands into her hip. "I mean it wasn't my dream. It was my dad's dream."

"I thought your father died when you were little?"

Knife sharp, his voice all but cut off the end of her sentence. "Call it what it was. He didn't die. He was murdered. By Danny McGinty."

"I'm sorry," she said swiftly. Delaney had been there

when his brothers rocked his known truths and shared that nugget with him. She should've been more sensitive. It hadn't been nearly long enough, in the grand scheme of things, for him to come to terms with that news. "I shouldn't have brought it up."

"Don't say that. I don't want us being cautious with each other. One of the things that makes me so comfortable around you is the fact that I don't have to hold anything back. I guess that's what I was pointing out. Don't sugarcoat it. Don't pin on your badge and try to soothe your protectee."

"Point taken." Were they working to establish a new normal here? One that included TLC when necessary. Because wasn't that one of the foundations of a relationship, aka a total dating perk? Seeking and receiving comfort from each other?

It would be nice to enjoy that, for once. Even if for only a few weeks. Enjoy not holding back the stress of her job, and maybe even being comforted. It would all have to end when the casual, better-be-spectacular sex did, but until then? Why not have it all?

Delaney reached up to caress his cheek. "Can I soothe you as a woman? One who doesn't like it when the man she cares about is visibly shaken?"

That trademark, quicksilver grin of his flashed across his face. "By all means."

"You get to be pissed about the murder. You get to be hurt." Standing on tiptoe, Delaney kissed the outside corners of his mouth, and then lingered in the center. "I get to do what I can to fix it."

"Just listening does a lot. Because Rafe and Flynn won't talk about it."

"They're probably still trying to shield you."

"Don't need it. Don't want it."

How did they not see the fierce independence that burned in Kellan? They weren't shielding that flame. They were smothering it. Whereas Delaney felt a feminine thrill all the way down her spine every time Kellan revealed his immense depth of inner strength. "I don't doubt either of those things."

"I was almost nine. Dad was a mobster my whole life. I just didn't know it. What I know now, in hindsight, is that he wanted one of two things. Either he saw the writing on the wall, knew he'd need a lawyer one day and wanted it to be someone he could trust? Or he picked lawyering as the safest, furthest thing possible from McGinty's taint."

Uh-oh. This had all the markings of a tale guaranteed to make her well up. Delaney didn't cry on the job—and didn't have patience for anyone who did. But she was clinically incapable of not welling up at returning vets surprising their kids at school and dead parent stories.

"Did he extract some sort of deathbed promise from you?"

"No. But from day one, he shoved lawyering down my

throat. My first Halloween costume was a tiny set of black judge's robes. When I wanted to go out and play with my friends, he'd tell me that was no way to get to be a lawyer, and sit me back on the couch to read. There was never mention of playing pro ball in my house, or becoming a chef or a banker. No mention of college, just law school."

"I think you're right. I think he was trying to push you to safety." She took long sips of her calming tea as they strolled.

"We'll never know. But once he did die, my going to law school somehow turned into his legacy. Like I'd let him down if I did anything else."

It said so much about Kellan that he'd crafted his life as a gift to honor the wish of a dead man. That took loyalty to one's family to the extreme—and the Maguire brothers had proven again and again that family loyalty was pretty much their wheelhouse.

God, how she envied it.

How she craved having a family that was *worth* her loyalty.

Delaney looked over at the shimmering water as they passed an empty lot. Someone must've sprinkled wildflower seeds in the spring because they popped up haphazardly between tall swathes of knee-high grass. The natural beauty, the happy vacation murmur of the tourists they passed, and most of all, the big warm hand wrapped around hers all helped to fill the empty hole that seemed to drain her heart whenever her mind shifted to thoughts of her own father.

Which was *not* something she'd dump on Kellan on a first date.

"What you've laid out for me is a powerful motivation. Choosing your career to honor someone else makes it a selfless dream. Double points for that goodness. And really, isn't being a deputy the next best thing?"

"You think my dad would be okay with this choice?"

"Absolutely. I think you're *still* honoring him. It'd be smart if you shared it at your interview. Just, you know, leaving out the part about the mob."

"Natch." A wink paired with his fast grin this time. But it vanished before Delaney could even smile back. "Going to law school made my brothers so proud. If I become a deputy, will *they* still be proud of me?"

"Kellan, of course they will. You could put cockroaches in their Christmas stockings and they'd compliment you on finding a gift they never would've guessed. You can do no wrong in their eyes."

He shrugged those big wide shoulders. "They've spent their whole lives dodging and/or reviling the cops. Looking at the entire profession from behind . . . what's the opposite of rose-tinted glasses?"

"I don't know." Delaney tickled her fingers across his ribs. "Skunk-stained?"

"Gross. Well played, but gross. And don't think for a second that I enjoy being up on a pedestal. I wouldn't mind if they took me off it. I just don't want my new career choice to split us apart."

"You haven't told them yet?" Delaney thought the

Maguire brothers were open books to each other. Aside from the whole lying about the mob for over a decade thing . . .

"Nothing to tell, yet. Not until I get the job."

My, how his tune had changed. "The job you assured me not five minutes ago was a done deal?"

Kellan pulled her off the sidewalk, over past a small park with benches and greenery filling out underneath the pine trees. It was quaint and cute—but not as much so as Bandon. Delaney was falling for the Maguires' new town every bit as much as she saw them doing so.

He tucked her hair behind her ear. Then he licked a wet line following the curve of it to end in a sharp tug of his teeth on her lobe. "Different crowd, different show."

Oh, but he was nimble. But Delaney had a sidestep of her own to take. "Your brothers will never do anything but love you wholeheartedly. Is there a chance they'll be disappointed by your decision? Unlikely. But even so, here's a radical thought—it doesn't matter. You have to make the best choice for you, for your own life."

"It sounds selfish, put like that."

It was time to vent a little of what she'd been holding in all these months. Because it had been burning inside her, ever since that first real connection she'd made with Kellan on the street when she'd just been a woman talking to an interesting man.

Delaney bit her lip. She slipped her hand from his and widened her stance a little, as if bracing for a fight. The Maguires had each other's backs, and it was possible what she was about to say would piss Kellan off mightily. But he'd just said they needed to be open and not sugarcoat things and it was worth the risk.

"*Rafe* was the selfish one, destroying the life you knew, the life you'd built, without consulting you. Witness Protection is a big deal. It shouldn't be inflicted on someone without their knowledge or consent."

His head tilted, his expression an unreadable mask of blankness. "Didn't know that was a rule."

"It isn't. Not officially. But I feel it strongly. And I've felt strongly, since the day Rafe walked into the Chicago field office and asked for immunity in exchange for protection for all three of you, that he didn't have the *right* to make that choice for you."

Kellan pulled her wordlessly beneath the cover of an old-timey white gazebo. He moved so quickly that she stumbled a little, her stiletto heels catching in the uneven floorboards. Delaney pitched toward him. She dropped her empty mug, her free hand bracing on his chest. Kellan used her momentum, spun them to the wide post in the corner. His other hand tunneled through her hair.

Then he kissed her.

Fiercely.

Roughly.

With so much desire that it made Delaney's head swim.

She'd *thought* he'd kissed her before. She'd *thought* she'd felt the full force of his lust, the full impact it had on her want for him.

She'd been wrong.

This was a hundred times more. More hot. More tingling. More exciting.

More toe-curlingly fantastic. Because yes, her toes were curling beneath the thin straps of her sandals. Had that ever happened before? Delaney didn't know. Delaney couldn't really think. She could only *feel*.

Feel the leashed strength vibrating in his thighs.

Feel the heat of his skin burning along hers.

Feel the thick hardness of his cock pressing against her belly.

Her fingers fisted around the silkiness of his green polo shirt. Where their hands joined, they gripped each other so hard that her knuckles ached.

Delaney didn't want it to stop. Didn't want to let up the pressure even a little. That pain, along with the burn of his stubble scraping against her cheek, the dull ache where her calf pressed against what must be a bench— all those things just added to her heightened senses. Because Kellan's onslaught kicked each of her senses into overdrive.

She smelled the wet tang in the air, overlaid with the sweetness of fresh waffle cones at the ice cream store across the street. Heard the steady, dull rush of the river, the lap of it against the shore, the squawk of a cluster of ducks somewhere between them and the water. Tasted the herbs of her tea mingling with the faint, salty tang along Kellan's tongue. Her nipples, hardened to painful tautness, rubbed against the unlined lace of her "date" bra.

Most of all, Delaney saw Kellan.

She saw the brightness of the early evening sun casting a halo behind his dark head. She saw the azure flecks that rimmed his pupils. The pale corona of blue that she could almost float in. That she wanted to stare at forever to see deep behind the quick smile and automatic friendliness to the intense soul of a man who struggled to balance the love in his heart with what his brain knew to be right and just and fair.

Delaney was hit with the certainty that she never wanted to look away. Never wanted to distance herself from the smart, complicated, thoughtful man he rarely showed in entirety to the rest of the world.

Kellan's tongue danced along the inside of her mouth, his hips moving in a rhythmic echo. His hand caressed down her neck, down over her shoulder to graze the side of her breast. Instantly, Delaney arched into his palm, wanting him to press harder. To take more. But all she got was a small squeeze before his hand continued its slow slide down her body.

His thumb bumped along each rib, leaving goose bumps in its wake. Fingers spread wide, they dug in to the high curve of her ass where it hit the railing. His knee lifted, sweeping her legs across his. Effortlessly Kellan shifted them from standing to balancing Delaney across his lap as he sat on the built-in bench.

"Thank you," he said hoarsely.

"You're welcome? I mean, with that kind of thanks, you are really, *seriously* welcome." His heartbeat thudded against her bare arm. "But for what? Because I want to do it again."

Reaching up, he cradled her face in his palms. "Thank you for seeing my side of it. Thank you for seeing me as a man with choices that deserve to be respected. Thank you for understanding. Nobody else has. Nobody else has even come close. I didn't even realize how much I needed that until you said the words."

A warm rush of caring radiated from her heart. She couldn't, *wouldn't* hide it. Or worry about it. About how not-casual this all felt. About how right it had felt to share such a serious discussion. About how right being with Kellan felt.

"I meant them. I *am* on your side."

"Team Kellan, huh?"

"I think not. That makes us sound like some horrible reality TV show love triangle."

"You're right. I can do better. Got a pen?"

Huh. Guess her purse had slid to the floor of the gazebo at some point, too. Delaney snagged it with her fingertips and handed him a deep green rollerball. Because even field notes deserved a little color.

Kellan leaned over to the bottom of the slats that encircled the gazebo. He drew a heart and put *D+K* in the middle of it. And Delaney's own heart melted.

"I'm not the focal point. We're the team. Together. You and me, figuring out what matters, figuring out how to be with each other, how to be there for each other."

"That is beyond romantic. It is ridiculously romantic."

"Too much?" He hovered the pen right over their initials, as if willing to scratch them out.

Delaney snatched the pen. "Not at all. Just because I'm carrying two firearms doesn't mean I don't enjoy a good romantic gesture."

"Then let's go have dinner while we watch the sun set. Tell each other silly secrets. Laugh. Drink some wine."

"You mean have the most perfect first date ever?"

"That's the plan."

"Then I'm going to tell you a secret right now." Delaney put her lips right on his ear. Whispered, "Mission accomplished."

Chapter Six

KELLAN HAD BEEN in some great theaters in Chicago. He'd laughed at Shrek's fart jokes under the golden dome of the Cadillac Palace. Come up with the idea for a trip to NYC after watching *Rent* at the ornately gilded Ford Oriental.

A trip to the theater, complete with a swanky dinner and champagne at intermission, added up to a night guaranteed to get a date to put out. And yeah, he was secure enough in the size of his dick to admit he liked the shows, too.

Bandon was a whole different playing field. He knew it wasn't Chicago. Knew making comparisons was pointless. But every once in a while, the vast differences between his old home and his new one really jolted him.

Like right now. Sitting in the Cranberry Community Playhouse on vinyl seats that squeaked every time his ass twitched. Instead of the usual big red velvet drape across the stage, Bandon had a white one with gigantic red cranberries painted in the center.

But he didn't even roll his eyes. Progress, right? Kellan just snickered and snapped a quick pic to text to Delaney.

K: Points for consistent branding? Or demerits for being cheesy as fuck?

D: OMG. That's . . . uh, not exactly elegant? Where are you? I mean, Bandon, obviously. And my vote's for cheesy.

K: Agreed. Demerits appropriately awarded to my new hometown. And I'm fulfilling my duty by sitting through a town meeting about the Cranberry Festival.

D: As your government-appointed handler, I applaud your willingness to participate.

K: How about as my

Kellan's thumbs froze, right above the screen. His what?

His girlfriend? That was pretty fucking weighted down with both meaning and expectations. Friend? Not enough to go with the hot kisses—or the surprisingly deep feelings—they'd shared. Hookup? Not yet, damn it. He lived with his brothers. Delaney lived two hours away. That made getting to a mattress logistically tough.

Solving *that* problem was high on his to-do list.

K: How about as my personal handler?

He hoped she'd appreciate the double entendre. And that it would make Delaney think about putting her hands all over him for the rest of the night.

Rafe knocked his elbow off the armrest. "Pay attention," he whispered. "You're up."

Shit. That *had* been his name Floyd just called. Kellan stood as a stack of papers got handed down each row of the auditorium. To avoid looking at Floyd in his god-awful fishing hat, bristling with lures even though he clearly wasn't about to hop on a boat, Kellan grabbed a sheet.

"What you're looking at is a mock-up of this year's Festival brochure. If you flip the page, you'll see the same basic design incorporated into the website's home page." At the last second he stopped from mentioning Sierra's name as the artist. Since she'd only agreed to do the beautiful refresh of the logo if he promised not to give her credit. Weird.

The microphone snapped and crackled as Floyd practically deep-throated it. Talk about a disturbing image. "We want to thank Mr. Maguire for volunteering his time to modernize our look."

Kellan had redone the text while he watched a Mariners game. This thing took no time. He enjoyed making words flow together. And it checked off his third of Delaney's community service requirement for the Maguires.

He flipped to the back and pointed to the tabs marching across the page. "I broke everything out into individual pages, so people can search for vendors, or the band lineup more easily for the whole weekend. There's a page with hotel and restaurant links, too."

Jacinta, the high school sophomore who maintained the website but had zero talent for turning an elegant phrase, piped up. "Website traffic has spiked since this went live three days ago. By spiked, I mean quadrupled over this time last year. And my mom said that she got seven reservations at the Face Rock Motel just this morning for Festival weekend."

A murmur of praise spread around the room as people burst into applause. That praise made Kellan itchy. They were making a big deal out of nothing. At least, *nothing* was the sum total of effort he'd put into it. So he didn't deserve this.

"See, Floyd?" Rafe's unlikely friend Mick, an ex-Marine colonel, whipped off his USMC cap as he stood and pointed with it. "I've told you for years to loosen your death grip on every damned aspect of the festival. We bring in new blood, new ideas, and it's already going better."

"I'm always open to new ideas. If they're good," Floyd said stiffly.

"That's a bunch of baloney. You hold this thing closer to your chest than I used to hold my rifle." Mick sat down in the seat next to Rafe and muttered, "How soon can I get you to run for mayor against this blowhard?"

Rafe snorted. Which turned into a full-out chortle. "I'm not the kind of guy people would elect to office."

Wasn't that the truth.

Hell, if the good folks of Bandon *knew* there were two ex-mobsters living here, they'd probably run them out of town on a rail.

Although . . . aside from the whole former poor career choice issue, Kellan had to admit that Rafe would be a great mayor. The kind of guy who looked out for everyone, not just his own agenda. One who wouldn't put up with bullshit jockeying and politicking.

He'd probably been a *great* second-in-command to McGinty.

Not that anyone would ever know.

His phone vibrated.

D: As your personal handler, I can't wait to hear all the details tomorrow of how you heroically held back from calling Floyd an idiot. From what Rafe says, he deserves a swift kick in the ass.

K: Small town bureaucracy at its clichéd best.

D: Speaking of small towns, any hints on our mystery date? Like how I should dress?

K: Casual sexy

D: So . . . naked?

Why wasn't there an emoji for a fist pump/victory dance combo?

Resentment at being called out dripped off Floyd's every facial feature. "This has the potential to significantly increase our revenue. Good work, Mr. Maguire." Floyd held up his ever-present clipboard to start another round of applause. "Now we'll take a quick coffee and cookie break before diving into discussion of the selection process for the Cranberry Court."

How was this his life?

The thought hit Kellan with the force of a meteor to the gut. Like it did every week or so, with the same force every time.

How had Rafe's actions brought them to a meeting with midafternoon cookie breaks on a summer Saturday? Sure, Kellan was all for scarfing down two oatmeal raisins. But in what *freaking* universe was he qualified to sit there and decide how to choose a high school senior to be queen of a festival?

Instead of spending a Saturday—as had been the original plan for, oh, the last ten years—prepping for a trial. Writing up motions. Researching case law. Stretching his legs with a run along Lake Michigan and then hitting a club to find a pretty woman who'd warm his sheets a few hours later.

Kellan was trying to make the best of fitting into Bandon because he didn't have a fucking choice.

Sure, he liked hanging with Lucien. Really, truly wanted to nail his interview and get the job as a deputy. Not to mention all the interesting . . . developments . . . with Delaney. So he wasn't saying that his life sucked.

Just that it wasn't the life he'd chosen. A dissatisfaction he'd never, ah, fully *expressed* to his brothers. For fear that once he started, it'd have to end with him balling his fists and turning it into a knockdown, drag out fight. He could either let it all out, or keep it all buttoned up.

Letting it all out would hurt Rafe and Flynn, and he loved his brothers, no matter how much fucking resentment built up at what they'd done to him.

Kellan couldn't tell them. Which was so damned hard. They weren't just his brothers. They were his best friends. They told each other everything.

Or so he'd thought.

But Kellan was liking this new alternative—letting it all out to Delaney. She'd been a great listener on their date two days ago. It'd felt as refreshing as a cold shower on a sticky day.

Still, times like these, his annoyance at Rafe crept out from behind the steel cage where he kept it locked most days.

"This is great." Rafe thwacked the paper with the back of his hand. A huge, proud smile took up residence on his face.

It was the same smile he wore every time Kellan had brought home an all A report card. When he won a debate. Or showed up with magna cum laude cords draped over his graduation gown.

"Did you hear how much people liked your redesign? They weren't being polite. They sounded really impressed by what you've done." Rafe gave a light punch to his shoulder, as though Kellan wasn't paying enough attention. "Hey, maybe that could be your new job. Your escape hatch from the cranberry plant. You could go into PR/Marketing."

Oh, for fuck's sake. Like he'd let Rafe steamroll him into anything else, ever again. Voice low, Kellan ordered, "Stop right there."

"We get the marshal to jazz up your fake résumé a little, you could slide into a PR job no problem." Rafe clapped and shot guns with both index fingers. "I'll bet firms all up and down the coast would get in line to hire you."

He could practically hear the pedestal Rafe dragged out for him to stand on. Passing the LSAT didn't make him a certified genius. Writing interesting content for one freaking website didn't make him a marketing guru. His brothers constantly smothered him under this cloak of purported perfection.

Kellan *hated* it.

"I said stop, Rafe." He crumpled up the paper and tossed it under the seats in front of them. "This was no big deal. That's not false modesty. That's my telling you

I'm nothing special when it comes to finessing a website. When will you stop seeing me as perfect?"

"I don't. Not after you burned the shit out of your last attempt at making pizza so bad that we had to throw the pan out."

Oh, yeah. That had been, well, not just *bad*. A certifiable kitchen disaster. How was deep dish pizza so hard to make? Maybe he should give up on trying to recreate their favorite Chicago foods.

"Look, I'm nothing special. Especially here in Bandon, working at the cranberry plant. I need you to dial back the over-the-top praise."

Confusion drew together dark brows that were a mirror image of his own. "But I'm proud of you."

Yup. Rafe and Flynn practically gave Kellan a standing ovation for getting out of bed in the morning.

He knew why.

He knew it was because everything he did was untainted by crime or violence. But being good wasn't supposed to be such a huge damn deal. It was *supposed* to be normal.

"Not for the right reasons."

"You've got that giant brain. Not to mention muscles and coordination almost as good as Flynn's. You do a lot of things right."

"Not anymore. Because there's been fucking nothing for me to do for months. Ever since we left Chicago."

Rafe's head practically whipped around like an owl's,

checking to see if anyone overheard. "Christ, K. Don't say that out loud!"

Funny how he'd been paranoid like that for so long, and his brothers had been so casual about dropping references to their old life whenever they decided it was safe. "This auditorium is empty. The lure of cookies cleared the place out. I could recite your old address and nobody would give two shits."

Stroking a hand down his chin, Rafe asked, "What's wrong with you?" And those eyes two shades darker than his peered closer, like he was trying to see past Kellan's walls.

Guess he'd let a little of that bitterness out of the vault after all. Of *course* Rafe wouldn't understand where this flare of temper originated. Because Kellan never, ever let him see the depth of his resentment.

It wouldn't be fair to Rafe and Flynn. Not when they'd stayed *in* the mob to help give him a good life. A perfect life.

One that he now resented the *fuck* out of.

"Sorry. Listening to Floyd is really as bad as you guys warned me." Kellan pulled a crazy face, crossing his eyes and twerking his mouth to the side. Rafe wouldn't see past his lighthearted antics. He never did. "Guess he just annoyed me."

"He's a trip. And by that, I mean a *bad* trip. Like one you'd get on that kitchen cleanser they used to sell as fake heroin on Clark Street."

Flynn and Rafe barely ever interjected stories from their old profession. But when they did, it never failed to shock Kellan. To knock him back with the force of exactly how bad that organization had been. How lucky they were to have gotten out alive with all its inherent dangers.

"How do you know that? I thought you guys stayed clear of drugs?"

"We did. But we were in the fucking mob, K. Not everyone was clean. Not by a long shot." Rafe clapped him on the shoulder in commiseration. "Let's go grab some cookies. Because you're sure as shit not ready to try baking 'em for us anytime soon."

They barely made it under the exit sign before Lucien saw them and waved from the other end of the hall. Or rather, he managed to wave and smile at Kellan while shooting his usual stink-eye at Rafe.

It only took a few steps in polished loafers for Lucien to reach them. "Hey, I saw you on the driving range this morning. You looked good. Not as good as me, of course."

It'd felt great to wrap his hands around a club again. Even a borrowed one. Like he'd reclaimed some small piece of his old life. Kellan grinned and shook his hand. "Well, you shot out of the womb with your umbilical cord wrapped around a nine iron. You've got an advantage." Then he coughed out the word *privileged*.

"We're still on for Monday?" He mimed taking a swing.

Hell, yes. Kellan used to golf with his friends all

the time. The single-minded focus required to sink a twenty-foot putt didn't leave any room for case law to crowd his brain. It'd been a great stress reliever. And he hadn't found a replacement for that mix of friendship and competition and relaxation here.

"As soon as I get off my shift," Kellan promised. Even though he didn't like his job screening cranberries for detritus and stacking crates, he wouldn't blow it off. That'd be wrong. Kellan was already pushing the karmic limits of doing wrong by dating Delaney. "It should stay light long enough for us to get in at least nine holes."

Rafe elbowed Kellan in the ribs. "Are you going to wear those stupid plaid golf knickers?"

"No." Lucien shot him a dirty look. Or, as Kellan had noticed, pretty much the only kind of look he *ever* aimed at his oldest brother. The guy was—hilariously—still not okay with Rafe dating his best friend. "Because it's not Scotland, and oh, it isn't *1937*."

Realizing his joke had fallen flatter than Wisconsin farmland, Rafe held up his hands and backed up. "Hey, you own the club. Figured you might make your own rules."

"My father owns the club." Lucien's reply was terse. And a little bit on the wrong side of spoiling for a fight. "I just work like a dog at it, ten hours a day."

Kellan pulled out the big guns to make them stop. "You know Mollie would be pissed, no, *disappointed* if she heard you two fighting. All she wants is for you two to get along."

"I'm friends with the *good* Maguire brother. That oughtta cover me. See you Monday." Lucien cut sideways past Rafe.

The *good* brother. Fuck. Lucien didn't even know about Rafe and Flynn being bad in their former lives. Yet he still somehow managed to peg Kellan with the one adjective he was trying desperately to shake.

Rafe gave him so side-eye so sharp it made Kellan wince. "Since when are you friendly with Lucien?"

Seriously? They lived in a town with fewer people in it than Kellan's undergrad class. Options for friends were far from vast. And yet Rafe was copping a 'tude? Rafe, who'd spent the past two months lecturing him and Flynn on making friends and fitting in?

This was bullshit.

But, as usual, Kellan swallowed his annoyance. Swallowed harder past the lump of Rafe's hypocrisy. Because rocking the boat, fighting with Rafe, might escalate into Kellan actually spilling how he felt.

About *everything*. Starting with how Rafe and Flynn had known their parents were fucking murdered by the mob and kept it from Kellan.

He headed for the water fountain and took a long slurp. "We hung out the other night. Lucien's a good guy. He's letting me borrow a set of clubs." Friendly and generous. Yet Rafe still acted like Lucien was worse than Dr. Evil. And Doc Oc. Combined.

"What's his motive?"

It was getting harder to fake playing cool about all

this. Kellan spun on his heel to confront Rafe. "Uh, I'm a fun guy? A good sportsman?"

That outburst just earned him a raised eyebrow from his oldest brother. "What are you up to?"

"Oh, for Christ's sake." He was done with this interrogation. Bad coffee and the cookies in the lobby sounded like heaven. Kellan marched down the hallway, yelling over his shoulder, "Which is it? Is Lucien up to something, or am I?"

"You tell me, K."

Kellen knew what he damn well wouldn't tell Rafe. *Anything* about the poker game which had bumped him into Lucien in the first place. Or his interview next week with Mateo.

Come to think of it, he definitely wouldn't tell him about what was going on with Delaney, either. No way, no how. Not since he and Delaney were breaking a rule big enough to get them tossed out of the program. Rafe would lose his shit if he found out. Flynn, too.

They'd make him call it off with Delaney.

Which was not, under any circumstance, an option. Not when he'd finally cracked through her knee-jerk iciness and discovered how well matched they were.

It felt fucking *amazing* to have his own secrets for once. And that little nugget was something he intended to tell Delaney when they FaceTimed later. When he hoped to start pulling a few secrets out of her. Fair was fair.

Kellan leaned his ass against the metal bar across the middle of the door. "Look, you and Flynn have better lives now. Great. Hooray for love. Yippy-fucking-skippy that you like your new jobs, rev 5.0. But me? I'm so bored I could chart my ass hairs into constellations. So the only thing that's going on is me trying to find my way. A place to belong. People that understand me."

He banged open the door with a swift shove, not waiting for a response. Because whatever Rafe said, it wouldn't be right. Wouldn't be enough.

It wouldn't be *I'm sorry for not trusting you enough to tell you the truth.*

Which was all Kellan wanted to hear.

Chapter Seven

DELANEY'S EMAIL NOTIFICATION pinged on her phone for about the tenth time since meeting Kellan in the parking lot in Florence. *Whoops.*

Before she could pull it from her jeans pocket, Kellan nipped it out, adding a firm squeeze to her ass as he did so. He raised it in the air, way above her reach. "Nope. We're done with this."

"Kellan." It was useless to try and jump for it, so Delaney crossed her arms and tried to look stern. She'd glared at him hundreds of times since November. The look, however, was super hard to conjure up with the feel of his palm still heating her skin. "That's government property. And I'm on the government dime. Hand it over."

"You're not on the government dime right now. It's Sunday. Long established as a rest day through centuries and, oh, the entire world."

"Not for me." Guilt surged through her—also for about the tenth time today. Because she'd thought about canceling, oh, *twenty* times since agreeing to this second date. "People's lives literally depend on my doing my job. Expertly. Just showing up, nine-to-five isn't good enough. I have more free time on Sunday, so I usually do a workout that's twice as long. Followed up by extra target practice."

"I'll make sure you get a workout, Laney." Those bedroom eyes of his shuttered halfway as his voice dropped to a low growl. "It won't be conventional, but I guarantee it'll leave you hot and sweaty."

Delaney wasn't sure if heat flooded through her at the obviously naughty suggestion, or the way Kellan shortened her name. The intimacy it conveyed, the connection, touched her heart in a way nobody ever had before. Probably because she never risked letting down her guard around men.

That's what happened when you had a role model of a mother who threw away her entire life to love the wrong man. You swore never to let the same thing happen to you. Never to let that kind of intimacy, that kind of dependency, happen to you. So nobody saw Delaney as a nickname kind of woman. An ass-kicker, a hard worker, but not a playful "Laney."

Until Kellan.

And the surprise was that she really, really liked it.

"The generosity of that unselfish offer is duly noted,"

she said, tongue in cheek. "However, I really am torn about being here with you."

"Is there anything you need to do about this string of emails? I mean, it's all out of your control, right? You said it's all just chatter."

"Yes, about the appointment about the new marshal in charge of the Illinois Northern District." Whoever it was could affect her promotion. It was driving her crazy not being back there for the announcement.

Kellan arched one eyebrow in utter dismissal. "Basically, it's a string of suppositions."

It annoyed her just how right Kellan was. Years of jumping onto every email, staying up-to-date on every ongoing investigation rather than just her own had turned into Delaney's single focus. Em not-so-jokingly called work her only hobby. That un-joke usually occurred during the quarterly lectures about how all work and no play made for boring texts with her BFF.

Delaney had sent her a photo of the gym at the FBI headquarters in DC, full of sweaty six-packed agents working out (with their permission, of course) when she'd been there for a training session. It had shut down the "boring" lectures for *months*.

She dug the toe of her sneaker into the wooden decking. "You're really pulling the big guns of lawyerly logic on me?"

"Yes. Because you deserve a break. You deserve to loosen up and have some fun." Kellan scooted her over

a few steps in front of the giant statue of cavorting sea lions. Then he threw an arm around her neck and snapped a picture of them. "Proof for later of your day of fun."

Delaney peered at the photo. Her hair was wind-blown, Kellan's lips were smacked onto her cheek, and her mouth was caught in a wide-open laugh. They looked carefree. Happy.

When was the last time she'd looked so happy in a picture?

When was the last time she'd even snapped a selfie? There'd been that awful haircut back in New Mexico in February. She'd sent Em a picture to get input on whether or not she needed to buy a cowboy hat to hide under until it grew out.

Defensively, she muttered, "Target practice can be fun."

"Today will be more fun. I promise." He stashed her phone in his own pocket and took her hands. "I swear I get it. I was on law review my second year at North-western. It was practically a full-time job on top of the already grueling schedule of law school. We're both people who go nose to the grindstone to get results."

"It's all I've ever done," she confessed. "Let's just say the gender split of the Marshals Service isn't anywhere close to fifty/fifty. I always knew I'd need to work harder than everyone to stay on top, to get hired first, promoted first. I'm only twenty-eight, Kellan. Nobody else who started when I did is in on something as big as this Mc-

Ginty sting. My supervisors saw my efforts and took a chance on me. That's why I can't let up."

"Like I said, I get it. But I've also seen people burn out. Big-time. Everything from pill-popping to booze to attempted suicide. I'm not saying those things are in your future. But I am saying that if you don't balance your life with a little fun, a little brain R&R, then your work will ultimately suffer. It's like pulling three all-nighters with no naps. You get things done, sure. You also start getting sloppy and stupid."

Maybe it was that Kellan wasn't lecturing, like Em did. Or because she knew that he completely empathized.

Either way, his words got through to her and Delaney let go of her guilt about taking a day wholly for herself. She could almost feel it lift off her shoulders and float up into the cloudless June sky.

Then she turned to look down the coastline behind them. The ocean was the flat blue of an old pair of jeans. White streaks of surf diagonally met the strip of golden sand. Enormous rocks marched in long rows up to the highway, and then the forest beyond.

"I need my phone back."

With a snort, Kellan said, "Fat chance."

Grabbing his shoulders, she turned him and pointed at the vista. "This is a postcard-esque view. I want to use it as my screensaver. I won't even open email—just the camera."

"It'll cost you. Another throw-caution-to-the-wind moment. To be used at my discretion."

However unlikely, Delaney felt a flutter of anticipation at how Kellan might call it in. "Deal." She snapped at least five photos. Then fired one off with a quick text to Em.

#dayoff shenanigans. Try not to faint in shock.

It actually felt good to hand her phone to Kellan for safekeeping. It removed all temptation. Kellan taking charge of the day *freed* her in such a liberating way. Delaney even swung their clasped hands as they strolled down the weathered boards to a small building. This was already fun.

Fun was good. Fun made it worth her while to . . . well, she wouldn't say *break*. No, she was *bending* the rules. Breaking them would be falling in love with him.

Delaney had zero intention of going down that road.

Kellan sucked in a sharp breath. "Are you claustrophobic?"

"No. Is this the part of the date where we ask each other weirdly random questions? Like, um, do you know how to fence?"

"No, it isn't. And yes, as a matter of fact, I do know my way around a sword."

"I was totally kidding. That's crazy." Her laughter died almost instantly as Delaney pictured Kellan in one of those puffy shirts from the Renaissance, tight breeches, and a blue velvet cape. Basically a musketeer. God, he'd look hot, wielding a sword. Wouldn't it be fun to see him in that on Halloween?

Not that she'd still be seeing him by then. That's what made it more, ah, acceptable to her strict ethical code to bend the rules. Or so she'd told herself in endless rationalizations over this crazy half plan to date him.

Half plan only, since they had *no* plan for what to do long-term. The trial would no doubt be over by Halloween. She'd be assigned to a different case, and they'd probably never communicate again.

So much for feeling lighthearted.

Kellan led her into the building and straight to a small crowd at the elevator. "We're headed down to a sea cave. It's the largest one in America, but still a cave. I needed to be sure you'd be okay down there."

They packed into the elevator with at least three too many other people. While not claustrophobic, Delaney didn't want to be squished into suffocation, either. The elevator showed feet instead of floors, bottoming out at two hundred. And it moved *slowly*. "Why on earth do you know how to fence?"

"I did plays in high school. Including *Romeo and Juliet*. My counselor, knowing I'd do everything and anything to give me a leg up on the competition for law school, told me that honing my dramatic skills would bolster my public speaking confidence and delivery."

Talk about an unexpected nugget of information. "Did it work?"

Kellan raised his hand, stopping with his fingers almost touching her lips. His gaze fixed there, too, and his voice was low, with just a tinge of a British accent.

"If I profane with my unworthiest hand
This holy shrine, the gentle fine is this:
My lips, two blushing pilgrims, ready stand
To smooth that rough touch with a
       tender kiss."

He finished with the lightest brush possible of his thumb, tracing the contours of her mouth.

Talk about sexy. Talk about panty-melting. Talk about romance personified.

Nobody had ever quoted Shakespeare to Delaney before. It was powerful stuff. Almost as powerful as the need and lust burning in Kellan's eyes like a blue fire.

This was why she was risking so much to be with him. Risking her self-respect, her career, and the series of thick, steel barriers around her heart.

Kellan surprised her. Delighted her. Charmed her. Challenged her.

He was everything she didn't know she needed.

The doors opened with a ding. Thank goodness for all the other people crammed in the elevator, bumping and shoving in their hurry to disembark. Or else Delaney might've stood there, frozen in, yes, *bliss* and let the elevator take them right back up.

She went up on tiptoe to whisper in his ear, "It sure works on me."

And then, even as heady and potent as it was to be with Kellan, Delaney jerked back. Because the *smell* hit her. Smell . . . stench . . . noxious odor. Kellan recoiled, too.

He pulled the top of his orange tee up to mask his nose. "Jesus. There should be a hazmat warning topside."

Giggles poured out of Delaney as they left the clean, ventilated air of the elevator. The thought of the most perfectly romantic moment of her life being ruined by the smell of sea lion poop was, well, par for the course. A reminder, some might say, from Karma that what she was doing with Kellan was very wrong, no matter how good it felt. A reminder that it could get her in a literal shit-ton of trouble.

She couldn't wait to text Em about the irony. If she could figure out a way to do it without flat out confessing that she and a protectee were dating.

Em knew her messed-up history, the reason why she chose career over cock—a phrase of Em's she *loathed* but which her BFF liked to use to powerfully hammer home the point—every time. Knowing all that, Em would probably do something crazy like jump on a plane and come kick Kellan in the nuts to keep him away and protect Delaney from herself.

She pinched her nose shut. "C'mon. I want to gawk at *a lot* of adorable sea lions to make up for this torture."

The cave walls were utterly natural, sharp, and craggy. It made her very aware that they were underground. The steady rush of water was audible before they crowded up through a darkened doorway to press against wide-spaced bars.

Suddenly, the smell didn't matter anymore. Because they were at the edge of an enormous cave that looked like it belonged in a movie about a distant planet. It had to be several stories high around a wide pool, dotted with rocks and continually slammed with incoming waves from one side. On the other it was also open to the ocean via a long tunnel, where she could just glimpse sunlight.

At first, Delaney thought the wide rock in the middle was moving. And at least the top of it was, covered in a mass of sleek, slippery sea lions, rolling and pushing, their sharp barks echoing off the cavern's ceiling. A few thrashed in the surf. Dozens more jockeyed for position along the rocky perimeter of the circle. A small black bird with white chevrons on its wings and bright orange feet soared in a zigzag pattern.

"This is . . . beyond."

"Beyond smelly? Beyond majestic? Beyond adorable?"

"Beyond anything I expected. It's completely worth taking the whole day off."

"I'm sorry, that's not good enough. I'm going to need you to repeat that. On video. For posterity." Kellan waggled his phone at her.

He was teasing. He probably thought she didn't have the guts. Couldn't relax enough, be playful enough to follow through.

Maybe that was true. In the past. But Kellan was showing her that it was possible to be laser focused, work at a hundred and ten percent, and yet still take breaks to enjoy life. The concept didn't come easily to Delaney. But when having fun felt like a novelty, it was clearly time to pencil in more of it.

So she could meet his challenge. She could be spontaneous, damn it. Or, at least, this baby step version of spontaneity.

Delaney snatched the phone and clicked on the camera, holding it at arm's length. She even raised her voice to be sure it'd be picked up over the sloshing water and sea lion barks.

"Kellan Maguire deserves a medal for planning the best date ever. I don't regret a minute of time spent on it, away from work and training. Because he's showing me such a good time, I don't ever want it to end."

The grin that had engulfed his face at the start of her speech had morphed into something much more serious. More . . . deliberative. As if she'd made him think. Dark eyebrows slashed upward. "That's quite a testimonial."

Whoops. Overshare much? She kept everything inside so tightly buttoned up that trying to unfasten just one had popped open the whole darn thing. Em would laugh herself silly over this.

But Delaney was embarrassed. Vulnerable. Stripped bare. And more than a little annoyed at herself for revealing so much. They were having fun—the last thing she wanted to do was scare Kellan away. About a zillion magazines and blogs all swore that men checked out as soon as emotions got shared. Without having a ton of her own experience Delaney had to rely on popular opinion.

So she tried to smudge out the level of honesty she'd put out there. "I, uh, must be a little high from all the sea lion poop. Ammonia fumes, you know. Very dangerous."

"Don't." Kellan put an index finger to her lips. "Don't do that. Don't pull back. For God's sake, I can feel the regret crawling over your skin like an army of ants."

"I said too much," she murmured.

A vein popped at his temple as Kellan ground his jaw shut. Then he scrubbed a hand over the top of his head. "That's so the opposite of the truth its almost funny. You hardly say *anything*, Laney. Not about yourself. You're a terrific listener. A great sounding board. You're blunt and an unbelievable hard-ass when it comes to work. You've got a heart that's sweeter than cotton candy when you do care about something. But you don't reveal anything about yourself. And I've been too damn nervous about this going well to push until now."

She turned away, back to the frolicking animals. The mist of sea water on her face didn't do much to cool the heat thrumming through her from his pushing. Because suddenly this wasn't fun at all. "There's not much to say."

Shoulder to shoulder with her, butted up against the bars, Kellan said, "It isn't the quantity that matters. It's the quality."

Desperate to change the subject, Delaney flashed a teasing smile. "Is that a warning about sex? That you won't be able to elicit those multiple orgasms you promised me?"

"Don't deflect," he said, with more than a little aggravation cutting each word off sharply. "Oh, and don't insult me, while you're at it."

Her hands tightened on the bars. He'd seen right through her attempt to not answer him. Her attempt to distract him from digging any deeper into her head and her heart.

Damn it all to hell, Kellan was right.

The right way, the mature way, to deal with handing over the truth of how she felt about him—accidental or not—wasn't to drop it like a flaming bag of crap and run away.

Delaney could have sex with . . . well, not anyone, but she'd never walked into a club and left by her lonesome if she was in the mood. To be honest—with herself, first and foremost—she wasn't risking her entire career to be with him just to scratch an itch.

It was more. Kellan was more.

Delaney had this *need* to connect with him churning up inside her. No, they'd already connected. All those months spent watching each other, circling and growling at each other, had netted lots of information.

She'd gotten to know him by watching his interaction with his brothers. She'd grown to respect him by watching him hide his gritted teeth behind an easy smile each time she yanked him from yet another town. Each time she stuck him with yet another crappy job.

And now that the hands-off approach had ended? Now that they interacted without any audience, without any constraints of the job or the rules? She wanted *more*.

To know more about him. To laugh more with him.

To share so much more time, amassing memories

and kisses and sweetness against the day when this inevitably would end.

She sucked in a breath. Through her mouth, because holy God, the smell was still acridly strong. "I'm sorry. About both things. This is progress, though. I wasn't lashing out at you this time—even if you were the unwitting victim. I was lashing out at my own stupidity." Delaney touched her forehead to the cool bars. "I can command a tactical squad in the field. I can wrangle hardened criminals. Why is this so much harder?"

Kellan rubbed a wide, outstretched hand in slow circles around her back. "Because this, what's happening between us, matters so much more."

"It can't," she breathed as little more than a whisper.

They had no future. Their time together had an expiration date. One that would literally pull them geographically apart.

Ohhhhhh.

Maybe *that's* what made opening up to Kellan so hard. Because the deeper they connected, the more it would hurt when she had to leave him.

His hand stilled. "But it does." Kellan gently prodded up her chin until her view was of the beautiful azure pool and the delightfully adorable creatures. "Stop concentrating on the bad, the future, on what could go wrong. Just enjoy the right now. That's what spontaneity is about. Not doing something wild and crazy that'll go viral. Being in the moment."

Delaney couldn't help it. She knew they were having a serious moment. A moment of growth.

Nevertheless, a giggle slipped out. *Spurted* out, with more behind it. "Funny, that's the same advice I got my first day at a firing range. Be in the moment." She waved her hand furiously in front of her face. Her mom had done that move to stop tears from falling. She'd done it a lot. Pretty much on a daily basis, when Delaney walked in from school and caught her with tears in her eyes as she scanned texts on her phone. "Sorry. Veered off topic there."

With a mischievous twinkle in his eye and a smart-ass quirk to his lips, Kellan doubled down. "I think it's a fair characterization to say that what's happening between us, what's happened since day one on Superior Street, is fairly explosive."

"Although hopefully not lethal." Biting her lip was as ineffective as the hand waving thing. The giggles kept pouring out. "Kellan, you're just making it worse. Don't play along, for heaven's sake!"

"Why not? Why shouldn't there be laughter in the middle of a serious discussion? Why can't we have fun?"

That suggestion sobered her up with the force of a battering ram to her belly. Because it was *brilliant*. "You think other people do that? Or are you simply a relationship expert *par excellence*?"

"I think I don't care what other people do. Only what works for us."

Okay. She'd repay that gift with one of her own. "I call my best friend, Em, every night as I drive the last two miles home and go inside."

"Why?"

"Why am I telling you, or why do I do it?"

"I got a 179 on the LSAT. I can use deductive reasoning to ascertain that you're—finally—sharing something private about yourself. Why do you call her?"

"She read a study that claimed most car accidents happen within two miles of home." Delaney held up a hand. "It's not accurate. Em doesn't care. She worries because I not only live alone, but live in random hotels half the time. So we chat for those 'dangerous' two miles and the scary walk into the dark apartment, and she has peace of mind."

Grabbing her hand, he pressed a light kiss to the back of it. Then he gave her a knowing look from beneath heavy-lidded eyes. "You, too, I'll bet."

"Kellan, I carry my service weapon with me every day. If there was someone waiting in my dark house, they'd end up far more surprised than me—and with a slug in their shoulder."

"I don't doubt you can take care of yourself. I meant that you get peace of mind from checking in with your friend on a daily basis. Your job, all the secrecy, it seems lonely. Knowing you have a daily connection must help."

He got it. Delaney had wondered if sharing what could seem like an inconsequential habit would resonate with Kellan. That she did it as much to stop Em from worrying as she did to have that caring touchstone to close out the day.

"It does."

"Hang on—didn't you tell me that she travels all over the world for her job?" His jaw dropped in exaggerated horror. "So you might end up calling her at three in the morning?"

Delaney giggled. "Yep. We don't discuss anything deeper than ice cream flavors when I wake her up. But she's made me promise to do it every single night, no matter what."

"Then I'll remind you tonight. Although I may be guessing about the exact two mile radius when we get close."

"Close to where?

With a tug on her hand, Kellan said, "Come with me."

They went back into the main room, then up several flights of shallow wooden stairs to a viewing area. It was just another natural opening in the cave wall. The wind whipped, and gulls squawked as they circled overhead. The air was so thickly tinged with salt that Delaney felt as though she could lick it from her lips. Moss provided a thick green wallpaper up the black face of the rock wall. It was wild and rugged and spectacular.

Kellan pointed up the coastline, to a white lighthouse perched between the edge of rock and pines. Three squat buildings, also white with red roofs, sat next to it. "That's where I'm taking you."

"More stairs? Is this a date or a training session?"

"It'll be a workout. But not from the stairs. That lighthouse is a B&B."

Another glance told Delaney that its unobstructed view of the sunset would be stunning. That it looked private and romantic and she was bowled over yet again by his plan for today.

Their . . . situation meant that she couldn't spend the night at the house he shared with his brothers. And Kellan certainly couldn't stay with her in the long-term hotel suite she shared with another marshal. Yet he'd managed to give them the gift of being alone with each other.

"We get to spend the night together?"

"Yes. It seemed like the right thing to do, for our first time."

It was. Maybe she should've thought of that. It was her job to think of every tiny detail when creating people's lives from scratch. Delaney planned. Came up with multiple scenarios. Left no possible development unaccounted for. But this relationship stuff . . . well, she sucked at it. Good thing Kellan already knew how well she kicked ass at keeping her protectees alive. Maybe he'd forgive her weak showing in the romance department.

"You're a gentleman. And a romantic."

That cocky look that she'd fallen for on day one smirked across his face. "Is that good?"

"It's mind-bogglingly good." Delaney threw her arms around him. "Thank you."

Kellan pulled out of her hug abruptly. "Okay, stop that."

"Why?" Nobody had followed them up the steps. The space only held enough room for a handful of people, anyway. They'd hear anyone on their way up.

"This is all a surprise to you, but I've been planning it for days." His arms caged her in against the edge of the rock wall. His breath felt like fire on her cheek, in contrast to the icy whip of wet wind on the other. "I've been thinking about being alone with you. Thinking about all the things we'd do. Imagining what you'll look like and sound like and taste like. I'm a man on the edge, Laney."

Finally. A moment where Delaney could shine. Or at least pull her own weight in this relationship. Because she knew her own strengths in the field. In a split second, she could assess, determine options, choose the best, and implement it on the fly. So she'd solve this problem for him.

"Let's do something about that."

"I don't want to shortchange you on the sea lions. Plus, we can't check into the lighthouse for another hour."

"Don't worry about what happens in an hour. Be in the moment," she teased, smugly throwing his own words back at him. "We've got this."

Chapter Eight

WHIPLASH. COULD YOU get it just in your brain and not your skeleton? Because Kellan had it from watching Delaney turn from a vulnerable, self-doubting mess back into a take-charge, in-control woman.

The weirdest part was that he liked *both* versions.

In the past, a woman navel-gazing slapped wings on his feet. Women were fun. Dating was fun. When the serious and hard parts hit, that signaled it was time to move on, *fast*. Kellan's life was too busy, his focus too laser sharp on his own priorities, to waste any of his precious down time watching a woman fall to pieces.

Was that selfish? Only a little. By getting out before things hit that point, he saved the woman from building any fantasies about the depth of their relationship. His timely exit did them both a favor.

But he wasn't looking for an exit sign with Delaney. It was the complete opposite. Kellan was trying his damnedest to find the key that unlocked all of her layers. Being able to help her through her confusion, her introspection had made him feel about ten-freaking-feet tall. *Anything* he could do to reassure her, to tease that smile back on her face—that was his new focus.

Seeing the side of her he'd first fallen for, though? The side that had strong-armed the Maguire brothers out of the mob and into not one, but five brand-new versions of their lives? The side that stood up for them, defended them, and bent over backward to keep them in WITSEC no matter how badly they screwed up because—and here's the kicker—she *believed* in them?

That was fucking *hot.*

The wooden stairs clattered and shook as Delaney took them at a dead run. The dedicated public servant part of her remembered to mutter *I'm sorry* to the dozen people she elbowed and shouldered out of her way.

It cracked Kellan up and he stayed hot on her heels.

"Why don't you just whip out your badge? Maybe wave your gun around? That'd clear people out of your way."

Delaney skidded to a stop right by the entrance to the sea lion cave. And damned if a gull didn't let out a squawk that perfectly tracked with the look of chagrin on her face. "There are multiple things egregiously wrong with your suggestions."

Oh, yeah. The side of Delaney that got all righteously ticked off at him? That might be the hottest sight of all.

Totally worth enduring another wallop to his nose from the shit stank. Kellan crossed his arms, settling in for the show. "Enlighten me."

"First of all, it would be a blatant abuse of power." She tugged at his shirt to bring his ear right to her lips. In a stage whisper, she said, "My badge is a *privilege*. I carry it with honor."

"I've noticed. Honor . . . with a side of swagger."

Delaney's teeth nipped at his earlobe. "Secondly, I'm undercover. In general. But doubly undercover in that I really shouldn't be spotted with my protectee. It'd be very, very bad. For both of us."

"Yep. Especially if you were holding the badge while I was, oh, say, holding your ass." Kellan punctuated his comment by reaching around to squeeze the luscious seat of her jeans.

In some lightning-fast move probably rooted in martial arts, Delaney twisted from his grasp and twisted his arm up behind his back. Huffing out an exasperated laugh, she teased, "Is there any boundary you won't push?"

"I've never . . . well, hang on, that's a fun game. We'll save strip Never Have I Ever for another time."

Delaney let go and headed toward the elevator as Kellan's laughter echoed off the rocks. "The third thing wrong with your suggestion? You didn't tell me where we were going."

"That's pretty much the definition of a surprise date."

"Yes, but I couldn't look up the restrictions of this tourist attraction ahead of time." Inside the elevator, she repeatedly punched the close door button. It earned her frowns as more people crowded in to capacity. "So I had to leave the, *you know—*" she made a gun out of her thumb and forefinger "—in the car."

He had to wipe his hand across his mouth to keep in the laughter. Good God, but she cracked him the fuck up.

"You were worried that your latent big game hunter tendencies would come roaring to the forefront when you saw the sea lions?"

"No. I was worried there'd be a metal detector." Delaney went on tiptoe to deliver the last two words into his ear.

Oh, yeah. She was real slick with the undercover stuff. "In a big city, maybe. Here? In some tiny hick town on the literal edge of the continent? Fat chance."

"Hey!" A short, mustached guy in a trucker's cap gave him a heated glare. "How about a little respect?"

"Sorry." And he was. Sometimes these knee-jerk comments came out. They weren't really insults to Oregon. Which he liked, quite a bit. Kellan figured they slipped out as an homage to his old hometown. An acknowledgement that nothing could ever live up to the Windy City.

Delaney sniffed at him. "Don't be rude."

"It was a slip of the tongue. But you're giving the Sea Lion Cave—as awesome as it is—credit for being more safety conscious than a movie theatre. The risk wasn't even minimal. It was infinitesimal."

"Nevertheless, it was one I was unwilling to take."

The doors opened and everyone pushed to exit simultaneously, so Delaney didn't finish her thought until they were back outside. At least there she didn't have to whisper.

She drew herself up, straight as a flagpole. Her actual badge might be locked in the car, but Delaney wore what it stood for like an invisible superhero cloak. "That's what I do, Kellan. I assess risk. Weigh the options." Stiffly, like she was in a military parade, she moved from one side of the boardwalk to the other. "Balance the threat of danger against the worry about being discovered."

"It's a date, not a walk under the Armitage Avenue El stop at two a.m." Kellan gave a lazy shrug. Just for the fun of watching her go from righteous indignation to a fully ignited burn aimed straight at him. For months, they'd fought and snapped at each other and not had any outlet for all that pent-up heat. Today, he'd give her an outlet. "There's no danger here. Unless you're worried about aggressive sea gulls. Which are probably protected. So don't shoot them."

"You don't know that." Delaney stabbed him in the chest with her index finger. But her tone wasn't heated, merely earnest. "*You* can assume it, because I need you to be happy and comfortable in your new life." She tapped her own sternum. "But *I* don't have that luxury. I have to constantly be on the lookout, assuming that a previous associate of your brothers' could've shown up in that elevator with us."

Fighting back laughter—not to mention a fierce desire to rip down her jeans, bend her over the wooden railing and plunge into her right the fuck there— Kellan said, "Then you would've wished you'd waved your gun and badge. Which makes me right."

"I swear to God, Kellan," The minute her voice rose, she bit her lip. "Damn it. We're not supposed to be bickering anymore."

"It's fine . . . when it's foreplay."

Her eyes widened. Kellan could see the awareness of his plan click into her consciousness. "You did this on purpose."

"I did. All those *I'm yelling at you because I can't kiss you* vibes we had going on for so long? Figured we needed to get them out of our system for once and for all."

"That's really brilliant. Definitely twisted." She threw back her head and laughed into the wind. "It's exactly perfect for us."

Thank God. Kellan grabbed her shoulder to turn her away from the water and back to him. Need made the motion a little rough. Jerky and fast. So when she spun, her lips parted in surprise. "Are you as turned on as I am right now?"

"I'm crazy hot for you. Ten times more than when we were down in the cave, and I thought that was pretty freaking intense." Delaney dodged around him and took off at a steady jog down the long wooden walkway. Over her shoulder, she yelled, "Come and get me, Maguire!"

She ran with a graceful ease that was almost as fun to

watch as the twitch of her ass in those tight jeans. Then Delaney put on a burst of speed that caught him by surprise. It shouldn't have. Marshals probably trained just like FBI agents and cops to be able to run for as damned long as it took to get the job done.

Even with his longer legs, Kellan had to step up his efforts to catch her. After running on the beach for seven weeks, the flat boards were easy.

Kellan stayed right behind her across the highway, then up the hill to the parking lot. When he saw the car, he pushed hard enough to get four steps ahead, using that distance to unlock and open Delaney's car. By the time she poured herself into the passenger seat, he was behind the wheel with the engine running.

Except that she kept moving. All the way over to lie across his chest. And she rained fast kisses and quick little bites up his neck while tugging at his shirt.

"Whoa. We can't do this here."

"Why not?"

"The sun's out. People keep coming in and out of this lot. We'd get arrested for public indecency, at the very least. Talk about something that'd blow your cover."

Delaney yanked his tee over his head. She stared for a couple of seconds and gave him that gratifying double blink as her eyes raked up and down his torso. "I told you. I've got this problem solved." After rubbing her palms in circles over his nipples, she slid back into her seat. "Drive."

"To where?"

"Like I said before, my job is to notice things. And I noticed when you drove us up here that there's a sign for overflow parking." She twisted to point out the sign to him. "This lot's not even half full. Nobody'll head for the other one but us."

"You're pretty smug when you show off your awesomeness as a marshal. It's fucking sexy, too." Gravel sprayed as Kellan backed out of the space. Fast.

"We already covered foreplay with our fight. You don't need to compliment me, too. I'm ready for this." Delaney tossed his shirt into the back seat.

More gravel sprayed as Kellan stomped on the brakes. Because this needed to be addressed *right the fuck* now.

"Listen up, beautiful. My compliments aren't foreplay. They aren't part of a planned seduction. When I give you a compliment, it's because I'm bowled over by you. By your smarts. By your ability to cut through the bullshit and get straight to a point. By the smile that turns your face into something so beautiful you're practically angelic. By the fucking amazing way you listen and understand things I'm trying to say when I haven't figured them out for myself. They're *fact*."

Then he floored it.

OKAY, THEN. DELANEY was legitimately torn about what to do next. Half of her wanted to get out of the car, race to the nearest store, and buy Kellan two dozen red roses in thanks for that amazing speech.

The other half of her just wanted to tear his clothes off. Even *more*. This man kept surprising her.

She loved what he'd said. Her entire life was spent working her butt off to do better, to be better, to get ahead. Kellan made her feel like she'd already won every race in the world, aced every test, and bested every competitor. He made her feel special.

It was *wonderful*.

"I think you're pretty amazing, too."

Quick as a blink, in his signature style, Kellan's mood shifted from serious to smug. "You only think so? Just wait until we've had sex. Then you'll know. Then you'll lose the ability to form words to describe my amazingness."

"You deserve more."

"Your finely honed organizational skills found us a place to have sex outdoors in the middle of the afternoon. Trust me when I say I need nothing more than that." Kellan sped them up another hill, across a vacant lot to park on the far side of what looked like a double-wide garden shed. It didn't completely hide them from view, but it made their lone car less obvious.

The parking brake ratcheted into place as Delaney whipped off her shirt. A smarter person might have left it on, in case they were discovered.

The fact that she was in this car with Kellan at all proved that Delaney was far from smart where he was concerned. Because the smartest thing she could think to do right now was facilitate his touching her bare skin.

Before she could climb across the console, Kellan reached for her. His hands stroked up and down her exposed abdomen. His touch was rougher than before. Not in a bad or harmful way. No, this fast, harder approach, almost skidding across her skin, inflamed her need.

Not to mention that it proved the level of *his*. Kellan wanting her was incendiary all by itself.

"Do your back seats fold down?" Even his question was sexy. Because he whispered it in her ear, and then licked along the curve of it.

She fought for her own chance to play while she answered. Seeing as how she'd exposed his chest a whole minute ago and hadn't gotten to touch it yet. With clothes on, Kellan looked less bulked up than his older brothers.

But stripped down? His lean muscles were readily apparent. His pecs popped. They were covered in a light layer of hair that Delaney couldn't wait to feel rub against her. His abs were ridged in a six-pack. And there was a trail of dark hair down the center of his abdomen, disappearing into the waistband of his jeans, that positively made her mouth water.

"No. This car's been, ah, modified for the Marshals Service. There's a steel sort of gate that rises up behind the back seats to contain a prisoner. And a hidden compartment with tools of the trade." Delaney tasted the warmth of the skin along his collarbone, sun baked and slightly salty from their run to the car. God, she could lick at that all day.

A laugh chuffed out. "What tools? Your gun lockbox?"

"Among other things, yes." Then she remembered the best feature for an afternoon car quickie. Delaney dug her nails into his side for emphasis. "But this bad boy does have tinted windows."

"God bless the U.S. Government," Kellan said fervently, unclasping her bra with a single flick of his hand. He swiped the straps down off her wrists. Then he latched right on to her nipple.

His sucking was hard. *Perfectly* hard and focused, and it pointed both her nipples and her toes simultaneously. "Keep going," she said, twining her fingers through his thick dark hair to hold him in place.

Kellan's response was to, indeed, keep going. But he added two things. A hand kneading her other bare breast. And just enough pressure from his teeth to shoot her ass off the seat.

It was like he'd set off a tripwire directly to where heat already pulsed between her legs. *Everything* on her body tightened. Her fingers in his hair. Her eyelids slamming shut as her eyes rolled back. Her thighs spasmed closed. Not having his own legs between hers was a serious lack, though.

"We're not touching enough." Delaney's hands scrabbled at his shoulders, pushing him away. "I need to touch you everywhere." Then she swung a leg up high, over the steering wheel, and straddled Kellan. It rubbed her core directly on the steel of his cock. Holy hell, she'd felt it before while they kissed. But feeling it bump against her belly while standing was nowhere close to the sensation of pressing its length directly on her clit.

This was going to be *good*.

"I've barely begun." Kellan's eyes smoldered. She could *see* the banked heat behind them, darkening the pale blue surrounding his pupils to the color of the sky overhead. The heat from his gaze seared Delaney's skin in prickling awareness as he stared at her bare breasts.

"We can take our time when we get to the B&B. But neither of us can wait that long. So I'm literally begging you to get inside me. Right now." Deft fingers that could reload a gun in 1.3 seconds had his jeans undone before she finished speaking.

He shoved his hand down the back of her pants. Grabbed her ass and squeezed in a rolling grip that jerked her hips forward, back onto that cock Delaney needed so badly. "Condom's in the bag in the trunk."

"Don't need it. I'm on the pill. And you're—"

All the heat and passion fell from his face as Kellan cut her off. "And you've studied my medical records. You know I'm clean. You know I haven't been with anyone since leaving Chicago." His lips quirked into something that was halfway between a sneer and a smirk. "I'm not wild about you knowing all that about me. About you bugging my laptop so you can spot check us. Seems like those are facts a couple should get to discover about each other."

Shit.

Shit. Kellan was right. She'd plowed ahead, secure

in the knowledge of not only his blood type and lack of STDs, but also a lack of dates.

The job, doing what was best for it, that was second nature to Delaney. Those instincts were strong. Because she'd spent so many years telling herself it was the only thing that mattered.

But now, something else, *someone* mattered. A lot. More than Delaney had figured out how to deal with, apparently. She'd damned well try, though. To put more thoughtfulness into what she said to Kellan.

"You're right. I saw a problem—not wanting to wait—and solved it. I'm sorry. But you should know that your computer's not bugged."

Kellan gave her the *don't lie to me* eyeball roll. "Of course it is. That's how you caught Rafe checking on the mob a few months ago."

"*His* is. Flynn's is. We deactivated the bug on yours three months ago." It was so important that he hear her, that he believe. "Because I trust you, Kellan." Holding her breath, Delaney slowly asked, "Do you trust me?"

"Hell, yes." Kellan surged up to take her mouth. Just like everything about this encounter, his kiss was fast and rough and exactly what Delaney needed at that moment. "But you've got to stop talking."

"What?"

He put a palm over her mouth. Long fingers wrapped around beneath her chin. "I'm crazy about you. We have the whole night to sit on the porch and drink wine and tell stories. Right now, though? Respectfully? Shut up and let me fuck you."

His command *excited* Delaney. The feeling of being dominated was just that—a feeling, since she knew at least six different ways to break out of his hold. That feeling *drenched* her panties.

So when Kellan removed his hand, she stayed silent. She waited for his next command.

And the waiting snaked chills of excitement up through her skin, and turned into goose bumps that covered her entire body.

Kellan pointed past the center console. "Get that sweet ass of yours up there. Plant a knee. Balance your hands on the back seat."

As soon as she got one hand on the wide bench seat, Delany saw his plan. This position would enable him to take off her jeans with the least amount of banged elbows and knees for both of them.

Clearly she wasn't the only one who could strategize the shit out of a moment.

Her jeans and panties only made it to her knees, however. Kellan paused. Blew a stream of air down the crack between her cheeks. Delaney shivered, her knee almost slipping off. Kellan caught her, steadied her with a big hand wrapped around her thigh. And then he bit her ass.

It was *good*. He licked, bit, and sucked in a wide circle and her other leg fell open as far as the jeans would allow.

He didn't take the hint, though. Didn't put his hands or his lips between her legs. Simply took his time repeating the sensuous circle of nips on her other cheek. Finally, he finished by blowing another stream of cool air, aimed directly at the narrow strip of hair at her center.

It wasn't enough.

It was enough to make her arch her back, though. To arch and mewl her need for more of him.

Kellan stripped her jeans off the rest of the way. A firm slap to her ass sent her scrambling onto the back seat. "Flip around," he ordered. As she did so, he put one knee in each of the floor wells. His feet disappeared under the front seats. Oh, and his pants were down around his ankles. There was his cock, jutting straight up and *beautiful*. Long and thick, with a big vein that she slowly followed from his engorged balls up to the tip of it, beaded with a drop of pre-cum Delaney wanted to taste.

He grabbed her ankles. One tug slid her to the edge of the seat. The next put her legs over his shoulders. "Are you sure about this, Laney?"

Was he asking about not wearing a condom? About the finality, the no-turning-back of breaking the biggest rule in the WITSEC book? About being with him?

It didn't matter. The answer would be the same to all of them.

"Yes."

Kellan positioned himself right at her opening. Just let the tip sit there for a moment, driving her wild. Then he pushed. Inch by glorious inch. Inch by excruciatingly slow inch. Delaney swore she could feel every millimeter of taut, velvety skin all the way around him as he sank in with such deliberation.

He stretched her.

He filled her.

And then, just when he'd seated himself all the way in, Kellan reared back and *drove* into her.

Fast.

Hard.

Deliberate.

Perfect.

With Kellan taking charge, Delaney could completely let go in a way that she never, ever did. Her brain turned off. She lost herself in the pleasure of the moment. In the spiraling sensations that tugged her up toward a peak.

There was nothing but his warm skin against hers. The sensual slap of their bodies moving together. The fierce passion burning in his pale blue eyes. His grunts of pleasure that made Delaney unself-conscious about the constant stream of moans coming from her own mouth. And the heat that engulfed every last nerve, threatening to burn her up from the inside out.

Kellan squeezed her breast. Twisted the nipple just enough to send a bolt of excitement through her entire torso. "Do you want it harder?"

"I want everything you can give me," she panted.

As if her words had unleashed the most primal part

of him, Kellan growled and surged forward, pounding into her almost savagely.

His strength, his raw power, and most of all, the unceasing thrusts of his huge cock pushed her right over the edge. She dug her nails into his ass, wanting him impossibly deeper. Delaney screamed as her vision blurred when each and every cell in her body exploded in satisfaction.

Kellan didn't let up until she stopped shaking against him. The moment her hips stopped rolling forward, Kellan gave three thrusts and then buried his face in her neck as his cock jerked inside of her. His long, drawn-out groan was loud right in her ear. Delaney didn't turn away. She relished knowing that she'd pulled it out of him.

"That was even better than I imagined. And I gotta tell you, I've imagined this a lot since November."

His reminder of when, and how, they met, set off a tiny warning bell in Delaney's brain. A warning that this couldn't last. That she could be fired if anyone found out what they'd just done.

No. She slammed those thoughts into a mental vault. She'd follow his lead and enjoy this stolen moment. Save the worries for when the sexy, muscled, amazing lover wasn't still tracing circles with his thumb around her breast.

"You were exceptional. We get to do this all night long?" she murmured softly.

"As many times as you want."

Delaney smiled in anticipation of what promised to

be a night to remember. "I want a lot." Licking her dry lips, she said, "Okay, I'd kill for some water first. But then, *all* the sex."

"I can do better than water." Kellan handed her a thermos that had been wedged in the webbing behind the driver's seat. "I brought you more of Norah's calming tea. You seemed to like it."

"I loved the flavor. I don't know how calming it was, but I could drink it every day." Delaney scooted over as he pulled out and sat next to her. He kept an arm locked across her stomach, as if making sure she wouldn't go anywhere. "So you're not only thoughtful, but you're also a fantastic lover? You're too good to be true, Kellan Maguire."

"Wait'll you see what I can do in a bed. Lots more room to get . . . *inventive.*" His voice dropped on the last word in a husky promise that raced chills across her body.

Delaney closed her eyes as she sipped at the tea. Yep, she was going to Scarlett O'Hara the heck out of this date. Tomorrow was another day, indeed. Today, and tonight, with Kellan—that was all that mattered.

For now.

Chapter Nine

KELLAN LOOKED AT himself in the bathroom mirror at the sheriff's office. It was like looking at a different person. Guess he was. The *ghost of Kieran Mullaney*.

The man in that navy tie with a purple paisley design cinched into a perfect Windsor knot, gelled back hair, and navy blazer who stared back at him was the man he'd seen before prom. Before every graduation. Before slick dates that started with steaks at Gibson's and ended up cruising the clubs on Rush Street and dancing at Spybar.

That man had a purpose. A plan. But that plan had always been rooted in someone else's dreams. Pursuing justice as a lawyer was a way to honor his father.

Today, Kellan planned to put that ghost to rest. By putting his own twist on the pursuit of justice. By going after a dream that felt right to *him*. By finally, after eight long months of pretending to be different people, embracing who he was now.

To hell with that reflection in the mirror. Kellan grabbed his comb and attacked his part, moving his hair to the opposite side. First time in twenty-five years that he parted it on the left. Nobody would notice the difference. But he needed to look different—even just that little bit—from Kieran Mullaney.

Some water coaxed it into staying. Now he felt ready. Ready to kick some interview *ass*.

Because when Kellan put his mind to something, he got it. Aside from finishing law school. He'd never failed at anything in his life, and didn't intend to start now.

Which probably explained the faint skitter of nerves in his belly. This interview with Mateo mattered. Not just because it got him out of the fucking cranberry plant, but because becoming a deputy felt *right*.

As right as Delaney had felt, wrapped around him two nights ago.

He shouldered open the door before his mind went any further down that road. Thoughts of Delaney inevitably led to his dick springing to attention. Interview 101 best practices was *not* sporting a half chub.

Halfway down the hall, Sheriff Mateo Rogers beckoned to him. "My office is here. Let's do this thing."

Nice to not be in the conference/interrogation room where the Maguire brothers always sat through their lectures from the marshal. Kellan straightened his tie. Threw his shoulders back and took a deep breath as the heels of his dress shoes clicked against the concrete floor. This could be the start, the *real* start, of his new life.

Hopefully Kellan Maguire was just as impressive in person—even lacking all the straight-A transcripts and glowing recommendations—as Kieran Mullaney used to be.

Mateo shut the door behind him. "How about we get the awkward stuff out of the way first?"

"Isn't everything about a job interview awkward?"

"Good observation." Mateo shook his hand. "We've seen each other around town—and around this jail—but it's nice to officially meet you, Kellan."

That wasn't awkward at all. The usual small-town pleasantry. Piece o' cake. "Likewise."

They both sat. Mateo took off his dark green uniform hat. Then he drummed his fingers across the leather blotter on his desk. "I'm dialed in to the fact that you're lying to every person in this town about who you really are."

Kellan winced. Awkward, indeed. About as awkward as singing the anthem stark naked before a World Series game. But thanks to prepping with Delaney, he had an answer.

"That's technically untrue. I really am Kellan Maguire. Now, that is. Who I was, well, that's a different story. One I'll tell you today, to get this job, and then never mention again. As long as I can count on your discretion."

Closing the manila folder in front of him, Mateo

shoved it to the side. "This whole conversation is off the record. Officially. Which put my hackles up, at first, I'll admit. But I've got a personal recommendation from Marshal Evans, and a letter from the director of the Marshals Office in Chicago vouching for your innocence and good standing. And I'm desperate as hell for a new deputy. So I'm willing to listen and give you this *one* shot."

The sheriff had a sharper edge than he let on as he ambled around town with a smile and a handshake for everyone. Which made Kellan want to work for him even more. "What do you want to know?"

"I need a deputy I can trust. One who'll prioritize the safety of the people of Bandon over everything else. One who understands, in his gut, the difference between right and wrong and all of its shades of gray."

"Do you want to know what I did to be put under witness protection?" Because, damn if Kellan didn't want to tell him. If he didn't want to blurt out the whole story to *somebody*.

Mateo held up a hand. "I understand I can't ask what has you in WITSEC. But I do want to know what put you in that chair across from me. And if any of that motivation comes from who you used to be, I need to hear it."

"Fair enough." Kellan leaned back in his chair, no longer nervous. Not because he'd practiced a speech, but because his motivation was easy to share. He'd done a lot of soul searching since asking for this chance.

Admittedly, it'd been weird not going to Rafe or

Flynn to get their take. They'd always been his sounding board. But Kellan hadn't been able to gauge what their reaction would be to this interview. If they'd see him as the enemy once he put on a badge.

So for the first time in his life, he was molding his future by himself. Without a single thought to what would've made his parents happy, or his brothers. This was all about his own choice, his own decision. And now he'd get to share his reason.

"My mom was killed when I was seven. The story I got back then was that she was an accidental victim of a random shooting. It didn't make sense. It didn't make sense that they never caught the perpetrator. That she could be gone from our lives for no reason, with no explanation. It made even less sense when my dad was murdered less than four years later."

Mateo grimaced. "Jesus, that's awful."

"It was. Got even worse when I found out last year that the same man was responsible for killing them both." Kellan had flown into a rage that first day, when Rafe and Flynn revealed the truth about McGinty and their parents' murders.

He'd kicked a file cabinet in the downtown Chicago marshals' office. Turned over a desk. Until they got to the part where the raid had worked. How McGinty, thanks to them, was now behind bars.

That made it . . . well, not *right*. Not by a long shot. But it gave Kellan some measure of satisfaction.

"Was he caught?"

"Yes. He's locked up, and hopefully won't ever see the light of day again without bars in front of his eyes." Kellan planned to be there, in the courtroom, to see McGinty's face when they announced his life sentence. "Knowing that, it helps."

With a nod of acknowledgement, Mateo said, "I'll bet."

"I want to do that for other people." Kellan stood. There was too much emotion in him to contain without pacing. "People whose lives are turned upside down by crime. Whether it's a dinged fender or a burglarized house or, yeah, even a violent crime. I want to be the one who stands up for them. Who makes them feel safe again. Who makes them feel vindicated by finding whoever caused that pain and locking them up."

Mateo steepled his fingers. Stared at him for a long moment, as though he could see right through to Kellan's heart and soul and measure the strength of his conviction. Then he tapped the gold star pinned to his uniform shirt. "You realize there's a limit to what we can do with this badge?"

"Indeed. Here's the other thing you need to know about me." Kellan held up his thumb and index finger, pinched together. "I came this close to finishing a law degree. I was good at it, too. Top of my class. So I know all about the difference between catching a criminal and putting them away for good."

"And you're okay with only being able to carry out half of that?"

Okay? Hell, no. But Kellan couldn't live with himself anymore if he kept doing *nothing*.

He sank back into the wooden chair. "The biggest thing I learned in law school wasn't how to put a guy away. It was how easy it could be to establish reasonable doubt in even the most concrete of cases. The law has gaps like a chain link fence."

On a snort, Mateo said, "Gaps as big as a football field is more like it."

"Law enforcement, on the other hand, is a steel wall. There are good guys and bad guys. Period. You follow the evidence, you nab the perp. I want to be holding up that wall against bad guys."

There was another long stare-down. It didn't make Kellan sweat even a little. He'd put up with his law school professors giving him the stink-eye while waiting for answers from day one. He'd even put up with Delaney's pointed and iced-over frowns every time he tossed a compliment her way for eight long months.

Oh, yeah—and he'd been taught not to squirm under pressure by his—*apparently*—high-level mobster big brother.

Finally, Mateo double-tapped Kellan's file. "I'm impressed."

"Don't be. Because these are all just words. Wait and watch." Kellan thumped his chest. "Tell me you're impressed when I've actually done something to merit it. I promise that if you give me that chance, I won't let you down."

More importantly? He wouldn't let himself down.

KELLAN STUCK HIS hands in his pockets and started whistling as he strolled down the sidewalk. Then he realized it was the Northwestern University fight song, so he stopped dead in his tracks, right in front of a nail salon that had lethal fumes wafting out the door. He waited until he pulled up a fragment of an Ed Sheeran song that wouldn't disclose a piece of his history that needed to remain hidden to anyone else walking past.

Safe to assume Bandon residents wouldn't have recognized the rouser. But it was June 21. The town was lousy with tourists from all over. He wouldn't risk it. Not on the cusp of a whole new career that Kellan *wanted* so damned much.

Defiant, feeling like he'd just kicked the ass of his memories and his stolen life, Kellan started whistling again. Until Lucien came out of the post office and waved him down. "Hey, you're just the man I wanted to see."

Huh. It didn't suck at all running into a friend while walking around town. It'd almost never happened in Chicago with its nine million people. Yeah, everything about today was falling into place like hitting a row of drop targets on a pinball machine.

Making a big show of looking at his watch, Kellan

shook his head. "Sorry, Lucien. Office hours are over for the day. I'm already late for about seven beers and trash-talking whatever game's on the TV at the Gorse."

His friend flipped him off. "Very funny."

"I do like to thread some humor into my trash talk. Tell me your favorite baseball team and I'll show you how it's done."

Lucien's grimace looked . . . embarrassed? "The Red Sox are my team. And before you even try, I guarantee there's nothing you could say about them that hasn't been said a hundred other times, and with more cursing."

Shit. Well, at least he hadn't said the White Sox. Otherwise Kellan would've been obligated to be his mortal enemy on principle. "Give me a month, and we'll do this again when football season starts."

Loosening his pale green tie, Lucien said, "How about we grab a beer now so I can say I wined and dined you into this favor?"

Uh-oh. Favors made him think of that line from *The Godfather*. Which made him think of Rafe and Flynn . . . and wonder what the hell kind of favors *they* used to bestow. It reminded him just how little they'd told him about their day-to-day lives in the mob.

Lucien, on the other hand, was straightforward. Wasn't that fucking refreshing? Kellan nodded. "I'm game. What kind of a favor?" He fell into step with Lucien's green boat shoes as they crossed the street to angle toward the Gorse.

"Are you interested in a little side hustle?"

"As long as it isn't related to the cranberry plant, you bet." He didn't know how long it'd be before the sheriff made up his mind. And even if he did get the job, there'd be a training class to wait for and join after the trial.

Because everything in the Maguire brothers' lives was supposed to be on hold until after the trial. Kellan was just fucking tired of waiting. Felt like he'd done nothing but sit around with his thumb up his ass since November 1. Lucien could ask him to count the blades of grass on the resort's three premier golf courses to be sure each had the same number and Kellan would scream *I'm your man!*

Almost.

"Should we do this like gentlemen, over thick slabs of red meat?" Lucien hooked his thumb in the direction of the Gorse. "Or get the business out of the way first so we can just shoot the breeze over beers?"

Kellan thought about the Gorse and the thought of Flynn overhearing this proposal. Flynn, who'd immediately tell Rafe, who *hated* Lucien.

No. Hell, no. He was done with looking for his brothers' approbation, let alone their approval. "Mixing business with beer's a surefire way to do bad business. Shoot."

"I need someone to help with marketing at Sunset Shoals. We started revamping everything—website, brochures, you name it. Hired a boutique firm up in Portland. My dad hated them. Bunch of tattooed hipsters who needed to wash their hair, that's what he called them. But this is my department, so he contained himself to making snide comments."

Kellan ducked under one of the fifty Cranberry Festival banners already hanging from light poles, even though it wasn't for two months. "Let me guess. Things went south."

"Like taking a bullet train to Antarctica. Boutique firms can be awesome. And I knew the partners from college. But they made the mistake of sleeping together. Then when John decided he wanted to stop sleeping with women altogether, Alice didn't handle the news well. They imploded. And I lost my new campaign."

Ouch. "Guessing you lost a friend, too."

"TBD." Lucien screwed up his face and waggled a hand back and forth. "At this point, I'm not sure which one I want to keep. Because there's a ticking clock relative to our annual golf tournament push. They've fucked me up royally. After seeing what you did for the Festival, though, I figured you might be able to bail me out."

Sure.

In a heartbeat.

Yeah, it was ironic as hell that he'd refused when Rafe pushed him to find a job in marketing, and yet wanted to jump at this one. Kellan figured that, aside from doing the immature knee-jerk thing just because Rafe suggested it, he'd pushed back because the idea didn't interest him as a career.

But as a way to re-engage his brain for a few weeks

before moving on to the job he truly wanted? It sounded great. Helping out a friend made it a double play of goodness.

Except . . .

Kellan shoved his hands in his pockets. "Rafe asked me to tweak the Festival page. On a strictly volunteer basis. I don't have the qualifications required for your resort's needs. No PR degree."

Lucien blew a raspberry so wet that the middle-aged woman walking past them recoiled. He just winked at her and kept walking. "I don't give two shits about qualifications on paper. You know how to make a pitch. You made love to the words on the page like they were a stacked blonde at the end of a bachelor party."

"That's one hell of a weird compliment, but I'll take it."

"Will you take the job, too?"

Kellan was *beyond* intrigued. First of all, the money wouldn't hurt. The trouble with having a secret girl-friend who lived two and a half hours away was finding a private place to meet. Hotels made the most sense. But they weren't cheap. Not ones nice enough for Delaney.

The Maguires had money, but it was all in a joint account. Two, actually. One that held their allowance from the Feds and their paychecks. Another that held their money from Chicago, that they couldn't access until after the trial.

Oh, yeah. And there was that unknown amount of cash that Rafe and Flynn stole from the mob the night before entering WITSEC. They hadn't bothered to tell him about it until last month. Kellan still didn't know all the details, just that it was still hidden somewhere in Chicago.

Kellan didn't want anything to do with that money. Blood money. Sure, he understood that they'd taken it as insurance. Something to live off in case the mob came after the Maguires and the federal protection fell apart.

But he'd never, ever be okay with using money that came from taking advantage of people. Possibly—no, probably—hurting them, or at least threatening them to get it.

Yeah, side-hustle cash would be welcome. More than the money, though, Kellan liked the idea of taking on a new challenge. He was fucking tired of not *thinking*. Of spending all day, every day, with his brain stuck in Park. He wanted to rev it up and take it for a spin.

He'd owe Rafe one hell of an apology. Turned out big brother *had* known what was best for him, after all. Kellan didn't mind—too much—manning up and giving Rafe credit. Just not until after he was done. Anything to do with Lucien was a powder keg about to explode as far as Rafe was concerned.

And keeping another secret from them evened the score a tiny bit. Which didn't suck at all.

"We should probably negotiate over terms."

"Terms? Discussion's over." Lucien made a snap/slap combo with his hands. "You're helping me. I'll make it worth your while. Starting with a free dinner at the Gorse."

Talk about a sudden switch. Was it a coincidence that as soon as he'd slept with Delaney, his life started turning around? Hell, even before that. As soon as he'd kissed her. That was the same week he got the idea to become a deputy. The same time he'd become friends with Lucien.

No doubt about it, Marshal Delaney Evans was his own personal good luck charm. He needed to find a way to repay her. Fast, since they had a secret date planned for tomorrow night.

Kellan grabbed Lucien's hand and shook. When life handed you . . . well, not lemons. Who the hell wanted lemonade all the time? When life handed you . . . a '79 Château Lafitte Rothschild, you didn't ask questions. You fucking drank it down.

"I'll do it. FYI, I'd do it for free to help you out. But since you offered, I'll take the money, *this* time."

"I recognize the look in your eyes. You want to spend your salary all in one place? And by one place, I mean on one person? A certain nameless woman?"

"Yeah." His brain had already started tinkering with the idea of something he could give Delaney that'd mean finding a jewelry store between here and Eugene. "And she's going to continue to remain nameless, so don't even try."

Lucien flicked open another button on his shirt as the Gorse came into sight. Finger combed his hair, too. Guess he'd need Kellan to play the role of his wingman tonight, as yet *another* favor. "You're just scared I'd steal her from you. Because I'm guessing you have excellent taste in women. But mystery girl would have good enough taste to realize that I'd give her a better time."

It was all Kellan could do not to double over in laughter. Delaney would eat Lucien alive and spit him out without so much as breaking a sweat. But it'd be fun tonight to trade some stories, at least half of them true. And even more fun to contemplate his new semi-job. This offer of Lucien's would at least quell his boredom.

Although that had dialed back a few notches, too, as soon as he'd started seeing D. There. That'd work. "You can call her D," he announced to Lucien.

"D for *delectable*? D-cups?"

"D for *danger*." Talk about an understatement. Delaney had driven home all the dire things that could go wrong if anyone sniffed out their relationship. No point worrying about a scenario he wouldn't let happen, though. "There'd be hell to pay if anyone found out about us."

"You dog. Is she married?"

"No. And didn't I tell you not to try and weasel anything out of me?"

"D for *not-quite-divorcée*?" Then Lucien shot him a look of concern. "Please tell me the D doesn't stand for *debutante*. You've checked her ID to make sure she's official?"

Funny. He'd done *exactly* that on the day they met. Except he hadn't been checking for jailbait status. No, Kellan had checked her credentials to be sure that they were official, standard government issue. Lucien couldn't have picked a more ironic phrasing if he'd actually known the truth about Kellan and Delaney.

"She's the real deal," he murmured. With one hand on the brass handle in the shape of a gorse bush, Kellan said, "You've gotta drop this before we go in. My brothers don't—*can't*—know about her."

"A secret hookup." Lucien winked. "No, a clandestine hookup. That sounds seedier. Or more globe-trotting spy thriller."

Kellan put his tongue firmly in his cheek. "Yeah. That's just what I've always hoped to become. The next James Bond. Spending every day on the edge, chasing danger."

Delaney would *definitely* get a laugh out of that.

Chapter Ten

THE FOUR DAYS since Delaney's last date with Kellan
had been spent anticipating the *next* one. Wondering
how on earth he could top it. Not that he needed to. Delaney didn't need the kind of romance that filled rom-
coms. She didn't need anything more than time with
him. Hanging out. Just talking. Holding hands.

Naked, preferably.

Or so she'd *thought* . . .

Delaney knew how to drive a motorcycle. It'd been
part of her personal homework to ready herself to
become the most qualified candidate for the U.S. Marshals. She'd learned how to drive automatic and stick,
motorcycles, buses, and big rigs. Because you never
knew what might be the only vehicle at hand when
keeping a protectee safe.

At the time, she'd decided that bikes weren't her thing.

But that was before riding *behind* Kellan Maguire on one.

Every sensation was dialed up to eleven. The powerful vibration of the machine between her legs. The loud rumble that perfectly overlaid the thrumming of the engine. The strength of the wind pushing against her body, even wrapped up for safety in a helmet and jacket. The steely hardness of Kellan's abs where she gripped him with both hands.

For a second—okay, for five seconds that felt like five hundred—Delaney shut her eyes against the bright summer sun. Just to feel the disorientation, the speed, and to have an excuse to cling a little harder to the solid strength that was Kellan.

All too soon, gravel spattered as he circled into a showy stop on a driveway next to an enormous white flowering bush. Hedge? Plants in different shades of pink bumped up against it in varying heights. Including a spiky almost-fern thing that looked like it belonged in a prehistoric rain forest. Of course, Oregon *was* a rain forest—just a significantly cooler version. They were surrounded on three sides by hills covered in a solid wall of pine trees. The fourth side held an unassuming house with a peaked roof.

Kellan yanked off his helmet, then used considerable more care to remove hers. He was grinning ear to ear. "Welcome to our celebration."

And here Delaney thought it was just a normal, utterly clandestine Thursday night date. Go in to work two hours early so she could leave midafternoon, drive for an hour, hide her car, then get picked up by her secret boyfriend to keep driving to an undisclosed location.

She scrubbed her fingers to fluff up her undoubtedly hopeless helmet hair. "What are we celebrating?"

"Well, I'm not up on all the protocol yet. I don't know if we should salute each other, or if there's a secret handshake for fellow members of government agencies . . ." Kellan's voice trailed off as his grin got impossibly wider.

No. Already? The wheels, and more importantly, the red tape of the government never moved that fast. But there was only one thing this could be. Delaney realized her mouth was agape.

No jumping to conclusions, though. That had been drummed into her from the first day on the job. *Especially* when it came to protectees. Boyfriends were probably another ten levels of "don't assume" beyond that.

Cautiously, she asked, "Does this mean you got the job?"

"You're looking at a soon-to-be deputy for the great state of Oregon."

Delaney jumped up onto him, wrapping her legs around that lean waist and covering his stubbled face with fast kisses. "You are such a great, big, smart, sexy, stud of a man!"

Deep laughter rolled out of Kellan as his head fell back. "Yeah, that's pretty much word-for-word what Mateo said."

"Smartass." Then she thumped him. Well, more that the flat of her hand bounced off his defined pec. "I'm complimenting you. Let me finish."

"Keep going. In fact, I can set a timer so you can be reminded to compliment me every hour on the hour, if that'd help."

Delaney slid down to put her feet back on the ground. This was Kellan in rare form. Full of himself. Certain that she'd fall all over him. Pretty much how he'd acted in all of their confrontations. The difference was that now she could admit how much it amused—and aroused—her.

At least, she'd admit it to *herself*. Kellan didn't need any additional encouragement at this point.

"Wow. You're pretty cocky already." Delaney raised her hands, palms up, feigning confusion. "I just don't know how womankind will be able to handle your swagger once you put on a uniform. It'll be potent."

With an exaggerated leer, he said, "I'll let you sample my potency tonight."

"See, I know that should sound dirty, but it really makes you sound like an eighteenth-century back-alley alchemist."

"You say that as if it's a bad thing." Kellan held his straight face.

Delaney couldn't. Her chin fell to her chest as she gave in to the laughter she'd been fighting to hold back. "This is fun."

"What is?"

"You and me." Pointing back and forth between them, she said, "Even when we're debating about ridiculous things, it's fun." It was probably sad that it still surprised her. Emily certainly carped at her often enough about taking a fun break.

Delaney had always worried that breaks would make her soft. Weaken her. Make her a less effective marshal. Having fun with Kellan, though, was like . . . taking a nap.

God, that sounded *horrible*. It wasn't—at *all*—that he was boring. Just that she felt rejuvenated and twice as ready to dive into life after being with him.

One hand at the small of her back, Kellan pushed her up the driveway. "There's nothing ridiculous about an alchemist. I'm guessing he'd have a cape, like a musketeer, and, obviously, be able to transmute any base metal into gold. That's pretty kick-ass."

She halted and framed his face with her hands. The teasing was, indeed, all kinds of fun. But this was a moment—a *huge* moment—that needed to be properly recognized. Both as a woman who cared for him and as the marshal in charge of his attempts at a new life.

Looking deeply into those ice-blue eyes, Delaney said, "Seriously, Kellan. I'm so very proud of you. This is a *huge* step. And I'm quite certain you're the first WITSEC alum to ever go into law enforcement. I think you just broke every record for succeeding in the Program. Congratulations."

"Thanks." Kellan took her hands and kissed the

backs of them before squeezing tightly. "But tonight's a celebration for *both* of us. I couldn't have gotten through that interview without your help. This was a team effort."

His attempt to share credit was thoughtful. It was also ridiculous. "Hardly. You were top of your class, in every class. You were on the law review. You're one of the most naturally charming people I've ever encountered. And you've got a passion lighting you up to serve and protect. You earned that job on your own merits, fair and square."

"Oh, I know I deserve the job." Fingers entwined in the sweetest way, Kellan angled her toward a path that cut past the side of the house.

"Glad that's cleared up." Hopefully an explanation would be coming soon for their location. Before the owners called the police on them for trespassing. Wouldn't that just be a *typical* Maguire brother move? Getting arrested the same day he got hired?

"But the interview, man, that was tough. It was one hell of a tap dance, telling Mateo what he deserved to know, what it was safe to share, and what I wanted to say to be sure I got the job. You taught me the steps, helped me practice. When it was time, the dance was simple."

Talk about a smooth metaphor. Then a thought struck her. "Can you dance?"

"I can bust a move. Why? Don't tell me there's actually a random fact about my life that you people failed to mine?"

"There are still plenty of unknowns about you." Finding out this way, rather than reading them in a dry report, was, well, again it was *fun*. "Let's start with the most obvious unknown. Where are we, and why?"

They rounded the side of the house. It was like stepping into a different world from the standard suburban view of the front. The yard had a fire pit, a table laid out with snacks and wineglasses, and deep Adirondack chairs. Grass sloped down to a dock on a wide river. Everywhere she looked was nothing but pines and water and peace.

"The 'where' is a B&B on the edge of the mighty Umpqua River."

"It's spectacular." Beautiful and romantic and, yet again, *thoughtful*. How on earth did she get so lucky?

Oh, yeah. *Not* actually lucky. Because in a couple of months, Kellan and his thoughtfulness would disappear from her life forever.

That thought was getting harder and harder to stomach. Even though it was the only way forward. Living in the moment was more challenging than she'd expected, because all these good moments just made Delaney crave more.

He led her through thick grass to the chairs. Plopping down with a sigh, Kellan said, "The 'why' we already covered—it's a celebration. Can't celebrate at my house, on account of it being a secret. Can't celebrate at your place on account of *me* being a secret."

"You're keeping this from your brothers?" That news was enough to distract her from the breathtaking view.

Kellan pulled a dripping bottle of sauvignon blanc from a standing ice bucket and poured. "You bet I am."

Really? She snorted her disbelief. "Don't you think they'll cop to it the first time they see you in a uniform?"

"Of course. That won't happen for a while, though. I need to go through training at the academy up in Eugene before I can become official. I'll be temping as an acting deputy with them until then. Mostly desk work. And I told the sheriff that I wouldn't be able to join a training class until after October." Every line on his face hardened. Every angle of his body stiffened beneath the worn jeans and soft red tee. "No point wasting the taxpayers' money just to have me shot by a mobster during the trial."

"Nobody's getting shot." The words popped out automatically. It was a reassurance Delaney had given all her other protectees. This time, however, it was less a statement of fact. More of a solemn blood vow.

Nothing would happen to Kellan. Or his brothers. Not on her watch. Even if it was the last thing she did for him.

Which it probably would be.

"I explained to Mateo that the holdup was related to why we're in WITSEC, and he's cool with it."

Delaney didn't care what the sheriff thought. She cared that the Maguires might be worrying themselves into sleeplessness every night for no good reason. "Kellan, I don't want you to be scared about the trial. This is what we do. Marshals *protect*. You and your brothers will be safe."

"I'm not scared. I'm pragmatic." He reached across the table to lay a hand on top of hers. "There's no doubting your abilities. The way you got us out of Chicago was a minor miracle. I've just learned the hard way that life can piss all over you without warning."

In all the time they'd spent together, all the towns, all the interaction with different people and officers, Kellan always, *always* radiated an easy comfort with life. A willingness—unlike his far surlier brothers—to roll with the punches. A knack for finding some silver lining in every situation.

Now he'd dropped that happy-go-lucky mask. Shown her another, deeper side to his true self. It felt important. It felt like a gift. But before she could respond, he shifted, like quicksilver and all that hardness relaxed. Then he waved an arm at the rushing river like a game show hostess. "Well, what do you think of our place?"

"Our place? I'm guessing we have to share it with the other guests."

"Nope. It only has a single suite. The whole upstairs. I stopped by before picking you up. Our hosts headed to the coast. We're solo here until breakfast. The ultimate secret getaway."

"Here I thought I was the expert in those. Are you gunning for my job next?"

"No fucking way. I want to lock up criminals. You have to be nice to them. Take care of them. I don't know how you do it."

No kidding. Delaney had been struggling with that

more and more. "I don't either, sometimes. I mean, not all of my protectees are criminals. Not by a long shot. There are whistleblowers. They're totally innocent, like you. Then there are people who accidentally got pulled into bad situations and are trying to do the right thing. And people like your brothers, who *are* criminals, but . . ." Her voice trailed off.

Kellan shook his head. Stared out at the rippling river. "Don't hold back on my account. You know I'm still far from comfortable with that fact. Pissed as hell, actually, that the men who helped drum ethics and morals into me apparently have a whole *do as I say not as I do* thing going."

That had to be so hard for him. Another thread of darkness that he kept hidden from the world.

Delaney was relieved that she didn't have to choose her words carefully. She never, ever got to talk about her work with anyone outside the Marshals Service. And even in the office, everything was segmented and confidential. Being able to unload her thoughts to Kellan felt luxuriously freeing. Especially with his unique, insider viewpoint.

"Rafe and Flynn are good men. It's why I fought to keep all of you in the program even as they kept screwing up and getting in trouble. The mob was their job. It didn't define them. It's so easy to pigeonhole everyone who walks in wearing handcuffs as a bad guy. A lot of my colleagues do." She certainly had, as a brand-new recruit. But she'd quickly discovered that protectees were so much more than just the deeds in their files. "When you really get to know people, you realize what they *do* isn't necessarily who they *are*."

"Yeah. That's what's kept me from kicking their lying asses and walking away." Kellan wiped his hands up and down the smooth green wood of the armrests. "I love those idiots. I'd lay down my life for them. They'd do the same for me. Hell, they stayed in the mob partly to keep me safe, to give me the best shot possible. Which makes me feel guilty as fuck. And then mad about it."

Her heart hurt for the complex emotions roiling beneath Kellan's surface. "What did they say when you told them that?"

"I can't tell them."

That was . . . shocking. The Maguire brothers had lost their tempers with each other repeatedly as they adjusted to WITSEC. She knew they were brawlers. Knew that Rafe and Kellan had regularly sparred with Flynn as he prepped for his MMA matches, and continued to now as a workout. With all those fists flying, how had his pent-up fury not been unleashed on them?

As their official handler, Delaney should be thrilled he was keeping the peace. But she cared too much to let Kellan burn up from the inside out, even if it did rub his brothers the wrong way. "I'm pretty sure you've *got* to. It isn't healthy to hold it all back. Festering wounds and all that."

"I thought about it. About a hundred times, that first week alone. I kept flipping from shell-shocked to fucking furious ten times a day. Every time something went wrong with our placement, I considered unloading on them. When Rafe or Flynn whine about missing Chicago, or the Cubs, or a deep dish pie from Lou Malnatis, I'm tempted to go postal." His voice roughened, like the words were being choked out over ground glass. "Tempted to remind them *they* made all the choices that landed us here. Choices that ripped us from our lives."

Wow. He was voicing the kinds of things she swallowed back at least once a week in her job. All protectees, good or bad, had one thing in common—they complained about missing their old lives. And yes, it got annoying to not ever be able to lose it a little and tell them to suck it up.

Except that Kellan didn't have to be professional. He *could* let it all out. Truly curious, she asked, "Why don't you?"

"Like I said, they made those choices for me." Kellan pushed out of his chair. He circled the flagstone border of the small brick patio, finally stopping at a large bush exploding with magenta flowers. His hands flexed and fisted at his sides. "When Dad was killed, we could've— *should've* gone into foster care. Rafe knew the only way to keep us together was for him to go all in with Mc-Ginty. It was his love for his brothers that pushed him into the mob. His love for Flynn that pushed him to turn evidence and put us in WITSEC. That's the most fucking selfless, noble thing in the world. I can't punish him for that. Or Flynn."

Her heart fluttered. If Emily was here, she would've been dabbing at her eyes at that speech. Delaney mocked Em every time her friend texted that she'd had to grab for tissues as she finished the latest book club weep-fest.

But now she got it. Because listening to Kellan describe the purity of the love the Maguires shared had literally made her forget to breathe. Delaney belatedly sucked in a deep breath. And blinked way too fast, just to be sure no wetness lingered in the corners of her eyes.

"The three of you have an amazing bond. I'm a little awed by how you make it work."

KELLAN APPRECIATED DELANEY's words. He appreciated how she'd listened without judging as he let slip the emotions he worked so hard to lock away. And yeah, it felt good to open up to her. But her eyes sparkled with . . . tears? Nah. His tough-as-nails marshal couldn't be crying over him. Talk about setting the wrong tone for their romantic escape.

He crossed the patio in two long strides to kneel on the grass just beyond her feet. "Enough about my brothers. I didn't bring you here to bitch about them, or about the past. I brought you here to celebrate the present. Actually, to *give* you a present."

"I'm not allowed to accept gifts from my protectees."

Kellan threw back his head and laughed, the sound echoing off the pine-covered hill across the river and bouncing right back. "You're not allowed to sleep with them, either. In for a penny, in for a pound, right?"

"You've got a point," she said dryly. "Just what we need. Another reminder of how dangerous and wrong being together is."

"Meh." He waggled one hand side to side. "*Slightly* dangerous. Living on the edge. A little bad, a lot exciting. Not at all wrong. God, Laney, nothing's ever felt as right as being with you. Are you telling me you don't feel the same?"

"If I didn't, I wouldn't be risking my entire career to be sitting here with you."

"Good. So here's your reward." Kellan leaned back on his heels to dig in his pocket. "This new job probably won't go over well with Rafe and Flynn. They've been trained for years to dislike and distrust the police."

In a measured tone, she said, "It's a safe bet that there will be yelling when you break the news."

"Worrying about how they'd react might've stopped me from taking this leap. I would've stayed at the cranberry plant, fucking miserable."

"No. You're too smart for that. You would've found another way out, given time."

The woman categorically refused to take a damned compliment. Kellan barreled on. She might fight his words of thanks, but he'd put money on Delaney not refusing the gift that went along with them.

"Your belief in me—that I can still be a good man and carve out a whole new path for myself—gave me the push I needed to pursue being a deputy. Because I think I can make a difference. Because I think I'll be good at it."

"You will be. Or else I wouldn't have recommended you." She playfully wrinkled her nose. "I can't risk getting a reputation as someone who's a bad judge of character."

"Yes, my career as a deputy will be all about making you look good for having such a successful protectee. Give me your hand." Kellan clasped a thin bracelet around her left wrist. A silver key and a heart-shaped lock dangled from it. "This is my way of saying thank you. A reminder that you've got my heart all locked up now."

All that thick blond hair hid her face as she stared down at her wrist wordlessly. For a while. For too long. Long enough that Kellan focused on the rushing of the river and the squawk from ducks at its edge.

Shit. Was it too much? Had he pushed too fast?

Delaney slid out of the chair to her knees. Then she threw her arms around his neck, locking her crossed wrists at the back of his head. "Thank you. I . . . I never planned on having someone feel like this about me. I was sure I didn't want it to happen. But I'm genuinely thrilled to hear you say all this."

Never planned on—what did that mean? How many secrets had she still not shared?

This near whisper of an admission sounded as if it was wrenched from deep inside of her. Pushing for more seemed like a sure-fire way to set off one of their old habitual fights. And Kellan was damn pleased that it'd been a while since they'd fallen into that trap. They deserved one of those OSHA safety signs—*It has been 10 days since our last incident*. "Any time I can provide a thrill, I call it a good date."

"I'm truly touched. I wish I had something to give you. For making me feel so special."

"No way. That's like writing a thank you note *for* a thank you note." On the other hand, he could press his luck a little more. Because Delaney was damned hard to read. "You could maybe let me know if and/or when you feel the same way."

Her eyes flew wide open. "Can't you tell?"

Maybe? The thing was, "maybe" didn't cut it. Kellan needed to *know*. "I don't like to raise at the poker table unless I'm damned sure of what I'm holding—and what everyone else is holding."

"Oh, for God's sake." Delaney rolled her eyes and dropped her head back. But to Kellan, her oh-so-habitual look of annoyance was simply adorable. "What is it with men? Not every analogy has to come down to poker or *The Godfather*."

"That movie actually never played in my house. I guess now I know why."

"Ironic." Delaney wriggled up against him. Then she kissed him, slowly. Softly. When she started to pull away, Kellan tightened one arm around her waist. Okay, sort of her waist. More that he started there before immediately moving down to anchor his hand on her sweet ass. Then he took charge of the kiss.

He liked to take charge in the bedroom. And, surprisingly, his hard-as-nails, normally take-charge marshal seemed to relish it when he did. Just more proof that they were right for each other.

So Kellan drew out the kiss. Kept it soft. Tender. Romantic, to suit the day and the setting. He wanted Delaney to go back over these kisses, these stolen moments, a hundred times a day on all the days when they were stuck hundreds of miles apart. Until he figured out a way to keep them together.

There *had* to be a way.

He licked his lips, savoring the residual sweetness from Norah's special tea she'd downed in the car. "That's you showing me how you feel?"

"I'm more about action. Less about words. That's why the act of your giving me a gift absolutely brought me to my knees. Literally." As she tossed him a grin, her eyes sparkled more than the river behind them. "How do you feel?"

Fan-fucking-tastic. "I feel like myself again. Life is good, I've got a plan, a girl, a job, and I'm in control."

"Really?" Delaney looked away. Far, far away, not just physically but as though she was leaving him and retreating inside her own mind. She started to pull out of his embrace, but Kellan solved that by rolling them both to the side and pinning her beneath him on the grass. "Because I've never felt more *out* of control. Being with you is so risky. It's so unlike me. And there's no good outcome."

"The Maguires always find a way." Or, this time, the one Maguire. He couldn't ask his brothers for help. But with all the times they'd lauded his giant brain, Kellan could damn well believe he'd solve this problem on his own.

He had to.

Delaney barreled on with recounting how badly the deck was stacked against them. Man, it was almost like she took comfort in it. Like it was an evil rosary that had to be said once a day or they'd be struck down by lightning.

"Once the trial is over, I'll be assigned a new case. We'll never see each other again."

"You need to end that sentence with #worstcasescenario. Or maybe an emoji of a cartoon character falling off a cliff."

Blue eyes snapped to his like a rubber band. "You're not taking this seriously."

"No need. For two reasons. I try not to get bogged down in being serious, and because you're serious enough to depress all of Death Row." Kellan tucked her head against his chest and stroked her hair. He was going to live in the moment, because they didn't get a lot of them together. For now. And it promised to be a damned fine moment. "It'll be okay. Trust me, babe."

"That's not really my natural state."

"Let's start small. You trust I'm going to show you a

good time tonight, right? Wine? Cheese? A river as the background soundtrack to drown out your screams of pleasure?"

One blond eyebrow arched up. "I'm willing to give you a shot."

Delaney never gave him an inch without making him work for it.

Nothing excited Kellan more than a good challenge. Especially one with the promise of sex as the reward . . .

Chapter Eleven

IT HAD BEEN a little over a week since Delaney's wonderful overnight with Kellan. A week of swapping favorite playlists—after the obligatory debate about the legality of Spotify and infringement on artists' intellectual rights. A week of sharing the minutiae of least favorite sport to watch—they agreed on NASCAR because it was just driving around in a circle—and most favorite food—they didn't agree at *all*.

Which was fine. They were used to not agreeing. Doing it without rancor was new and delightful, though. Delaney promised to give sushi another try (*once*) and Kellan reluctantly agreed to try lemon meringue pie again, despite railing against its texture. Everything was fun.

Even the nightly FaceTime sessions that ended with the cameras aimed someplace about two feet below the face while they simultaneously talked each other to climax. That was shatteringly sexy, but *fun*. Laughter and panting and breathy murmurs all meshed together into complex chords Delaney wasn't sure she'd ever heard before. And it was absolutely beautiful.

Which is why she should've been braced for something to go wrong. For this idyll to end. Abruptly. Because life wasn't smooth-sailing perfection.

Delaney couldn't even blame Fate for ruining her truly excellent run of days. Days of texting and daydreaming a ridiculous amount and staying up way too late because neither of them wanted the conversation to end. Nope, Fate didn't toss the stink bomb into her cocoon of happiness.

It was the Maguire brothers.

All of 'em.

They'd screwed up yet again. Not a huge surprise, after spending the last eight months riding herd on them. Frustrating, yes. But Rafe and Flynn not sticking to the rules wasn't a shock.

The shock was that Kellan, her secret boyfriend, the man who'd pushed her to open up and not keep things hidden . . . *he'd* been a willing participant in their idiocy. So after a long drive to read Flynn the riot act, now she was supposed to meet Kellan for a hiking date.

Except that learning he'd kept *important, WITSEC-related, vital-to-the-continued-safety-of-the-Maguires information* from her didn't put Delaney in a romantic mood.

It put her in the mood to push him over the waterfall that was their planned destination.

Delaney spotted Kellan right off as she pulled into the small parking area at the trailhead. The sight of him jacked her temper right back up to a full boil. The long drive from the surprise meeting with his brother hadn't exactly cooled her off. Especially not with the last three miles jarring her way down a single lane gravel road.

He looked handsome as ever. Sexy as sin, with long tanned legs showing between his hiking boots and cargo shorts. He looked happy. Well, she'd been happy too, anticipating this date to kick off the holiday weekend.

She should've realized things were going too well. That they were bound to implode far sooner rather than later.

After securing her backpack—the one with her service weapon in it, as well as sandwiches Delaney wasn't sure they'd even get to depending on how heated the discussion became—she got out of the car and slammed the door. Hard.

Kellan waved the deep green Coffee & 3 Leaves travel mug. "Brought you more of Norah's special tea. You know, to keep you calm enough you don't jump my bones before we hike up to the Gold and Silver Falls."

Fat chance of that. With or without the tea.

Wordlessly, Delaney took the tea. Swung open the top and drained the entire thing in six long gulps. Then she handed it back.

"Nope. Not calm. Not one fucking bit calm."

Kellan jumped off the wooden picnic table. "What's wrong?" He reached for her shoulders, but Delaney sidestepped away. She couldn't bear for him to touch her right now. His betrayal hurt too much.

Oh, and she was pissed enough that she just might let her combat training slip to the forefront of her brain and give him a few hard knocks.

Where to begin? Where to begin with this ruined, crappy day? To think that when she'd joined Flynn in his truck, she'd been a little bit frustrated. Yes, protectees were supposed to reach out all the time for reassurance and/or help from their marshals. Except the Maguires never did that. Not in all the months—and cites, and jobs—they'd weathered together. For Flynn to break that habit on the start of a holiday weekend when she got to spend actual consecutive days with her boyfriend? Well, he was lucky she hadn't knee-capped him in principal.

Not that she ever would. Not that she'd ever be vindictive or in any way judgmental to a protectee. But apparently being lied to brought out a caveman level of violence in her.

"Let's see. While I want to rail at you for about two days straight, I should put the blame where it belongs. On me. Because I'm the one who knowingly broke protocol. Broke the rules. Broke *my* rules."

"What are you talking about?"

Delaney pointed at the trailhead. "Start walking. We don't want to attract attention, standing here fighting."

After stuffing the mug into his own backpack, Kellan fell into step beside her. "How can we be fighting when I have no idea what you're talking about? And even if we are, why would it matter if people noticed us? We're not in hiding."

Wow. Talk about picking the *most* wrong thing to say. Delaney did a full three-sixty to make sure there were no other hikers around. Then she stopped and jabbed a finger at his chest.

Voice low and terse, she said, "You are, Kellan. You and your brothers *are* in hiding, and will be for the rest of your lives. More to the point, you're in hiding right now in the hopes we can keep the three of you alive long enough for Rafe and Flynn to testify against McGinty, his entire crew, and hopefully remove ninety percent of the threat against them."

"I know the drill." His eyes and his tone dropped, slightly sullen, as though she was reminding him of something as ingrained as looking both ways before crossing the street.

"Oh, do you? Then how about you tell me what flashed through your brain when you discovered a known mob associate *in your town*?" Fury flashed through her again, just as it had when Flynn had broken the news to her. That he'd met with her as the Maguire brothers' representative, to give her a heads up that Patrick O'Connor, a fellow freaking Chicago mobster, had shown up in Bandon.

Delaney had been blindsided by Flynn this morning.

Because there was a price on the Maguire brothers' heads.

Sure, the Chicago mob was splintered and struggling now. More than half were in jail already, or at least indicted. The others were too low down the totem pole and thus didn't have the leadership or balls to make a plan.

But someone could be dispatched. To take them out. *Finding* them was the hard part. *Killing* them was incredibly simple.

The fact that Kellan and his brothers hadn't raised the red flag, set off a flare and freaking called her and 911 simultaneously was a serious breach of not just the rules, but of *trust*.

"That's what you're mad about?" Kellan's whole demeanor relaxed. Like he honestly believed there was nothing to her obviously raging temper. "We told you about O'Connor. I mean, Flynn did tell you today, didn't he?"

"Yes. Flynn told me this morning. *Saturday* morning," she clarified, enunciating slowly so Kellan would get the clue about where they'd all gone wrong. "But he and Rafe spotted O'Connor on Thursday. Do you realize how much could've gone wrong in that amount of time that I was left in the dark? How can I protect you guys *if I don't know you're in danger*?"

That thought had twisted her belly into layers of knots. One layer of how if anything happened to them, she'd be responsible as a person for their deaths. Another layer about how she'd be responsible as a marshal, and possibly lose her job. The third, most twisty layer, was about losing Kellan.

The man she'd fallen for, completely.

No matter how dumb and wrong and self-defeating those emotions might be.

"We weren't in danger," Kellan insisted. "Rafe and Flynn told me. They'd followed him all around town. It was obvious O'Connor had zero idea we're living there."

She'd felt . . . impotent when Flynn said they'd spotted one of their known associates days ago. Powerless. Panicked. Those pent-up feelings exploded as Delany slammed the side of her fist into the nearest tree trunk. Bits of bark flew through the air.

"It is *not* your brothers' job to tail a known criminal. The point is *not* that this O'Connor character accidentally stumbled into Bandon, and happily stumbled back out none the wiser as to your presence. The point is that he just as easily could've been on a mission to kill all of you. That at any moment, he could've ducked around a corner and shot Rafe. That he could've been pretending to not know you were there, and then murdered you in your sleep."

Kellan's brows drew together in confusion. Either at her reaction or the way his brothers had brainwashed him into feeling safe enough to not tell their handler about the level of danger. "Rafe and Flynn know O'Connor. They know how he works, what to expect from him. He's a mean son of a bitch, but he's not the guy who gets sent to take people out."

Civilians. They couldn't see the forest for the trees. They didn't have the training to flash through every possible scenario, rather than just the obvious ones.

Delaney started walking again, one hand out to brush the softness of the waist-high ferns. Because as mad as she was? It was her job to make sure that Kellan learned from this mistake. That he fully understood why this was such a big deal.

"O'Connor didn't *used* to be that guy. But McGinty's crew is upended. Half of them are in jail, and the other half are charged but out on bail. That means the power structure changed. People end up doing different things after a shakeup like this. Put on your lawyer hat and think about the possibilities. What if Pat was the only one who could get out of the state? Maybe McGinty believes he's the only loyal soldier left, and sent him on one last mission of vengeance? Or promised that if he carried out this hit, all the charges would be dropped and O'Connor would be a hero to the mob."

Kellan tromped along silently for at least a hundred feet, twigs and dirt crunching beneath his boots. "Those are all worst-case scenarios. Highly unlikely." He shook his head. "Look, my brothers said it was handled. I trusted their judgment."

That was the problem. The one she had to make him see, no matter how much Kellan might hate her for it. The truth would hurt. A lot. But his continued safety was worth it.

Delaney swept her gaze left and right, taking in the

creeping vine that bordered both sides of the path, the variety of shades of green on the trees, and the steady whoosh of the creek to their right. It was picturesque and peaceful, but not nearly enough to cushion the blow she was about to inflict.

"At this point, you should trust me as much as your brothers. Hell, maybe more. Because I've never lied to you, Kellan. Never once endangered your life." Sucking in a deep breath, she asked, "Can you honestly say the same about them?"

His answer came as half snarl, half sentence. "That's fucking low."

"I told you, I'll do whatever it takes to keep you safe. That includes fighting dirty. You know the truth about how your parents died now. Your mom was collateral damage in a mob shootout. Your dad was a hit by the head of the mob. That means the whole time your brothers were not just involved, but integral to McGinty's crew, their actions put your life at risk. *Knowingly.* Because the mob isn't just a job. It isn't a glorified club. It is a dangerous, lethal way of life."

"Fucking A, I know that." Kellan slapped his palm over his sternum. "I've struggled with that since the day you ripped the blinders from my eyes. Rafe, and then Flynn, made choices. Choices that kept us together, but choices that weren't the smartest or safest."

"Exactly. I'll grant you that they had good intentions, to be sure."

Because Delaney honestly didn't know what she

would've told a teenaged Rafe to do when his dad died. Let his brothers get ripped away and put into foster homes? Maybe not see them again?

Since he was already working for McGinty, letting the man pay the mortgage and employ him full-time must've been a no-brainer. Didn't mean he had to *stay* in it once Kellan hit eighteen, though. Nope, she didn't approve of that one bit. "But they made dangerous choices from day one."

"Are you saying I'm supposed to never trust them again?"

The shattered pain in his roughened voice sliced through her righteous anger like a hot knife through ice cream. "No. Of course not. You know I like and respect your brothers. You'll always have that bond. But I *am* saying that when it comes to decisions regarding the mob, your status in WITSEC, and your safety—those are instances you should trust *me* above all else."

They continued walking in silence for a few more minutes. Only three other hikers passed them, with friendly nods. Kellan looked like he was brooding. Delaney poked at her own hurt feelings, going back to them like testing a sore spot on her tongue against her teeth.

This lecture she'd just delivered was necessary and appropriate as his marshal. As his girlfriend, though, she wanted to push harder.

It *hurt* that Kellan hadn't reached out to her. That they texted all day long, Skyped every night, and he didn't think to tell her that this big, scary development had crashed into his life. Whatever it said about their relationship, it wasn't good.

The one thing she couldn't do was carp at him about not volunteering to be the Maguire who officially told her about O'Connor. Flynn had a secret reason to reach out to her that even Rafe and Kellan didn't know about. The favor he'd requested from her was to protect his girlfriend, Sierra, who'd evidently witnessed a crime back in Wisconsin and had been on the run ever since.

Technically, Delaney was happy that Flynn had trusted her to take care of someone he cared about. But it just hammered home how much Kellan *hadn't* trusted her.

She'd spent the drive to meet him on the phone, organizing surveillance on O'Connor from the moment he stepped off the plane back in Chicago. And getting another agent to pull his file and go over it with a fine-tooth comb. Then she'd reported on Sierra's unwitting involvement in a counterfeit art ring to her boss and gotten things rolling with that investigation. It hadn't left a lot of time to pout.

Now was a good time for that, though.

She'd been an idiot. Let a man cloud her judgment.

Just like her mom had. Which is why Delaney had sworn to never, ever let that happen to her.

"I'm sorry, Laney."

Kellan's apology yanked her from her wallowing. Okay, she'd give him one shot at redeeming himself. "Sorry for what, specifically?"

"You want the bullet-point list?" He bit off the words and spat each one out.

Freaking engraved and gilt-edged. Yeah. "To make sure I got through to you? You bet I do."

His head whipped to the side, as if he was about to keep snapping at her. Something in her expression must've made him reconsider, though. Because Kellan looked up to where the sun filtered through the roof of leaves and took a deep breath. Much slower—and more earnestly—he said, "I'm sorry I held back from you. Sorry I listened to my brothers instead of thinking for myself. I swear I heard everything you said. I'm dialed into it all with the logical, lawyer side of my brain, not the emotional, Maguire-family side. I get it."

"Good."

That was a pretty darned decent apology. More importantly, Delaney believed that he knew what he'd done wrong. That it had been, indeed, dangerous. Her duty as a marshal had been dispatched.

As a girlfriend? She was still pouting. Maybe Emily would Skype a coffee-fudge-swirl ice cream eating session with her tonight. That'd turn her mood around.

"I'm not making an excuse." Kellan bent to pick up a rock, then winged it over into the creek. "But can I give you an explanation?"

"Alright." She'd listen. Even though it wouldn't fix anything.

"I was off-balance when Flynn told me about O'Connor. It took the two of them a day to fill me in, even after they'd sworn to never keep secrets again. Only this time, it was my fault. They didn't know where

I was on Thursday, when this all started. Because I was with you, on our overnight at the B&B. Flynn pounced on me, accused me of never being around anymore."

Uh-oh. Self-righteous anger didn't fly when she'd brought some of the hurt on herself. "I didn't think they'd notice. Not with Rafe so wrapped up with Mollie and Flynn with Sierra."

"Me, neither. Rafe's so lovestruck that he hasn't noticed that I've skipped out on doing the laundry for two weeks. But they did notice I've been scarce. So I was playing defense, from the get-go. Trying to distract Flynn from nailing down where I've been disappearing to."

"You didn't spill the beans, did you?"

"Of course not. Flynn was pretty anxious. More about telling me, even, than tailing O'Connor. It didn't take much to throw him off the scent. I did ask if they'd reported O'Connor to you. But they wanted to hold off, see what he was up to first."

Delaney yanked—viciously—at a pine branch. Then she crushed the needles in her palm and took a long sniff of the fresh scent. "That's what I don't understand. Why? Why risk themselves, when I could've had a team there to do it?"

"Because they're in love with Mollie and Sierra. Because they didn't want you to yank us out of Bandon before knowing if O'Connor was there for us, or for shits and giggles. When they laid it out like that, I had to agree. Can't ask them to leave their women behind." Kellan took her hand. Brushed the needles from it and laid a soft kiss on top of each knuckle while gazing into her eyes with a look so heated it melted her knees to jelly. "Not when I know what it feels like to care so much. Not when I'd do anything to stay with you, to protect you."

"Oh." This wasn't just an explanation. It was a declaration. One that Delaney wasn't at all prepared to hear. One that made her want to freeze the moment and memorize the way the wind lifted the shock of dark hair off his forehead. How the shadows from the thick foliage made the lightness of his eyes pop. How her heart felt like it was about to triple-time it right out of the two sports bras she'd layered for their hike.

Kellan winced. "I listened to my heart instead of my head. Something they tried to drum out of me in law school. The facts are supposed to be all-mighty. Emotions can't ever overbalance the facts. I never believed that, though."

"Really, Counselor?" They'd stopped walking. When had that happened?

"Nope. Emotions are facts all unto themselves. Ignoring them wipes out a powerful tool."

It pained her, just a bit, to hear Kellan's insightfulness. It highlighted the promising career that Rafe had denied him. "You would've been a great lawyer."

"Maybe." He shook his whole body, like a dog after getting out of the water, clearly sloughing off the what-ifs. "Doesn't matter. I'm going to work my ass off to be a great deputy sheriff. Later. Right now, I'm going to work my ass off apologizing. For not trusting you. For not being honest with you. And, I'm pretty sure I should also apologize for hurting you. I made Marshal Evans angry. But I hurt my girlfriend, Delaney, and that's inexcusable." Kellan put her hand on top of his heart and covered it with his own. "I'm sorry."

Let's see . . . an A for effort, and an A for execution. Not because of the hand-holding or the staring-into-her-soul gaze. No, it was the naked honesty that coated every single word that did her in. "Was there a whole semester in law school in how to always say the right thing?"

Quick as a flash, Kellan's signature rakish charm straightened his neck and popped out his pecs as he grinned. "Nah. That's pure, natural talent." He gathered her into his arms and hugged her tightly. "I'm truly sorry, Laney."

"Thank you." Her phone vibrated in her front pocket. Normally, she'd ignore it. A big, dramatic apology was sure to end with some truly fantastic kisses. Delaney wanted the whole package. But between the impending tail on O'Connor and the new case she'd started on Sierra, this was not the day to let it roll to voicemail. "Sorry. I have to check my phone."

"No big deal. As long as you're not signing up to look for a new boyfriend on some dating site. Are we okay?"

"Getting there. Or maybe it's just Norah's calming tea kicking in . . ." Delaney winked and smiled as she unlocked her phone's screen.

For all the time they'd spent fighting since they met, the fight today had felt weird and horrible. Probably because things had been relatively idyllic since they'd come to a truce and started dating. A little more grovel would be appreciated, but darn it, Delaney completely understood why he'd made those choices.

"Would a back rub help get me the rest of the way?" he offered.

Laughing, Delaney looked down again. And the email address that flashed across her phone was the last thing she expected to see.

No. That was wrong. The message *beneath* it was the last thing Delaney expected to see. It was a sucker punch to her gut. And it stopped everything. Her walking. Her finger hovering above the phone. Very possibly her breath. The moment froze around her, squeezing her, tightening unbearably—

"Laney. Laney!" The sharp crack of Kellan's voice brought her head up with a snap. "What is it?"

"I can't . . . I don't want to tell you. I don't want to think about it. I don't want this to be happening."

And yet, she reached out for him. For the comfort, for the safety of Kellan's embrace. Maybe the need for his touch was a weakness. But Delaney didn't care. Didn't care about leaving herself open to be hurt again.

If anyone could make her life being upended better, it was him.

But she still only gave it about a ten percent chance of actually happening.

Chapter Twelve

KELLAN MORE OR less pushed an unresisting Delaney over to a fallen log and sat her down. She was scaring him. Normally, the marshal was . . . well, calm, but vibrating with suppressed energy. Now she was flat. Deflated. Her muscles limp, her face a sheet-white shuttered mask.

"Can I see?" He pried the phone out of her hand. Normally, Kellan wouldn't risk even a side-eye glimpse of her phone. He got the sanctity of the utter privacy that had to be maintained with all of her cases, but Delaney looked a blink away from fainting. Whatever was on that phone had caused it and he couldn't help unless he knew the facts.

The short email displayed gave Kellan more questions than answers.

From: Pennsylvania Department of Corrections
Subject: Parole Hearing for Inmate 76582

It is our duty to inform you that inmate Roger
Brinker is eligible for parole. His hearing will be on
Monday, September 27, at 10:00 a.m. You are invited
to speak to his character in person, or you may send
in a statement.

"Who is this? Someone you tried to protect?"

"Hardly." The ghost of a smile twisted at her mouth. "Someone I tried to forget, is more like it."

"Delaney, I'm not asking you to break protocol." He dropped to one knee in front of her. "But you've got to find some way to let me know what this is about. You're scaring the hell out of me."

"There's no protocol to break. This isn't about a case. Roger Brinker is my father." Her voice dropped to a whisper, barely audible over the rushing creek below. "And I thought he'd rot to death in prison."

So the marshal had a criminal in *her* family tree, too. Kellan never would've guessed they had that in common.

He sure as hell wouldn't have wished it on her.

"How long's he been in there?"

"Since I was seventeen. Since he's the reason my mom was killed when I was sixteen." Delaney looked at him, her pretty blue eyes as dull as old jeans. "He got a life sentence, Kellan. I was promised he'd never be free. That I'd never have to worry about seeing him again."

Sadly, he could offer a basic explanation. "The prisons are overcrowded way beyond capacity. Older inmates, with good behavior and the right records, are getting sentences reduced. Even lifers."

"It's not right. I put him, all of it, behind me. This complicates *everything*."

"Tell me."

"It's a short story. An old one that repeats over and over again. Woman falls for a man. The man's handsome, a smooth talker. Full of empty promises. Ones he tries to fulfill by committing crimes, both petty and major. She stays with him even as he bounces in and out of jail. Until finally she's killed as a result of his stupid, reckless, thuggish actions. He gets life, she gets a headstone that reads *Loving Mother*, and their daughter gets left to pick up the pieces."

"That's a shitty story." His succinct review was enough to cut through her shock and finally pull his darling Laney back to life.

She snorted, chortled, and then grimaced. "It is, isn't it?

"Barely worthy of straight-to-video release." They both laughed, and the worst of the tension seeped from her stiff muscles.

"Nobody would sit through ninety minutes of a heroine that stupid."

If nothing else, their barely ended fight proved that anyone and everyone would do, ah, *less than smart* things because they cared. Rubbing her knee, Kellan said quietly, "She must have loved him a lot."

"Too much. Too much for her own good, anyway." Delaney steepled her hands around her nose and just breathed for a few moments. "Kellan, my mother wasn't blind to what he did. She didn't deny he was guilty of all the crimes he got caught for, along with dozens more that he got away with. She just believed that her life would be nothing without him."

Ouch. "Nothing? What about you?" What kind of a mother left her own kid out of the equation?

This time her smile was bitter, and so brittle it looked like a single pine needle floating by on the breeze would shatter her entire face. "See, that's the same thing I asked myself all those nights she cried herself to sleep, alone, while he was in jail. The same thing I screamed at her every time I begged her to leave him, to forget him, to focus on our life."

Kellan had thought that growing up without his mom was the worst. But . . . growing up with a mom who didn't see you, who didn't make you feel like the best damn kid in the world . . . maybe *that* was the worst. Even though he'd had her for only seven years, the strength and comfort of his mother's love lasted to this day and beyond.

"You got a raw deal. You deserve about a thousand percent better. You know that, don't you?"

She swallowed hard, bobbed a couple of nods. "I do. That's why I made my life on my own terms. I went into law enforcement to atone for all the criminal things my father did. And I swore I'd never be one of those weak women who throws everything away for a man. Swore that I'd always stand on my own two feet. Not lean on anyone else."

Delaney was strong, all right. But that strength was compressed so tightly that little stress fractures were bound to develop. Kellan didn't want her to topple over one day from relying solely on herself. "You know how they earthquake-proof skyscrapers?"

The corners of her mouth quirked. "Ah, no. I can honestly say I have no idea."

"At first, they just tried reinforcing the shit out of them. It didn't hold up. So they went the other way. Added ball bearings and springs at the base to act like shock absorbers. Now buildings sway instead of toppling over."

"Is this your way of telling me that if we have to relocate you again, you want to be an architect?"

In the dirt, Kellan sketched a square with a roof and an X inside of it, all without lifting his finger once. "In undergrad, we called them squareheads."

"You can't malign an entire profession like that." Her lips twitched.

Which he counted as a win. He had to jostle her out of that scared, shattered version of Delaney any way possible. "Oh, yeah? Like there aren't a thousand and one dead lawyer jokes?"

"Touché. I suppose you've heard them all?"

He cleared his throat loudly. "Graveyard tombstone reads: Here lies a lawyer and an honest man. A passer-by remarks 'It doesn't look big enough for two people.'"

After snickering, Delaney covered her mouth with her hand. "That's so bad."

"Guess I need to start learning sheriff jokes."

"There aren't many. They're mostly about the uniform hats."

Kellan eased the backpack down her arms, and stuffed the phone inside, right on top of her gun. A little weird to think that he'd be carrying his every day, officially, soon enough. He set it to the side. Then he pulled her off the log to sit next to him, leaning back against it. "Do you want to make a statement at his parole hearing?"

"I don't know." She picked up a single leaf and methodically ripped it in half, then half again, until the pieces were too tiny to continue. "I've literally never even thought about it, because there wasn't supposed to be any chance of this happening."

That might be true, on the surface. But there were still a lot of emotions roiling down deep for her to be so stricken by that email.

Kellan decided to keep pushing, for her own good. He had a feeling that Delaney rarely opened up to anyone, and that she *never* let herself be pushed. And if he could help her with this, maybe it'd go toward working off what an idiotic jackass he'd been to not immediately go to her about O'Connor.

Very gently, he placed her on his mental witness stand and began the interrogation. The key was always asking not *every* possible question. Just the pertinent ones. He'd have to button up his curiosity to get through this the right way. "Do you have any contact with him?"

"None."

"Did you say everything you wanted to before he was sentenced?"

"No. I cut him off. Completely. I didn't want to let him cast a shadow on the life I was building for myself." She picked up another leaf.

He didn't need a second pile of green confetti on his thigh, so Kellan took her hand and began to trace idle patterns across her palm, up and down each thin finger. "Did he try to reach out to you?"

"Yes. Repeatedly. But what he wanted no longer mattered to me. Doing what he wanted, whenever he wanted, led to my mother's murder."

About a dozen questions instantly barraged his brain. But those would have to wait. "Do you maybe want to let it all out? Give him a piece of your mind?"

Or, you know, hire some jailhouse rat to jump him on the way to the cafeteria one day. Nothing lethal. But a really sharp shiv to the biceps with a few whispered words might make the scumbag realize at least a portion of the pain he'd caused this beautiful woman.

Wow. He'd never had fantasies of hurting someone before he found out that violent mobsters ran in the Maguire family. Was it catching, like the flu?

Or was it just that he'd never felt such an intense need to protect someone before?

Had Delaney brought out all of his base, animal instincts? If so . . . Kellan didn't so much mind.

White teeth sank into the pink perfection of her bottom lip, worrying it while Kellan's self-judgment grew stronger. Finally, Delaney said slowly, "I'm not sure. It took me a while to put all this behind me. I don't want to give him any power by letting it all flood back and keep me up nights again."

That all sounded reasonable. *Too* reasonable. But it wouldn't purge the bloodless fear that had taken over Delaney's body at the first glimpse of her father's name. If it took all afternoon, he'd keep poking at her until she got it out of her system. "Do you want to actively assist on his *not* getting parole?"

Delaney gave a slow nod. "If Mom doesn't get to have a life anymore, because of him, his actions, his choices, then he shouldn't be allowed that freedom, either."

Maybe he could get through to the law enforcement part of her to make the decision. "Even though you haven't interacted, what do you think of his recidivism chances?"

This answer came swiftly. "He's dangerous, Kellan. Older now, without his network of criminals. But he proved time and again that he was incapable of changing his ways. I truly believe that he'd seek out criminal opportunities. Not only to make a living, but because he enjoys it." Tugging on the end of her ponytail, as if the question were as simple as asking Kellan if he was ready for a snack, she asked, "What do *you* think I should do?"

He laughed so loudly that a trio of brown birds lofted out of the trees above them, squawking like crazy. "Hell, no. It'd be safer for me to strap on one of those dynamite vests from the Bugs Bunny cartoons and then strike a match."

"No, really. I want to know." Delaney turned, curling her legs underneath her. "You're ridiculously smart. You have a uniquely pertinent vantage point on the whole family criminal angle. What's your advice?"

Oh, he had some all teed up and ready to go. But it'd come back and bite him in the ass, no doubt about it.

There were still about a billion things he wanted to discover about Delaney, but her self-sufficiency and iron will had been easy to see from day one. It was a big part of who she was and Kellan wouldn't ever infringe on that.

"Remember my shock absorber analogy? I'm here to absorb whatever you need to work through. You can vent and yell and cry and scream at me. I'll take it all. Today, tomorrow, as often as the need hits. When you're done, I'll bet you'll have your answer. And I'll support that decision, whatever it is."

HER COMPLETELY OUT of character, out of control shock had passed. Delaney chalked it up to a combination of letting herself fall apart to Kellan, his calm logic, and that hypnotic magic created by his tracing her fingers, and raising every tiny, invisible hair on her hand in the process.

Or maybe it was the aftereffects of Norah's special tea. If so, the woman should open one of those food trucks and sell it outside prisons and courthouses. She could make a ton of money.

Although she felt better, Delaney also felt embarrassed. She'd looked to Kellan for the answer, rather than asking him to help her find it.

Screwing up her face as if a skunk had just sashayed by, Delaney said, "See? I suck at asking for advice, probably because I do it so infrequently. Emily would throw every dollar in her wallet at you if she were here now, just for getting me to break down and do it. She rolls her eyes so often when I insist on making my own decisions, I think they're permanently sprained."

Yup, she'd officially begun babbling. Just when she thought the humiliation couldn't get any worse . . .

"Come on. Don't tighten up again." Kellan lifted her hand. And then he put her index finger in his mouth, twirled his tongue around it, and sucked it slowly from base to tip. Just as her eyelids fluttered shut, he asked, "Is asking for advice *so* terrible?"

The man was such a flirt and he used it to distract her until he pounced in for the kill. So freaking smart and strategic. Her eyes flew back open. "If you're going to force me to admit it, then, no. And after I mull it over a little bit, I think I will still want to hear your opinion."

"Fair enough. We can have the discussion. As long

as I'm not handing down a decision that you'd accept without deliberation."

"No chance of that, Counselor, I guarantee. Consider it part of the discovery phase of an investigation." Delaney delved a little deeper, dug around in her psyche for any discomfort, like poking a potentially sore tooth. But that emotional trigger that had always reminded her to stand solely on her own two feet was . . . gone. Her instinct to shun help seemed to have shrunk considerably over the course of their conversation. "I don't think it'll make me weak to lean on you, like I always imagined."

"Don't you know? It makes you twice as *strong*."

Like a brace on an injured limb. Interesting. Turn her whole life mantra upside down–interesting. "I may not know what I'm going to do about my dad, but I feel strong enough to figure it out," she murmured. "Not so gobsmacked, anymore."

Delaney stretched her neck up to peek beyond the tree at their back. Still nobody coming down the trail. The off-the-beaten-path-edness of this park was one of the reasons they'd chosen it. Less chance of accidentally running into anyone, even on a holiday weekend. In front of them was a gentle slope down to the creek with lots of undergrowth and ferns and bushes.

Lots of *cover* for what she had in mind. She cinched her arms around Kellan and yanked him prone on top of her. Then she rolled, both of them, over and over and over.

"What the hell are you doing?"

"Celebrating how strong you make me feel." She pointed at a cluster of giant tree ferns a few feet to the right. "Scoot over. Nobody will be able to see us behind there."

Kellan's eyebrows shot up to his dark hairline. "Are you suggesting we engage in an act of public indecency?"

"Very much so." She pounced on top of him the moment he stopped butt-wriggling into place. Straddling his calves, Delaney unzipped his shorts. "I'm also suggesting we try for a land speed record at this, so as not to push our luck too far."

His penis was . . . *spectacular* in the dappled sunlight. Long and veined, with a drop of pre-cum already glistening at the tip just from anticipation. Only fair, since she was already wet from the mere idea of this, too. With the tip of her index finger, she traced the velvety steel of his shaft. The dichotomy of all that soft hardness made her want it stroked all over her body. For now, however, she'd settle for getting a mouthful of it.

Delaney stroked again, this time with all of her fingers in a superlight, twisting circular motion. She settled her palm against the head and rubbed for about half a second. Kellan let out a groan.

"Don't tease me. If you're going to blow me, put that pretty mouth around me right now."

She absolutely loved hearing the harshness in his command. Loved knowing that she'd provoked his lust, pushed him to insistence already. All wide-eyed innocence, Delaney blinked at him while continue to rub in tiny circles. "I'm just making sure you're ready. Interested. In the mood."

"Let's be clear. There is never a time I'm not in the mood to have sex with you. Every day, I have to walk around town hiding a half boner because I can't stop thinking about how good it is when I'm inside you. If you say you're ready, I'm sure as hell ready."

"Well, if we're having a quickie, you need to be *very* ready. I think I should just make doubly sure . . ." She reached up, underneath his shirt, and raked her nails lightly from his collarbones, across his nipples, and all the way down his rippling abs. Gratifyingly, goose bumps arose on the thin strip of belly that was exposed by his open shorts.

And then Delaney took him in her mouth. All at once, practically swallowing his length. Kellan let out a moan that was about eight hundred times too loud for two people hiding in a forest. Biting back a laugh, she let him fall out of her mouth. "None of that. You've got to be quiet. Or I won't climb on top of you."

"That's a solid threat."

She wrapped her lips back around just the tip as she swept one hand underneath to cup his balls. To squeeze them in rhythm to the hard sucking. They were tight and hard and hot and she couldn't wait to feel the hairs on them slapping against her ass.

One hand grabbed at her head. Kellan got a grip on her ponytail and applied pressure downward. "More, Laney," he pleaded hoarsely. "Take more of me."

Usually he was the one giving the orders. This was a fun change of pace. Could she make him come like this? Her guess was probably, but she wanted the pleasure, too. And was amazed by how blazingly hot she was just from sucking him off. Delaney pulled him deeper, raking her teeth gently with each downward pull of her mouth. Felt all that hardness bucking and jerking against her tongue. It was powerfully arousing.

"I'll take all of you," she promised.

Hurriedly, Delaney pushed her shorts down and off one foot. It wasn't worth taking the time to get them around her other sneaker. Because the idea of this quickie was turning her on as much as the heat pouring off Kellan.

It was like her body wanted her to orgasm immediately and every sense was jacked up to overdrive. She relished the softness of the springy moss beneath her knees. The way the breeze caressed her skin. The damp and earthy mix of scents rolling up from the creek. It was primal and basic and sensual.

Kellan lifted his hips to shove his shorts halfway down his thighs. And then she pushed down onto him in one long stroke, just like she had with her mouth. Delaney sank onto his penis all the way, until her butt did indeed brush against the wiry soft hairs covering his balls.

He filled her so completely. Part of her wanted to stay, frozen on top of him, taking it all in. Enjoying the solid feel of connection. Enjoying the sight of that dark line of hair arrowing down his belly to where they touched. Enjoying the look of concentrated bliss that had Kellan's eyes scrunched shut, and his mouth slightly open.

Then his eyes flew open and met hers. Delaney could swear an arc of heat, need, *desire* flew between them before singeing her heart in a brand that, in that instant, she knew would be permanent.

That whatever happened, that despite the inevitability of their breakup, she would always, *always* carry Kellan Maguire in her heart.

The moment fractured as he dug his fingers into her hips. "Ride me, Laney. 'Cause I'm ready when you are. I could come just from looking at you sitting on top of me."

"I'll race you to the finish," she said on a breathless laugh. And then she planted her hands on the dirt, canted her body forward, and pumped up and down. Fast. Hard. Kellan helped, his hands guiding her even faster. It was fun. It wasn't practiced or elaborate or careful. It was just plain hot and fun and exciting. Just like Kellan himself.

So it took fewer than a dozen strokes before the gathering tidal wave of pleasure crested into a solid wall of heat that flooded through her entire body. Delaney opened her mouth to scream. Kellan arched up, capturing her lips and swallowing her cry with a deep kiss that extended her orgasm as he finished with two violent surges of his hips.

Their panting couldn't be muted, however. Delaney

collapsed on top of him, her breath labored and fast. And it wasn't just from the exertion. This was supposed to be a casual forest quickie. Instead, she'd been blindsided by the strength of her emotion, her caring, her connection to this man.

She was falling in love with Kellan.

Had fallen already, if truth be told. The way he'd helped her today had pushed her over the edge. There was no turning back, no ignoring these feelings.

Despite the fact that she couldn't tell him about this huge new case Flynn had gift wrapped and handed to her about his girlfriend. Despite the fact she'd have to lie and hide things from him as she fielded emails even over the holiday weekend as they were supposed to be enjoying rare downtime.

Delaney didn't want to lie to him. She didn't want to put her job first. She wanted to put Kellan first.

And that realization was even more dangerous than the threat of them being discovered any second.

Chapter Thirteen

KELLAN DID SOME mental calculations. His cards were crap, with only a possibility of a low two pair. The guy in an actual fucking *visor* sitting across from him looked like an idiot, but played poker as though they were in a high rollers room in Vegas. Better to fold now and wait for a better hand to suss out his tells.

Especially since he was playing with Lucien's money. His friend was officially—albeit off the record and definitely off the books—bank rolling him to be a ringer in the monthly poker game. Lucien wanted to be sure the idiot Kellan had caught last month didn't have a group of similarly inclined-to-cheat friends. Kellan liked the idea of being poker's version of Robin Hood.

And it felt kind of good to see some of the guys from the plant. Bandon was too small for him to be one of those tight asses who ignored old colleagues. He'd given his notice almost a month ago. For the past two weeks Kellan had been part-time on dispatch and chipping away at the backlog of paperwork at the sheriff's department. The rest of his paycheck—which helped tide him over until he got trained and could draw a full-time deputy salary—came from helping out here at the resort.

So all the cranberry plant guys knew about his new job. Lucien knew, along with a bunch of people at Sunset Shoals. The sheriff knew.

It was only Rafe and Flynn, the two people he'd always been closest to in the world, who had no clue that he'd changed jobs.

Figuring out how to break it to them was a problem for another day. Tonight he had the chance of a decent run of cards, some not-sucky beer, and a spread of barbecue left over from a big party at the resort. No better way to spend a Wednesday night.

Aside from spending it with Delaney. But it was hard enough to steal time with her on the weekend.

If he got up now, though, he could ping her. See what she was up to. Pretend like chatting online made up for being more than a hundred miles apart and unable to see each other without a shit-ton of advance planning.

Who was he kidding? He'd take what he could get when it came to Delaney. And even if she was here, in Bandon? Having dinner with him every night and waking up next to him every morning?

It still wouldn't be enough.

Which was a big-ass problem he'd have to figure out ASAP.

Kellan threw his cards on top of the pile of green and red chips in the center of the table. "I fold."

"Don't be a pussy," whined VisorMan. "The game's no fun unless the pot gets fat."

Interesting. Maybe this guy *was* trying to pull something. "I need to refill my plate more than I need to watch you play out this hand, George." No time to chat with Delaney after all. Kellan was here to do a job. So he'd grab another scoop of mac and cheese, a pulled pork slider, and hurry back to the table to keep tabs on the newcomer.

That plan went out the window exactly one scoop of coleslaw later, when the door to the clubhouse opened to reveal Rafe in the doorway, with Flynn right behind him.

Oh, shit.

There was a moment that could've been funny—okay, it was funny, but Kellan figured he'd only make a volatile situation worse by laughing at the identical, eyebrows-high expressions of shock on his brothers' faces. One that he was pretty damn sure was echoed on his own. He couldn't let the rest of the room see it, though, so he ditched the plate and made it to the door in three long strides while they stood, frozen.

One hand planted in the middle of Rafe's classic Springsteen concert tee—that Mollie had gotten for him on eBay to make up for all the carefully collected concert shirts he'd been forced to leave behind in

Chicago—Kellan pushed them back into the dark and kicked the door shut with his foot.

"What's up?" Yeah, his casual greeting fell flatter than a leaf under the 876-page tome Intro to Contract Law.

Rafe gave him a return shove. "What the fuck is up with you? What are you doing here at the resort, after hours?"

Part of Kellan—about 99.999 percent of him— wanted to remind his older brother that he was an adult who could go wherever he wanted, whenever he wanted. But that wouldn't shut down this interrogation and get him back to the poker game anytime soon. Or remind them that he wasn't a kid anymore.

Maybe they'd treat him like an equal once he strapped on his badge, holster, and service weapon.

Then again, maybe they'd hate him for it.

On a shrug, Kellan said, "I'm hanging with my friends."

"What friends?" Flynn asked.

"Guys from the cranberry plant." This was stupid. There wasn't any reason for Rafe and Flynn to be here, after hours, either—unless they'd somehow heard about the game. But they didn't want to get caught dipping back into anything even semisecret so they were hassling Kellan.

Clearly, they didn't know that *he* knew that *they* knew.

Rafe pounced with the next question. "Since when do you hang out with them?"

"Since you two are too busy *getting* busy with your

women to hang with me anymore." There. A good dose of guilt ought to wrap this up.

Flynn looked down and away, fast. If he made a move that obviously guilt ridden on the witness stand in October, he'd be toast. Then he knocked his elbow against Rafe's. "Why don't you get Mollie to set K up with Lily? She's pretty. Good job as an elementary school teacher. I'll bet they'd hit it off."

Talk about an awkward—and obvious—attempt at redirection. "I don't need a setup," Kellan said swiftly. "I just need you two to go away and let me throw some damn cards in peace. Nobody needs brotherly bickering in a poker game. I know all your tells, anyway. I'd empty your pockets in three hands."

Rafe stared at him for a long minute. Then he jerked his head so they'd follow as he tramped off the grass and up over the dune onto the tenth hole of the famous course. Kellan was tempted to mention that most people had to pay more than five hundred bucks to set foot on the perfectly manicured grass.

Maybe he'd just tell Lucien and have him send Rafe a bill. As a joke.

Mostly.

At the top of the dune, the moon glinted off the dark ocean. Rolling sand dunes stretched all the way along the narrow course, with the water on the other side.

"Are you running a scam in there?"

Kellan was not at all surprised that Rafe had semi-figured it out. After all, he'd spent his whole life in the mob. An underground poker game was as basic and obvious to him as a quadratic equation to an astrophysicist. So he changed tactics. Went with the truth.

They'd never see that coming.

"A legal one. I'm playing to catch cheats. I've got Lucien's blessing."

Flynn turned to face him, backlit by the moon, so the harsh edges of his face were in shadow. But no light was necessary to see the anger tightening every muscle, making his stance rigid and his words fly out like bullets.

"Don't try to weasel out of this with technicalities." He jabbed his fingers against his sternum, fast. "I lived my life on that knife's edge and almost ended up in prison for five years."

Wow. The attack coming from Flynn instead of Rafe was . . . unexpected. Flynn, even after nine months had gone by, was obviously still raw from his near miss with prison. It almost took the edge off Kellan's annoyance at them being overprotective.

"Look, it's cute you want to be bad like us, but you're the *good* Maguire brother." Rafe crossed his arms over his chest in a wide-legged Superman pose. Then he threw him the *do it or die* look that Kellan had always associated with orders to do his chores or make it home by curfew. The underbelly of Chicago probably knew the look as a threat far more serious. "Keep it that way."

It wasn't the patronizing tone that pushed him over

the edge. It was the clear fact that they still viewed him as living inside a glass bubble.

Well, fuck that.

He'd had enough. Enough of them being in their oh-so-secret club and keeping him out of the loop. Enough of them treating him like a freaking museum exhibit of *Perfect Brothers*.

Enough of Rafe and Flynn not *seeing* him at all. They saw only what they wanted to when it came to Kellan. He got that they did it to make them feel better about their crap life choices of being mobsters, but he was done being their morality savior.

"I'm not!" he exploded. "Stop seeing me through this funhouse mirror that makes me look perfect. Just because I wasn't a professional thug doesn't mean I'm one-dimensional."

"Ooh—you can count cards. You're a real rule breaker," Rafe mocked. No, he didn't even mock. He was just teasing. The same way he'd teased when Kellan was eight and solemnly stated that he would be the first ever astronaut to talk to aliens.

Fine. They thought he was so perfect? So incapable of bending, let alone fucking *shattering*, the rules?

He'd tell them.

He'd tell them about breaking one of the biggest rules of their continued participation in WITSEC.

Kellan planted one foot at the top of the soft dune and leaned in, one hand bracing on his thigh. "I break one hell of a rule every day. You two turned over a new leaf when we moved here. Tried to be good. Tried to stick to the straight and narrow. Well, I went the other way."

Flynn rolled his eyes. "Dude, stop trying to keep up with us. We'll always be older than you. You're not a badass. It's just dumb pretending to top being in the mob."

Rafe's eyes, however, narrowed. With both belief and suspicion. "What have you done?"

Unable to resist, Kellan lobbed back, "Delaney."

"I don't . . . what does the marshal have to do with any of this?"

It was just sad that they didn't get his word play. "I'm *with* Delaney. We're dating. We're together."

Two sets of almost identical blue eyes blinked at him. The full moon made it easy to read the shock washing across their faces.

For a split second, Kellan wanted to take it back. Because he didn't want to see the inevitable disappointment paint their faces next.

Then all hell broke loose. Rafe looked around, as if trying to find something to heave at a nonexistent wall. It's what usually happened when he lost it. He leapt down the slope, grabbed the flag out of the hole, and chucked it toward the ocean.

Being a tiny flag on a pole, it didn't go very far. And when he was back in the privacy of his room, Kellan planned to laugh hysterically at the memory of his hulking brother heaving that teensy white flag.

Flynn, meanwhile, paced in a tight circle, one hand drilled through his hair as if trying to pluck Kellan's words straight from his skull. Oh, and he muttered. Every single curse word Kellan had ever heard, and then a string of them put together in . . . *interesting* combinations.

God, he wanted to take a video of the two of them losing it and send it to Delaney. But first he'd have to wade through the filthy aftermath of the truth bomb he'd dropped.

Rafe stalked back up to him, grim determination set in every frown line across his forehead and bracketing his mouth. "Have you lost your fucking mind?"

Hot on his heels, Flynn demanded, "How could you not tell us?"

Whoa. Talk about pulling exactly the wrong string.

Kellan started to lift his arms, then just let them fall back to his sides. "Are you fucking kidding me? After you hid *everything* from me for fifteen years?"

Rafe jabbed a finger in the three inches of air between them. "You didn't need to know what we did. How we earned the money that kept pizza on the table and new Nikes on your feet."

"And you didn't need to know about Delaney," he shot back.

"We damn well did. Do. We deserve to know when we're in danger. Your inability to keep your pants zipped could get us kicked out of WITSEC."

Unbelievable. Did they really think he'd given that zero consideration? That his dick was the only part of him making decisions?

Kellan wasn't flaunting their relationship on social media. They were careful not to meet where anyone would know them. For God's sake, he'd kept it a secret for seven weeks *from the people he lived with*. No way would a federal agency suddenly figure out their dating status. Not with the precautions they took.

"No, I won't. I'm smarter than that. We're careful," he insisted.

Flynn grabbed his shoulder, fingers digging in deep. His voice was a low rumble beneath the constant background noise of the pounding surf. "Careful like you double wrap with condoms and the pill? Or careful like you actually think an entire office of trained government spooks won't figure out that one of their own is skulking around fucking her protectee?"

One quick twist got him out of Flynn's grip. But Kellan didn't back away. He crowded closer, getting right in his brother's face. "Don't," he warned, in more of a growl than an actual word.

"Don't what? State the obvious?"

Rafe tightened their triangle. Not even an insomniac seagull would be able to overhear their conversation. "We've both watched you drooling over the marshal from day one. Believe me, there are plenty of other hot blondes in the world, even out here in this hiccup of a town."

Kellan stood his ground. Literally. "I don't want a blonde. Or a brunette, for that matter. I want *Delaney*."

One hand stroking his chin, Flynn asked, "What if we offered you twins, instead?"

Rafe's jaw dropped. "Do you know any twins?"

"No. But I know how to work a Google search." He scrubbed a hand through his hair. "What about maybe a gymnast, or an ice skater?"

Hands thrown up in the air, Rafe said, "Christ, Flynn, finding a woman isn't like building a pizza on the Domino's app."

Kellan refused to listen to any more of this even though it was pretty damned funny. He needed to make a point, right the hell now. "Look, you both gave speeches about demanding respect when you fell for your women. I'm asking for the same. Delaney's *mine*. You'll just have to get used to it."

"Does she know this?" Rafe hooked a thumb over his shoulder, in the direction of their house. "Or is she back home, locked in our basement?"

On a snort, Flynn asked, "Did you make a secret sex dungeon, K?"

Okay, it was nice that they'd stopped yelling at him. Their lame attempts at humor were at least better than fighting.

Kellan hated being at odds with his brothers and they'd been that way for *months*. He loved 'em, but Kellan still wanted to lay a haymaker on each of them for being mobsters.

It was something he'd started to work out of his

system by talking with Delaney. Her listening, her flat-out support and total understanding of how it killed him to see both sides of their decision, smoothed out the rawness of it.

So he was able to say, calmly, "I told you, we're together. We're crazy about each other."

"Crazy, that's for sure." Flynn shook his head. "I like the marshal. A lot. We respect her, too. But if this is more serious than an easy bed bounce, what's the end game? How do you guys end up together? Breaking a rule's not that hard. Living with the repercussions of doing it is what gets tricky."

Kellan stared out at the choppy water. It wasn't anywhere close to as choppy as the frenetic, off-kilter beat of his heart right now. Because he realized he'd just lied to his brothers. Again. When he said he was crazy about Delaney.

That wasn't true. He was in love with her. He'd been falling in love with her through all the months he watched her, noticed everything about her, and fought with her. Actually *being* with her just pushed him over the edge.

One thing was sure. He couldn't tell Rafe and Flynn before he told Delaney. And he had no idea when she'd be able to hear it. She was crazy skittish just at the thought of dating. So Kellan locked that brand-new, startling revelation in the back recess of his brain. Calmly, he said, "I'm working on a plan."

That lie was as big as Lake Michigan. Between

changing jobs and driving all over the state to steal time with Delaney, Kellan had been busy. And when he was with Delaney, the last thing he wanted to do was hash out depressing *what-ifs*.

They still had time. It was only July 19. The trial wasn't until October.

Plenty of time.

So why did his gut clench just thinking about it?

Rafe cracked his neck. Rolled his shoulders. Stepped farther out onto the sand, like he needed room to breathe before continuing. "You know, Flynn and I promised that we'd never lie to you again."

Uh-oh. Cautiously, Kellan said with a nod of his head, "I appreciate it."

"Guess we left out one important thing." He crouched, and used his finger to draw two lines that met in a V shape. "Kellan, you need to promise that *you* won't lie to us again." Then he drew another line, connecting all three. "We can only stay safe by fully trusting each other."

Shit. They were right.

But it meant launching another truth bomb. He locked his hands behind his head and let out a big sigh. "Then I guess I should mention that I got a new job. A month ago. Now I can promise not to lie to you with a clean conscience."

Flynn clapped him on the back, with a big-ass smile. "That's great. Why didn't you tell us?"

"What is it?" There it was again, that instant recognition by Rafe of the need to be suspicious. Man, he must've been one hell of a mobster.

Kellan had thought about how he'd tell them, eventually. After all, he'd had a month to come up with a way that would piss them off the least. Easing into the news was the key. "It won't fully kick in until after the trial, but I'm getting a head start there. Sort of unofficially taking it for a test drive. In the meantime, I've been helping Lucien on the side with a PR reboot for the resort."

Rafe held up one hand, palm out. "Quit stalling. What the hell's your new job?"

Shit. Okay. "I'm going to be a deputy in the Sheriff's Department. I'll join the training class up in Eugene in the fall. Since Mateo's so short staffed, until then I'm subbing in. Like a much better paid intern."

In a flashback to five minutes ago, two sets of blue eyes blinked at him, while identical jaws dropped. Flynn recovered first. His brows came together in almost a single line of confusion. "Why've you lied about it, hidden it from us, for a month?"

"Did you lie to us to get even?" Rafe demanded.

It was tempting to say yes. They'd certainly earned that treatment after fifteen years of lies about the mob.

But no, he'd promised to tell the truth. Petty vengeance had nothing to do with it. "I didn't tell you because I didn't know *how* to tell you. Because I thought you'd hate me."

"When have we ever been anything but proud of you, K?"

Not the point. Following Rafe's lead, he drew a long line in the sand that put Flynn and Rafe on one side, and himself on the other. "I'm joining the opposite team. Putting on a white hat and chasing down the bad guys."

Flynn pulled him in for a rough hug, followed up by three slaps on the back. "Way to go, K. I can't think of anyone more qualified. Except for maybe a Navy Seal. Or an army sniper. A ranger?" A proud grin split his face in half as he said it.

Rafe looked up at the web of stars in the inky sky. "It's not an excuse when Flynn and I say that we showed up just to get a paycheck in the mob. It's the truth. We didn't see a way out. But we probably didn't look hard enough, either. We never got a thrill out of threatening people, or breaking the law." He swung back around to look at Kellan, to reveal the naked honesty in his expression. "It took some getting used to, but I'm damn happier living on the right side of it."

"Me, too," Flynn added swiftly.

"Even if we were still neck deep in McGinty's crew? I'd say the same thing—I couldn't be more fucking proud of you, Kellan. The job requires a man who's brave and caring and smart. The people of Bandon will be lucky to have you protecting them."

Emotion clawed its way up Kellan's throat from his heart. Luckily, he didn't have to try and get words past it, because Rafe grabbed him in a giant bear hug. The kind they only shared once a year when they'd visited their parents' graves.

The kind they hadn't shared at all since leaving Chicago.

Flynn let out a yell, ran the few steps to them, and leapt onto Rafe's back. It toppled them over in a pile onto the sand. Kellan gave a strong push with his foot, and they rolled in a weird, flailing, laughing mass down the dune to land on the damp flat sand at the shore.

Almost all the rest of Kellan's pent-up anger washed away with the next outgoing curl of tide. He had the best brothers in the world.

"Hey, can I borrow your deputy uniform now and again?" Flynn asked as he pushed himself up to his elbows. "You know, for a role play with Sierra? The Big, Bad Cop and the Naughty Teacher?"

"Pervert." Rafe slapped a puddle at Flynn.

"Really? This from the man who's done Doc Mollie in more than half the hospital rooms?"

"We did it in the X-ray room last week. That whole table moves up and down with a foot pedal. So useful."

Yeah. The best, idiotic, depraved, ridiculous, *awesome* brothers in the world. Nothing could go wrong as long as the three of them stuck together.

Chapter Fourteen

THE SPECIAL, "EYES-ONLY" conference room in the Eugene field office of the U.S. Marshals didn't have any one-way glass disguised as a mirror or discreet cameras in the corner. It was utterly plain.

Delaney had explained that every field office had an identical room. That way, when they needed to bring in witnesses or protectees for a video conference, like to-day's, it was impossible to discern anything about the location.

That, and she'd cautioned/threatened Kellan about wearing anything Oregon, or even West Coast branded. He'd tried to make a joke that his bitching new tan would give away their location.

She hadn't appreciated it. Delaney had her marshal game face on, and humor wasn't anywhere strapped onto her utility/weapons belt.

Probably for the best. It'd help keep them from accidentally slipping into the role of boyfriend/girlfriend that felt so natural after almost two months together.

Nah, that sounded too juvenile for what they had going.

Lovers? Too middle-aged and smarmy.

Consenting adults with a mutually shared and acted-upon attraction?

When they checked into the target range in the basement before this meeting, she'd made him call her *marshal*, and Delaney had called him *deputy*. It'd been one hell of a kick to realize that wasn't a cover. It was his new reality. Just as much as the hour they'd spent at the range, working on his aim.

Kellan flexed his right hand in his lap, beneath the long metal conference table. The gun she'd given him didn't have much of a kick, but his trigger finger and palm ached from repetition. He'd get better. Fast. And not just to be at the top of his training class.

The days until the trial were trickling away faster than a handful of sand in the wind. If McGinty could find them—which was unlikely, yada yada yada—and was planning an attack, it'd come between now and October.

Or back in the mean streets of Chicago. The odds were much higher that McGinty would make his move there. On his own territory. Get one of his few henchmen who hadn't run away peeing themselves in fear of indictments, or who was not already jailed, to do it.

When and if it happened? Kellan would be on guard. And he'd be damn well ready.

One more flex, then Kellan reached for his water. They'd been in here for almost an hour already. It was a planning summit about getting the Maguire brothers physically *to* the trial.

Kellan was here as the representative for the family. They'd learned quickly last November that Rafe didn't do well when submerged in a sea of red tape and lawyer speak, surrounded by government agents. Kellan had taken over back then, and he was happy to do so now. It gave him the excuse to drive up to Eugene and see Delaney.

Now, though? FBI agent Darius Hegger had mounted his high horse about some snitty way the marshals office had done him wrong on their last case. It was small and petty and off topic, and Kellan was done with it.

He tapped the end of his pen against the yellow legal pad. "How about we come back to our list of requests? When not actively testifying, the Mullaneys would prefer not to stay in the holding room." Man, it was weird using their real last name again after all this time. "They want to remain in the court room. Strategically, it could be a smart move to keep McGinty off-balance."

"We came to the same conclusion." State's Attorney Linda Braunstein nodded over the iPad screen. "They won't be at the prosecution's table, but we'll have seats for Ryan and Frank in the front row."

It was even more odd to *hear* their original names

used, after all this time with their new identities. Kellan waggled his fingers in the air. "What about me? I know this is the trial of the century and the courtroom will be packed, but do I really have to sit behind them?"

Under the table, Delaney's foot pressed into the top of his. She wore her boring semi-uniform blue pumps, so it wasn't a sexy stiletto gouging him, but it still hurt. What the hell?

The reason became clear when Agent Hegger laughed. Threw back his shaved head and guffawed. There was a thin, mean slant to his lips when he looked back at them. "You mean you want us to waste a seat propping up an iPad so you can watch?"

They thought he wouldn't be there? That he wouldn't support his brothers through this entire, horribly hard, brave event? Shit, even before they'd patched things up two weeks ago on the golf course, Kellan had always planned to be there for them. These federal agents didn't understand what it meant to be a family at *all*.

He flicked his pen against the screen. "Sorry to increase your official head count, but I'll be there. If not next to Ryan and Frank, then in the back or wedged behind the flagpole, if necessary."

Linda frowned in her tiny window. She tugged at the discreet pearl stud in her ear. "Kieran, this is a change we didn't expect. We have you down as not attending. Not only that, but with your own full protective detail and a temporary stay in a safe house for the duration of the trial."

"That's bullshit. What is it—SOP for family members not testifying? Well, guess what? The Mullaneys don't do things by the book. And it should've become abundantly clear to all of you over the past nine months that whatever we do, it's with all three of us. Together."

Another frown from Linda. But this one came with a slight shift of her head, toward Delaney, who bumped shoulders with Kellan to share the screen. "You didn't tell him? That's rather unorthodox of you, marshal."

Kellan barely stopped himself from jolting in surprise. "You knew?" Delaney must've fought to have him in there and lost. Didn't want to admit that there was a dragon that she couldn't slay for her guy.

A bark of derision came from Hegger. "Knew? It was her damn idea. What's the matter, Evans? Do you not talk to your protectee?"

"This particular assignment has a lot of moving parts," she said, slick as ice on the steps up to an El stop in February.

Her idea? Delaney's?

Shock and anger warred for dominance inside of Kellan. Why—how—had she come up with this stupid-as-shit plan? Delaney knew him. She knew all of them. She *knew* they wouldn't want to be separated. That they wouldn't *tolerate* being separated.

He leaned back, kicking his legs out and crossing his arms over his mint green Oxford shirt. "I don't care whose idea it was. Not all ideas are keepers. So adjust your seating chart, because I'll be in Chicago come October."

"Actually, let's put a pin in that for now. We're running out of time and we need to go over the nightly hotel changes. We've booked a different hotel every night for three weeks. Different names, different parts of the city. There will be marshals flanking the Mullaneys, as well as across the hall. All of those reservations were made sporadically over the course of three months. There's no way to tie them together."

"It sounds like a solid plan," Hegger admitted, grudgingly.

It sounded like a crap plan. Kellan was still reeling, both from the news and the way Delaney had adroitly sidestepped a fight about it and rolled forward.

It was also clear she was the one setting down the rules. Neither Hegger nor the ADA had seemed to give a single rat's ass about *his* take on it. About *his* need to stay with his brothers.

Kellan still held an ace in the hole. There was no way in hell Rafe and Flynn would leave him behind during the trial. He could dial them in to this video call right now and Kellan had zero doubt they'd balk at testifying without him there.

Linda had to get back to court, so they wrapped up just a few minutes later. The second the call disconnected, Kellan pushed to his feet.

Delaney held up one hand. "Not here."

"I thought this was a secure room?"

"It is. But I'm not having a fight with my secret and highly illegal boyfriend *at my office*."

As if to prove her point, the door creaked open. A big man with black hair to his waist leaned in halfway. "Nguyen needs this room in five. And I'm wondering why you're trying to poison me."

"That's just silly, Kono." She gave him the one-two combo of a condescending chin tilt and a head shake. "If I was *trying*, you'd already be on the floor and foaming from the mouth. What are you talking about?"

"This salted caramel soda you gave me." He wiggled a cream-and-brown can back and forth. "It's disgusting. All the sugar in it's going to eat away the glue holding in the crown on my back tooth."

As if it was a normal day, as if he was nothing more than her freaking *assignment*, Delaney closed her computer and gave Kellan a wry smile. "Emily sent me samples of her company's new holiday soda to get honest feedback. Marshals offices all across the country have been independent test groups for her. She says she trusts our integrity."

Kellan did not care. Not about her best friend, not about fucking soda. All he cared about was getting out of this room and to where they could hash out why the fuck she'd tried to pull this over on him. But he also didn't want to be seen as a temperamental troublemaker.

He walked over to the man and plucked the soda can. "Why don't you try it yourself? That should put to rest the potential poisoning allegations." Hell, he'd pop a hole in it with a Bic and shoot the whole thing in one gulp if it'd get them out of there faster.

Delaney gave an overly dramatic shudder. "I wouldn't touch that stuff if you had a gun on me. I'm fairly certain its target demographic is kids who think pop rocks are haute cuisine."

"Speaking of popping, I heard you got in some practice this morning at the target range." Kono tapped his chest, between the lapels of a navy blue blazer almost identical to Delaney's. "Why didn't you come get me? I'd have practiced with you."

"It wasn't practice. Not for me. I was walking the soon-to-be deputy here through the basics."

"Ah." There was a long moment of silence as Kono gave Kellan a slow once-over. "This is your guy?"

"He's not my guy." Her retort came out faster and harder than a bullet.

"The one you got the gun for?"

"Yes."

"Kono Cheeska." He nodded at Delaney, sending his sheet of hair waving. "I'm her partner as long as she's assigned here."

Kellan shook his hand. But didn't give his name—and knew that it wasn't expected. That was the constant level of secrecy under which this office worked. "Nice to meet you."

Another long stare that lasted about four beats past uncomfortable gave Kellan the certainty that there was much more to her partner than the Hawaiian surfer looks. "Interesting to meet you." Then he turned on his heel and left.

Whatever. "Can we get out of here?"

"If you'll promise to keep your . . . *opinions* to yourself until we get out of the building. No, until we get to the hotel."

"Fine." It'd give Kellan time to line up his opening statement. A list of the rock-solid reasons her plan was crap, not to mention that she'd cut off his balls and served them up on a doily-covered plate by not telling him before the video conference.

The handwritten sign Kellan kept in his room that said *67 days without an incident*? Yeah, that was going to have to be reset. To zero.

THE SIDE WALL of Rose Cottage was, aptly, covered in lush pink climbing roses. The front had striking navy and orange window frames that played off the matching flowers painted all across the gray wall. It was adorable, quirky, and private. Everything you wanted from a rental for romance—or for what promised to be a very loud fight.

Kellan didn't slam the door behind them. But he did drop his overnight bag with a distinct thud on the dull orange Spanish tile. "Can we talk now?"

"Do we need to?" Anger emanated off him more strongly than heat from a volcano. It was a lame joke, but Delaney just wanted to keep putting off the inevitable.

"You can't be serious."

Lame jokes apparently fell flat when Kellan was in a snit. Duly noted. Delaney crossed to the glass-front cabinets and grabbed for a water glass. What she got was a mug with a picture of Lionel Ritchie on it that said *Hello—is it TEA you're looking for.*

That was definitely going in their Airbnb review. Geez. So cheesy it should come with a sleeve of Ritz crackers.

"Delaney." Kellan crossed to her in two long strides. He snatched away the mug before she could fill it, then crowded her against the sink, glowering down at her. "You wouldn't talk at your office. You wouldn't let me talk in the car. We're all alone now. What the actual fuck?"

She'd been dreading this for the last three days, ever since making the decision after coming out of a nightmare in a cold sweat. Because the minute Delaney sent the email requesting a separate detail for Kellan, this fight had been inevitable. There'd been a faint sliver of hope that his finding out in the planning session would've mitigated his anger.

That had *not* worked.

So this was uncomfortable and sticky—despite the fact that Delaney knew she'd made the right decision. The appropriate decision as a U.S. Marshal. Because Kellan's *girlfriend* Delaney didn't get a say.

"Our working relationship, the one where I'm responsible for keeping you and your brothers alive, has to stay separate from this relationship." She tried to wave a finger between them, but there wasn't any space. There was just the breadth of his chest, brushing against the front of her white shirt. Just the space of a breath between their lips. And nothing but heat, like the waves off asphalt in the summer, burning up the air between their eyes.

With an eerie, fierce calm, Kellan said, "It is separate. I treated you with, hell, *more* professionalism than I have since we met. I turned off the flirting. I did nothing to muddy the waters."

If only it was that simple. "You did. You do," she insisted.

"This high-handed decision you made to split me from my brothers for the trial isn't right. I'm not a kid to be left at home while the grown-ups do the dirty work."

"Is that what you think this is about? That I'm not trusting you?" Kellan didn't understand at all.

"What else is it?"

"You're a distraction," she burst out. "I can't keep your brothers safe if I'm worried about keeping *you* safe."

The realization had hit her on their holiday hike almost three weeks ago. That she didn't want to lie to him, to keep her other cases secret from him. That she wanted to prioritize Kellan over everything else.

She'd told Emily. There'd been a long night of sleeplessness, followed by an hour-long chat with Em where she told her . . . well, not *everything*, but enough.

The gist being that she'd gone all googly-eyed for her boyfriend. That she'd—gulp—fallen in love with him. Which was fine and right in the real world, but it didn't work at all when she was equally responsible for him along with his brothers.

Em said it sounded like love. She'd even mentioned cutting her business trip to Zurich short to come back and give Kellan a once-over to be sure he was worth it.

Not. Helpful.

But talking it over with her best friend had made it clear to Delaney that she cared too much for Kellan. Too much to do her job right. So she took steps to make sure he stayed safe while she protected her primaries.

"You've kept us safe for nine months, Laney. I have absolute faith in you."

Even in the middle of their fight, his voice resonated with truth and respect. "That's appreciated. I have faith in my abilities as a marshal. I don't have faith in being able to make hard decisions in a firefight without factoring in what would keep you the safest. *Only* you. You raise the danger level unnecessarily."

His eyes narrowed to an annoyed squint. "My presence is far from unnecessary. Rafe and Flynn need me there."

"Technically? Officially? They don't." Delaney *knew* how hard that would be for Kellan to accept. It pained her to spell it out for him. "You're not testifying. By your own admission, you knew zero about the mob or their involvement. I'd be putting you more at risk if I let you near two people who are known targets."

"Uh, it's in your job description to keep me safe."

Nope. He still wasn't getting it. Because Kellan saw the best in her. Which zinged straight to her heart, even in the middle of this fight.

"My job description technically is to protect Rafe and Flynn, first and foremost. If we do get attacked by McGinty's crew, I should be making assessments based on number of assailants, bullet trajectory, the most optimal chances of walking away with federal assets intact. Because that's what the Maguire brothers are. People I've sworn to give my life to defend. But bottom line? Rafe and Flynn are assets. *They're* supposed to be my top priority."

"You want to wrap me in Styrofoam peanuts, stick me in a fortified bunker with armed guards, and keep me safe?"

God, it sounded awful put like that. "Desperately."

"Because you care about me?"

She bit her lip and nodded. "Desperately."

"Because you're worried you'd let Rafe take a bullet that was meant for me?"

"Yes."

"I'm pretty sure that's the sweetest thing anyone's ever said to me." A slow, smug grin poured across Kellan's face like warmed hot fudge. "*Almost.* I'm going to interpolate the rest. About how you love me."

Feeling it and saying it, or sharing it with him, were two completely different things. And Delaney was definitely not ready to take that leap. Not without knowing where he stood, at least.

"I didn't say that."

His hands smoothed up and down her sides while his grin grew impossibly bigger. "You didn't say you didn't. And there's no way you worked your ass off to rise through the ranks and snag a big case like this to let just a hot man distract you. Even one as hot as me. Nope. The only possible extrapolation is that you've fallen in love with me."

"Assumptions don't count. Not in my line of work, and not in yours, Counselor. I mean, Deputy."

"Here's a fact: I love you. I've held off saying it because I was worried you'd think I was moving too fast. That we're already fighting an uphill battle with a secret relationship and no possible good outcome, and that telling you how much I love you would just make everything harder."

The rehash of the down side of their relationship didn't even register. Delaney's brain pretty much melted like glaze on hot donuts as soon as Kellan said those three surprising and all-important words. "You do?"

Kellan's quick, clever fingers unbuttoned her blouse as he spoke. "I love that you care enough about keeping my brothers safe to risk a fight with me. I love that you've got the integrity to do what's right, instead of what's easy. I love the way you guzzle down Norah's special tea and then sigh like you've finished an hour of yoga. I love the way you shiver when I lick the back of your neck."

Wow. Kellan hadn't just unlocked the vault door to her heart with that declaration. He'd laid out a red carpet in invitation for her to reciprocate. Both hands tugged at the back of his collar, whipping his shirt over his head.

"Why are you stripping us?"

"Because we're done fighting. I get why you did it, and we can talk through it later. Right now, we're going to celebrate that we're officially in love."

Oh, he was far too smug. Delaney put an edge in her voice. Just a little. Like the knife crease on pants fresh from the cleaners. "I haven't said it yet."

"You will. Because you love me." He bunched up her skirt above her butt, then lifted her to the edge of the counter.

True. So ridiculously true. But making him work for it—while he ripped off her panties with one swipe of his hand—seemed deserved. "Kellan Maguire, that's beyond presumptuous of you."

"Again, that's not a denial." Kellan unzipped his dress pants and let them slide to the floor. And then he was inside her with one long stroke.

Delaney's head fell back in sheer pleasure at the fullness, the way he stretched her. His hands clamped on her hipbones as he began to move. It was fast and unexpected—just like their falling in love.

She locked her ankles around his bunching thighs. Rubbed her palms up and over his shoulders, relishing the tautness of those muscles beneath his warm skin. She sucked in sharp, shallow breaths as Kellan literally drove his point home.

Delaney met his intense blue gaze and saw not just need, desire, but also all that love blasting out at her. She couldn't let Kellan do it alone. Even though she needed every ounce of oxygen just to keep pace with him as their skin slapped together frantically. Even though her orgasm was barreling fast along her nerves.

Hands cradling his face, Delaney took the leap and said, "I love you."

His bellow of satisfaction bounced off the exposed wooden beams. And as her own world shattered into joy, she drowned in a new and better kind of satisfaction as Kellan repeated, "I love you, too."

Chapter Fifteen

DELANEY PUT THE box of cranberry streusel muffins at the coffee station, then leaned her upper body through the doorway of her office. "It is August 14th. One month until the Cranberry Festival. Your belly profits from my growing excitement."

Kono slowly swung his head around, his waterfall of hair following in a rippling wave. "You're going native."

"No. Well, blending in. I mean, I've been here in Oregon since May. What's wrong with feeling the spirit of the place?"

"It can be good. It can be bad."

Nope. His low word-count wisdom couldn't penetrate her love bubble. It'd been two weeks since she and Kellan admitted their true feelings. How come she'd never been told it would get better every single day? Grow stronger, more true, deeper?

Delaney grabbed a muffin and waved it in a slow circle in the doorway. "Nothing can be bad topped with nutmeg, sugar, and cinnamon."

Sure enough, the lure worked. Kono got up and joined her. "Thanks for the afternoon snack. This'll make it harder to say goodbye to you."

"Goodbye?" Her trial didn't start for another six weeks. But so many marshals' postings were transient. "Did you catch a case? Are you headed out?"

"You are." He peeled back the paper from the muffin stump with agonizing slowness. "You're being loaned to a joint investigation with the FBI, ATF and state police down in Coos Bay. A serial bomber. Started small, at the Vietnam memorial in a local park. Scaled up to IEDs at the county prosecutor's office and a judge's house. That's how the Marshals Service got pulled into it. Judicial Security Division."

Well, that proved her theory that Kono was officially her *are you worthy of promotion* watchdog, as well as her partner. It was the only explanation for him knowing about the assignment before she did.

A multi-agency case wasn't unheard of. But it was unusual. A joint task force assignment could last a long time. It might not be wrapped up by the time she headed back to Chicago. "Me? Why me?"

"We needed someone. I suggested you."

"I don't have any experience with bombers. Are you

trying to get rid of me?" she joked, but with a burgeoning bubble of self-consciousness pressing up her esophagus.

"Not exactly."

Uh-oh. Uneasiness piggybacked on top of the self-consciousness. This had better not impact her promotion. She'd thought they had an easy rapport. What hadn't Kono told her?

Delaney loaded the coffeemaker to direct her sudden burst of nervous energy *at* something. "Well, that's not exactly reassuring. What's the deal? Do I click my teeth without realizing it? Pace too much?"

"This is an ideal posting. Coos Bay gets you much closer to your protectees. Being stuck this far away was never optimal. You've logged too many hours in the car riding herd on them."

All good points. Also? A pivot away from her actual question, which proved there was something more to Kono's recommendation that she take this assignment. Delaney pushed past him into their office. Once he followed, she deliberately shut the door.

"What's the real reason?"

"On the record? I told Supervisory Deputy Marshal Lomax exactly what I just told you. He agreed you'd be the best fit."

Fine. But Delaney wasn't done digging. "What about *off* the record?"

As he sat, a sustained sigh came out, like a tiny hole popped in a pool toy. "You care about your protectees. You treat them like people, not just a job."

"Yes. Basic human kindness, etc. What's your point?"

"You're seeing them as people, not as criminals," he said bluntly.

And suddenly Delaney knew exactly what this was about. She'd told him about how the Maguires had affected her. How she'd pushed to keep them in the program despite a dozen good reasons to cut them loose. How she *believed* in them. How she was now torn about the giant swath of gray she'd discovered in a job that used to be black or white.

Kono was worried she'd gone soft. Burnout could manifest in either disgust or too-great attachment. He was worried she'd lost her objectivity.

Wow. He didn't know the *half* of it.

Delaney leaned over his desk, tapping emphatically on the edge of his monitor. "We protect plenty of innocents. Whistleblowers. Spouses. Children."

"Criminals who may or may not have turned over a new leaf."

Self-defense reared its hammer-shaped head. It knocked the double hump of unease and self-consciousness right out of her. "I do my job—"

He cut her off by lifting a hand as big as a paw. "You're a top-notch marshal. I did some digging when I found out I'd be sharing my office with you. Your cases are buttoned up tight. Everyone likes working with you, even if you are a control freak. If this trial goes off without a hitch, there'll be a promotion in it for you."

"That's my hope."

Dusting crumbs from his hands, Kono leaned back, making the chair squeak in protest. "Is it?"

"Yes. Of course." He was probing, which she'd normally resent. But now she knew for sure that he had the ear of people up the ladder, so an explanation was necessary. "My dad was a bad guy. Through and through. In prison for life, as long as the parole board doesn't fuck up. I'm atoning for what he did, righting his wrongs, balancing the scales, by being in law enforcement."

"There's more than one way to fold a towel."

"Don't get folksy with me."

The chair creaked again. "I thought this joint task force might be a good change of pace. Give you a chance to explore your options, work on a different aspect of the Marshals Service. Think about how else you could tip the scales."

Delaney had let that thought slither around her brain only a few times in the last four months. The black-and-white distinctions being called for didn't always apply. A lot of people landed in gray areas. Like the Maguires. Officially bad boys, but deep down, good guys.

Still, she always came back to the same point. One that was impossible to move past. "But I've always wanted to be a marshal."

"I always wanted to ski. Was in a cast for six weeks the one time I tried. Stop being a lone wolf. Take my advice and think about what you really want. Because it looks to me like you want to help people. Help them not have their whole lives defined by one bad action, one bad day."

It was too much to contemplate with his sharp black gaze on her. "I . . . I don't know."

"Exactly. Take the day off."

"You don't have the authority to give me the day off. I can't play hooky, even if you cover for me."

Kono crossed his arms with a snort. "I like you, Delaney, but I wouldn't cover for anyone not doing their job. Lomax told me to pass that on to you. He knows you won't be able to take any time with the trial getting closer. Don't think about it. Do something different. Clear your head. They're expecting you in Coos Bay on Wednesday."

Delaney didn't know what to say. Or think. She sort of wanted to give him a hug. "This whole having a partner thing is working out differently than I imagined. Am I going to receive a bill for *life wisdom imparted*?"

"You've already paid in full." He crumpled up the muffin wrapper and lobbed it into the trash can. "This job is hard. Just because you're good at it doesn't mean it's good for you. There's nothing wrong with caring." His gaze sharpened. "Until it crosses a line. Until it clouds your judgment. I'd hate for that to happen to you."

He knew. Kono knew—somehow—about her and Kellan. Or did he?

"Thank you. For the opportunity. And watching out for me." Then she almost jumped when a knock sounded.

After barely a second, the door opened. Sierra Williams waved and gave a shy smile. "Hi."

Delaney had set up Sierra with a different marshal. As Flynn's girlfriend, there was too much of a conflict of interest for Delaney to take on her case. But she liked the brave woman who had found the strength to get herself out of a horrible situation, to move past the fear and still see the good in people. "What are you doing here?"

"Training with a sketch artist. It was a great morning. He taught me ways to make a witness think about shapes and faces. I took a ton of notes. There's a lot to practice."

"I'm glad it went well." As soon as she'd seen Sierra's quick and precise talent with a pencil, she'd known it could be put to good use. Doing something far more rewarding than her current job serving beers at the Gorse.

Crossing to squeeze her arm, Sierra said, "Thank you, again, for hooking me up. I never dreamed my art would make a difference. That it could save someone's life, or help put away criminals. I kind of feel like a superhero."

"Mild mannered, unassuming, but with a secret, glorious red cape?"

"More or less. Hey, do you have time for a coffee?"

Hanging out with a friend sounded like a great distraction from thinking about her new assignment. Especially the one person besides Kellan that she didn't have to lie to about what she did. "Yes. It turns out I've got the whole afternoon."

Sierra's mouth rounded into an O of excitement. "What if we do something more fun than just coffee?"

An hour later, Delaney regretted acquiescing to Sierra's suggestion. Regretted it like walking into the ocean with fresh razor burn. Because it turned out that Sierra wanted to hang at a paint-your-own-pottery place.

She pulled her phone out and shot off a quick text to Em while Sierra grabbed more paint bottles.

D: You know what you should never do with a professionally trained artist? Make art.

E: How would that translate to your job? Like if a bodyguard-to-the-stars came up and hulked over you with muscles and shades and a bulky holster showing?

D: Are you confusing me with the Secret Service? What exactly do you think I do all day?

E: Not entirely clear. I've got a picture of you in my head with a shotgun trained on the bad guys and a badass smirk. Or this sad version of you in a government-issue ill-fitting suit, at a desk stacked with papers higher than your head, in a cubicle with those annoying buzzing fluorescent lights overhead.

That was . . . unsettling. Delaney looked up as Sierra set more bottles—*seven* more, god help her—of paint on the table. "Do you know what your best friend does for a living?"

"Of course. Flynn's a bartender."

"Not your boyfriend. Your best friend."

A sort of private, knowing smile slid onto Sierra's face. "That's what I said. Flynn is my best friend."

"That's . . . well, that's lovely."

"What about your boyfriend? The one who gave you that?" Sierra stroked a finger along the bracelet Delaney now wore every single day.

"Oh. Well." Delaney swirled her brush in the little pot of water, buying time. No, not buying time. More like trying to figure out the answer. "I talk to him every night. Text all the time. I tell him things that I've never told my best friend, Emily. He's become very important to me."

Sierra clasped her hands over her heart. "You love him."

"How did you know?"

"The way you're talking around it. Like you don't want to admit the truth, but you can't deny it."

Admitting it to Kellan hadn't actually been that hard. Figuring out what to do next, now that was *hard*. But she didn't want to get sidetracked. This question Emily had accidentally planted in Delaney's brain about her job still bothered her. "What about a best friend you had back in art school?"

"Well, since I turned into a fugitive—" Sierra

dropped her voice to a whisper on the *F* word "—I don't exactly have a profile on LinkedIn to keep up with everyone."

"Not even your very best friend? No midnight Googling?"

Sierra took the half-painted plate in front of Delaney and made a tsking sound. "Did you have a plan when you started this? A vision?"

"No. I'm trying to go with the flow. Be spontaneous." It had some circles—the same blue as Kellan's eyes. A few wavy lines.

"That's not really your style, is it?"

A laugh erupted from Delaney. "Not at all. But I'm giving it a whirl."

"Be spontaneous with ice cream flavors. Or places to have sex. Not with paint." Expertly, Sierra dabbed and swirled while she continued talking. "It isn't just the being in hiding thing. I was a bit of a loner at college. You know my history. A string of bad foster home experiences doesn't give you a big circle of friends to trust. That's what I love about Bandon. I have friends there. I'm not lonely anymore. And I'd never realized just how lonely I was, being all strong and self-sufficient, until I moved. And, of course until Flynn."

Good thing Sierra had taken her plate because Delaney would've dropped it the moment Sierra mentioned being lonely. It was like not realizing you needed glasses until suddenly putting on your first pair and realizing the trees had leaves, not just green blotches.

She'd been *lonely*. For so long.

There wasn't the kind of built-in camaraderie with the Marshals as with other law enforcement agencies. That was impossible with the layers of secrecy and constant moving around the country. Back in college she'd been too focused on keeping her scholarship, training to be ready to hit the ground running for the six-month-long stint at the Federal Law Enforcement Training Center in Georgia.

Not being able to reveal what she truly felt, or even what she did on a daily basis, had worn her down. Emily not knowing how she spent her days? That proved she'd been too buttoned up, too isolated. For too darned long.

"My best friend that I've had since college just told me she has no idea what I do every day as a marshal. Is it weird to ask how you see me?"

Sierra dropped the brush on the table. Palms flat, she leaned forward with wide eyes. "Omigosh, you're the one who's a superhero."

"Hardly." Delaney tugged at the polyester lapel of her blazer. "Don't you think I'd be rocking a cape and a good pair of red knee-high boots if I could?"

"You protect people. You're a living shield against not just violence, but against fear."

That was a shock. Flattering, over-the-top, and so surprising to hear from someone that she hadn't actually protected at all. "I haven't caught a bullet between my teeth in at least two months," Delaney joked.

"It's not that. You've got this air of competence—I'm

quite sure you can run and fight and shoot as well as, if not better, than everyone else. But it's the way you listen and lay out facts and options. You hand over this supreme surety like a giant safety blanket. To someone who's scared of the present and petrified of the future, that's invaluable."

The heartfelt compliment flashed the beginning of an idea into Delaney's brain. What if Sierra was right? The woman had a heart the size of a small Baltic country, so obviously what she'd said was overblown, but what if the foundations were true? What if Delaney used that compassion and empathy that she'd braced against? Rather than being a weakness, it could be an asset.

What if she used it to help witnesses feel secure enough to testify? Witnesses who weren't necessarily victims, but whose testimony would ultimately help the government make their case. People like that were often sneered at by prosecutors, agents, cops, all because they weren't purely innocent.

If she became an official advocate for them, she'd still be doing good. Still be on the side of right, and yet also celebrating the good she saw shining in people who were far from paragons.

Was this even a real thing? Victim advocates, sure, but for witnesses who were on the wrong side of the law? Delaney didn't know. But insider testimony often proved to be the most important. If it wasn't a thing already, it *should* be.

Her fingers flexed, almost reaching for her phone to

tell Kellan. That had become her first instinct for every-thing. Telling him. Sharing with him. In a little more than two months together, they'd melded into what she'd never aspired to be—a *couple*. It turned out there was a reason for all the hype. That sharing with another person didn't weaken you. It doubled everything. The joy. The strength. The fun.

The love.

Then she remembered that she couldn't tell Kellan, at least not without coming up with an alternate version of how she got the idea. Delaney didn't know if Sierra's training to be a sketch artist with the marshals was con-fidential or not. And in her work, the go-to assumption was always to err on the side of caution and confiden-tiality.

Was that what their relationship would be like? Hiding things from Kellan all the time? They had this unique opportunity for her to talk about her current case because he was in it, but that wouldn't continue. This glimpse into the future . . . *sucked*.

Sierra tickled her arm with a dry brush. "Delaney? It feels like I lost you there for a minute. Are you okay?"

"I will be." She squeezed the tube of blue paint. Hard. Good thing the cap was on. "Thanks for what you said. It helped more than you know."

"I'm sorry that you have to hide so much from your friends."

"It's not that hard. I don't have very many." Wow.

Delaney had never let herself think about it before. Not really. Because why brood about something that couldn't change? But now that she'd released the floodgates on all of her buttoned-up feelings—thanks to the whole falling in love thing—she could admit that it bothered her. "One of the hazards of the job, of always being on the move and under a gag order."

"I know the feeling." Sierra's wry smile was the only hint at how hard her life had been while she spent six months alone, running from an ex-boyfriend who'd duped her into art forgery. "But you've got me, now. Not just for as long as you're here. For as long as you want."

She made it sound so simple. "Will that still hold after you see how ugly I make this plate?"

"Don't worry about that. I fixed it." Sierra pushed it back in front of her. The lopsided blue circles were now quirky, adorable flowers. The wavy lines had become a field of grass blowing in the wind.

"How did you do that?"

"Your cape says superhero. Mine says super with a paint brush. We've all got our thing. Mollie can literally save lives, so I always thought her talent was the coolest. But then I tasted Lily's chocolate rum cake, and now I'm wavering."

"That sounds amazing."

Sierra squeezed her arm. "I wish you didn't live so far away. You could come to our next girls' night and try it yourself."

"I'm actually moving much closer—to Coos Bay. For at least six weeks." With a half-shake of her head, Delaney said, "Don't ask why."

"That's wonderful. I mean, unless there's a serial killer that you're stalking."

"As far as I know, your boyfriend and his brother are the only criminals in Bandon." It felt good to tease Sierra. To talk about the Maguires.

"Criminally handsome, that's for sure. Ooh, you'll be nearby to help with the Cranberry Festival."

"Hasn't your whole town been working on that all year?" Rafe certainly complained about it enough at every briefing. And Kellan had worked hard to draft a new brochure and website for it.

"Mmm-hmm. But there are so many different events over the three-day festival that the to-do list is endless. And it doesn't feel like work when you're hanging out with your friends. Like us, today. With more wine and chocolate. My Bandon friends seem to require that every time we get together. It's awesome."

"I like their style. I'm much better at providing wine than I am at painting."

Sticking her tongue out, Sierra said wryly, "I can believe that."

The Festival was the biggest event in Bandon. It drew hundreds of thousands of tourists to town, which meant she and Kellan could interact normally. They'd blend into the crowds and there wouldn't have to be a cover story, or a pretend date with the sheriff. Delaney wouldn't have to lie. It could be three days of carefree fun before the reality of the trial hit.

"You know what? I'd love to meet your new friends. I'll even liaise with your handler to make it count as a check-in. We can use today as our cover story."

"Cover story for what?"

Delaney loved the streak of optimistic innocence that ran deep in Sierra. "You can't introduce me as a federal marshal."

"Why not? Policemen say what they do. As long as you don't tell anyone that you met me doing your job as a marshal, why do we have to lie?"

Because it was second nature? Because it cut down, even if by a minuscule percentage, on anyone wondering why a marshal would be in the area, and then maybe telling their cousin back in Chicago that there was a marshal roaming loose? Because dating Kellan constituted going off the rails enough when it came to following the rules?

Short answers were always best. "For safety. Besides, this is an adorable meet-cute. Both of us killing an afternoon painting pottery. You rescued me from my own horrible lack of talent."

"Aren't meet-cutes supposed to be in dating?"

"I'm appropriating it. A good marshal makes use of whatever tool or situation is handy. Consider it a lesser version of my superpower."

Friends. Fun. More chances to see Kellan. Suddenly, this new assignment that had felt like a punishment seemed more like a gift.

Grabbing her phone—because resisting the urge to talk to Kellan was about as difficult as resisting a bowl full of spaghetti and meatballs heaped with parmesan—she shot off a quick text.

Having a good day. Plan on it being an even better night if you can meet me in Coos Bay. I'll explain later. Just say yes.

His answer took no time at all. My answer to you will always be yes. Especially if it involves getting naked.

D: If you're lucky . . .

But she felt like the lucky one. This living in the moment thing, ignoring the impossibility of their future, it was working.

For today, anyway.

Chapter Sixteen

KELLAN RUBBED THE heels of his hands against his eyes. "I miss Chicago."

"What set you off this time?" Delaney asked. She flicked her glance from the dark road to give him a very disdainful side-eye. "The predawn air doesn't smell enough like the spilled beer puddles outside Wrigley? The sky's too dark and not lit with enough ambient lighting from the Hancock Building?"

Okay, he got it. There were times when he bitched about missing stupid little stuff about his hometown. And since Delaney was one of only three people in the world he could complain to, she probably heard too much of it. Especially in the week since their planning summit, which had brought up all sorts of Chicago memories now that Kellan knew he wouldn't get to see it one more time after all.

He'd do better. Dial it back. Because he intended to be the best damned boyfriend to her in the world. That was step one in his elaborate plan to convince Delaney there was a way for them to keep dating after the trial. Without any repercussions.

Okay, it was his only step planned so far. But he was *killing* it at step one.

Smugly, Kellan remembered the three orgasms he'd given her last night. Right after he'd magnanimously ordered in Chinese to make up for his attempt to cook her dinner. It'd been his first try at recreating Chicago's famous Chicken Vesuvio. Chicken baked with potatoes and artichoke hearts and peas seemed impossible to ruin. Unless your pot holder hit the flame and started a small fire . . .

Rafe and Flynn always gave him shit about his failed cooking attempts. Delaney, on the other hand, covered him in kisses and thanked him for making the effort. Man, she'd make a great mother someday.

Kellan jerked in his seat at the thought. Technically, they had no way to be together by Thanksgiving. What was he doing thinking about kids with her?

"Sorry, Laney. What set me off is, well, it's how I miss the routine of my life there. I worked out in the afternoons. After class, to get the blood pumping before hitting the books for eight more hours." He wrapped his knuckles against the car window. "This running on the beach at zero dark thirty isn't my speed."

"You said you wanted to do more things with your

brothers. This is the best time to work out as a unit. It's good for you in a lot of ways."

"I feel bad that you got up so early to drive me to the beach."

She reached over to slide a hand languorously up and down his thigh. "It was worth it to spend the night together. And I'm doing some work around here today, anyway."

Kellan didn't ask for details. He was just thrilled that her new assignment put her so much closer. "You'll be careful?"

"Kind of in my job description, babe. Hey, how about *I* try cooking for us tonight?" Delaney turned off her lights as she coasted into the parking lot. That way Rafe and Flynn wouldn't know that he'd been dropped off.

They wouldn't care. But explaining to Delaney that his brothers knew about the two of them was a fight he wasn't ready to have yet. "Can you cook better than me?"

Laughing, she pointed out the window at a shore bird digging its beak in the sand. "That gull can cook better than you. It won't be fancy, but it won't catch on fire, either."

"Where's the fun in that?" Kellan opened the door. "You need more adventure in your life."

"You're all the adventure I can handle." With that she kissed him and pushed him out of the car.

If he had to run on the beach at the crack of ass, doing it with a kiss from Delaney was the way to go. Kellan trudged up the dune and over to a towering rock formation, at least twelve feet tall. Rafe and Flynn waited for him, stretching against the rocks.

"I didn't see a car," Rafe said.

"That's the idea. Your not seeing it means—to Delaney—that you guys don't know about us."

"When are you going to man up and tell her?"

He bent over to stretch his hammies. "Don't hassle me. You lied every day you were in the Chicago mob. Don't act like truth is encoded in the Maguire genes."

"The longer you wait to tell the truth, the worse the fight. Trust me on that." Flynn stripped off his wind shirt and left it piled at the bottom of the rocks. "I waited too long to tell Sierra. I almost lost her because of it."

"Since when do you give dating advice? What makes you think you know more about women than I do?"

Flynn's sharp laugh echoed off the rocks. "I'm older. More handsome. And my street smarts beat the living shit out of your book smarts when it comes to women."

"Still using your fists every chance you get, huh, Frank?" A bald, stocky man stood at the edge of the farthest rock.

And he was holding a gun, trained right on Kellan.

Wow. Just when he thought a dawn run couldn't suck any more . . .

Kellan's mind instantly flew to Delaney, hoping that she'd left the parking lot without any interaction with this goon. Then he spared a thought for his gun, safely tucked away in his dresser drawer. He hoped his socks felt safe, because he sure as shit didn't.

That's when time sped back up to normal and it fully registered that one twitch of a finger could mean his death. Because this wasn't some random mugging. No, this guy had used his brother's *real* name. Original name. That made him a mobster.

Holy shit.

"It's Flynn, now, actually. Try to keep up." Flynn sounded calm. Looked perfectly still. But Kellan had seen him like that at MMA fights, right before he executed a crazy windup kick that put his opponent six feet across the floor. Did the calm mean he was ready to strike? Or that Kellan didn't need to be panicked about the gun pointed at his chest?

"Davey O'Brien. This is a surprise," Rafe said.

"The fuck it is. You've known from day one that we'd be coming after you for that money."

Oh. This was about the money his brothers stole from the mob the night before going into WITSEC. That could be good. This O'Brien guy would need to keep them alive to find out where they'd hidden the cash.

Or at least, keep one of them alive.

Shit. Yeah, that didn't reassure Kellan at all.

"We didn't steal any money," Rafe said calmly.

"Right. Just like you and I didn't fuck up that asshole Dwyer with a baseball bat when he skimmed off the top of McGinty's take after the Super Bowl. Jesus, I'm not an idiot. You took the money. We can stand here lying to each other all day, but it won't change that I'm the one with the gun aimed at your little brother. You really want me to start shooting parts of him to jiggle your memory?"

"You might get off one shot." Rafe lifted one shoulder in a halfhearted shrug. "Then we'd be all over you."

"One's all it takes."

Kellan really didn't like where this conversation was heading.

His brothers might be calm, might think they could take this guy down. But in the meanwhile, even if it didn't kill him, one bullet could do a hell of a lot of damage. "Do I get a vote?"

Simultaneously, his brothers shouted, "No!"

Flynn reached out an open hand, palm up. Which would look nonthreatening to anyone who hadn't seen him use his thumb as the leading edge of an uppercut to the underside of a jaw. "Leave the kid out of this. He's got nothing to do with McGinty or the money. You know damn well we kept him in the dark about all of it."

"Doesn't look like he's in the dark now." O'Brien flicked his gun up and down at Kellan. "Not if he's living with you on the government dime."

He couldn't keep quiet any longer. "Believe me, I don't know anything. They won't tell me much."

"I hear you're the brains of the family. Why don't you use those smarts to convince your brothers to play nice? I don't want to shoot anyone. Hell, I don't even want to disrupt your cushy deal with WITSEC. I just want the money. Then I'll vanish."

"You'll vanish?" Rafe straightened as though that

news had stuck a coat hanger up his ass. "You're not here on orders from McGinty?"

O'Brien swatted at the air like that suggestion was as annoying as sand fleas. "Why should I share with a washed-up old guy on house arrest?"

"He's out of jail?" Now Flynn straightened up, too.

"Yeah. After he got sick again this month, they put an ankle monitor on him and moved him home."

Interesting that Delaney hadn't shared that fact with them. Not that Kellan blamed her. The news would've sent Rafe and Flynn into a lather.

But as her boyfriend, yeah, it rankled a little that she'd held back, no matter how logical it was to keep McGinty's change in status on a need-to-know basis.

Rafe shook his head, squinting. "After ten months locked up? How'd he finally convince a judge to be lenient?"

"There was a shake-up because of that scandal with the bailiffs, oh, and that other thing with the night court bribery ring. It left a few judges' seats empty. They had to bring some out of retirement to keep the dockets clear. Judge Fitzpatrick, who was always in our pocket, came on board and had McGinty back in his recliner within a week."

This was a lot of gossipy catching up that in no way moved the barrel of the gun away from Kellan. Couldn't they go grab a beer and talk mob stuff *without* him being in mortal peril?

"Fitzpatrick's a tool," Rafe said companionably, as if they were sucking on cigars after a bone-in ribeye back at Sullivan's Steakhouse.

"Sure is."

Head cocked, Flynn asked, "How'd you find us?"

Now they were getting somewhere. Because however Davey found them could lead other mobsters here, too. It could be make Delaney yank and relocate them immediately.

Well, *immediately* after they got rid of this joker and his fucking gun that was still, unwaveringly, pointed at Kellan.

"Pat O'Connor. He came out here about six weeks ago. He knows I've been working on my golf all summer, so being the prick that he is, he bragged about the courses at Sunset Shoals."

"They're pretty great." Kellan snapped his fingers. "Tell you what—I'll get you a free round if you put the gun away." Yeah, it was desperate and stupid. But a bribe seemed like something a mobster would appreciate.

O'Brien smirked. "I can play a lot more than one round once I get my hands on that two million."

The *what*? Kellan knew they'd stolen money as a backup, in case WITSEC didn't work out for them. But they'd never told him the actual amount. Funny to think that Rafe and Flynn were millionaires.

For a second.

The whole loaded gun thing seriously dampened his sense of humor.

Rafe cleared his throat. "You're not getting one red cent unless you explain how you found us."

"My wife hates Arizona. This sounded like a better

place to bring her for winter golf. I looked on the web and found the site for the Cranberry Festival. How hokey is that? I was laughing my ass off about it when I saw your picture."

"On the website? Impossible," Rafe said flatly. "There aren't any photos of us." They were all cautious about that—even in this era of smart phones capturing every damn second of life in a tourist town.

"It was you, Rafe. Bending over a half-done stage with a hammer. I wasn't sure, until I recognized your tattoo."

"Fourth of July. You helped set up for the concert." Flynn tunneled his hand through his dark hair. "Fucking Floyd. He must've added photos to the website Kellan designed after the holiday."

If that was true, it'd be easy enough to take down. Or just creatively blur Rafe's face and tat. Kellan could do it in less than five minutes.

If he got off this beach.

Alive.

"Enough jawing. Where's the cash?"

Cash? They'd stolen two million in *cash*? That had to be . . . well, a lot of bundles of bills. You couldn't just stick two million in your coat pocket and walk down the street unnoticed. Kellan was suddenly very curious exactly *where* they had stashed that much money.

"It's in Chicago." Rafe crossed his arms. "You're not getting it today, no matter what."

A bark of surprised laughter burst out of Davey. "You left it back home? What the hell good does it do you there?"

Flynn mirrored Rafe's pose. "Well, right now, it's keeping you from shooting our brother, so I'd say it's doing a fuck ton of good."

O'Brien's head swiveled back and forth between them. Frowning, he growled, "You're lying."

"Are you serious about vanishing after you take the money? Not telling anyone about us?" Rafe asked.

"Of course." Davey double-thumped his chest, looking pissed that he'd been challenged. "What the hell, Ryan? Fuck, I mean Rafe? You always trusted me to do a job right, not skim off the top, not be rough with women. We worked side by side for years. You know I'm a man of my word."

Ah. The famed *honor among thieves.*

It was like watching every clichéd mobster flick being acted out right in front of him. Again, it'd be amusing as fuck in hindsight. Once this was all over. After Kellan did about seventeen shots of Johnnie Walker.

"And you know the same goes for me. I've never lied to you, Davey. Never treated you badly." After a quick glance at Flynn, and getting a nod, Rafe said, "We'll give it to you. It's worth your keeping our secret."

"Fair enough.

"We don't need it, anyway. It was just backup in case this WITSEC deal went south and we had to run." Flynn rubbed at his temple. "It's been weighing on my conscience. Giving it to you will clear the books. With the added win that prick McGinty won't see a cent of it."

Kellan couldn't believe that O'Brien was actually buying this load of crap.

Sure, it was true they'd stolen it as security. But Flynn saying they didn't *need* to be millionaires? This from a guy who used to drop five hundred on fancy sneakers without blinking, but hadn't worn anything more than Nikes in ten months? And the guilty conscience thing almost made him laugh out loud.

Rafe actually backed up a few steps, farther away from O'Brien, to lean against a rock. It gave the impression he was totally chill with the conversation going down. That he didn't give a rat's ass about the gun.

Kellan hoped like hell that was only an impression, and not reality.

"I'm telling you, straight up, Davey—all the cash is in Chicago." Rafe shrugged. "You can have it. But we'll have to go and get it when we go back for the trial."

"October, right? I'll meet you at O'Hare. We'll go right to wherever you stashed it."

Flynn held up a hand. "No can do. We'll need to shake our marshal. That'll be tricky. Having you around would make it impossible. We'll meet you at the Water Tower after we've retrieved it."

Smart. Smack dab in the middle of the Magnificent Mile, the Water Tower was a landmark. Always well lit, with both tourists and locals constantly streaming by. No chance for any funny business so out in the open.

A low, threatening laugh gurgled out of Davey. "Oh, I'll take care of your bodyguard. It'll be fun. Consider it a welcome-home present."

Kellan's blood ran cold at the breezy threat against Delaney's life.

Flynn, too, backed off to lean against another rock. Even gave a nod of his head in . . . *gratitude*? "That's a generous offer, Davey. But the marshal's off-limits. If you're taking our security stash, we'll need our monthly check from WITSEC. Gotta play it smart and safe."

"No wonder you boys left the mob." O'Brien pulled his mouth downward into a smirk. "Pussies, all of you!"

"Toeing the line doesn't net us a lot of cash. That extra padding from WITSEC makes all the difference."

"You *would* say that, Flynn," the mobster sneered. "I remember all your fancy ties and sneakers. No wonder you sat behind a desk and never got your hands dirty like your brother."

"Work's work, Davey. Everyone contributed. Now, do we have a deal?"

"Yeah. Get a burner phone before you text me about the handoff."

"We're not amateurs. You'll get the money before the trial starts. You'll learn the date in the *Chicago Star-Trib,* I'm sure. Book your flight for the next day to whatever acre of the Mexican coast you plan to retire to."

"Deal." He tucked the gun into his pants and stuck out

his hand. At a measured pace, Rafe came forward, shook, and then they both spit sideways over their crossed hands. Then Davey jerked his chin toward Kellan. "Crazy how much the kid looks like you two."

"Not so much." Rafe winced. "He's about to be a deputy sheriff."

"Ha! No shit? That'll keep me laughing all the way back to Chi-town." Davey headed for the parking lot.

Not a one of the Maguires moved or a said a word. They all stared at each other, frozen, until a car door slammed, an engine revved, and the car peeled out of the lot.

Rafe broke first, running to Kellan and grabbing his shoulders. "Are you okay?"

"Yeah." Better than okay. Amazing how great it felt to *not* have a gun pointed at him. Like finding out you won the lottery while getting a blow job.

Flynn slapped him on the back, and then left his hand there. "Jesus, you were amazing. You didn't blink. You didn't freak out."

"Well, I'm about to be a deputy. Gotta be calm under pressure."

"I'm sorry, so *fucking* sorry you went through that."

Before he got bitter, Kellan figured he'd better assuage his curiosity about his brothers' complete lack of saving him. "Did you guys have a plan? You know, to jump him and get the gun away at any point?"

With a hard squeeze of his shoulder, Rafe finally let go. "A plan? Yeah. But not to jump Davey."

"We needed to hear him out. Get *his* whole plan."

Flynn's eyes widened. "You thought . . . you thought he was going to shoot you?"

Only every single second. Kellan paced in a tight circle, needing to move. Residual adrenaline burst through him like a horse through a starting gate. "It seemed like a distinct possibility."

"We never would've let that happen," Rafe said, low and rough.

Right on top of him, Flynn said, "Davey wouldn't have done it, either. He knew we'd be on him the moment he touched the trigger. But holding that gun on you made him feel like he had the upper hand."

"He did," Kellan bit out.

He believed them. Saw the logic to their strategy, even. But he still wasn't thrilled with how long he'd been held at gunpoint.

"Nah. You were always safe, K. We'd never let anything happen to you."

Kellan pulled out his phone. "I'll call Delaney."

Rafe grabbed it from him. "No, you won't."

"Are you kidding? The mob knows we're here. That's the number one reason for an extraction."

Flynn shook his head. "The mob doesn't know we're here. Davey O'Brien does. If we're reading him right, he's the *only* one who knows."

If?

There was a whole lot riding on those two little letters. Kellan wasn't sure that he had the faith that his brothers did.

Maybe because he'd grown up believing that you couldn't—and shouldn't—trust the bad guys. "What if you're not reading him right?"

"We've got six weeks to find out." Rafe stiff-armed Kellan's biceps to force him to stop pacing. "Look, there's almost no chance he'd tell anyone else. Davey doesn't want to split the money. Now we've got time to figure out what to do. Do you want to leave Bandon?"

If they left, he'd never get the chance to be a deputy. That career would always be off-limits to Kellan in a new life, just like lawyering. He'd miss Lucien, the beach, the new and awesome proximity to Delaney. His brothers might have to leave their women. Or Mollie and Sierra would have to leave their lives here that they adored so much.

God, he didn't want to keep this a secret from Delaney. Didn't want to lie to her. But she'd have zero choice about yanking them out of here if she knew. She'd have to follow the rules.

Guess he'd have to break them in order to get more time with her.

"No. I don't want to leave," he said firmly. "But I don't want to stick my head in the sand either."

"We'll make a plan," Flynn promised.

Rafe clapped him on the shoulder. "Hell, we're taking down McGinty and the entire Chicago mob. Finding a way to deal with Davey'll be a piece of cake, compared to that."

Kellan just hoped the plan they came up with would be half as strong as his brother's ego.

Chapter Seventeen

DELANEY HOLSTERED HER gun, then she pulled off her goggles and electronic earmuffs. Next to her, Kellan did the same as Mateo ripped off their target sheets. The sheriff let out a long, low whistle.

"Damn, you're good."

"Which one of us?" Kellan asked, one dark eyebrow arched. She loved seeing his competitive spirit. It was sexy and fun . . . and nothing that she'd ever felt at a shooting range before.

"Both of you." Mateo lifted one sheet a little higher. "Delaney got all fancy, adding a kill shot to the forehead—"

"That's execution, mobster style. Trying to stay topical."

"You're adorable," Kellan whispered.

"But Kellan did great. Seven solid shots, straight to the heart. Three right on top of each other. You're a natural."

"Video games. Lots of hours on Grand Theft Auto gave me a leg up."

He joked, but Delaney knew he'd put in countless hours at this range in the forest. Kellan swore he needed to be ready to protect and serve by the Cranberry Festival. She saw through that, though. It was obvious he was pushing himself to be able to protect his brothers, should anyone come nosing around Bandon.

It was touching. Endearing. She wondered if Rafe and Flynn knew how hard he'd been working to ensure that they'd all be safe.

"You're going to do us proud when you head up to the academy." Mateo stuck out his hand. "Thanks for sending this one my way, Delaney. You could've kept him for yourself and the marshals."

Biting back a laugh, she shook. "Ah, the Marshals Service doesn't hire protectees as employees."

"How do you know?" Kellan asked with a waggle of his eyebrows. "Maybe there's a marshal in Eugene who's on his third new life."

"Very funny."

"He's got a point. I like your out-of-the-box thinking, Maguire." Mateo clapped him on the shoulder before walking to his car. "See you at the station on Monday?"

"I can't wait."

Delaney bent over to retrieve their spent cartridges. It was great to have this semiprivate range just outside of Bandon, but it didn't have the amenities she was used to at an official governmental range. No attendant. Even worse, no *bathrooms*. When she straightened, Kellan was grinning from ear to ear.

"What's up with you?"

"It hit me how . . . normal this feels. Spending a Saturday afternoon hanging out with my boss and my woman. Excited to show up for work on Monday. Looking forward to tonight with you. It feels like real life."

"As opposed to?" She dropped the shells into a coffee can. Finally, a way that old-fashioned coffee was more versatile than a Keurig.

"I'd been treading water, going nowhere since you plucked me off that street in Chicago. Now I finally have a purpose. A plan." He put his hands on her waist and beamed down at her. "A future."

Uh-oh. Because Delaney loved him, she loved seeing Kellan so happy. But *also* because she loved him, she'd have to step out of the role of girlfriend and use her marshal's badge to burst that bubble of happiness.

"Remember, we don't have a future," she warned. It hurt to say. In a perfect world, Delaney could wish on a star and make everything work out. But the sun was still out.

She'd accepted the ticking clock on their dating. Accepted that he was giving her a love she'd never dreamed of experiencing. The only "forever" they could share was the memory of this summer. "There's only a really, truly fantastic right now."

It got harder and harder every time Delaney reminded him of that. Seeing Kellan embrace the reality of his new career, though, made it even more imperative for him to acknowledge the looming end of their relationship.

"Don't be so defeatist." He nuzzled at her neck, pushing aside her hair to trail kisses down to the collar of her navy-and-white-striped dress. She'd taken off the holster-hiding jacket before they started.

God, Kellan was as stubborn as she was. And yes, it was romantic and sweet and melted her heart that he believed he'd figure out a solution to the impossible.

Grabbing his chin, Delaney tugged his head up to look into those arctic light blue eyes. "If anyone found out, you'd have to leave the program."

"Nobody knows." But his gaze flicked to the side. Just for a second.

It was enough.

Oh. My. God. That tell could only mean one thing. He'd told his freaking brothers about them. "Kellan. No. You didn't."

"Didn't lock the door? Not yet. But I can lock it *and* have you down to your bra before you can say please."

"Don't. Don't dissemble. We've always been honest with each other, even when we keep lying to the rest of the world. You told your brothers, didn't you?"

To his credit, he owned up without pausing or flinching. Although he did let go of her waist and take two large steps back. "Yes. I did."

There weren't many times in her life when Delaney wished she'd lived in another century. This one had antibiotics and air-conditioning. Almost nothing else compared to the goodness of that. But right now? She wished it was the eighteenth century, so it would be perfectly acceptable to twitch at her skirts, fan herself furiously . . . and then let dramatic tears slip down her cheeks as she pounded at Kellan's chest.

"Kellan. How could you?"

He tunneled a hand through his hair. With a face set in harsh lines, he asked, "The more pertinent question is, how could I have lied to them for so long?"

Oh, for fuck's sake. Enough.

Loyalty was one thing. Admirable, definitely. But Delaney didn't believe Rafe and Flynn deserved as much loyalty as Kellan was willing to give them. Especially when he'd bitched about this very thing for *months*. "They both lied to you for literally years!"

"Tit for tat? That's really your response?"

Not her finest retort. And embarrassment at her poor choice immediately put her on the defensive, when she had every right to be on offense.

Delaney fisted her hands on her hips. "At least I'm having a conversation. Whereas you went off and did this without so much as telling me before *or* after the fact. On a need-to-know basis, this is information I damned well needed to know!"

"They promised to keep it a secret."

It hurt that he was missing the point. "It wasn't *your* secret to share. It was ours. Jointly."

Kellan just stared at her. It was so quiet that the buzz from the fluorescent lights overhead might as well have been a hornet's nest. Then he banged through the door into the square of grass that acted as a parking lot, taking in a gulp of air that worked his Adam's apple up and down.

Still not looking at her, he ground out, "The rift between me and my brothers went deeper than the San Andreas Fault. Everything looked solid on the surface, sure. This whole new life, though, left some enormous chasms underneath. The only solution was the vow they made to not lie anymore."

Agreed. But it was Rafe and Flynn who made that vow, who needed to atone and damn well grovel to Kellan. He didn't need to do anything. "*They* made that. To you. Because they repeatedly lied on a daily basis about the very basics of their life."

He whipped around. "My love for you is a basic. As integral as breathing and eating and sleeping. I had to tell them about it, Laney."

Delaney hadn't wanted to make him choose between herself and his brothers. But it looked like he had, nonetheless.

That choice had broken them. It meant Delaney couldn't trust him. Not with their secret. Not with her heart. It didn't even matter that Rafe and Flynn certainly wouldn't risk their exposure and tell anyone.

It didn't matter that her parents had been the worst role models ever for a healthy relationship. She still knew, beyond a shadow of a doubt, that love couldn't exist without trust.

Which meant she knew, beyond a shadow of a doubt, that this, *they*, were over.

Her mother had—foolishly—trusted her father, blindly, despite how many times he shattered that trust. Trusted that he wouldn't keep cheating on her, wouldn't do drugs again, wouldn't keep doing bad things that sent him to jail. And she never learned. Her mom never drew a line in the sand to protect herself. It had ultimately gotten her killed by the man it turned out she couldn't trust at all.

Delaney refused to repeat that pattern. She was smarter than that.

She wouldn't give Kellan any more chances to hurt her, to betray her trust.

She *couldn't*.

Heaving in a breath, Delaney said, "You didn't have the right, Kellan. Not to expose me like that."

"I did it to put things right with Rafe and Flynn. Not to put you at risk."

"But you did." And that choice he made would be the cause of everything that happened next. That choice shoehorned Delaney into exactly one course of action. "If you get thrown out of the program, you'll still have Rafe and Flynn. I could lose my job, Kellan. That would mean starting from scratch, without a reference. Without any connection to law enforcement, which is all I know. I don't have a family. My career is all I have."

"No. That's not true. You have me." He reached for her again, but she slipped sideways, out of his grasp.

They'd never be this close again, this connected again. It hurt already and Delaney hadn't even told him. Hadn't made the break that would never, could never, be repaired.

Sadly, she semi-whispered, "I don't. I can't."

Kellan Maguire was no dummy. His brain must've whizzed ahead to the final words she couldn't bear yet to speak out loud. His eyes widened. Words hammered out of him in fast desperation. "You can't keep lying, just like I couldn't. So we'll stop sneaking around. No more cars or hotels. We need to stop the secrecy."

"We need to stop all of it. That's the only way."

"No, Laney! You're not a quitter. And you don't run scared. So don't give up on us just because I screwed up."

"I'm not doing this to punish you. We have to end things to keep both of us safe. You used to make me feel safe, Kellan. But not anymore. That trust is gone." It took seconds to reach through the doorway and grab her purse and jacket off the wall hook. "Our breaking up was inevitable. Better to do it sooner rather than later."

"Laney. I love you."

Which was exactly why this hurt so much. "I love you, too." Delaney got in her car and peeled out of the lot without another word. Five miles down the road, she pulled over and *sobbed*. She'd never loved anyone the way she loved Kellan.

She'd also never felt this depth of pain, of betrayal before.

Well, her time with Kellan had been about trying new experiences.

This one *sucked*.

KELLAN BANGED THE wooden spoon inside the giant stock pot. The noise was a little satisfying—a signifier of how badly he wanted to take a metal bat and bang it around all the walls of their house.

While swearing.

He wanted to beat things and break things very, very loudly.

While swearing. Because he couldn't figure out a better way to let out all the rawness, all the burning pain bleeding out from the spot where Delaney had ripped his heart four days ago.

Luckily, he was plenty mad at the Chicago mob— one mobster in particular—so he could focus on anger rather than heartbreak.

"It's been six days since O'Brien showed up and fucked with us. Got a plan yet, Wonder Twins?"

Flynn looked up from where he was scribbling in a notebook at the wooden table. "That's hurtful. You could've referenced any super hero. But you skip over Batman and the Flash and go with the Junior Super-Friends?"

"Yeah, and which one of us is supposed to be the girl Wonder Twin?" Rafe kicked off his second work boot at the front door. "Jesus, Kellan, that's a double layer of insulting. I had a bitch of a struggle with a dirty carburetor today. Then you attack me the moment I come home?"

"I'm tired of waiting." Tired of missing Delaney, was more like it. But it wasn't fair to take that out on his brothers, so he gave another vicious stir to the pot. More than a couple of popcorn kernels flew out to land on the counter. "I'm tired of not knowing what happens next. You two said you'd keep me in the loop."

"You *are* in. This is the loop—just waiting." Rafe disappeared down the hall with his boots.

Kellan thought about dropping it. Following their lead, not butting in. Yeah, that might've happened a year ago when he looked up to his brothers with something akin to hero worship. But now he knew just how fallible they were. He could contribute, maybe keep them from missing something, or come up with a better solution.

Plus, he was in a shit mood and itching for a fight.

He followed Rafe around the corner. "That's your plan? Wait for the next shitty thing to happen?"

"Not exactly." Rafe was already changing into shorts and an official Cranberry Festival tee that Floyd had passed out at the last meeting. "But waiting a week has proven that Davey's keeping his word. We've done the rotating watch every night, so nobody could catch us by surprise again. If he'd told anyone he found us, there would've been an attempt by now."

"But you said you trusted Davey? That he was low level enough to not try to pick up the reins and reassemble McGinty's crew by telling them he'd found you? That all he wanted *was* the money?" He'd made Rafe and Flynn go over their laundry list of reasons to believe a criminal who had everything to gain by revealing their location. Repeatedly.

"Trust—but verify."

"You know, that's a Russian proverb. Don't tell me you're moving on to the Russian mob next?"

"Nah." Rafe pushed past him to rejoin Flynn in the living room. He flopped down on the dark green sofa. "I saw it in that Bond flick that came out in July."

Flynn lifted his head. Sniffed at the air. "What smells so good?"

"Chicago food experiment #137."

"Thought you gave up on trying to give us a taste of home. Your experiments slacked off once you started up with the marshal."

"Well, that's no longer occupying my time, is it?" Kellan snapped. "And don't look a gift horse in the mouth. Or I won't fill yours."

Flynn's brows knitted together into a frown. "Hey, you know we feel bad about your breakup. We should be the ones cheering you up. I mean, not by cooking dinner. That'd just be cruel. But . . . something."

"You want to take a road trip?" Rafe offered. "T-Top off in the Camaro, tunes blasting, no women allowed?

Maybe go down to San Francisco for the weekend? Blow off some steam, get drunk off our asses?"

Kellan shook his head. "I appreciate the offer. But if all three of us bug out of town, we'll have to notify the marshals service. That's a contact—and an interrogation—I just don't need." He did appreciate the offer. They were trying.

Trying to do an impossible task, because Delaney Evans was not a woman easily forgotten. Kellan headed back into the kitchen and emptied his pot into a blue mixing bowl.

"How about an abbreviated version?" Rafe offered. "Raise one night of hell at the Gorse?"

"You mean where I work?" Flynn elbowed Rafe's side. "Why do you always have to stir up trouble for me at work? Remember that time you brought in a bag with 5K in singles and told me to 'do something with it'?"

"Hey, cash money is good any way you get it. I don't know why you thought the construction crew would complain about getting their pay in ones."

"Because the IRS can't track a foot-high stack of ones. The whole point of the construction company was to be legit. To be able to send out a W-2 every January." Flynn's voice grew louder with what was obviously an old and much-repeated frustration.

It fascinated Kellan. After all these months, it was one of the first stories about their years in the mob that his brothers had let slip in front of him. It showed that they weren't sheltering him anymore, not treating him like a kid that needed protecting from the big, bad world. That cheered him up more than any night of shots and burgers could.

Rafe bumped Flynn's shoulder with his own. "Your solution of using it to pay bribes to the city's inspectors was brilliant. It impressed the hell out of McGinty."

"I impressed myself with that one. Might've used one of the stacks to buy beer at Wrigley, too. As a reward for dealing with you."

"Here's another reward. For surviving our move—no, our *five* moves," Kellan corrected himself, thinking of the long road they'd traveled. He plunked the bowl on the coffee table. "That popcorn's a near-perfect replica of Chicago's famous Garrett Mix—cheddar and caramel."

"No way." Rafe and Flynn both grabbed handfuls and jammed them in their mouths.

"I realized I'd been shooting for the moon, trying to copy a Malnati's pie, when I'd never made pizza before in my life. But you know what I have made through a hundred study sessions? Popcorn. Found a hacked recipe online for the flavors and went for it."

"You nailed it," Rafe mumbled around another mouthful. "It tastes like I'm back on Randolph Street, right next to the Oriental Theatre. I can almost smell the taxi fumes and river mold." Then he closed his eyes and smiled.

It was a small win—fucking *popcorn*, for God's sake—but Kellan needed it this week, and he'd take it. "Thanks."

"That makes one thing we can scratch off our required foods list when we go back for the trial. We're limited to five per week. The marshal wouldn't agree to any more special requests than that. Something about how her agency wasn't a delivery service."

Kellan sat down opposite them in the big wing chair. Flynn had handed him the perfect segue on a silver platter. "Since you mentioned Delaney, I've got to make another pitch to tell her the truth about O'Brien."

"Thought you didn't want to talk to her at all?"

No kidding. The idea of seeing her and treating her as just their handler instead of the woman he loved? Well, it'd take a life or death circumstance to force him into that situation.

Unfortunately, that's exactly what they were in. And his brothers damn well knew it.

Kellan leaned forward, bracing his arms on his thighs. "We should tell her about O'Brien finding us. She can't protect us from a threat she doesn't know exists."

"We're not telling her," Rafe said flatly. It was in the same voice that he'd ordered Kellan not to break his curfew and go to the Jay-Z concert in ninth grade.

That voice might've worked on mobsters who never bothered to think for themselves, who only took orders. It didn't work on Kellan. Not when he was fourteen, and not now. "It's the right thing to do."

Flynn pushed off the sofa and was in Kellan's face in four long, fast strides. "If we tell her, there's a better than fifty percent chance that we get extracted immediately. Leave Bandon, get dumped who knows where doing who knows what shit job. So if we tell her, that's conceding that we're out of options."

There you go—Flynn had just made his point for him. "We *are* out of options. We're walking around with not just targets on our backs, but with the knowledge that someone's actively aiming at us!"

"That's where you're wrong. I get that you're scared—"

Kellan jabbed his hand in the air, finger pointed accusingly at Rafe. "This isn't about being scared. This is about being smart."

"See, you trust your brains." Rafe tapped a finger to his head. Then he moved down and thumped his whole fist against his belly. "I trust my gut. And it tells me that O'Brien's on the up-and-up. There's nothing for him in Chicago. He doesn't want some office job. Most of his buddies are in jail or in hiding. Our money's an easy solution. He wouldn't screw that up by telling *anyone* where we are."

Just like all the other times Rafe had laid that out, it made sense. As much sense as, oh, say, *telling their marshal they'd been found.* So Kellan pushed harder, because their lives were at stake. This wasn't some discussion about going with your gut to place a ten-dollar bet at a racetrack, for fuck's sake.

"You pulled Delaney in the other times. When you got that blackmail letter you thought was from the FBI, and when that other mobster showed up in town out of the blue."

"Those were different. The danger of extraction wasn't definite."

Oh, he got it now. The real reason was definitely *not* because of how much they trusted Davey to keep his mouth shut.

Kellan stood, pacing the length of the room and back as he spoke. "You don't want to leave. You've gotten comfortable. You know Mollie loves it here. And Sierra. You don't want to risk leaving them behind."

Flynn and Rafe shared one of those looks that used to be—in hindsight—a whole secret conversation about what not to tell him about their mob lives. No surprise they'd obviously talked about this behind his back, too.

On the other hand, Kellan didn't entirely blame them. Not after falling for Delaney. He would've done anything to stay with her.

If there *was* anything to be done.

"Yeah, we want to stay. We've put down roots. The Festival's coming, and we've worked hard on it." Rafe got up, grabbed napkins off the big stack in the middle of the dining table, and brought them back. "You're right. We won't leave our women behind. There's no guarantee that the Marshals Service would let them come with us."

Flynn grimaced. "Even if they did, I wouldn't do that to Sierra. She had such a rough life, growing up in foster care. She's happy here, probably for the first time.

I won't rip that away from her. I'm sorry, K, but she matters too much."

"I just needed to hear you say it. To lay all the truth out for me, not just what you thought I *ought* to hear."

They both had the good sense to look embarrassed. Flynn swiped his hand like he was erasing what they'd originally said from a blackboard. "Shit. Yeah. You're right. It's sixty percent Rafe's gut, and forty percent true love. Happy now?"

Not entirely. Uneasy was more like it. Like the mild queasiness of too much coffee on an empty stomach versus the full-blown puke clench of eating bad sushi. "Do we keep up the round-the-clock watch, at least?"

"Nah." Rafe dug back in to the popcorn up to his wrist. "Nobody in McGinty's crew is that patient. Or strategic. Not the ones still roaming free, anyway. Just . . . be normal."

Normal would be spending every free minute he could to sneak away with Delaney.

That normal was never coming back.

Jittery from the need to do *something* coupled with the lack of immediate action, Kellan paced another long circle. "Maybe I should skip golf with Lucien on Friday. It spreads us thin, my being all the way out at the resort. Should I stay in town, by you guys?"

"Nope. Act cool." Flynn mimed combing his hair back on both sides like a fifties' movie star leaning on a jukebox. "That's the whole plan at this point."

Hard to be cool when he was freaking out that Delaney broke up with him. But Kellan still had his brothers. In a better way, a better place, than they'd been in a long time. That should be enough.

It had always been enough.

But Kellan had the feeling it might not be, anymore.

Chapter Eighteen

FOUR ANGUISHED DAYS after walking away from Kellan, Delaney sat on a bench thinking about her mentor from the Federal Law Enforcement Training Center. Clint Jackson was hard-nosed, old-school, and didn't have a second to waste on stupid questions. He did have all the time in the world to help trainees he thought had potential, though.

He'd believed that marshals should sleep with their guns, never trust anyone, and be able to outdrink any criminal in case they tried to "get one over on you" at a bar.

She'd never asked what bad experience he had with a protectee slipping past him after a few drinks. Out of respect, of course. But she did know that if Clint were here today, watching her do arts and crafts with the girlfriends of her protectees, he'd probably grab her by the collar and drag her away. Then make her run sprints and practice shooting until her arms and legs were limper than a wet toupee.

His analogy, of course, and yet another thing she'd never asked about, out of respect.

Faux floral crowns were soooo not her bailiwick. Which was apparently clear to Mollie and Sierra, since they'd taken the hot glue gun away from her after two minutes. Now they had her cutting lengths of twine for whatever Cranberry Festival Court adornment they'd move on to next.

Scissors were good. They were a weapon, and Delaney felt comfortable with weapons. And she hadn't felt anywhere in the vicinity of comfortable since breaking up with Kellan. Desperate, mad, heartbroken, hurt, angry, distraught . . . pretty much any word that was the antonym of *comfortable* summed up her mindset.

Mollie let the screen door slam as she came into the backyard. Her hands were full of wineglasses and a bottle of sparkling wine. "We can't be expected to work this hard on a Wednesday night—on Sierra's only night off from waitressing—without having some fun, too."

"I should volunteer for things with you more often," Sierra said, giggling.

"I haven't even gotten to the best part. I'm forcing my nephew to cook us dinner."

Delaney had done a full background check on Mollie's relatives as soon as Rafe told her they were serious. Which had been about a minute after Rafe went and

comatose denial. Sparkling wine, with grass under her bare feet and a glorious summer evening overhead, *had* to be good for her. Restorative. Healing.

Who was she kidding?

Her heart would never heal from the loss of Kellan Maguire.

The door slammed again as Mollie did, indeed, come back with another bottle. "This one's not cold yet."

Sierra snorted. "Believe me when I say I won't notice."

"The only champagne you've ever had was the super expensive stuff Lucien served at my birthday party. Believe *me* when I say this will taste absolutely nothing like that."

Delaney set the scissors down on the picnic table. "Can we suspend the crown-making for a few minutes? I have a feeling my hands might start shaking, and I don't want to be the cause of ruining the Cranberry Festival in even a tiny way."

"Omigosh, what's wrong?"

Like they didn't know. Like Kellan hadn't run straight home to his brothers and told them all the ways their marshal had trampled his heart. Which would've led to Rafe and Flynn telling their girlfriends, and probably immediately to rounds of *aren't we lucky we found each other and aren't miserable like them* sex.

What they didn't know—probably—was how much it hurt. "I'm assuming I got painted as the villain in the version you heard. But breaking up with Kellan wasn't easy. It was the hardest thing I've ever done. And his emotional betrayal hurts worse than anything I've ever experienced. Including the time a three-hundred-pound meth head broke my wrist by slamming it against a light pole."

Mollie blinked. Slowly. Then twice more, before finally saying, "That's . . . a lot of information."

Sierra dropped her half-finished crown to the grass. "You're dating Kellan? Or, you were, and you two broke up?"

Whoops. And wow. Kellan's brothers had *actually* kept their promise not to tell anyone about them.

That was a surprise. And now, it was a gigantic problem she'd have to manage. Delaney winced, scratching her right temple. "You, ah, didn't know?"

"Of course not." Rapid fire questions burst from Mollie. "How is that even possible? Isn't there a rule against it? How can you keep what you do a secret and have a normal relationship with him?"

Delaney let her chin drop to her chest. "I can't."

This reaction was good. Helpful. It pretty much took a grater to the infinitesimal scab over her bleeding heart, and then rubbed sand and salt water in the emotional gash. But that just reinforced the rightness of her decision.

Daily reinforcement was necessary. It was pretty much the only thing that kept her from jumping in her car and begging Kellan to take her back every minute of every hour. She started each day by staring in the mirror at the dark puffy circles under her eyes and reciting the mantra of exactly why her only option had been to break up with him. That Kellan had *shattered* her trust in him.

Sierra pushed the piles of wire, fake flowers, cranberries, and glue to the end of the table. Then she crossed her arms and leaned forward. A curtain of light brown hair shadowed her face. "This is . . . this is messed up. How could Kellan do this? How could he risk his brother's lives?"

"He didn't." Delaney couldn't help the intense surge of defensiveness. "Nobody's in any danger right now from us seeing each other."

"But how can you protect all three of them if you're in love with Kellan?"

How was it that these women spotted the problem *immediately*, when Kellan had been poo-pooing it for *months*?

Nevertheless, it was still hard to push the truth out. Delaney's fingers tightened on the stem of her glass. "I can't. Well, I can't do it to the fullest extent required."

Sierra interlaced her fingers and clenched them into a giant fist. After biting her lower lip, she asked, "This was so risky. Was he seen with you at all where people know that you're a marshal? What if there's a mole or a spy or a double agent at your office?"

Yikes. She should've realized this would hit Sierra hard. After all, her own safety from her violent past was now in the hands of the marshals. Delaney reached over to pat her white knuckles. "We were careful. Yes, people saw us together, but only in his capacity as a deputy trainee."

"We were careful." Mollie made air quotes with her fingers. "You know, that's what every teenager with an unplanned pregnancy says when I break the news to them in the exam room." Anger vibrated off her like steam off a pizza.

She had every right to be mad. Hearing their fear and anger reminded Delaney of why she'd insisted this couldn't work from the very beginning. Between the two of them, she and Kellan were overflowing with book and street smarts. There was no excuse. Just the explanation that it'd been easy, *too* easy, to be caught up in all the good moments to worry about whatever bad might come in the future.

"We didn't do it on purpose. It just sort of . . . happened."

Mollie raised one dark brown eyebrow. "*Also* what those unexpectedly pregnant teenagers say."

"Yes, we were dumb. There was no conscious choice to break the rules, to flout protocol, to risk anyone's safety. But you know what did happen? We fell in love."

"Damn it." Mollie tugged at the bottom of her green scrub shirt. "That's the one thing you could've said to calm me down."

"Real love? Both of you? Not just really hot sex?" A light pink flush spread across Sierra's cheeks and neck. "Because, um, all the Maguire brothers are drop-dead sexy. We'd certainly understand if you were just in this for a hot hookup."

That was the original, ideal scenario. Two or three amazing orgasms and then put it behind them forever. "I wish. That'd be easy. Manageable. I'd be able to move on without feeling like I've been run over by a tractor trailer. But Kellan lied to me. Broke my trust. And I'm absolutely devastated by his emotional betrayal."

Sierra came around the table and sat down, then she put her arms around Delaney. "When love makes you hurt as much as it makes you happy, then you know it's the real thing. I'm so sorry."

Mollie sat on her other side. And leaned her head against Delaney's shoulder. "What are you going to do?"

"Well, I broke it off with Kellan. Completely. I'm going to continue on as the official Maguire handler. Unless Rafe or Flynn isn't okay with it. If they request another marshal, I'll understand."

It'd sink her career, unless she could come up with a viable excuse for why they'd make that request. But it was their right. It was what she deserved for letting Kellan turn her head, get under her skin and so deep inside her heart.

"No, what are you going to do about being in love with Kellan?" Mollie asked.

That was an easy question. Because Delaney had known the answer from day one. "Never see him again after October."

And then she held on to Sierra and just wept.

KELLAN HAD THOUGHT he was living a double life while dating Delaney. And yeah, it'd been cool. He'd been a bad boy, breaking a big-ass rule and technically risking their new lives. He'd been just as bad as Rafe and Flynn.

Or so he'd thought.

It turned out that he'd been kidding himself. Because swinging a nine iron on Labor Day weekend under a cloudless sky with the ocean cresting a hundred yards away? That was fucking *work* to pull off when a mobster—Jesus, an actual gun-toting *mobster*—knew who he was, where he lived, and could technically show up again at any moment.

This was a real double life.

He hated it.

"You're slicing the ball a little to the left today." Lucien pulled a driver out of his golf bag and walked to the tee. "Have you been doing bicep curls with only one arm since the last time we played?"

Kellan hadn't been sleeping. Or really eating. But he *had* been working out every spare minute. Pushing himself physically, sweating and panting and basically being on the edge of puking—those were the only times he managed to forget about Delaney.

How she'd just given up on them.

How she wouldn't even try to let him fight for their future.

So his golf sucked because his head was anything but in the game. Instead of spilling the truth, Kellan rubbed his arm and winced dramatically. "The kids that are helping Flynn build the float for the festival? One of them lost control of his hoverboard. Damned thing nailed me right above the elbow."

"I think if you'll check Floyd's ever-present clipboard, you'll find a form you signed absolving the Cranberry Festival and the Town of Bandon from any and all injuries."

"I'll bet he's got a form to check in and out of the porta-potties," Kellan said grimly.

Lucien swung, then gave a tight nod as he watched the ball arc through the air. "If your arm keeps hurting, don't be a hero. Go see Mollie at the hospital. You're on the friends and family list at this point. No waiting, no forms, and no insurance. She'll fix you right up."

"It's a hoverboard bruise, not a bear mauling. I'll be fine." The last thing he needed was sympathy and TLC from his brother's girlfriend for his made-up injury.

Lucien jabbed his club at Kellan as they walked back to the cart. "Maybe I just want an excuse to get you together with Mollie. God knows I'd rather see *you* with my best friend than your brother."

Enough was enough. It'd been four months. You'd think Lucien actually *knew* about Rafe's sketchy past the way he held a grudge against him. There was a part of Kellan that enjoyed Rafe not being fucking hero worshipped for once, but Bandon was a small town. Everyone he liked needed to get along. 'Cause they were all he had with Delaney gone.

So he shot Lucien a sidelong frown. "Come on. How

long are you going to make Rafe jump through hoops before you admit he's a pretty decent guy? One who treats Mollie like a queen?"

"The jury's still out." After another shot of side-eye, Lucien huffed out a laugh and continued. "Honestly? I'm having too much fun hassling him to quit."

That he understood. "Well, cut loose that fantasy about me ending up with the Doc. I've got a girl already. Sort of."

Shit. That had popped out automatically.

Kellan's heart still one hundred percent belonged to Delaney. But while loving her kept him sidelined, it—sadly—didn't mean he *had* the girl. The "sort of" had meant their secret relationship. Had to face facts, though. There wasn't even a "sort of" anymore.

Lucien dropped into the driver's seat and rumbled them slowly down the cart path. Being Lucien, he had to wave and nod at every cart they passed, so their speed was at about Mach snail. "Didn't you say that same thing a couple of months ago? Can't you seal the deal?"

Well, that was fucking insulting. "I did. Until a week ago. Then it got . . . complicated. And now it's over."

"Man, I'm sorry. What happened?"

"It's a long story." He guzzled ice water from the metal bottle stamped with the resort logo. Guess they justified charging an arm and a leg per round when they provided a bottle that kept water cold for the whole thing. Technology rocked. "But it boils down to one cold, hard fact. Us being together? Impossible."

"Bullshit." Lucien stopped them with a jolt at the next tee. Then he leaned his arms on the steering wheel. "Nothing's impossible. Aside from you winning this hole."

"Don't be an asshole."

With a cool, challenging stare, he tossed a final insult at Kellan. "I thought you were smarter than that."

Those words rocketed Kellan out of the cart. Because that's exactly what he'd thought the whole time. There'd never been a doubt that once he stopped wallowing in the awesomeness of dating Delaney and focused? He'd be smart enough to figure out a way they could be together forever.

Instead, he'd been dumb enough, cocky enough, to tell his brothers. It'd been stupid. Kellan's way of proving he could run with the bad boys.

What a joke. And it was all his fault. Oh, yeah, he saw that now. He'd absolutely shattered her trust when he'd revealed their secret to Rafe and Flynn.

For what? To resolve the age-old question of whose dick was bigger? To prove that he was truly a Maguire, every bit as bad as them?

All he'd proven was that he was an idiot.

He didn't need to be bad. He didn't need to be a hero, either. Or compete with his brothers. Life wasn't about being top dog. Kellan just needed to be the best version of himself. That's who Delaney had fallen for.

Too bad he'd realized that too late.

"Being smart doesn't solve everything. You can't think your way out of every single problem." Talk about learning that one the hard way. Kellan grabbed his wedge. Because, of course, since everything sucked in the six days since Delaney dumped him, his ball sat on the side of a sand trap.

"Brains or brawn? One of the two works every time. And you've got both."

Kellan would—maybe—someday appreciate the way his friend was trying to help him. But Lucien didn't know the complicated story. Didn't realize that some problems just couldn't be fixed. So he snarled, "Consider this to be the exception to that rule."

Lucien didn't *need* to follow him over to the crater of sand. Not when his ball sat fifty yards away on the lush, perfectly manicured grass with a straight shot to the cup. But evidently he was in the mood to be relentlessly helpful. Or just drive Kellan crazy so he did, indeed, lose the hole.

"Okay." He waited while Kellan scrambled into the sand. Lucien even crouched to point at a better angle of attack. He was so damned annoying with all that good-natured helpfulness. Especially given that, in Kellan's current mood, he'd probably be pissed at a firefighter wielding the jaws of life to cut him out of a burning car. "Then we come to the less often used option three—breaking the rules. Can you get your mystery woman back by doing that? Can you cross to the dark side?"

What a question. That's what had gotten him to this self-pity-fest. Bitter laughter rolled out of him like fog off the ocean that morning. "I'm already there. Apparently? I suck the schwang at being bad."

"Then embrace your wheelhouse. Be good and smart and figure out how to get your woman back."

Funny. That was the one thing Kellan hadn't second-guessed to pieces over the past six days. Delaney made it clear they were done, so he hadn't bothered to keep trying to come up with a solution.

But what if he did?

A tiny spark of hope flared in Kellan's desiccated heart. He swiveled to stare across the rolling dunes at the vast blue spread of the Pacific. What if he groveled profusely—obviously—and apologized and charmed her into forgiving him? Into giving them another chance?

And then put his mind to work on how they could stay together?

The first, hell, the only *real* stumbling block, the reason he'd avoided thinking about this for so many months leapt out of his mouth. "It could mean leaving my brothers."

Lucien bent over to pluck a rogue dandelion. Wonder how he listed that under his resort heir job duties? "I'll say this for Rafe—it's clear he'll always be there for you. Whether you still share a house with him, or go live on the wrong coast. But will mystery girl?"

That couldn't be the solution. Lucien drilled it down to simplicity because he didn't know all the facts. As much as Kellan loved Delaney, as much as he wanted to go wherever made her happy? The immensity of Rafe's actions in joining WITSEC to maintain the three of them as a unit couldn't be sloughed off.

Searching for just the right words that wouldn't give anything away, Kellan said, "He and Flynn sacrificed a lot to keep us together."

"You guys are tight. Tighter than a full body tan on a supermodel. So tight that a little thing like distance wouldn't matter. Talk to them. Or her. Just fix it."

Kellan mulled it over on the short drive to Lucien's ball. Loyalty and love were supposed to be good things. Having too much of them shouldn't ruin everything. But it did. "I can't. Somebody gets hurt any way this shakes out."

Lucien lifted his hands from the wheel, palms up. "Does it have to be you, though?"

Chapter Nineteen

THE PREVIOUS HOLIDAY weekend, Delaney had found out about her dad's parole hearing. Surprisingly, the news hadn't spoiled the weekend because she'd spent it with Kellan. Because he'd listened to her and soothed her . . . .and then screwed her senseless. And she'd wished that they could've been out in the open, back in Bandon, watching the fireworks with his brothers. Like a normal couple.

Now here she was on Labor Day weekend, in Bandon. No fireworks. No Kellan.

Guess it proved the old adage about being careful what you wished for.

Not that she was ungrateful for spending the afternoon at a vibrant coffeeshop, rather than sitting alone in her very much *too* quiet room in Coos Bay. Mollie was helping her gran choose new winter blends for Coffee

& 3 Leaves. The invite to join them was a dose of normalcy Delaney badly needed. A reminder that she had new and awesome friends, even if her love life was demolished.

Plus, it gave her a reason not to stay in yoga pants with the blinds drawn feeling sorry for herself.

Norah used her prosthetic pincher to tap on the edge of the thick green mug. "Do you think the chocolate mint French roast is too much a reminder of Christmas? Will people still want to drink it in February?"

"I would drink this every day of the year." Mollie licked her lips and gave a low hum of contentment. "In fact, can I take the rest of the sample bag home with me?"

Norah reached across the wide wooden counter to tap her granddaughter's nose. "Greedy."

"Appreciative," Mollie corrected as she took another long sip.

Delaney told herself to stop watching and longing for their easy interplay. She'd stopped pining for a mother figure a long time ago. Losing Kellan, the hole he'd left in her life and her heart, certainly shouldn't bring up old wounds long-since scarred over.

So she focused on the steady stream of customers at the front of the shop, where the more questionable medicinal products were stocked. It was about an even mix between millennials who probably wanted a hit for fun, and middle-aged people who actually needed the relief that marijuana would provide from their aches and pains.

This shop itself was a gray area. Here, it was legal. In most other states, it wasn't. Delaney had spent her early years of law enforcement *positive* that there was only black and white when it came to crime. Now? Her whole outlook had gradually changed over the past year. She was actually drawn to the gray areas. To helping people who might be dismissed otherwise from a single black mark, no matter how big.

She'd need to snap a selfie for Em before leaving. Her friend would laugh herself silly over the self-righteous Marshal Evans chilling in a marijuana dispensary—even with the coffee and cookies that were, for Delaney, the real draw.

"Norah, I think a peppermint cocoa would give people a holiday hangover. But this coffee is subtle. Delicious. I vote you put it on the menu." Not that she'd be here in February. Unless the task force assignment lasted that long. And wouldn't that be painful? Being in Bandon—but not with Kellan anymore.

"Do you like it enough to fight my Mollie here for the sample bag?"

Mollie curved her arms around her mug and glared a warning. "Don't even think about it."

"Don't worry. I'd actually like to take back a few bags of the calming tea blend. I can't get enough of it." Best to stock up now, while she could. Bags of loose tea were easy enough to stash in her suitcase when she moved on to the next assignment.

"Glad you like it so much. I'll fill you a couple right

now." Norah spun around to the glass apothecary jars lining the shelves next to the espresso machines and pulled one down. It looked like regular tea leaves, but with spiky lighter brown shards, fuzzy yellow flowers, and wrinkled red things that almost looked like cranberries throughout. Not nearly as pretty as the dark glossy coffee beans in the jar next to it.

But Delaney knew these next few months would be beyond stressful. Getting over Kellan without resorting to a pint of ice cream a night followed by a bottle of wine the next night meant trying to survive this heartbreak the healthy way.

Less caffeine. Lots of workouts. Soothing things like fleece blankets and stupid comedies and this tea.

"I mean, it tastes great. But I was shocked at how much it actually smooths out my stress levels. You've blended some magic in there."

Norah quickly filled two bags and labeled them. "Old folk magic—the best kind. People try to dismiss herbal medicine, but the results can't be denied. The St. John's wort in it packs a powerful punch. Powerful enough to take down modern medicine, even."

Well, it calmed her down, sure. But stronger than modern medicine? Hardly. With an indulgent smile, Delaney asked, "What do you mean?"

Mollie jumped in with the answer. "Oh, it's true. St. John's wort is similar to antibiotics in that it can very much diminish the efficacy of birth control pills. I keep telling Gran that she should put up a warning label. If you were dating anyone—" Mollie bit her lip and winced "—I'd tell you not to have this more often than once a month, just to be safe."

It was as if time suddenly stopped. The espresso machine still spluttered. The giggly teens who looked like they were on a first date still chattered at the table on the left. Afternoon sunlight still poured in the front window.

But all Delaney saw was her Google calendar in her mind. The box on it, specifically, that reminded her each month that she was in the last week of her pill pack and should add tampons to her bag.

She hadn't needed to add any tampons last month. That little pocket in her purse had still been full from the month before. Lots of people said their period just went away when on the pill, but Delaney had never been that lucky in nine years.

Until now. Was it luck, though?

Or had her period not shown up for two months for an entirely different reason?

Oh. My. God.

Grabbing Mollie's arm, Delaney said, "I have to go. I'm sorry."

"Are you okay?" The ingrained doctor in Mollie had her reaching one hand to feel Delaney's forehead.

"I have absolutely no idea. I just . . . I have to go." Without so much as a thank you to Norah, Delaney stumbled out of the shop and broke into a half jog to get to the drugstore three blocks over. Her hands shook as she stood in front of the shelf with way too many choices in pregnancy tests.

This wasn't in the plan. Not in any version of the plan. Delaney had focused on her career trajectory, because it was something she could do all by herself. Without relying on her criminal father or dead mother or some nameless man the universe might eventually send her way.

She only admitted to Emily last year—after several whisky sours—that having a baby was her secret dream. One that would remain only a dream because it didn't fit into the life she'd crafted. A satisfying life. And Delaney was a strong believer that you should only be a parent if you were one hundred and ten percent committed to that choice. So more of a fantasy than a dream, really. Like winning the lottery. It'd be nice, but you knew it'd never actually happen.

But . . . but . . . deep down? Delaney had never stopped wishing. Hoping. At least a little.

She'd never, ever wished or hoped, however, about becoming pregnant at the culmination of the biggest case of her life, right after breaking up with the man she loved.

Kellan.

The mere thought of his name was a visceral punch. Kellan *had* to know. She had to do this *with* him. That one thought of him was enough to stop the shakes, make her swat five different tests into her basket, and race to the checkout counter.

There were three places he could be right now. Hanging out at home, hanging at the Gorse watching Flynn juggle the busy holiday crowd, or . . .

He could be at the station. Mateo had promised Kellan shifts this weekend to prep him for the influx of tourists with the Cranberry Festival. And it was just around the corner.

Delaney broke into a full-out sprint to get there. She didn't care about blending in, about not making people wonder what the heck was going on with the crazy woman bolting down the street.

She needed Kellan.

Who was she kidding? She'd *always* need Kellan. A week away from him had proven that in spades.

The admin gaped at her dramatic entrance, but waved her on back without a word. And there he was, at the first desk. The one with a giant bouquet of flowers stuffed into a water pitcher. Kellan looked so official in his tan uniform, with his hat balanced on the corner of his monitor. So serious. So *wonderful*. Then he looked up and saw her.

"Delaney, what's wrong?" He jolted out of his seat, sending it rolling across the floor.

At the clatter, Mateo poked his head out of his office, and also hurried to her side. "Were you identified, Marshal? Attacked?"

She shook her head.

Kellan almost reached for her shoulder, but then dropped his hand back to his side. "Are my brothers okay?"

Finally, Delaney found her words. "Everyone's safe. There's no danger. I'm sorry for causing a fuss. I just . . . Sheriff, I need a few minutes alone with your deputy."

To his credit, Mateo didn't ask any questions. "His shift's over in five, anyway. Go ahead and use the room in the back."

Delaney's sandals slapped against the concrete. She watched Kellan in front of her, his walk a little looser with the equipment belt weighing him down. He looked official, determined, and sexy as hell.

Guess even sheer, life-changing panic couldn't block her brain from noticing that.

She closed the door of the interrogation room behind her. Immediately, Kellan grabbed her hands.

A little piece of her world stabilized at his touch.

Eyes flashing, dark brows knitted together, he asked, "What's going on? What can I do? What do you need?"

His worry, his tender care washed over her in a soothing wave. It took her panic down from a stammering ten to a let's-do-this two. "I'm sorry to barge in on you like this—"

"Laney, there's nothing I've wished for more over the past week than to have you barge back into my life. I just wish it wasn't happening when your face looks like you just saw a ten-foot-tall Transformer firing bazookas."

Now that she was here, in front of him? Delaney wished the same thing. Wished she'd realized without the need for a panic prompter that she'd made a horrible mistake sending him away. And they'd get to that—

hopefully. If he was still willing to listen to her after the bomb she simply *had* to drop first.

Delaney licked her dry lips. "I have something—maybe—to tell you."

"I have something to tell you, too. That I was wrong." His words rushed out, like Kellan was worried she might turn and leave at any second. "That I know exactly how stupid it was to tell my brothers anything about you. That I lied to you, that I made you not trust me. I was a thoughtless idiot, and it wasn't fair to you and I'm so very, very sorry. I was on my way to track you down and tell you all this tonight. That's what the flowers on my desk are for. I'll apologize until I lose my voice, and then I'll keep writing it in the sand until you forgive me."

Oh, my. The unexpected surprises just kept coming today. That was beyond lovely. Gratifying. Heart melting. And she wanted to have that conversation with him.

After.

"I might be pregnant," she blurted out.

His hands tightened to the point of pain around hers. Then he let go, and pulled her in tight against him. His lips brushed the rim of her ear. "When will you know?"

"As soon as I take one of the five tests I just bought. I wanted—I *needed*—to do it with you."

"Let's go." Hand in hand, they banged out of the room and down five more steps to the bathroom door. Delaney fumbled one box out of her purse. Kellan reached in and grabbed another.

"Might as well try two at a time." He made quick

work of the packaging and handed her the two sticks. Then he gave an encouraging nod as she slipped inside.

It was all happening so fast. Life never moved this fast. Schooling took so long to finish, and then the marshals training. Even falling in love with Kellan had taken a few weeks. How could her entire life be about to change with a two-minute test?

Delaney set both tests on the institutional metal sink and let Kellan in. "Now we wait."

"God, I've missed you."

Those words grated against the raw wound of her heart. It didn't matter anymore if she was like her mother, dependent on a man. If it was perhaps a *weakness* to be this in love with a man.

Delaney was done with that mantra, the fear that had guided her entire life. Loving Kellan, being with him, had only made her stronger. So she told him the truth. "I've missed you, too."

"I want this settled before we know the results." He grabbed her shoulders to turn her away from the tests. To her dismay, he immediately dropped his hands. "I don't want anything but the truth of our feelings between us. Can you forgive me? I don't care how long it takes. Will you give us another chance? Let me rebuild that trust? Will you take me back?"

The truth?

Was that her heart had never let him go.

"You've already got your answer." Delaney put a hand over his heart. Even through the starched polyester and the cotton of his undershirt, she could feel it thumping outrageously hard and fast. "I came to find you, Kellan. Not because I needed to lean on you. But because something momentous was about to happen to me, and I had to share it with you. Because everything is better when I share it with you."

He cupped his hand around hers. "Babe, I completely agree. I don't want to be one of those couples who lead separate lives. I want to share our work, our successes, our failures, our laughter. Our *everything*."

Oh, they were so completely on the same page. The fact that there was a toilet running behind them and the room reeked of nauseatingly strong pine air freshener didn't diminish the romance of the moment one bit.

Delaney tilted her head up to stare directly into those sky blue eyes. "I don't have any solutions. Yet. But I do have an answer. I forgive you, and I love you. I'm sorry I walked away. We should've fought, hashed it out, and tried again."

"That sounds like a much better plan than breaking up."

"Let me finish apologizing. I reacted, well, *over-*reacted. I was scared, upset, so hurt. Instantly, I saw myself making the same wrong choices my mother had. I focused on all the things that could go wrong, all the worst-case scenarios, because that's what I'm trained to do every moment of every day."

With a lopsided grin, Kellan said, "Maybe that's one of those things you should try to leave at the office. And

I won't automatically arrest everyone I see jaywalking when I'm off duty."

His talent to reset the mood of a room with a single, carefree comment should be bottled and sold to SWAT team negotiators. Her laughter chased away the tears thickly lining the back of her throat. "That's a good plan. Except . . . has anyone actually been arrested for jaywalking in this century?"

"Dunno. But I'll get right on it after we solve the more burning question of *are you pregnant*."

Delaney curled her fingers around the placket of his shirt, keeping him from turning to learn the answer. "Do you want me to be?" she asked in a near whisper.

"I love you."

Was he stonewalling her? Now? About this? "That's not an answer."

"It's the intro to my thoughtful and heartfelt answer. Don't rush me, woman!"

Had she actually forgotten in the past week his love of language? The way he used words the way other men used chocolates and roses to melt a woman into a puddle of longing? Grinning, she urged, "Do go on."

Kellan kept up the slow, reassuring strokes up and down her back. "I always planned for a family someday. My ties to my brothers are so strong, I want to pass that on to the next generation. I don't want your life to be any more complicated right now, but if you are pregnant, I'd be thrilled. We'll roll with it, whatever happens."

"You know that's exactly the right answer, don't you?"

"Marshal, I was valedictorian of my class."

Delaney challenged him just for the fun of hearing the answer, even though it was in his file that she'd memorized so long ago. "Which one?"

"All of 'em. I only give right answers. Now what about you? What do you want the test to say?"

"In my head I know this isn't the right time. It would complicate my next assignment, or maybe even this one, depending on how bad the morning sickness gets. A baby wasn't on my career path. But in my heart? Of course I want it. I'd want our baby whenever it decided to come."

"Also the right answer." Kellan squeezed her hand, then split them apart to face the sink. "Ready?"

They both stepped forward and leaned over to see a double pink line on one test, and the word *pregnant* on the other.

Guessing that it was possible was worlds away from actually seeing the confirmation. Stunned to her core, Delaney met Kellan's gaze in the mirror. "We did it. We made a baby."

"We did, Laney. I can't believe it." Then he whooped so loudly the sound clanged around the room as he lifted her and swung her in circles. Delaney squealed and they laughed and it felt like the whole station would burst open with their joy.

"We should be quieter. Mateo's going to think we've lost our minds."

He set her down carefully. "Are you kidding? I want

to shout it from the top of the lighthouse so the whole town knows."

The logistics and reality of what had to happen next smothered her joy like a heavy fire blanket. "One step at a time. We shouldn't say anything. It isn't safe. I'm not three months along yet."

"How far along are you?" Kellan rubbed a hand over her belly with a bemused expression. "How did this even happen?"

"You'll need to be sitting down for that explanation. But I meant that we shouldn't tell *anyone* yet. Not my work, not Emily, not even your brothers." With all her good intentions of not forcing him to choose between her and his brothers? That's exactly what had to happen. Kellan had to lie to them. A lie of omission. A lie expectant parents routinely used every day. But still a lie. "Not until we figure everything out."

Because this changed . . . everything. Delaney had sworn to guard her protectees with her life. Had ordered Kellan to stay away from the trial so that she wouldn't be distracted from protecting his brothers.

But with a life growing inside her? Could she knowingly put it at risk? Would she still throw herself willingly in front of a bullet headed for Rafe if it meant injuring their baby? Delaney didn't know the answer to that. And it was an answer she'd have to come up with before heading back to Chicago.

Kellan must've sensed that she was spinning out, because he pulled her in for a tight hug, rubbing circles on her back. "We will. I promise. You won't be able to shake me again. I'll be your date to your dad's parole hearing—or sit at home with you on the couch eating popcorn if you want to avoid it. I'll be at every ultrasound, every end of a long day when you need a foot rub. We'll figure out how to have a future together."

"That might not even be possible until after the trial." If things went south and one or both of his brothers didn't come back to Bandon, would Kellan stay?

Worse yet, would he be able to forgive her if she couldn't keep them safe in the end? That fear crushed down on Delaney, stealing her breath.

She never discussed with the Maguires the full extent of the danger they were putting themselves in by going back to testify. The day Rafe came to WITSEC, the agent who signed him on board read him the standard disclosures.

But Delaney's job was to keep them safe mentally as well as physically. So she downplayed the risk, keeping them focused on getting through it and starting their lives for good once the trial was over. The harsh reality, though, was that she couldn't promise them absolute safety.

Kellan pulled back to cradle her face in his wide palms. "We've got the rest of our lives together. Nothing has to happen right now. Nothing starts the moment we walk out of this bathroom except celebrating that we're back together, and we're going to be parents. Let's take the rest of tonight, even the rest of the week, to take that in."

He was right. And she was all over the place. Delaney happily checked off pregnancy hormones as an excuse for the first time. "I never expected this. But then, I never expected you, either."

As they kissed, Delaney hoped that all the surprises in store for them were this good.

But the one thing she knew, that she saw day in and day out, was that life came with no guarantees.

Chapter Twenty

MATEO DOUBLE-THUMPED HIS knuckles on the scarred wood of Kellan's desk. "Isn't it time for you to clock out, Deputy?"

Whoa. A glance at the corner of his monitor told Kellan he should've changed ten minutes ago. This was just like all the times the library closed around him in law school. His concentration totally wiped out his inner clock.

"I lost track of time." He logged out with an apologetic grin. "Memorizing rules and regs so I'm ready to hit the Academy."

"I'm beginning to think the Academy won't know what hit *it* when you walk through the door. Try not to show up every other recruit, okay? Leave a few of them their pride?"

"I'll play it cool, I promise. Just . . . excited and itching to get started full-time." Kellan was in the *zone* with his deputy training. Beyond ready to jump into the deep end.

"You'll get plenty of full-time helping out at the festival this weekend. Expect twelve-hour shifts, minimum, even if some of it is babysitting the drunk tank."

"Whatever you need."

Mateo placed a gun, holster, and ammunition in a pile in front of Kellan. "Be sure you fully suit up for it."

Talk about a surprise. Kellan curled his fingers around the snub-nosed barrel of the Smith & Wesson. "I thought I couldn't carry until I finish the Academy training?"

"It's the Wild West out here. We've been deputizing citizens since the first wagon trains rumbled down the Oregon trail." Mateo hooked his thumbs in his own gun belt. "You passed your shooting certification last week, officially. The Cranberry Festival's got all the ingredients for trouble—lots of people, lots of drinking, and competitions. I want you armed. And I trust you to know to keep it holstered in ninety-nine out of a hundred situations."

This nod of approval from the sheriff meant more than getting his official certificate would in a few months. Today, September 5, was Kellan's personal graduation day. "Thanks for trusting me. I won't let you down."

"I know. I've been watching you. You've got the book smarts down cold, but it's the way you respect the people in this town that makes the difference for me. Like everyone matters."

"Isn't that what the law is all about? Making sure everyone gets treated equally?"

A laugh that practically shook the building roared out of Mateo. "There's still a part of you that's wet behind the ears and naive as all hell. But sure. Go with that mindset. I hope it lasts." Still chuckling, he headed out the front door, tossing a wave at Rafe and Flynn as they entered.

Flynn was in his usual uniform of a black tee and jeans, despite the fact that it was pushing eighty-five outside. He'd been doing that ever since O'Brien hit town. He could get away with wearing his steel-toed boots with jeans. Those boots and his killer MMA moves were more than enough protection.

But Rafe wore a dark green scrub top over his jeans. Jeans that meant *he* was hiding a knife or two somewhere on his body for added protection. That scrub top gave Kellan the perfect opening to poke at his oldest brother. "What's with the shirt? Is this your less-than-subtle way of announcing to the world that you snuck into the hospital again at lunch for a quickie with your hot doctor girlfriend?"

Smirking, Rafe said, "Who said I was trying to be subtle?"

Flynn gave him an up and down and sighed. "Dude, it wouldn't be any more obvious if you had a used condom caught in your zipper."

"I'm the head of this family. I'm just setting a good example for you two. Proving that you can have a fulfilling career and still squeeze in time on a random Tuesday for a nooner with your woman. Living the dream over here. Watch and learn."

Man, would Rafe *ever* drop the older and wiser routine? Because, if you objectively asked a hundred people, Kellan was sure the overwhelming vote would be that the wisest Maguire was the one who had never voluntarily joined a freaking crime syndicate.

He jammed on his hat. "You know, Mollie needs the people of Bandon to respect her. Not think that you're turning her into some perverted addict to hospital bed sex."

"Honestly?" Flynn chuckled and shook his head. "The people of Bandon are just off-kilter enough to probably respect her *more* for that."

Rafe jangled his keys. "You ready to hit the road, K?"

"I need a minute to lock this up." He lifted the service weapon and showed it off before securing it in the weapons safe at the back of the room.

Flynn whistled. "You're the real deal now, Deputy Maguire. Very impressive."

They were the right words, but Kellan needed to know if they were sincere. He didn't want his brothers looking at him and seeing not *him*, but the crime fighters they'd worked to evade for so many years. "Is it, ah, uncomfortable for you guys to see me here?" He waved his hand to encompass the station as they walked out. "Chasing down criminals?"

"Not at all." The answer came without the slightest hesitation on Flynn's part. "Maybe weirded out a little. At first. But we never wanted you to share the life we fell into. We wanted you to do whatever made you happy."

"And we're so damn proud of you." Rafe gave Kellan's shoulder a hard squeeze. "This is a better fit than lawyering. Lawyers are sharks. Sheriffs are just good guys, through and through."

"Not all the way through. I've got a little of the Maguire bad boy streak in my veins. So I'll keep up the poker scam and live on the edge a little. Helping the little guy while cheating the cheaters."

Flynn opened the passenger door of Rafe's beloved Camaro. "You get shotgun. To celebrate getting your service weapon."

Just . . . *wow*. Flynn hadn't ceded shotgun to him, well, ever. Talk about proof that they finally saw him as an equal instead of their kid brother. "Thanks." As Kellan buckled up, he asked, "Why are we squishing Flynn into the back? Why not take his huge truck on this mystery road trip?"

"Because I need to drive. I need to do it myself. I need to do all of this myself." Rafe spoke through near-gritted teeth. A desperate determination roughened his voice, like he was talking about dismantling a bomb instead of pulling out onto Highway 101.

"I'm with K. What are you trying to prove that's got me losing feeling in my nuts back here?"

Rafe's knuckles whitened on the steering wheel. "I'm proving that nobody coerced me. That this whole trip was my idea, my plan."

"Okay, now you sound like we're off to rob a bank." Kellan kept his tone light, but wasn't at all joking. "Which, given your past histories, isn't outside the realm of possibility."

"I already hit the bank. Emptied out half my pay from since we got here." Rafe stomped on the gas two blocks later, when they passed the start of forest that marked the end of town.

"The last time you acted this strange was when you showed up at my door to tell me you'd thrown us in WITSEC," Flynn said slowly. "What the hell have you done?"

"Something just as life-changing. Or it will be. I hope." He nipped around a couple of cars and floored it as they came to Bullards Bridge. The blue water frothed beneath them. "We're going to Coos Bay to buy Mollie an engagement ring. I'm proposing to her. And hoping to fucking God that she says yes."

The whole mood of the car changed. Flynn laughed, clapping Rafe on the shoulder. And Kellan let out a whoop that was as much happiness for Rafe's decision as it was relief that they weren't doing something crazy.

"Way to go, bro," Flynn said. "You don't deserve the

awesomeness of the Doc, but it'll be great to have her as part of the family."

Kellan elbowed his big brother in the biceps. "I guess some of my smarts finally rubbed off on you. Because proposing to Mollie will be the smartest thing you've ever done."

"Don't I know it. I shouldn't have waited this long to buy the ring, but I was worried about not giving it away. I can't lie to that woman. I'll barely be able to survive the next four days."

Now Kellan was lost. "What happens in four days?"

"Weren't you listening? I'm proposing. At the Cranberry Festival, because it'll be special for her."

Wow. That really *was* a gesture of love. Rafe had sworn up and down from day one in Bandon that he hated cranberries, and hated the crazy-ass festival. The timing, however, shocked Kellan to his core.

"What happened to no major changes until after the trial? Not until we're free and clear of the whole thing. Not until we know we're safe and *have* the rest of our lives ahead of us."

"Yep. That was the plan. Plans change."

Plans changed. The reality of being in the same real estate as a bunch of pissed-off, vengeful mobsters did *not*.

More quietly, Kellan asked, "Aren't you scared?"

"To go back to Chicago and testify? Hell, yes." Oddly, talking about the trial seemed to take the edge off Rafe's nerves. His grip loosened, and the cadence of his voice was far less forced. This was familiar territory. Love and marriage? Totally not. "I'm no idiot. I've read the stats on witnesses being taken out just between the car and the courtroom door. Or being trailed to the hotel and ambushed. I know it's dangerous."

"For the record, I'm pretty fucking scared, too," Flynn added from the back seat. "And I can't tell Sierra that. I can't give her any more reason to worry. But yeah, there will be flop sweat from the moment our plane lifts off at PDX and heads to O'Hare."

"Then I'm glad I won't be sitting next to you and your stink." Kellan had been looking for a time—and a way—to tell his brothers he wouldn't be going along. They talked about the trial so rarely that this was suddenly the best option. "The marshals have benched me. I'll be in a safe house the whole time you're in Chicago."

"Good," Flynn said, shocking the hell out of him. "I didn't like the idea of your being in danger just because you want to support us. Anyone by our side is painted with an automatic target. This will give me one less thing to worry about."

Huh. Almost identical to the argument Delaney had laid out. "Rafe? Is this okay with you?"

After a couple of beats, Rafe shot him a sidelong glance that saw way too much in that split second. "Did the marshals bench you? Or did *our* marshal, specifically, tell you to stay behind?"

Man, *nothing* got past him. Which would make his testimony so damning to McGinty and his crew. "Delaney's in charge of us, so, yeah, it was her decision. It's important to her, so she can do her best to protect you two. I don't want to put up a fight." Not anymore, at least. And if it seemed that he was siding with her over his brothers? Well, this time he *was*. Zero regrets on that score, too.

"Then that's how it needs to be. You know we want you with us, but we'd rather be safe and smart than selfish."

Kellan seized on those words. If they were finally, actually talking about this, he needed to hammer home a point. Because he was fucking scared, too.

Rafe and Flynn needed to bury the Chicago mob, but more importantly, they needed to come back home afterward.

"You will be, right? Safe and smart? Not bullheaded and all *I know this town, I know these people, I'm in charge?*"

Rafe punched on the radio. "Don't be an asshole."

"Don't be arrogant," he shot back. "And don't assume it'll be easy."

"I know," Rafe muttered. "I know to keep my head down, to follow Delaney's instructions to the letter."

Flynn stuck an arm between the seats and counted off on his fingers. "We won't sneak out to catch a game at Wrigley. We won't sneak out for Italian beef, or ask the marshals to do a drive-by of our old house. We won't even visit Mom and Dad's graves."

That all sounded good. But Kellan needed one more—specific—reassurance. "What about Lakeside

Cemetery? Will you try and go retrieve the two mil you hid there?"

"No." Rafe's response was swift and decisive.

"What we've found here in Bandon is worth way more than some stacks of cash," Flynn elaborated. "The future with Mollie and Sierra—and Jesus Christ, *you*, K—it isn't worth risking."

Good answer. It just didn't touch on all the aspects of his question. "What about Davey?"

"We've gotta get through the festival this weekend. All of us are working overtime and being pulled in crazy fucking directions for it. After, it'll be easier to figure out what to do about him. Worst case, we just tell Davey where it is when we get there."

That was . . . simple. Kellan drummed his fingers on the smooth black leather seat. "Why not tell him now, then?"

"We won't risk grabbing it this trip. But—" Rafe raised his index finger "—it *is* nice to know that it's out there as insurance. If anything goes wrong in October, it'll be yours to get and share with Mollie and Sierra."

Casually discussing their death as a real-to-fucking-God possibility, his brothers were still looking after him. Kellan loved them. And if anything did go wrong? He might roll up to Chicago with *both* of his guns and take out whoever hurt them.

"What a fucking crap ball of a plan. How about you make sure nothing goes wrong?"

Rafe circled his hand in the air. "Which is why I'm

proposing to Mollie on Saturday. Once you help me pick out a rock."

"One big enough to guarantee she overlooks all your flaws and says yes?" Flynn snickered. "It'll need to be at least three carats to pull off that miracle."

The forest blurred on both sides of the car with Rafe's foot so heavy on the pedal, putting them in a dark green bubble. Maybe it put Kellan in a trance. Maybe he was dog tired from making this same commute to be with Delaney most nights. Or maybe just talking life and death put everything into perspective.

Whatever the reason, he opened his mouth and said, "I'm buying one, too."

"One what?"

"An engagement ring. For Delaney." It felt . . . right to say that. Not scary. Not a knee-jerk reaction to the pregnancy. Just . . . right. It popped everything back into focus. The trees. The smell of day-old coffee from the travel mug in the cup holder. "But don't worry—I won't rain on your parade. I'll do it in a couple of weeks."

Rafe's foot stuttered on the gas. "Are you serious?"

Flynn leaned his whole body between the seats to get right up in Kellan's face. "You only patched things up three days ago. How about waiting to see if it sticks this time around?"

Nope. "I know that you're trying to look out for me. I appreciate it. But Delaney's the right woman for me." He also knew that if he disclosed Delaney's pregnancy, they'd get on board immediately. But Kellan didn't ever want them to think *that* was the reason for the proposal. So he shared the simple truth that had hit him on this drive. "When you know, you know. No point waiting."

"I know," Flynn said quietly. "I know that Sierra's the one for me. I still want to wait until after the trial. Go ahead and laugh at me, but I don't want to jinx anything. Everything to do with McGinty's got to be behind us before I officially start the rest of my life with her."

"And that makes sense—for *you*. But for me?" Kellan shook his head. "Waiting until after the trial would feel like a jinx to me. The mob was never *my* life, so I damn well won't start letting it influence me now."

Rafe slapped his palm against the wheel. "Well said."

There was only one glitch in this spontaneous plan. "I don't suppose you guys have any other hidden money you haven't told me about? Or want to float me a loan to get her the ring she deserves?"

"Shit." Flynn banged his fist against the door. "You have money, K. All your savings from Chicago and what's left of dad's insurance."

"I thought that was untouchable?"

"*Ours* is," Rafe corrected. "Because of the whole us being material witnesses thing. But *yours* is accessible. We didn't tell you at first because we were worried you were so pissed at us that you'd bolt."

Kellan struggled, balancing a knee-jerk anger at being treated like a child against the fact that, yet again, Rafe and Flynn had worked to keep the three of them together. To not let him go off in a huff and be unprotected. Good intentions, yes. Badly handled, hell yes. But they'd all come a long way since November.

"Okay," he said slowly. "It might've been the right call back then. Doesn't explain why you didn't mention this since things smoothed out between all of us over the past few months."

Rafe tugged at the neckline of his tee. "We forgot."

"Come again?" Kellan gave himself a mental high five for not screaming *what the actual FUCK?*

Rafe explained in a rush. "We're living off the WITSEC monthly stipend, in WITSEC paid-for housing. Which is all we've been doing for ten months. Haven't given money a thought. We've kept our heads down. No expensive concerts, ballgames, trips. Quiet life in a town the size of a freckle."

"If you'd told us that you needed money, we would've said something," Flynn added. "Money hasn't really mattered."

Well, damn. He'd just about scraped dry his savings from the cranberry plant, meeting Delaney in hotels up and down the Oregon coast. Guess he should be grateful that the situation wasn't as dire as he'd thought.

In fact, the whole thing was so ridiculous that Kellan started laughing. They *forgot* about his money?

He twisted around in his seat. "Pull out your phone," he ordered Flynn. "Delaney can't know about this. Call the marshal's office in Chicago and get me access to that account."

"They emptied the Chicago account. For safety. It's at a bank here in Oregon."

Fucking *ridiculous*. And hilarious. "I want that money by the time Rafe's done picking out his fifteen-carat rock. Get started."

As he wriggled his phone out of his pocket, Flynn said, "I'm sorry, K. We should've told you."

"Yeah? That's been your motto for a while now. Both of you. How about this be the last time you ever say that to me? Or is there anything else? A sister I don't know about? A secret house in the Caymans?"

"There's Rafe's third nipple. He sliced it off when he tried to juggle knives for an eighth-grade talent show."

Laughing even harder, Kellan let go of the residual anger. They were doing this. Starting over. Clean slates, women they loved, a baby on the way. Everything was going to be great. Starting with the *has to be seen to be believed* epicness of the Cranberry Festival. Getting through the trial would just be a tiny blip after that.

He had to believe it.

Chapter Twenty-one

THIS WAS ACTUALLY one of those rare times when an event didn't just live up to the hype, but surpassed it.

Bandon's Cranberry Festival had more people in its streets than Kellan had seen in total the whole four-plus months he'd been here. People dressed like pirates. One woman had an inflatable shark strapped to her waist and fake legs dangling from it. People in giant puffy cranberries that reminded Kellan of the sumo wrestling suits used in bars. The 5K fun run at dawn had a group of at least fifty in fluffy red tutus.

Flynn tipped a cranberry slush drink into his mouth. He wore an official Festival tee that all of his float-building kids had signed on the back. "It may not be the Chicago Blues Festival or the Windy City Ribfest, but this is damn awesome in its own right."

Rafe continued to tinker with the huge electric box that controlled the stage and the strings of lights spanning the street overhead. It was a little quieter here, but once the live music started in two hours, the bulk of the people would tilt to this end of town. "Are you seriously drinking a cranberry daiquiri? *And* still expect to call yourself a real bartender after you drain it?"

"It's a cranberry margarita," Flynn corrected in a know-it-all tone. "If you can't beat 'em, join 'em."

Snickering, Kellan asked, "Isn't that the same motto that turned you into a mobster?"

"Shut up," he said, with no heat behind it. "The Gorse is closed today. I'm here as a solid town citizen, sampling all aspects of the festival. Did you swing by the Food Fair yet? They've got some cranberry-sauced meatballs that will change your worldview. I think I saw Mick put away an even dozen."

Kellan patted the silver star on his uniform shirt. "Missed my lunch break. I spent it helping the paramedics and Mollie finish dealing with the injuries from the race. One guy dressed as a pirate got stabbed by his fake parrot's beak when he tripped and fell. Thing went right through his cheek."

Ripping off a piece of black electrical tape with his teeth, Rafe said, "You know, as much as we bitch about Floyd, this really is a fucking big-ass deal. He did a great job juggling everything into place."

"You gonna tell him that?"

"Nah. He's enough of a pain in the ass without me making his head any bigger. But I'll give him less grief next year. This thing is pretty damned fun."

"Rafe Maguire, you've finally crossed to the dark side!" Laughing hysterically, Mollie ran up to Rafe and tickled his ribs. "You just praised the Cranberry Festival. Wow. My work here is clearly done." With a toss of her long brown hair onto the back of her cranberry red tank top, she turned to dart off.

But Rafe's hand shot out, grabbing her wrist to stop her. "Don't. Don't even joke about being done with me, Doc."

"I was only teasing—"

He cut her off with a finger to her lips. "Doesn't matter. Can't stand the thought of losing you. Hell—" he dropped his pliers on the ground "—I can't wait any longer."

"To do what? Finally smile and lick your lips when you eat cranberries?"

"I've got a better use for them." Off the top of the electrical box, he grabbed the cranberry-and-flower wreath Sierra made that Flynn had just handed off. Red and white ribbons trailed off the back. After holding it at eye level long enough for her to register, Rafe settled it gently on her head.

Holy shit. He was going for it. Right here, right now.

Kellan exchanged an excited glance with Flynn. Gave his big brother a silent-thumbs up. And was grateful as hell that he got to witness Rafe taking such a monumental step. This was heads and tails better than sitting next to him at the trial.

"I tried to wait, Doc. I wanted to do this tonight, on the stage, and make a big deal out of it. But I can't wait. I can't live another minute without hearing you promise that you won't ever walk away from me."

"Rafe, no, I wouldn't leave you. What's going on?" Mollie's hands floated up to pat the wreath. "You look so serious."

"This damned thing's burning a hole in my pocket. If it stays in there any longer, I won't be any use to you in bed."

"Well, we can't have that . . . oh . . . ." Her voice trailed off when she saw him pull out the square red leather box. "You don't have to do this. We can wait. Until, you know, after everything's settled. After October."

That, right there? Proved that Mollie really was the one for Rafe. How many women would try and slough off an obvious diamond ring to keep their man calm?

"Fuck October." Rafe's expression was fierce. Like his whole life distilled down to this moment, this question. "It can't mess with how much I love you. There's no waiting. There's only you and me. And I'm promising you forever, Doc, if you'll take it. You could find a richer man, one with a squeaky-clean past. But I swear you'll never find anyone who loves you more, who works harder every single day to make you happy. You're the best thing that's ever happened to me."

"I don't want a good man. Talk about boring." Eyes already brimming, Mollie caressed Rafe's cheek. "I love the streak of bad in you."

Rafe dropped to one knee. Thumbed open the box. And didn't seem to notice that his hip was up against a giant cranberry balloon, and that he had to shout a little to be heard over the din of the festival-goers packing the street. "Then will you marry me, Doctor Mollie Vickers? Will you let me kiss you awake every morning and fucking drench you in my love for the rest of our lives?"

Only his ex-mobster brother would find a way to use *fuck* in a marriage proposal—and make it sound good. Talk about legendary. Guess there were still a few things Kellan could learn from him.

Two tears tracked down Mollie's face, blurring the tiny cluster of cranberries painted on one cheek. "Yes. Yes, I love you. Yes, I want to share forever with you. Please be mine forever, Rafe Maguire." She held out a shaking hand and he slid on the pear-shaped diamond surrounded by a halo of rubies. Mollie gasped once she really eyeballed it.

She zoomed her ring finger up to right in front of her face. "Would those be cranberry red rubies, by any chance, you big softie?"

Rafe shifted from one foot to the other, clearly uncomfortable. "I know how important Bandon is to you. How much you love it here. How much the town did for you once your mom left. I thought, since it brought us together, it was only right to give it a nod."

That brought on a steady stream of tears. Kellan looked away while they kissed. Well, he watched it at first, until it quickly turned from romantic to way too R rated for a city street. In unspoken agreement, he and Flynn turned their backs and formed a bit of a shield for the lovebirds until the smooching sounds died down.

"We're thrilled to have you join the family." Flynn hugged Mollie with one arm, and gave Rafe a high-five with the other.

"Yeah—it's great to know that if I'm wounded in the line of duty, I'll have a doctor in residence to patch me up," Kellan joked as he hugged her, too.

"No. Hell, no," Rafe roared. "This whole house-sharing thing ends the moment we get back from our . . . ah . . . trip. You two can keep the place. Mollie's leaving her gran's, too. We'll find our own love nest."

This time her left hand sort of fluttered up to her face. "Oh, I have to tell Gran. I mean, I want to stay here and kiss you some more, but she'll be so tickled . . ."

"Go. Hurry back, but go take your victory lap past Elena, Karen, and Lily, too." Mollie gave Rafe one last wet smack before literally running off down the street, one hand clutched tight to her crown.

Kellan clapped him on the back. It wasn't enough. Even for the very much non-hugging Maguire brothers. He moved in front and gave a squeeze that Rafe's ribs would hopefully be protesting for days. "Way to go, bro."

Rafe looked down. Then he reeled back a few steps, off the sidewalk toward the elevated stage. "My hands are shaking. Holy fuck, it worked. She said yes."

Flynn pumped that shaking hand up and down at least five times, with a shit-eating grin on his face. "Best day's work you've ever done."

"Surprised you could cram it in after being so busy screwing me over." From deep in the shadows beneath the stage came Davey O'Brien's voice. This time he held two guns, both pointed at the tight cluster of the Maguires.

Shit. *Shit.* This was a hundred times worse than when he'd surprised them on the beach. Because of two words—*collateral damage.*

He was here for the Maguires, but their lives weren't the only ones at risk. Any action Kellan took could end up with Davey shooting wild and endangering the tourists and townsfolk innocently walking by.

With the stage being at the far end of the festival area, nobody was really crossing behind them. Or looking their way, even. Davey was hidden pretty well. So Kellan needed to draw him out, get him visible. Attention was for sure the last thing the mobster wanted.

But Mateo was out there patrolling, along with a couple of deputies from Coquille helping out. No doubt Delaney was carrying, too, even though she was here unofficially, hanging out with Sierra.

He could try to edge behind Rafe for cover and dial

911 on the phone in his pocket. No guarantee he'd blindly hit the right numbers, though. The one thing Kellan knew that he couldn't do was fire on Davey. His aim was true, but his draw wasn't that fast yet. By the time he got a shot off, Davey would have more than enough time to fire both of his guns. And from this distance, chances of his missing were slim.

"What are you talking about, Davey?" Rafe's tone was calm, his voice steady. "And what are you doing here? We had a deal."

"We did. I was dumb enough to trust that you'd stick by your word."

"We will." Rafe held out his arms, palms up. He used the gesture to hide the fact that he took a couple of steps backward. Away from the stage, in an attempt to lure Davey out the same way Kellan had envisioned. "Nothing's changed. Soon as we get to Chicago, we'll get the money and hand it over."

"Everything's changed!" Droplets of spit flew from his mouth as Davey—gratifyingly—took three hurried steps forward. The guns wavered, too. "The money's gone. Didn't you see the news?"

Flynn spun in a wide circle, arms up, with much more dramatic flair than normal. Also trying to attract attention. It was like they'd all choreographed these moves to get Davey out on the street. "Buddy, you see this craziness we're in the middle of? This has been our whole world this week. So how about you clue us in as to why you're pissed enough to be holding us up?"

"Some kids found your stash. Trying to hold a séance or some dumb stunt. Two million in a grave at Lakeside Cemetery sound familiar? Because as soon as it hit the news, Danny McGinty knew right off what it was. He's pissed as hell that you used our hiding spot for it."

"Why?" Rafe bluffed. Another wave of his hands. Another couple of steps back, up onto the sidewalk. "He can't claim we stole anything when it's in a known mob spot. Danny should be thrilled that we thought to hide it there from the Feds."

"Nice try. I'm not buying it." As he jabbed the gun in his right hand, Davey came all the way to the edge of the stage overhang. "And the mob sure as hell can't touch it now. Those kids turned it over to the police. More to the point, you can't get at it anymore and give it to me. You fucking two-timers. You played me."

"For fuck's sake, Davey. We didn't hire ourselves some gullible teens to go ghost hunting. It was just bad luck that it was found. We didn't have jack shit to do with that."

Kellan's mind raced at this information. What did it mean? Was the deal off? What was O'Brien's plan now, aside from the whole gun-waving thing? And had he told Danny about the Maguires? Would they have to relocate if they survived the next ten minutes?

"You must have more money. You had to know there was a chance someone on McGinty's crew would think to check that tomb eventually. You're fucking still going to pay me off, or I'll squeal."

Rafe's voice arrowed out, razor sharp. "So, you didn't tell him about us?"

"Of course not. I want the damned money. I don't want to split it with a man who's going to spend the rest of his life in prison. But if you play me again, I *will* tell him. I'll tell him about that pretty woman you just put a ring on, too."

Sierra clutched Delaney's arm and pointed down the street. "Oh, look, Mollie's wearing the crown I made her. And she's running like she's trying to set a land speed record."

Nibbling around the edge of a cranberry double chocolate cookie the size of a dinner plate, Delaney said, "I guess that means Rafe popped the question early. Probably couldn't handle waiting. When I saw him this morning, he was already jittering around like a kid on meth. It was kind of adorable."

"Was it hard for you? Keeping the secret from her for three days? I know I could barely do it." Sierra grinned. "I canceled lunch with her yesterday just so I wouldn't be tempted to spill."

Delaney thought about the secret she and Kellan were keeping from *everyone*. For about the millionth time, she pushed down the impulse to put her hand on her belly. Because that gesture was one heck of a give-away as to what was going on in her body.

"Sierra, I keep secrets for a living, remember? Life

and death are pretty much riding on the line for me to hide what I know about my protectees. So no, I didn't have any trouble keeping the imminent proposal from Mollie."

Delaney was over-the-moon happy for Rafe and Mollie. Their big news, however, was about seventeenth down in her list of obsessions currently circling her brain like a swarm of bees.

She'd been beyond busy with the task force. They'd arrested someone on Thursday that not only tied to the bombings, but also opened up a lot of avenues to finding a drug distribution circle that had set up shop here on the coast.

Not to mention the small matter of thinking about being pregnant all the time, scheduling a doctor's visit for next week to make it official, and trying to figure out if she could still be not just an effective marshal, but the best possible marshal.

And, oh, *Kellan*. How crazy she was about him. How crazy it would be if they actually figured out a way to be together. How impossible it would be to stay a marshal and be living with a former protectee.

How impossible it would be to *not* be with him and raise this child together.

Sierra tugged on her arm, pulling Delaney up the street. "Let's go congratulate Rafe."

"Do you want to congratulate Rafe, or do you want to go give your own boyfriend a big old smooch?" she teased.

Flynn and Sierra were one of those couples that always stuck together, like magnets. It was sweet to watch. It also made Delaney more than a little jealous. In a perfect world, she and Kellan wouldn't be hiding anything, and they'd get to PDA all over the place in front of their friends and family, too.

"Both," Sierra admitted, laughing.

Delaney handed over the cookie in trade for Sierra's cranberry candied apple. "Didn't you walk with him in the parade next to his float just a couple of hours ago?"

Stopping in her tracks, Sierra threw back her head and dramatically put the back of her hand to her forehead. "Oh, geez, thanks for rubbing it in that I haven't kissed Flynn in *hours*. We'd better hurry."

"How do you plan to find them in this crowd?"

"Flynn said Rafe had to tinker with the electrical box by the stage. I think Kellan was meeting up with them, too."

That put a hustle in her step. Because Delaney hadn't seen Kellan in hours, either. Sure, he was working, but she'd hoped they'd get to hang out at least a little at the festival. Ogling him in his uniform was her new favorite thing to do. He filled it out like every sexy cliché of a law enforcement hottie.

Thanks to his height, it was easy to spot his hat in a relatively empty section by the stage. Automatically she scanned for two dark heads with his same height and build. Looked like Rafe and Flynn were with him.

But . . . her quick scan doubled back. The bald man

facing them, just out from the overhang of the stage, looked familiar. "Hang on a second," she said, grabbing Sierra probably a little too hard.

"What is it?"

"I need to think. Just . . . wait." Delaney closed her eyes. Tried to place the face that had sent a chill up her spine. And then it hit her. As SOP, she'd memorized the faces of everyone in McGinty's crew. It gave her an edge in protecting the Maguires while they were still in Chicago, and even five moves later, she still reviewed the photos once a month to stay sharp.

That man was a Chicago mobster. She didn't remember his name, but she'd swear he worked for McGinty. The fact that he was standing less than ten feet from the Maguire brothers couldn't be a coincidence.

And it couldn't be anything but dangerous.

But she'd stop whatever he had planned. There was no way she'd gone through so much to keep the Maguires safe for ten long months that she'd let some pissant mobster who evidently wasn't even important enough to be indicted and jailed bring them down.

Pissant *idiot* was more like it. Clearly, he wasn't smart enough to know what he was up against with the U.S. Marshals Service.

Delaney dropped the apple. Then she whipped her phone out of the pocket of her red shorts. "Call the sheriff. Not 911, just Mateo directly. He's in my contacts. Say I told you that I need immediate backup at the stage. He'll understand." She thrust Sierra at the nearest shop door. "Do it from inside. Don't come back out at all until I come and get you."

"What's wrong?"

She'd always suspected—but not been able to prove—that Sierra knew all of Flynn's secrets. Right now, she hoped it was true. Delaney needed her to be scared enough to heed the warning and stay safe.

"I think Flynn and Rafe's past just caught up with them. Now *go*."

Looking to her right, she saw the vast majority of people streaming off the street. It must be almost time for the Cranberry Bowl kickoff. Good news in terms of potential collateral damage, although even the handful of people left could be in danger. Delaney needed to take down the mobster before he even realized she was coming for him.

If only Rafe's big body wasn't blocking her view of anything besides his head. Did he have a gun? A knife? Or was he just here to threaten the Maguires? Maybe try to bribe them into not testifying?

Delaney reached into her purse. She angled her approach more to the right, to get around Rafe to make a full assessment. If she took her gun out now, the woman in the pink flowered hat might see, react, and freak out. Said freak-out could lead to a chain reaction of an attack that could be prevented. On the other hand, if she didn't take out her gun now and nameless mobster was armed, she'd be a minute too late in her reaction to whatever he had planned.

Rafe, Flynn, and *oh, God*, Kellan could all be victims.

Damn it. There wasn't time for fear. That'd flood in later, when this was over and she relived however it turned out a thousand times. Now there was only focus and training and the absolute belief that she could and *would* prevent any harm from coming to those three men.

Cursing her noisy red flip-flops, Delaney stepped out of them. And then kept walking, right at the stage as she pulled out her gun. She had it arcing up and out, her left hand moving to steady it while she identified herself as a marshal. But before she could wrap her left hand around the grip, a woman screamed *GUN* at the top of her lungs at the same moment a shot rang out.

It came from the mobster and the dull black gun he held out sideways, gangster style, pointed right at her.

Shit! Delaney squeezed and fired. Weirdly, it looked like she missed, since he didn't so much as waver, aside from the cruel smile spreading on his thin lips.

But she never missed a target.

Except . . . she wasn't standing still. She'd missed because she'd already started falling to the ground. Screams sounded all around her.

Confused, and, *ow*, suddenly on her knees on the hot asphalt, Delaney looked down.

Blood spilled out of a black-edged hole in the side of her white tank top.

Then she heard yet another gunshot. Looked back up to see Kellan, arms locked, service weapon smoking as he stood over the man who'd, *holy crap*, shot her. A second later, Flynn viciously kicked the prone body.

Good. The Maguires were safe. Delaney slipped from her knees the rest of the way to the ground. Falling didn't hurt. Nothing really hurt.

Oh.

She couldn't feel *anything*.

"Mollie!" Kellan screamed as he ran toward her, ripping his shirt over his head. "Mollie, she's pregnant. Help!" He wadded his shirt against her belly with one hand and he grabbed her hand with the other. "Delaney, just hang on. Look at me," he ordered. "Don't close your eyes. Look at mine and *hang on*."

They were such an unusually light shade of blue. It was a pretty color to be the last thing she saw.

"I love you," she whispered.

And then everything went black.

Chapter Twenty-two

DRESSED IN TOO-BIG scrubs that left plenty of room around her thick surgical dressing, Delaney leaned hard on Mollie's arm as she got out of the car at Sunset Shoals. "I've heard of doctors making house calls, but never taking a patient *to* a house. You're going way overboard with the TLC."

She slowly led her up the walkway of crushed shells. "You almost died protecting my town yesterday. There is no way for me to go overboard."

"Whoa, dial back that 'almost died' talk. You'll freak me out." Mollie had reassured Delaney backward and forward that the bullet narrowly missed hitting any organs. It simply went right through her side. And that—embarrassingly—she'd only lost feeling and blacked out from shock.

The gunshot wound still earned her a U.S. Marshals

Service Purple Heart. But it wasn't officially serious, and hadn't endangered the baby. The only reason she'd gotten an overnight stay in the hospital was due to Mollie throwing her weight around.

"It could've been far worse. You're lucky your baby is the size of a grain of rice. So while I don't want to scare you and have you pass out again—" Mollie grinned, as she'd teased Delaney mercilessly about her apparent aversion to pain and blood every time they ran tests and even took out her IV "—you've got to not rush the healing."

"I know. But I only wanted you to call Kellan to give me a ride back to Coos Bay. That wasn't a plea for you to finagle a free room at your bestie's five-star resort. I feel guilty."

"Hey, I'm your doctor. You have to do what I say. What's best for my patient is a peaceful view. Listening to the ocean. And, oh, not being forty minutes away from everyone who wants to help you. You're a part of Bandon, now that you bled for it." Mollie used a keycard on the private entrance to the Sunset Shoals Inn on the edge of the beach.

It opened into a large airy room with dark wood floors and whitewashed beams. Two sets of French doors led onto a private patio overlooking the ocean. A giant stone fireplace sat in the middle of the wall, and opposite the bed was a comfy-looking couch and chairs in the resort's signature driftwood color. It was easily three times as big as any of the hotel rooms she'd called home since last November.

Which almost made her burst into tears. That people she'd come to know and care about through the—technically—*criminals* whom she protected cared about her . . . well, that outcome was nothing Delaney would've envisioned in her entire career. The tears, though? She'd chalk those up to either hormones or the pain meds.

"Do you need me to help you into bed?" Mollie smoothed the skirt of her long pink sundress.

Delaney hated, *loathed* feeling sick and incapacitated. She took charge. She *did* things. "I'm headed to the couch. No help." Standing up straight pulled at her stitches with something substantially sharper than a twinge. But getting there on her own mattered.

So what if a sigh escaped as she sank into the cushions?

It was a win. A triumph over the fuckhead who'd shot her.

"Is Kellan coming soon? I need to talk to him. To all of them, actually." This living without a cell phone sucked. Yet another reason to stop being a patient and get back to being a person.

"I'm here." A door opened to her right. At the same time, Mollie slipped into the bathroom with the bag of Delaney's meds and extra dressings.

Carefully turning, Delaney glimpsed another entire room. But only that it existed before Kellan stepped through and shut it behind him. Talk about a sight for sore eyes. No uniform today, but a white shirt and tan slacks that made him look as beachy-elegant as the room itself. He leaned down and kissed her cheek. "How are you feeling?"

"Pretty buzzed still from cheating death." Delaney clung tight to his hand. "Thanks for saving me."

"You were trying to save me. It was just a matter of timing who did it first."

"Are you okay?" They'd barely talked since she regained consciousness in the hospital. After being assured she and the baby were fine, he'd had to leave. Kellan and Mateo had the not small matter of tying up loose ends pertaining to the dead mobster. With her out of commission, Mateo had been the go-between to the marshals. And that was all Mollie had relayed. Being out of the loop was driving Delaney crazy.

Most of all, for not being there while Kellan struggled with his first fatal takedown.

He ran his knuckles down her cheek with a soft smile. "You're walking and talking, so I'm fine."

So typical of him to deflect and put the focus back on her. "I mean, are you okay with shooting O'Brien? It's a big deal."

"To protect you, the town, my brothers—shooting him was the only course of action. I know it was the right thing. Do I feel bad for his family? Yeah. Will it probably keep me up at night for a while? Yeah." He dropped to one knee on the plush area rug in front of her. "Being with you will get me through it."

Now it was Delaney's turn to stroke *his* cheek. Because she'd hoped it would be a long, long time before he ever was forced to make that call. "I'm sorry you had to."

"Have you ever? Shot anyone?"

"Twice." Something she'd share down the road. Not today. Because Delaney wanted today to be about beginnings, not endings. "How about we save those stories for a rainy night?"

"Good call. I've got something I need to—"

Delaney cut him off. "Any chance you can hold that thought? I really, really need to tell you and your brothers something. Are they at the festival? Could you call them?"

Cocking his head to the side, Kellan stared at her, his face unreadable. Finally, he shrugged and said, "No problem."

Getting up, he disappeared through the same door and came back almost immediately with Rafe and Flynn. They both wore shirts and slacks that matched Kellan's. It was odd to see them out of tees and jeans. The three of them packed a visual punch with their dark hair and tans popping out the varying blues of their eyes.

Mollie reappeared, and opened the French doors to let in a fresh ocean breeze that felt wonderful.

"What are you guys doing here?"

"You put your life on the line to protect us, Marshal. We're here to thank you." Rafe handed her three pale pink roses held together with a satin bow. Then he dropped a kiss on top of her head.

Flynn handed over an identical trio of roses. He bent over to awkwardly encircle her shoulders. "You're a badass, Marshal Evans. Just like us."

All she'd done was pull O'Brien's focus away for a split second. "You know I didn't actually save you. Your brother did that." Kellan deserved full credit for stopping O'Brien from hurting anyone else.

"If we gave him roses, it'd be weird," Rafe joked. Then he dropped into the adjoining chair. "You risked yourself, and your baby. To keep us safe. We always believed that you would. But we're damn sorry that you had to, and that you got hurt by our fucked-up past."

She wafted the roses just beneath her nose and inhaled their sweet scent. "Hopefully it won't happen again."

"O'Brien wanted our money more than he wanted to curry favor with a dying man headed for a life sentence in prison. He didn't tell anyone where we are. The secret of our whereabouts died with him. We're safe here."

Talk about a perfect segue. "I want you to be safe when you go back to Chicago, too. Which is why I won't be your handler anymore. I'm handing you off."

"Why? You'll be healed by October. We won't trust anyone else as much."

"When I saw O'Brien's gun, I acted. I didn't think about my baby." This time, Delaney let her left hand flutter over her belly. She'd awakened somewhere right before dawn, stricken and gasping with guilt. Wondering if Kellan would ever forgive her for being so reckless with their baby's life. Wondering if *she* would ever forgive herself. "It was the right call, in the moment. To do what I had to, to protect all of you. But it isn't the right call going forward."

Kellan sat next to her. "You're quitting the Marshals Service?"

As usual, her smart man had jumped three steps ahead. "I'm stepping down from witness protection. I can't be one hundred percent focused on a protectee when I'm worried about the safety of my baby on board. Or later, risking my life and leaving this little one without a mother? I lived that. There's no way I'd knowingly open up that possibility with my own kid."

Mollie gaped at her as she perched on Rafe's knee. "You're sacrificing your whole career?"

Ouch. That sounded . . . *final*. "Hopefully not all of it. I want to do something working as an advocate for witnesses." It was an idea that had barely bloomed after her talks with Kono and Sierra. An idea that she'd use the rest of her time healing in this beautiful space to fully form.

"You know I'd never ask you to do that. Not for me." Dark brows knitted together, Kellan patted the hand still resting on her belly. "Not for our little surprise in there, either."

"I know. My quitting would've solved our problems from day one. And you never even suggested it. Because you so wonderfully respect how hard I've worked to get here. I love you for that. But this is the best decision for the three of us."

Delaney hoped he didn't feel pressured by her decision. Hoped the Maguires didn't feel abandoned. But she knew it was the right one, to her core.

Flynn sat in the other chair. "I can't wait to spoil the heck out of my niece or nephew. So I can't be anything but grateful that you're doing this."

"You've got our support, Marshal." Rafe arched an eyebrow hopefully. "Does this mean you're finally going to stop hassling me?"

"Doubtful." Everyone laughed. "I'll have a say in choosing my replacement. And all of our plans are already in place. You'll be safe when you testify."

Rafe leaned forward, one arm slung around Mollie. "Isn't that exactly what you said when you moved us to this podunk town? I think your exact words were *there's no place safer than a blip on the edge of the map*."

"Technically, I was right. You're all still in one piece and safely undercover. I'm putting that in the win column." But she waited, nervously, to hear what Kellan had to say.

He was looking at her again with that sideways tilt to his head. "You surprised me, Laney."

"We've made this beautiful gift together, you and I. From now on, I need to protect Baby Maguire every bit as fiercely as I protected the big Maguires."

"I'm glad to hear it." Kellan wiped a hand across his mouth. "You just made what happens next a whole lot more of a sure thing than I anticipated. Feels like I can toss about two pages' worth of a speech."

That was hysterical. Her man *never* skimped on using extra words. The bigger, the better, too. "What happens next?"

Kellan dropped back down to one knee. A small red leather box was in his palm. "I fell for you at first sight, Delaney. I was a different man then. Literally. You were pretending to be someone else, too. But this chemistry exploded between us. Who we are today? Together? That chemistry's even more explosive. Grounded in a deep love and respect."

Oh. *Ohhhhhh*. She couldn't believe he was doing this. It was crazy. She was wearing borrowed hospital scrubs, for god's sake. On the other hand, Delaney couldn't deny the tidal wave of joy that flooded through her at his words—and the symbolism of what she suspected to be in that box.

So she followed their pattern from day one. She poked at him. Just, you know, without the aggravation and rancor they'd originally had. With a teasing smile, Delaney sassed, "You're mixing your chemistry and electrical metaphors, Counselor."

"What can I say—you throw me off-balance. In all the best ways. You make me happy. You're who I want at my side, holding on as we tackle everything life brings our way. For a while there, it seemed like Fate was working overtime to keep us apart. But I think it was really just forcing us to realize how much we needed each other. How right we are together."

"Did we pass the test?"

He flicked open the box. An empire-cut diamond sparkled in an Art Deco design, flanked by four baguettes. It was *beautiful*. And not nearly as intense as the sparkle in Kellan's light blue eyes. "Marry me and find out. Be my wife, the mother to our children. Be my partner. My love. My future and my forever."

Thumbing away tears, Delaney whispered, "Yes." Kellan slid the ring onto her finger. Then she reached for him, to kiss him. But he pulled away and stood up.

"I've got another surprise for you now."

She waggled her finger. "Bigger than this? I doubt it."

"Oh, you're going to eat those words." Grinning from ear to ear, Kellan knocked on the door. This time Sierra and Lucien came out. Sierra wore a pink dress like Mollie's and held a bouquet of ivory roses. Lucien, who she'd met at the festival, carried an iPad.

Leaning on the armrest to crane around, Delaney asked, "How many people did you hide in that room? Does it have a secret tunnel directly to Norah's coffeeshop?"

"This is it. The bare minimum."

"For what?"

"For a wedding." Kellan's smile absolutely dazzled her. "For our wedding."

Delaney gaped at him. "You're crazy."

"Nope. I'm seizing the day. You said yes, so why wait? It's dangerous out there. We've both got jobs with a higher than average degree of injury and fatality.

There are—" Kellan cast a sidelong glance at Lucien and clearly rethought his next words "—unknown forces that may or may not be at work. We can't control what the world throws at us. We *can* control getting married so that we face it all together."

Sierra grouped the ivory roses around the pink ones that Delaney already held. Mollie stuck a jeweled headband attached to a veil on her head and helped her stand. It felt spontaneous and passionate and altogether naughty. Like she and Kellan were thumbing their noses at what should be and rules and convention. Like they had all along.

It was hilariously *perfect*.

Kellan touched her arm. "We can still have a big party when you're ready. White dress, tux, DJ, the whole nine yards. Oh, and the wedding rings. I didn't have time after you got shot to get back up to the jewelry store. But you don't have any family left. Mine's all here. What more do we need?"

Silly man. Guess that was another whole page of speech he should've ditched. "Stop selling me on it. I'm all in. This is a great idea. It fits us."

"Yeah. Exactly what I thought."

"Damn." Rafe pulled some crumpled bills out of his pocket and handed them to Flynn. "I had fifty bucks on you telling him hell to the no for this surprise wedding. You two really are right for each other."

The matching outfits. The flowers. It all made sense

now. Except for Lucien. Who'd thrown open the doors and stood on the patio, fiddling with his iPad. Suddenly music rang out—something lushly classical.

Mollie put her fingers on Delaney's pulse. "We're good to go, but this has to be bare bones. I don't want her standing for very long. I didn't bring my suture kit along if she passes out again and hits her head."

With a roll of her eyes, Delaney said, "Really? Is this going to be a forever thing with you? Assuming I'll pass out at the drop of a hat?"

"Well, I figure it'll stop being funny once your baby bump's the size of a bowling ball. But we're going to be sisters. That gives me license to tease you."

"Sisters sounds great." She reached out to Rafe and Flynn. "Brothers sound great, too. I didn't expect to like either one of you. But I do. I'm in awe of the strength it took to turn your lives around, and I'll be honored to be a part of the Maguire family."

Both of those big, bad guys ducked their heads in an *aw, shucks* gesture that tickled Delaney to no end.

"Hey." Kellan lifted her into his arms. "Save the mushy stuff for *our* vows."

Everyone else went out and lined up on the patio, with Lucien in the middle. "What's he doing?" Delaney whispered.

"My friend there got himself ordained online. He's marrying us."

Yet another surprise. "I didn't think he believed in marriage. Didn't you tell me he's a huge playboy?"

"That's the rumor. We're bucking convention top to bottom in this wedding. What do you think?"

She looped her arms around his neck. "I think I love it. I love you. I'd thought that falling for you was the biggest surprise of my life. The most unlikely thing that could happen. The worst, biggest risk I could take. Was I *ever* wrong. It turns out that I'm a little addicted to choosing a risky, uncharted path. As long as it's with you."

"I'll be right there with you on every path, for the rest of our lives," Kellan promised. And then he carried her outside to make that solemn vow official.

Epilogue

Five months later . . .
Valentine's Day

KELLAN PACED BACK and forth across the kitchen of the house he used to share with his brothers. "I'm nervous."

Delaney caressed the back of his neck. It was probably supposed to be soothing. In reality, it turned him on. Just like every single time she touched him. Including last week when she took out a splinter—painful—but the underside of her breast had brushed against his arm and totally distracted him from the extraction.

"You planned an entire surprise wedding in less than twenty-four hours after I was shot. How could a family dinner possibly throw you off your stride?"

The answer was so simple. But he loved any excuse to tell his bride how much he loved her. "I *knew* we'd work out. Because I loved you to pieces and refused to accept any other outcome. Tonight, though—it isn't about us. I'm feeling the heat."

"Then maybe move away from the stove." This time she pinched him. On the butt. Also not anything but a turn-on. "I married a cocky, borderline arrogant man who never saw a challenge he couldn't overcome."

"Almost true. You know I finally had to admit defeat on the whole deep dish pizza attempt." It still rankled Kellan. He'd never failed before. At anything. Over the past few months, he'd successfully recreated Chicken Vesuvio, Italian beef, and full-blown Chicago dogs for the Super Bowl two weeks ago. But the pizza was his white whale.

"Technically, you stopped because the fire department ordered you to not try again after their third response to your smoke alarm. Not a defeat, babe."

For the millionth time, Kellan reflected how lucky he'd been to marry Delaney. "I love you."

"Love you, too." They kissed, with him angled sideways around the growing bump of their baby girl.

A balled-up napkin hit the side of Kellan's face. "Hey," Rafe barked. "Stop making out for ten freaking seconds and come join us."

"Weren't you and Mollie literally still in the bedroom messing around when we got here?"

A shit-eating grin broke across his big brother's face. "Yeah. The one at our house reeks of paint fumes. The bed's covered in drywall dust. This is better."

Flynn pushed a rocks glass into everyone's hand. "Per Rafe's request, I've made a very special cocktail tonight. The Maguire."

Sierra and Mollie shifted into spots next to their guys as Delaney and Kellan came to the dining table. "There's no way it can be as delicious as the Sierra blackberry pie martini."

"We'll call it *different*. Because I think you're the only one in the room who likes something that sweet."

"What's the occasion?"

Kellan sniffed at his glass. "What's the drink?"

"Whiskey—to represent us Irish Maguires. A little lemon juice and simple syrup shaken with it, served on the rocks with a float of Oregon Pinot Noir on top to represent our wonderful women."

Rafe lifted his glass up to his head. "I have a toast. Well, a story that leads to a toast."

"Oh, boy. Can I sit down through the story part?" Delaney asked, rubbing the small of her back.

"Suck it up, Marshal," Kellan said with a wink. "You're strong as steel."

"I really wish I hadn't set the bar so high when I first met you."

Rafe cleared his throat. "As some of you know, I used to have a Valentine's Day tradition. One that had nothing to do with romance. My old boss and I would go to Clark Street, to the site of the 1929 Valentine's Day Massacre."

"Capone tried to take out the Irish mob," Flynn explained to Sierra. "It didn't work."

"Nope. But it did cause a lot of trouble. And the Irish mob never forgot it. So McGinty and I would go out there and toast to the murdered from a flask of whiskey. Then we'd drink a toast to his crew."

Mollie shuddered. "That's a horrible Valentine's Day tradition. I mean, not everyone goes for candy hearts, but you weren't even getting sex."

"Don't you worry about me, Doc. I made out okay." He shot her a rakish grin. "Afterward."

Impatient, Kellan tapped his knife against the table. "Could we get the short version, without the flirting, in deference to the pregnant lady?"

"Mollie's right. It was a suck-ass tradition. One I'm glad to put behind me. Just like we've put everything to do with the trial and McGinty behind us."

Flynn lifted his glass higher. "*Almost* everything. I do like to go on YouTube and replay that footage of the look on his face as he got his life sentence."

"The point is, I want to start a new tradition, for our new life here in Oregon. One that is purely about love, the way it should be on this day." Rafe beamed down at Mollie. "I love my brothers, and I love the family we've created out here. So happy Valentine's Day."

They all clinked glasses and drank. Kellan had been skeptical, but once again, Flynn's knack with a cocktail had knocked it out of the park.

"Before anyone asks, I didn't cook. We picked up this food from the chef at Sunset Shoals." He pointedly glared back and forth between his brothers. "So you can just swallow whatever cracks you were about to make at risking your lives eating a dinner I cooked."

Flynn held up his hands. "You're the only one of us licensed to carry a weapon, bro. I wouldn't dream of hassling you about your cooking."

If only that were true. He was just glad that Flynn was back to teasing him about the gun. Both of his brothers hadn't made a single jab at him for weeks after shooting O'Brien. It hadn't been until after they returned from the trial that things got back to normal.

Kellan hoped to God they stayed that way from now on.

Mollie pushed back her chair. "Should I go get the salad?"

"No." The answer exploded out of Flynn. Shaking his head, he said, "Sorry. I thought we'd do something fun tonight. Since Valentine's Day is all about sweetness. Start with dessert first."

At least it'd get Kellan's nervousness out of the way. "On it." He went into the kitchen and pulled the cake out of the fridge. "This, I did make. Also per Rafe's request. I'm giving up recreating Chicago food. All things Oregon, that's my new kitchen mantra. Salmon, probably. And, of course, cranberries. So I made a cranberry cheesecake."

Mollie's jaw dropped. "Rafe, *my* Rafe, asked you to make something with cranberries?"

Eyes squinted to angry slits, Rafe growled, "I abso-fuckinglutely did not."

"He asked for a purely Oregon dessert. I picked cranberries just to mess with him." Kellan made quick work of slicing and plating. And he made sure to put the slice with the big swirl of cranberry sauce right in front of Sierra.

Then he held his breath. Because if he'd screwed this up, not only would he feel bad, but Flynn would kick the shit out of him.

The women all dug in. The men all sat, forks hovering over their cake, eyes trained on Sierra.

"Oh!" She leaned down to peer at her slice. "There's something *in* my cake."

Thank *God*.

"What is it?" Flynn asked. The guy looked all knotted up, like he was in the midst of passing a kidney stone.

Sierra tapped and scraped on her plate. Then she dropped her fork. Her hands flew to cover her mouth. Slightly muffled, she said, "It's a ring."

"That's right." Flynn put it in his mouth, getting off all the cheesecake. Then he held it out. "It's *your* ring. If you'll accept it. The only clincher is that it's a package deal. I come with the ring. For better, for worse—or so they say. All I know is that everything about my life has been better since you came into it, Sierra. Please say you'll let me love you, and work my damnedest to make you happy, every single day for the rest of our lives."

She slid her finger through it. Love and happiness radiated from her, dulling the candle flames. "Only if you let me love you right back."

"Done."

And with that, their new family as the Maguires was

complete, their new lives officially on course. Kellan put one arm around Delaney as everyone clapped and cheered, and rested the other on the bump of their soon-to-be daughter. He didn't need a fancy lawyer's office in a Chicago skyscraper. Didn't need so much as a single bill from that two million that—for ten months—had belonged to all of them.

He had the love of his life and his brothers, safe and together.

Nothing could be better.

About the Author

USA Today bestseller **CHRISTI BARTH** earned a master's degree in vocal performance and embarked upon a career on the stage. A love of romance then drew her to wedding planning. Ultimately, she succumbed to her lifelong love of books and now writes award-winning contemporary romance.

Christi can always be found either whipping up gourmet meals (for fun, honest!) or with her nose in a book. She lives in Maryland with the best husband in the world.

www.christibarth.com

Discover great authors, exclusive offers, and more at hc.com.